The Suicide Club

The Suicide Club

ANDREW WILLIAMS

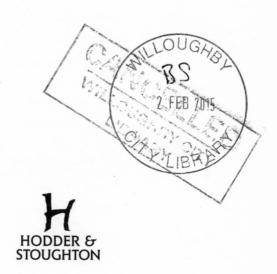

H
HODDER &
STOUGHTON

First published in Great Britain in 2014 by Hodder & Stoughton
An Hachette UK company

2

A CIP catalogue record for this title is available from the British Library

Hardback ISBN 978 1 848 54585 4
Trade Paperback ISBN 978 1 848 54586 1
Ebook ISBN 978 1 848 54587 8

Typeset in Celeste by Palimpsest Book Production Limited,
Falkirk, Stirlingshire

Printed and bound by Clays Ltd, St Ives plc

Hodder & Stoughton policy is to use papers that are natural, renewable and recyclable
products and made from wood grown in sustainable forests. The logging and
manufacturing processes are expected to conform to the environmental
regulations of the country of origin.

Hodder & Stoughton Ltd
338 Euston Road
London NW1 3BH

www.hodder.co.uk

Intelligence is about people and a study of people. It is not simply a question of studying people on the other side, but studying one's own as well. We have to learn about one another, not just about strangers.

Sir Maurice Oldfield,
Director of the Secret
Intelligence Service [MI6]

In memory of Dick and Millie Ellis from Sunderland.

July – August 1917

Every success brings us nearer to the end of the long and desperate struggle and we are now justified in believing that one more great victory may turn the scale finally.

The commander-in-chief of the British armies in France,
Field Marshal Sir Douglas Haig to his generals,
on the eve of the Passchendaele offensive,
5 June 1917.

1

Bakers and Thieves

Muzzle flash white and burnt. Twisting, falling in filth, gaping a *silent scream to stop. Then darkness. Smothering. Total. Pinned* *like a butterfly in a tray.* Phut, phut, *the dying respirator, dizzying* *wisps of memory condensing in its glass discs, familiar faces* *looming, dissipating, as if glimpsed in a cloud of gas. And voices,* *whispering in the Scots of those lost on the field at Loos in the* *battalion's first days. 'You've come tae us frae oot the battle,'* *they say. 'Frae hell tae emptiness, tae this purgatory.'*

Then he hears himself pray, 'Sweet Jesus, let me back.' But *Jesus doesn't answer, only the dead. 'Why? Why should you be* *saved?' they whisper. 'Why not us?'*

'CAPTAIN! CAPTAIN INNES!' Mertens was shaking him, his face tense with concern. 'You were calling out. You must be quiet.' He raised a piano finger to his lips. 'Are you sick?'

'A dream.' Innes touched his chest, feeling for the brass crucifix. His shirt was wringing wet.

'Bad dream, no? From before?'

'Yes, Joos, from before.'

Mertens squeezed his shoulder. 'The war will be over soon. You hear? British guns. It's the big attack. One of our men at the station heard a German *Oberst* say so.'

Ratchet after ratchet, the gears of the machine were turning again. British gun-crews, grimy, stripped and grunting with the effort, and the air thick with the smell of cordite; shell fire tearing the ground above the shattered city of Ypres, scooping gobbets of flesh and clay from the German line and rumbling on across roads and ditches into Flemish villages, leaving only brick and sludge in its wake. Flash, flash, the engine of war was sparking the night, rattling windows in distant cities where small children cowered beneath covers like the enemy in his concrete pillboxes.

'We must leave.' Mertens offered his hand, hauling Innes to his feet. 'The nuns are waiting.'

Boom! Innes flinched as the percussion trembled through the floorboards and lifted the dust from the picture rail.

'*Godverdomme*! That was big.' Mertens whistled. 'The gun at Moere?'

'Too close to be anything else.'

They had gazed at its barrel a few hours before, making a careful mental note: fifteen-inch howitzer; reinforced cement emplacement, its walls fifteen feet thick at least; underground ordnance gallery; electric security wire. A few minutes' observation that had taken days to organise. First a suitable café, a haughty Bavarian lieutenant, and then a brawl convincing enough to secure them a sentence of six weeks' forced labour in the forbidden zone. Their work gang had marched hard miles of *pavé* with pick and shovel, footsore, hungry and abused by the enemy's field police. Belgium's factories had been plundered in the first years of the war but its people could still be pressed into service. Innes had dug the foundations of a new reserve line, mixed concrete, repaired roads, and seen all a spy might hope to see. At the end of the fourth week he had run.

Boom! He frowned and touched his brow as the attic room shook again.

'Sorry, Joos. A little jumpy.' He wasn't sure why he said so.

He wouldn't have admitted it when he was in the line. Mertens nodded sympathetically. A decent sort, he was a baker and old enough to be Innes's father. 'They're managing two rounds every three or four minutes,' he said, reaching into his coat for a cigarette.

'Is that good?'

'A gun that size? Yes.'

'Ah.' Mertens took his watch from his waistcoat and peered at its shattered face by the thin light of the window. 'No time for a cigarette, Captain. Almost ten o'clock.'

The hall was dark but for a sliver of smoky light from the parlour. Members of the family would be gathered there, waiting for the click of the front door to signal they were free from the fear of sheltering a British spy.

The storm at Ypres flickered in the broken panes of the house opposite, its confused echo haunting the empty street.

'Are you all right?' Mertens whispered.

'Yes. Of course.' He was a little embarrassed. 'Fine. Really. It's nothing, I'm fine.'

'Keep close then, Captain.'

Mertens moved swiftly and lightly for a large man, holding to the shadow of the buildings opposite. Innes tried to follow, but wielding a pick for the Germans had aggravated the old wound in his leg. It was the electric-blue hour and still warm, but the village had drawn its blinds and fastened its shutters. Summer in the enemy's *Operationsgebiet* ended every evening with the eight o'clock curfew.

Mertens was waiting in an undertaker's doorway. 'Just the next corner. I'll check it's safe.'

'Together, my friend, let's go together.'

The abbey enclosure occupied almost a side of the street: a walled garden, the west end of the domestic range and the church, its stepped gable as black as a crow's wing. There was

5

a row of shops opposite, a post office and a small hotel, light spilling through its shutters on to the pavement.

Mertens bent closer, cupping his hands to Innes's ear. 'The door – there.' Weather-worn, studded with rust, it was set low and deep in the wall, a dozen paces from them. 'Please wait here, Captain.'

Innes tugged his sleeve. 'No.'

They were pressed against the ivy-clad wall of a house in their own no man's land between shadow and the sanctuary of the abbey.

'We must move.'

'I know, I know.' But it wasn't how it should be. The grumble of the battle, men and metal sucked from miles around into the maelstrom at Ypres, yet the village was so still and there was that careless light at the hotel, just a few yards along the street.

'Please, Captain. Let me try the door.'

'Joos, there's—'

There was a blinding flash and Innes shrank into the ivy as the enemy howitzer thundered another shell in the direction of Ypres. For a second the street palpitated in its afterglow. When he raised his eyes again the wicket in the church door was open and there was the bent silhouette of a man on the threshold – a priest, to judge by his robes. He was carrying a pillar candle like the one lit at the Easter altar to banish the darkness of the tomb. He took a few shuffling steps, glancing up to be sure perhaps that he was still beneath the arched portal. Then he sank slowly to his knees, grey head bowed in prayer with the candle a few inches from his chin, its troubled flame cutting deep lines in his face.

'What is he doing?' Mertens' voice cracked with fear. 'He'll lead them to us.'

'I don't—' No. The priest's face; it was a kindly light. 'We must go. Now! Quickly!'

Turning away, the hotel lights spilling into the street, Innes could hear the slap of military boots, and a moment later, the confusion of many feet, a shouted order, and as he ran, *crack!*, a single rifle shot. Mertens was a few yards in front, stumbling and almost falling, picking himself up and pushing on again. *Boom!* His face was sickly white in the gun flash as he glanced back along the street. *Bloody, bloody leg* – the rhythm of Innes's stride – *bloody, bloody leg.* He knew he wouldn't be able to run far, and he could hear the enemy, somewhere. Mertens was pulling away, disappearing at the bottom street. *Bloody, bloody leg.* Where were they going to hide? *Bloody, bloody . . .* where was he? But Mertens wouldn't desert him.

A woman steps into the street, beckons '*here*'. Mertens is at her door. '*Hurry,*' she urges, driving him along her dark hall and through her kitchen. A child is wailing there, a small crumpled face. Mertens has lost his cap. Drawing bolts, they go down to a yard, then neighbour to neighbour, weaving through washing poles, on without question until their guide leads them up steps to another door, another stranger; and as he catches his breath they whisper in Flemish, their guide, their saviour offering a shy smile, then she has gone.

'This is Pierre, another one of the network's *promeneurs,*' said Mertens. 'Ramble sent him here. Thank God for Ramble.' His voice trembled a little. 'Pierre is a baker, like me. Well, he used to be.'

Innes offered his hand. 'Ramble sent you to look after us?'

Pierre nodded curtly, his spectacles slipping down the bridge of his nose.

'We'll be safe here tonight,' said Mertens. 'No, not in the kitchen—' pulling a chair away from Innes, 'the parlour. There's a space behind the fireplace in there.'

They sat in silence, knees pressed to their chins. Innes slept for as long as he could, but in the coffin darkness there were dreams, those same Scots voices, whimpering, sweating, shaken awake. Pierre brought a little soup and the news that a German soldier had struck the priest with a rifle butt and he was unconscious. Innes touched the brass cross beneath his shirt and tried to pray for the old man, but it wasn't as easy as it used to be under shell-fire, the old words had come then with conviction and feeling. Everyone was a believer in the line.

Later, they heard the Germans clumping lazily around the house, shouting, turning over furniture. They left after only a few minutes.

The following morning Pierre moved them on in a farm wagon, by green lanes north-west towards Bruges, the grey sun too weak to dissipate a beard of mist from the fields, and for once the fighting was lost in the rumble of wheels and the clopping of the horses. 'To the market at Torhout,' they told Germans who asked, but most just marched by. The first night Innes was hidden by an elderly doctor and his daughter, the second on a farm, and the third with a carpenter near the border. Sleepless, his leg aching in the short sleigh bed the carpenter had made for his son, his thoughts drifted back to his old battalion and one of the last conversations he'd had with its officers. 1916. High Wood on the Somme. Shaken by three hours of shelling, and exhausted pretending not to be. When it lifted there was whisky. Dust motes dancing in a shaft of late sunshine. At the entrance to the dug-out, proper Clydeside cursing. Some of the men started up a chorus of 'We're Here Because We're Here,' although a good few wouldn't be by the end of the following day.

'Does anyone know?' Ferguson said.

'Know what, Major?' someone replied.

'Know what the hell we're doing here, of course.'

What a card, they'd laughed; only an old sweat would have the temerity to ask. But Fergie wasn't laughing.

8

Many times since, Innes had asked himself the same. From the parapet of a trench the depth of a well-cut grave, the world seemed a cruel, pitted place of blasted trees, wire tangles and rotting bodies, a place where men sang without reason, *we're here because we're here.*

He shifted on to his side, his cheek pressed to his coat. It smelt of sweat and the road, and the cement he'd mixed for the enemy. There was comfort, and good reason, and faith to make sense of the sacrifice. The old Belgian priest with his paschal flame, kneeling before his church in prayer, hands knotted like old oak about the candle. *A pillar of fire by night.* Priest, doctor, farmer, carpenter, risking their lives to shelter a British spy. To London they were numbers in Ramble's network, but to Innes they were the purpose of the whole bloody business. *Where are you, Ramble?* He reached beneath the blanket to touch his cross. Crafted from a fragment of brass shell-case, it left a green stain on his chest. 'But it will keep you safe,' Ramble had said; 'Safe, always.'

In the end he gave up trying to sleep and sat at the edge of the bed, rubbing the hollow in his right thigh left by the shrapnel he'd caught on the Somme. 'A Blighty one,' his surgeon had said, and he was right in a way. Tonight he was too far from the Front to hear the guns, only the rain pattering against the shutters and a startled blackbird. Was his old battalion at Ypres? Ferguson was dead. Milne and Low were dead. If he could speak to them he would say, 'You fought for freedom and justice. The flame you lit will never go out.' The thought brought him close to tears; thank goodness no one could see him. Mertens was snoring lightly. After two months of danger and companionship, they would go their separate ways in the morning. Just one more goodbye in a long series; in each an image of death, someone famous once said.

*

Sebastian Aerts had once made his living as a cracksman but now the laws were German he was a patriot, a *passeur*. Ramble turned a blind eye to his private enterprises because running lines in and out of the occupied territories called for his sort of nerve and attention to detail. Spies and intelligence one way, booze and cigarettes the other.

'Still don't trust me, eh?' he said, when Innes asked about the arrangements for his crossing.

'The forest border, like last time?'

'That's the one, Captain. Here . . .' Dipping into a canvas sack, he tossed Innes a pair of rubber gloves.

'So you don't fry on the fence . . .' His brown face was a wind-blown web of smile lines. 'The rubber boots you'll have to pay for this time.'

They stepped from the carpenter's house into a grey sheet of rain. 'German soldiers hate the rain,' Aerts observed, pulling the brim of his sou'wester lower.

'All soldiers hate the rain,' Innes replied.

Skirting fields, seeking the cover of hedgerows and trees, they worked their way round the town of Arendonk towards the forest at its northern edge, stopping only once to rest and shelter in a barn, and to share bread and beer with a farm labourer.

'That's lucky,' Aerts declared, as they were preparing to resume their journey. 'Our friend says the Huns have lifted the checkpoint on the canal between here and the forest.'

Dusk beneath the trees, the ground boggy and broken, Innes pitching forward on to his knees and jolting his thigh. 'You move like an elephant,' the *passeur* muttered.

His companions were waiting deep in the forest, in the shadows by a lake. Two of them were brothers, perhaps the *passeur*'s sons or nephews, and the third was an older man called Merckx.

'All right, Captain,' said Aerts, 'you rest. The boys and I will check on the guards.'

Wet and bone-weary, Innes sat on a stump and stared emptily at the rain circles on the water. He trusted Aerts to know his business. That's how it worked in the occupied territories. Trust. Links in a long chain. Ramble insisted they weren't spies. Spies lied and cheated and did 'immoral' things. No, they were Belgian soldiers fighting for their country's freedom, even old thieves like Aerts.

A heavy hand on his shoulder made him jump. 'For God's sake!'

Aerts was shaking with laughter. 'I might have been a Hun, Captain, then you would have had to swim for it,' he said, gesturing at the lake.

'I couldn't be wetter than I am now.'

Aerts threw him a pair of rubber boots. 'For free, because we're comrades. And there's this . . .' He slipped a waxed cotton package from his coat and gave it to Innes. 'From Ramble. The reports from the network in Antwerp, Brussels and Roulers. Ready?' Short but powerful, he hauled Innes back to his feet with ease. 'My boys are keeping watch. When it's clear, we'll run out with the frame. Once it's up . . . three minutes, that's all. Or you'll be caught up there and—well, you know they won't take chances, they'll shoot. Bad for all of us.'

'But especially me.'

Aerts chuckled and reached up to slap Innes's back. 'When you're across, remember to watch out for the Dutch guards. There aren't many but you don't want any trouble. If they try to stop you, say you work for Gasper. Most of them owe me. Walk due east towards Reusel. You have a compass?'

Innes nodded. He didn't anticipate trouble once he was over; the Dutch wanted to keep things quiet, head-down neutrality, see and hear no evil. It would be fine . . . once he was over.

'Last thing . . .' Aerts held up his gloved hands. 'Watch out. No trailing knees.'

Somewhere beyond the fringe of the forest there was the murmur of voices. Crawling on their bellies now, closer, closer, and Innes could hear two men speaking German. Saxons. One of the guards wanted a light for his pipe.

The border was only a dozen yards from the trees. The Germans had cut through the plantation and the ground was stippled with stumps. First a belt of wire, then a dimly lit fence ten feet high and laced with copper, carrying a charge of six thousand volts. There was no sign of the enemy, but it was impossible to be sure. Aerts took the ropes. Somewhere in the forest on either side, the brothers were gripping the other ends: a sharp tug when the sentries were out of sight, then *Go!* Merckx was quietly clearing branches from the frame they had left hidden there.

Aerts held up his right hand. 'Stand by.'

Innes's heart was beating faster with excitement, because it was still possible to feel it, in spite of everything.

The other rope rustled through the brambles like a snake, jerking Aerts' left hand. 'Wait here, Captain.' He began hauling the triangular frame clear of the trees. Like a garden toy or the top of a hangman's tree, there were rungs to a right angle, two rubber-covered rails to place over the electric fence, and a hypotenuse of supporting poles. A sheet of tarpaulin over the barbed wire, and Merckx was over, reaching back to lift the frame. Innes glanced at his watch. Seconds were ticking by. Like the trenches, the worst thing about going over – the time before – waiting with his imagination. Now, a minute.

But the frame was up at last and he was running, gaze fixed on the barbed wire, head first and over. He paused at the bottom of the ladder to make eye contact with Aerts – an unspoken thank-you – then he was climbing. One foot carefully in front of the other, his boot slipping on a rung, and swaying like a ship's stoker on Sauchiehall Street at closing time: God help him if they didn't have firm hold of the bottom. Hoisting knees and boots on to the rails at the top, his bad leg trembling with the effort. Above the fence now, the bright bones of an animal at its base. Left hand, right knee, right hand, left knee, and over at last. Climbing down, jumping the last few feet, he glanced back into Belgium and waved, but Aerts was too busy to notice. So he pressed on through thorns and bushes, then across the corner of a potato field, his boots so thickly caked in mud he had to swing his legs, but his spirits lifting with every heavy step, the refrain of a soldier's song the men sang on their way out of the line rolling round his head. After twenty minutes tramping steadily eastwards he reached the road, the faint glow of the border lights to his right and safety, a good meal, beer, a hot bath to the left – if he could rouse an inn-keeper. The tension of the last few months was draining from him: forget the beer and the bath, he thought, all he really wanted was a bed with thick white cotton sheets that rustled when you drew them back from a goose-feather pillow. He could see the silhouette of the church at Reusel and was impatient to be there.

Head bent to the gusting drizzle, he was concentrating so hard on putting one foot in front of the other he didn't notice the motor car until its lamps were spilling on the road in front of him. It looked expensive. A driver and a passenger. The road led into occupied Belgium and nowhere else. Germans? There was no time to hide even if he could find the strength to. The driver was closing the throttle, cruising to a halt, his face still lost behind the lamps. Innes kept walking. If he heard the passenger door open he would force it shut, then run for the hedge or the ditch.

Another few strides and he was level with the car. Something German; black; the engine still running. Both men were wearing Homburg hats. Thank God the driver's hands were gripping the wheel. Walking at the same steady pace, he passed by the passenger side. No sound; no movement. Then the squeaking of a door, and he rocked forward ready to run.

'*Oi*! Silly bugger. Where do you think you're going?'

Innes stopped and almost laughed out loud because, yes, he was a silly bugger, and the night was over at last. 'Oh, it's you, Tinsley.'

'Of course it is, who else?' Tinsley walked round the car to offer his hand. 'You're late. I 'ad word it would be midnight.'

'I wasn't expecting a reception.'

Captain Tinsley was an old Merchant Navy bruiser who tried not to venture further than his smoke-filled office in Rotterdam and the bar at the Hotel Weimar.

'Well, I'm 'ere now,' he said, 'get in.'

His driver was one of the Secret Service Bureau's locals. Innes climbed up to the back seat and arranged a blanket over his wet knees. 'Is there a good hotel nearby? Oh, and before I doze off . . .' he reached inside his coat for the packet of papers, 'The latest returns from the network. I'll do a report tomorrow.'

'Keep 'em. You can deliver them to London yourself.'

'What?'

'All right, let's go,' Tinsley said, addressing the driver. 'We'll 'ave to be quick.'

Innes leant forward to make himself heard over the engine. 'Where are we going?'

'To the Hook. You're to catch the first boat in the morning. Careful!'

The driver was trying to turn the car around without venturing on the muddy verge.

'But I've only just got here.'

'I know.' Tinsley shifted awkwardly in his seat to look back at him. 'Look, Innes, orders.'

'From whom?'

'Captain Cumming. Wants you in London at once . . . yesterday. Now, if I were you, I'd just sit quiet and think of old England.'

Innes leant back and pulled the blanket to his chin. 'Scotland, Tinsley. Scotland.'

September 1917

During 1917 a collection of agents was formed, known locally as the Suicide Club. Their mission was to penetrate the enemy line.

Lieutenant Colonel R. J. Drake, Head of Section B, Military Intelligence, GHQ

2

The Home Front

'ALEXANDER MACDONALD INNES.'
   'A Scot.'

Cumming glanced up from the file spread across his broad knees. 'As we discussed.'

'This coffee is undrinkable.' Hankey was contemplating his cup. 'Isn't it always at this club?'

'But they're good about me here, Sir Maurice. Discreet.' Cumming lifted the file. 'Do you want to know more?'

'Yes, yes.' Hankey flourished his hand like a concert impresario at an audition. 'Go on, please.'

'He's twenty-seven. He taught at Glasgow University, history, and a little philosophy I think . . . he used to be known in his battalion as "the Prof". After the Somme it changed to "Lazarus". We call him that at the Bureau: "Agent L".'

'Lazarus?'

'He was buried by a direct hit on a dug-out and they gave him up for dead, but his sergeant insisted on searching for his body. They found him under four feet of earth with just a few scratches. Unfortunately his luck ran out a month later when he was badly wounded in the leg.'

'I believe most of our soldiers would consider that lucky, too,' Hankey said, rising from his chair. 'And he's been working for you since?'

'In Belgium. He's grown the network there – speaks five

languages – the intelligence from our watchers in Belgium is better than it's ever been. He pulled off quite a coup: spent four weeks repairing the enemy's defences; mapping artillery strongpoints and reserve lines, and the harbour at Ostend.'

'The Army was grateful?'

Cumming grunted. 'To the Bureau? Never. Bloody ungrateful.'

'Yes, I imagine it was.' Hankey was standing at the window, gazing distractedly into a London square, a slight figure in charcoal grey, right hand tucked neatly behind his back. A lugubrious fellow, or so he seemed to Cumming, that right hand always cold to shake. He had a hang-dog face with brown eyes, like a Bassett, that hardly ever betrayed emotion. They'd known each other a little for years, first in Naval Intelligence – plain Hankey then – but now he was the great panjandrum of government. More. He was *Sir* Maurice, the prime minister, Mr Lloyd George's advisor and confidante.

'I'm sorry, Captain.' He took a deep breath, and turned to look at Cumming. 'A difficult meeting of the War Cabinet this morning. You've heard the news from the Front at Ypres? Of course you have, enough of it's in the newspapers. Well, as you can imagine, the Cabinet is losing its faith in this offensive. Lloyd George didn't have a great deal in the first place. The casualty figures . . . we're all desperate to prevent another Battle of the Somme.' Wearily he bent his head, bald and shining in the sunlight at the window – perfect for a civil servant's bowler.

'The weather's been atrocious. Drowning in mud. In September!' he said, reaching into his jacket for his cigarette case. 'I expect you know – it's your job to, isn't it? – but L.G. doesn't have much of an opinion of our commander-in-chief. "Field Marshal Haig is brilliant to the top of his cavalry boots," he says, "but with some very influential friends. Friends in the press, friends in parliament. The King."' Hankey lit his cigarette. 'I'm sorry, would you like—?'

Cumming held up a hand.

'Which is rather a long-winded way of saying, you can see how important this affair is to him . . .' Hankey's face seemed to droop a little more, 'and for your Secret Service too.'

'I understand the situation, yes. Although I'm bound to ask, if the Prime Minister didn't have any faith in this offensive why did he allow—?'

'He didn't think he could prevent it.' Hankey pursed his lips for a moment. 'Actually, I think he was ambushed . . . but that is by the by.' Lifting a glass ashtray from the chimney-piece, he walked back to the armchair opposite. 'Tell me more about your man. Who did he serve with?'

'The Cameron Highlanders. A queer chap. His battalion commander said he worried away at things. Serious, a certain fixity of purpose. Not exactly inflexible, but once he has the bit between his teeth . . . I had a devil of a job persuading him spying was worthwhile and decent. But Belgium – the people he met in our network there, and he saw with his own eyes what the Boche have done – well, he's changed his tune.'

'And an assignment to Field Marshal Haig's Staff, will he consider that worthwhile?'

'A short assignment, yes, I believe so.' Cumming removed his monocle and massaged the corners of his eyes with his thumb and forefinger. 'My people have freedom, of course, Sir Maurice, but he's a soldier and I expect him to obey an order.'

'May I?' Hankey pointed to the file on Cumming's knees. 'Or is it secret?'

'Not for the Secretary to the War Cabinet.'

Hankey took it, turning the pages slowly, lifting a photograph of Innes to the light from the window.

'A miracle he survived so long.' He glanced up at Cumming. 'Six feet, one inch. Too tall to be comfortable in a trench.'

'He does stoop a little. Habit, I suppose.'

'But no doubting his courage.'

'The Military Cross was for rescuing a wounded man under fire.'

Hankey's perfectly arched eyebrows collapsed in a frown. '"Suicidal" his colonel says; "broad daylight, full view of the enemy". A little too reckless?'

'I don't think so. A good officer. Religious, apparently. A Roman.'

'A firm faith is to his credit in my book.' Hankey drew heavily on his cigarette, then reached across to press the butt in the ashtray. 'And a couple of years at Göttingen University; that *is* useful.'

'I thought so.'

The sun was creeping across the polished floor towards the rug at their feet. The club was famous for the height of its ceilings, but it felt close, and Cumming was grateful for the draft stirring the curtains at the open window. *Thunder later.*

'I don't think lunch at the Rag is worse than anywhere else. Would you like to . . . ?'

Hankey didn't look up. 'No. No, thank you.'

'You're prepared to put your trust in Captain Innes?'

'Oh, yes. The Prime Minister's determined.' Hankey closed the file and offered it back to him with a polite half-smile. 'But it must be handled carefully. It would be damaging . . . actually, it would bring down the government if it became public knowledge.'

'Yes. Well, it will be handled carefully, of course.'

'When will you speak to him?'

'He's spending a few hours with his sister.' Cumming was straining on his stick and the arm of his chair to rise. 'No, no, I'm quite all right,' he said, waving Hankey away. 'He's staying at the Royal Automobile Club round the corner . . . it seems to be popular with the young. Ah. There.' A deep breath. 'Made it. Sitting in one place for too long.'

Hankey was on his feet too. 'I hear you use a scooter when you visit the War Office.'

'Useful in long corridors. You know . . .' Cumming chuckled. 'I heard someone on the Staff there say, "Watch out! Here comes that miserable Secret Service fart with the wooden leg. He's a damn menace."'

A gong was sounding somewhere, echoing up the Grand Stair, summoning one of the club's many committees perhaps, a resting place for the commodores and colonels of the last century.

'They don't clean this place as often as they used to.' Cumming ran a finger along the half-panelling by the door. 'I suppose that's the war. Three years and everything's dirtier, don't you think?'

Hankey was holding the door handle, the silhouette of his long face in the mahogany. 'It isn't the time for sentiment, we've lost too much. This place reeks of it.'

Cumming frowned. 'Not sentiment, standards. Old-fashioned, I grant you, but I'm fond of this place. But of course, I'm old enough to be your father, Maurice.'

'No doubt, no doubt.' Their eyes met for a moment, Hankey's drooping mournfully at the corners. 'I know I don't need to remind you, Captain: your man must know nothing of the Prime Minister's interest.'

'He won't. Of course.'

Hankey offered a faded smile. 'Innes seems a good choice.' He opened the door and stood aside for Cumming. 'And you can be sure I'll speak to L.G. about the future of your Bureau.'

Innes was tired of London. On leave from the battalion, he'd done the sort of things young officers were supposed to do.

He'd eaten in the right places, taken his sister and her friends to a show, danced and drunk and laughed, thankful to be alive and determined to prove it to everyone, and on his first visit he managed to. By the time his second furlough came he'd lost his appetite and did what was expected only to have a story to tell when he returned to the line. In truth, he hated the bustle and smoke, he hated scuttling across its streets, the horn-honking anarchy of the motor car, the impatience, the 'business as usual' insouciance, and the ignorance of the people he met who knew nothing of the real war. He took some pleasure in the Turkish bath at the R.A.C. – soaking and scraping away dirt that always felt more than skin deep – and in a soft bed, hot food, and the silence of his room. He wanted to walk with a warm breeze on his face. Home was too far but he thought of it often. Most of all he looked forward to seeing Jessie.

As always, they met at the Bureau de Change opposite Charing Cross Station. Innes watched her running through the traffic, pausing to apologise to a man pushing a handcart, ignoring the protests of a cab driver, tall and straight like their mother, with the same fine features and large blue eyes, but dark brown hair like their father's family, unruly wisps breaking free of her hat. Everyone said they were alike – in their temperaments, too.

He wanted to hug her but she held him away, her eyes pointedly falling from his peaked cap, down his tunic buttons to his trews. 'Oh, Sandy . . . why?'

'What's the matter?'

'You're in uniform.' Her face was beginning to crumple.

'Jessie. This doesn't mean anything. Here . . .' He folded his arms about her. 'They're sending me to GHQ in France for a few weeks. They won't let me near the Front. I'm crocked. I'm going to work for Field Marshal Haig.'

She pushed him away. 'You promise?'

'Yes, yes, I promise.' He laughed, glad he could tell her the truth even if his uniform was uncomfortable and he preferred a Belgian workman's beard to the army moustache the barber had conjured up for him that morning. Jessie didn't like face hair. A hint of red made him look like a bit of a lothario, she said; that and his weather-brown skin, the worldly care lines at the corners of his eyes.

He'd reserved a table at Romano's in the Strand to celebrate her birthday.

'It isn't for another six weeks,' she said.

'I'll be in France by then.'

People complained it wasn't the restaurant it used to be before the war but Innes couldn't say. Jessie was excited to be there, and they ate and drank well enough.

'I expect you're used to places like this,' he teased. 'A beautiful young nurse . . . so many officers . . .'

She tried to smile. 'The hospital allows us one day a week. We're too tired to go out.'

'But you must find time for friends, for laugher. You're almost twenty. This damn war may drag on for . . . oh, I don't know. Too long already. Here . . .' He poured her more wine.

'Let the waiter, Sandy.' She sounded embarrassed.

'Why?'

'Because you're supposed to.'

'Dug-out manners.' He didn't want to argue. 'Tell me what you're doing. Are you still playing the piano?'

'There's one in the hospital chapel.'

'But you haven't . . .'

'No. I told you; we're too busy.'

Bed pans and dressings, starched white aprons like the ones worn by the Romano's waiters; suppurating wounds and the last mumbled words of the dying: Innes was very familiar

with 'busy'. One more case drifting in and out of conscious-
ness. *Don't take my leg,* he'd pleaded with the doctors, and
they hadn't. Perhaps they'd forgotten they were going to. He
lifted his wine, trembling a little at his lip. In just a blink of
memory the restaurant had reeked of Jeyes Fluid and gangrene.

'Are you all right?' Her hand crept across the cloth to his.
'You've got black rings about your eyes. Are you sleeping?'

'A few aches, that's all.'

'Your leg? You look worn-out, Sandy.'

'It has been . . .' He hesitated. 'Busy.'

'You don't look well.'

He gave her hand another squeeze. 'I'm all right, nurse.'

After lunch they walked down to the embankment and along
the river towards Westminster. On the bridge, a steam lorry
had been knocked on its side and traffic was grinding round
it in a filthy haze. The pale stone face of Whitehall Court was
across the road and the gardens to their right; the fashionable
home of the great and good, of famous authors and suffragettes,
socialists and senior civil servants, and nesting discreetly in
the eaves beneath its green slate roof and turrets, the offices
of the Secret Service Bureau.

They chose a bench and sat facing the river. Father was
working at the infirmary again, Jessie said, even though he
was too old to be on his feet all day. Mother was spending her
empty hours fretting about her children and the war. '"Sandy's
safe in an office," I tell her, but she won't listen. She wants
me to come home. "You can nurse in Edinburgh," she says,
"your father can arrange a transfer." But I have my job here.'

'Do what is best for you.'

'It's not about me, Sandy. I'm needed here.'

He smiled and placed his arm round her shoulders. 'Do you
ever think of Dalibrog?'

'Sometimes. You spent more time there than me.'

'You know, I thought of Uncle and the island all the time in the trenches – I still do. The quiet routines of his life, prayer, the Mass: I used to think he was lonely in that draughty parish house – none of the windows fitted properly – but I'm not sure now. He knew and cared for everyone, and he liked his own company too. Out in no man's land with a wiring party, I would imagine him cutting and stacking his peat or preparing his rod on the banks of Loch Marulaigh. Calming, I suppose. There were three men from Uist in my battalion – until the Somme; they spoke well of Uncle Allan – *Maighstir Ailein* – although they were too young to have known very much of him. A worthwhile life, to be remembered so long after your death.'

'It was a hard life. Too hard for a sensitive man.'

'Not for a man with his strong faith.'

'No.' She reached into her coat for a handkerchief. 'Oh, Sandy, do you remember? When someone was sick on Eriskay, he'd walk seven miles to the Sound, light a fire on the shore and wait . . .' She swallowed hard, trying not to cry. 'Eventually one of the islanders would sail across to fetch him.'

'He almost drowned, more than once. Ionad-bhàis co e dha'n aithne?'

'I don't—' Jessie discreetly wiped a tear. 'I was never as good at Gaelic.'

'Something Uncle Allan wrote: "Who can tell his place of dying? Away abroad or amongst friends; is it to be engulfed by the waves or a death in bed that is in store for us?"'

'He knew it was his duty to go, no matter how dangerous,' she said, 'trusting in God's love.'

For a while they sat in silence, the tide of the brown river turning. Big Ben struck half past the hour, the traffic on the bridge was moving again and the first bowler-hatted civil servants were crossing to catch trains from Waterloo to their neat semi-detached homes in the suburbs. Jessie was rummaging in her bag. 'Here.' She opened her long fingers slowly, a miraculous medal cradled in her palm. 'Granny's. I wished I'd given it to you before.'

He smiled and squeezed her shoulders. 'You keep it,' and he tried to close her hand.

'No. Sandy. Take it, please.'

He could see she was determined he should have the medal. 'Thank you. I'll attach it to this,' he said, reaching for the chain round his neck.

'That's strange. Rough. Tarnished.' She leant closer to peer at his cross.

'Yes. Tarnished,' he said, 'but it's lucky. I promised someone I'd wear it.'

'Promised?'

'A comrade I became close to. We were all superstitious out there.'

'Not superstitious. Do you say your prayers?'

'No. Before, at the Front . . .'

'You don't go to church?'

'No.'

She kissed the medal and dropped it into his hand. 'With your cross, then. I'll pray for the both of us.'

Innes offered to pay for a taxicab but she refused, so he escorted her back to the Strand and waited with her for an omnibus. Back on duty at eight, she said, restless, anxious to be away. She hated saying goodbye and he felt the same, even after so much practice. The first bus to Bethnal Green was full.

'Here, blokes like you don't catch buses,' someone in the queue joked.

'Blokes like me do all sorts of strange things,' he replied.

When the next one came he hugged and kissed her and

promised to see her soon, then he watched her climb to the top, her eyes fixed to the front, only turning to raise her hand as the bus pulled away. She was crying. Why? He'd told her he was joining the Staff so he would be safe – or was that a foolish thing to take for granted in these times?

Bitheamaid 'nar faicill daonnan . . . Let us be watchful always, God has not given us a lease of life; when we go to rest at night we cannot be sure we will see the day.

More of his Uncle Allan's lines, spoken softly on the Prince's Beach at sunset to a boy with no cause to reflect upon their meaning until he became a soldier. As well to remember and mark them again before his visit to Captain Cumming.

Miss Groves met him with a cool smile and an apology. 'He's in a meeting,' she said, 'would you mind waiting for a few minutes?' She was an attractive young woman as all Cumming's secretaries seemed to be. Some of them were married, Tinsley said, which was rather unconventional for an officer who'd seen most of his service in the old Queen's Navy. Perhaps he'd changed in the eight years he'd been head of the Secret Service Bureau. Rules and conventions could hardly matter to a man required by his role to judge actions by their outcomes. No broad straight corridors in the Bureau; it was a maze, Innes reflected as he followed Miss Groves down steps and into another narrow passage. On his left, a room under the eaves, two men roughly his own age, dark suits, desks, a map of Europe; to his right, laughter, the clatter of typewriters, and passing the door, he saw four 'gels' in nice clothes, with nice hair.

'You know, we're opening a canteen,' Miss Groves said, 'Colonel Browning's idea. He's borrowed a chef from the Savoy.'

'Who's Colonel Browning?'

'You don't know?'

'No.'

'But here we are,' she said, pointing him to a chair in Cumming's outer office. 'C will be with you in a minute.' Everyone at the Bureau called him C. Innes wasn't sure why, but he seemed to approve. His door was ajar and Innes could hear the heavy fall of his wooden leg and the scuffing of his shoes, then the tinkle of something metal, and seconds later a crash and muttered curse. 'Groves,' he bellowed; 'Groves!' But she'd gone, so Innes answered.

'Innes.' He was bending over the pieces of some sort of instrument. 'One of my toys. Isn't Groves there?'

The rest of his collection was on a work table beneath the window.

'Rescue it, would you?' he said, pushing the mechanism with the end of his stick. 'Damn clumsy of me. A new electronic clock.'

Innes picked up the tangle of cogs and springs and put it back on the table. 'Is it beyond repair?'

C peered at it through his monocle; 'No, I don't think so, not if I can find the time.' He plainly relished the possibility. 'Sit down. Would you like a drink? Whisky, I suppose.'

'No, thank you.' Innes took the armchair in front of his desk. It was polished spotless; pens, blotter, inkwell, aligned to a perfect inch.

'You spent a little time with your sister? A nurse isn't she?' He was standing with his back to Innes at a dark green cupboard safe. 'Here it is.' Turning with a file, he carried it to the desk and sat down, his rough sailor's hands clasped in a fist on top of it. 'The War Office is pleased with your report . . .' He flipped the file open and ran his forefinger down the page. 'Delighted, actually – positions above Ypres, the Moere howitzer, Ostend Harbour – it's gone to Haig's headquarters. You *should* receive a warm welcome there.'

He lifted his head, his small grey eyes twinkling mischievously. 'I don't expect you will.'

'I don't . . .'

'Are you sure you wouldn't like a drink? It's after six.'

'Quite sure, thank you.'

'You can smoke if you like.'

Innes watched him turn the pages of the file. Thin white hair, a determined set to his jaw and pale straight lips, he was older than Innes remembered; a bruiser cut from the scarred timbers of some old warship. They'd only met twice before; he'd been genial, even kind to Innes. Tinsley said he was an unscrupulous old Tatar, but with Tinsley he would have to be. 'You'll meet scallywags and patriots in this work,' he'd warned Innes at their first meeting, 'rather more of the former, I'm afraid.'

But sitting back now, he said, 'Field Marshal Haig is going to clear the Germans from the whole Belgium coast and win the war at a stroke. That's what he says.'

'You sound sceptical.'

'I'm a naval officer, you're the soldier. What do you think?'

Innes shrugged. 'I'm a teacher.'

'A teacher, a soldier, a spy.'

'We've all had to do things we never thought we could.'

C smiled. 'And done them well. Your past, your record in the Army, your experience behind enemy lines. They could see you would be useful.'

'You persuaded the Army to take me back?'

'Yes.' He lifted the monocle from his eye and began to polish it with his handkerchief. 'Field Marshal Haig's head of intelligence has set up a new section of Army agents at general headquarters. If I understand him correctly, the Field Marshal hopes to exploit a break in the German line by sending in his cavalry. The new Army agents will be with 'em. Once the

31

agents are through the line they're expected to operate under-cover in Belgium, reporting on the enemy's activities.'

Innes looked down at his hands. 'You want me to become one of these Army agents?'

'Good God, no. Complete waste of time. Bound to fail.' He slipped the monocle back in his eye and leant a little closer. 'No, they want you to train these poor devils. *They* think it will work, and that's what matters.'

'I'm sorry, I don't understand.'

'I'm sure you do.' His eyes narrowed a little, appraising Innes carefully. 'The thing is, some important people have concerns about the intelligence operation at GHQ. They would like, well, an impartial view.'

Silence. Innes stared at him, or to be precise, at his twinkling eyeglass. It was disconcerting, like being at the wrong end of a microscope, something smeared on a slide. 'If I understand you correctly, Captain . . .' Deep breath . . . 'You're asking me to spy on our army – at headquarters?'

'I'm not *asking*, and I wouldn't put it like that, no. Investigate. You'll be in a position to observe the operation there.'

'I see.' Innes said. He didn't see at all. 'And our network in Belgium?'

'Invaluable, of course. You can be sure I wouldn't have brought you back if this wasn't absolutely necessary. Tinsley will have to manage things there without you, just for a few weeks.'

Silence. Innes was hunched at the edge of his chair, his arms tightly folded. 'I'm confused. This investigation, is it going to help us win the war?'

'Don't be simple, Innes.' Cumming's chin seemed to lift until it almost touched his nose. 'But as you ask, yes, I think it might. The Army wants to swallow up our service, take over direction of the Bureau. There are people – and I'm one of them – who think that would be disastrous for the country and the war effort.'

'I see.'

'No. This time I don't think you do.' One hand on the edge of his desk, he rose and took three stiff steps to the drinks tray. 'Damn it, I'm having one. Soda?' he said, pouring whisky into two glasses.

'Just a little water, please.'

'This isn't about me, if that's what you're thinking, or some petty internecine struggle – fighting for the bridge while the ship burns. Here . . .' He thrust the glass at Innes. 'I happen to think we are better at what we do than the Army, but that doesn't matter. What matters is good intelligence, sound intelligence; what matters is the security of our networks in Belgium and France and elsewhere. Your network, yours and Ramble's. There. Chin-chin.' He sank gratefully into his seat and took a sip of whisky. 'As I was saying, there are concerns in certain circles about the Army's intelligence operation.'

'What sort of concerns?'

'About the quality of its intelligence. You can see what the implications are – *might* be – I'm sure. Poor information makes for poor decisions that men pay for with their lives.'

Silence. Innes turned his glass on the arm of the chair. Miss Groves was back at her desk. Big Ben struck the half-hour and a few seconds later the carriage clock on the marble chimney-piece did the same.

'I'll have to do something about that,' Cumming said.

'These important people – concerned people – who are they, Captain?'

'People in Whitehall with access to *all* our intelligence sources.' He lifted his glass to his lips but lowered it again without drinking. 'That's all you need to know . . . all I can tell you.'

Another silence. Then he continued: 'It's just a case of keeping your eyes and ears open. Have you met Brigadier Charteris? Of course not. Well, he's Field Marshal Haig's head of intelligence at GHQ. With Haig for years in India first and everywhere since. A Scot.'

Innes smiled. 'I see. Was there anything else that recommended me for this job?'

'A good number of things, actually. Here . . .' He lifted a sheet from his file. 'John Charteris. Your new commanding officer. Clever, a good linguist, some say a good intelligence officer.'

'But not your friends in Whitehall?'

C pushed the sheet across the desk to Innes. 'He isn't popular with Haig's Army commanders either.'

Innes picked up the sheet. Aged forty. At school in Glasgow. Father a professor of medicine at Glasgow University.

'You see?' C was smiling broadly. 'Very tribal, the Army.'

There was a photograph: strongly built, regulation military moustache, a thoughtful face.

Innes asked: 'Is this more than a fishing trip? What am I supposed to be looking for?'

Cumming drained his glass and looked at his watch. 'They're expecting you tomorrow, so we don't have more than a few hours. I suggest we eat at the Army and Navy Club; you can still get a decent steak. You're staying round the corner aren't you, so that's easy. Let's talk over dinner . . . you weren't meeting your sister? Shall we say in two hours.'

Stepping from the entrance of the Court, a military motor car roared past and turned into Whitehall, a cloud of its exhaust fumes hanging in the air. Innes walked on, dirty London rain speckling his uniform. But in Horse Guards Parade he stopped for a moment to gaze at the rear of number 10 Downing Street.

How important were C's important people? Honourable or even Right Honourable Gentlemen? Big Ben was almost ready to strike six. At Ypres they'd be counting the dead and wounded from the day's action, the rations would be on their way up the line, perhaps someone in his old battalion was checking the pickets in the sap-heads overlooking no man's land. And beyond the Front, in the enemy's forbidden zone, Ramble's priests and teachers, bakers and station-masters were watching, writing returns, waiting for a tap at the door to signal the courier was there to collect.

3

At GHQ

INNES LEFT ON the boat train from Victoria Station at half past seven the next morning. In his compartment there was a Guards officer on his way out for the first time and an old sweat from the Royal Fusiliers. They talked of the new battle at Ypres and Innes listened just long enough to be polite. As they rattled through London's dreary brick suburbs he closed his eyes and tried to rest. He'd slept badly and dreamt again, waking with a start in the early hours, wrapped tightly in damp sheets. Unwilling to risk more of the same, he'd stood at the open window with a cigarette, listening to the hum of the city, straining, unconsciously at first, for the echo of the guns. Nothing, even on a still night. Of course not. But he'd stood there naked until the cigarette burnt his fingertips.

Sunshine glinted through the carriage's soot-stained window, and the warmth and motion helped him doze for a time. He woke with a start as the train rumbled across the swing bridge into Folkestone station. Judging by the flags flying from the boats slumped in the mud of the inner harbour, it was going to be a lively crossing: it always seemed to be. His first with the battalion had been two years before, with pipes and drums through the town, cheers for Jock, and, *Company . . . Step Short,* the order for the march down the hill to the harbour. Most of the men he'd marched with that day were crippled or dead. On another late summer day a year later he'd been carried down a companionway to the same quay, his leg in splints and weak with exhaustion after heaving into a bowl for an hour and a half.

'Wonder if there's time for breakfast?' the captain of Fusiliers said, tapping the ash from his pipe on to the carriage floor. 'The Pavilion Hotel's good.'

But the marshals were herding men straight to the pier. Shouldering kit-bags, the new recruits anxious for guidance; officers with wispy moustaches, struggling to fill their tunics; and veterans returning from leave, with hard times in the lines of their faces, a certain slouch and perhaps a little rectangle of ribbon.

Innes could see a subaltern in a Cameron kilt and glengarry edging towards him.

'Hello, sir,' he said, flashing a salute and an eager smile. A first-timer, a Surrey schoolboy whose grandfather had served with the regiment forty years before, when the enemy carried a spear.

Innes wished him luck. Meet, greet and move away. New men used to think he was unfriendly, but too many would arrive one week and disappear the next, leaving only their shadow, fine emotional scars, and perhaps the remains of a food parcel from home.

The ship sailed on time for once, her smoke a flat black plume to starboard. Innes found some shelter on the upper deck and settled beside his back-pack to watch a destroyer run patterns round them, dipping then rising to cut the top of a wave white. The wind was a whetted knife even on the leeward side, and she pitched and rolled without mercy. A colonel with a walrus moustache scuttled from a door to stand at the rail with two green-looking subalterns. Most of the officers elected for the open deck; other ranks were left to shift the best they could in the heaving, evil-smelling body of the ship.

Approaching the piers at the mouth of the port of Boulogne,

then into the channel, customs house, fish market, and somewhere in the streets beyond, Madame Paul's café and brothel, crowded at night with young soldiers hoping to prove themselves men before they died; woken on Sunday by the Matins Mass bells of Our Lady in the old town above, a basilica 'in the degraded Italian style' the guidebook said. The harbour basin was busier than he'd ever seen it, with food, artillery shells, and men for the mincer at Ypres. A train was making steam on the Quai Chanzy.

'Is it going south?' Innes enquired of the transport officer at the foot of the gangway.

'North to Poperinge,' he replied. 'To the Front.'

'Anyone driving to GHQ?'

The transport officer pointed across the basin. 'Try the Quartermaster's Office.'

The young Cameron had been sick on his tunic. He was holding his pack so tightly to his chest to cover the stain, he was struggling to negotiate the gangway. Innes caught his elbow as he tripped from the bottom step.

'Oh, I'm sorry, sir.' His breath smelt of vomit.

'Are you all right?'

He tried to smile. 'Glad to be ashore.'

'Boyd, isn't it? Look, don't worry about that . . .' Innes gestured to the stain on his uniform. 'Where are you going?'

'Wipers, sir. The sixth battalion.'

'Training at Étaples?'

'At the Front. The battalion's very short.'

'The sixth will look after you.' Innes offered to shake hands again and waited while the boy struggled to balance his pack on his knee.

'Done it,' he said, pulling his hand free at last. 'Sorry, sir.'

'Put your pack on your back where it belongs, Boyd.' Innes gestured to his uniform. 'It isn't worth the trouble.'

'I'm sorry, sir.'

'You don't need to apologise to me.' Innes gazed at him for a moment, then he said: 'Look, I'll give you a note for Colonel McCabe.' He slipped his own sack from his shoulders, took out a slim volume of poems and tore out the frontispiece. 'This is the only paper I have.' He scribbled a note and handed it to Boyd. 'It says we met. Good luck. Remember – keep your head down.'

There was no one in authority at the Quartermaster's Office with time for Innes, but a lieutenant from GHQ was queuing with a chit for stores. Business complete, he was proposing to buy delicacies in the old town then drive back to headquarters, and he was ready to take Innes too. Conversation was almost impossible above the roar of the engine and the tinkling of the loosely packed wine bottles the lieutenant had been sent to collect for the Officers' Club. They drove south through woods tinged with autumn colours, slowing for military traffic as they approached the base camp at Étaples, turning west to follow the twisting course of the Canche.

'Almost there,' the lieutenant shouted, 'the centre of it all.' Round a corner and the pink walls of Montreuil-sur-Mer flashed through the tree-lined banks of the river. Innes was surprised at how anxious his first glimpse of the town made him feel.

He'd been given orders and was on his way, but with a strong sense of embarking on a dubious enterprise. There hadn't been time to consider what it would be like rubbing shoulders with those 'at the centre of it all'. They forked right to the lower town, accelerating along a sun-dappled road. A Staff car approached and passed with a *woosh*, and he closed his eyes long enough to sweep the gas curtain aside again, the lamp above the plank table swinging in the draught, faces dipping in and out of the light, an empty whisky bottle and the sad echo of words spoken by young men who'd placed too much faith in those charged with the direction of the war. But someone has to take the responsibility for making decisions, he'd always argued.

'Does our commander-in-chief live in Montreuil?'

'Just outside,' the lieutenant said. 'The Château de Beaurepaire. Newspaper folk and senior officers out, the rest of us in the town.' On the road ahead there was a hay wagon. 'It's a small place. We've taken it over really. There!' Opening the throttle, he managed to slip past the wagon before the bridge. 'The locals don't seem to mind, they're paid quite handsomely for the inconvenience.' Across the railway track, the town above them, turning left and climbing. 'You'll probably be billeted here, sir. Captain Macrae's old room, I shouldn't wonder. He was with your lot.'

'He was intelligence?'

'Yes. Captain Macrae—' The road was receiving his full atten-tion. 'He left. Very sudden.'

Coaching inn beneath the walls, paint peeling from its facade; fork right, the engine straining as they climbed the curve of the hill, the valley of the Canche below, smoke spirals rising from the woodland to the north. 'Our Chinese labourers,' the lieutenant said, following the direction of Innes's gaze. 'The locals complain we're taking too much timber, too much of everything. But the Boche wouldn't pay 'em, would they, sir?'

Innes smiled. 'No. The Germans don't pay.'

Ahead of them the road narrowed to a cart's width as it approached a gate in brick ramparts scarred and patched with white stone. A military policeman waved them down and inspected Innes's papers: new arrivals to report their presence at the École Militaire.

'Most of us are in the old military school,' the lieutenant

said. 'Intelligence has the large courtyard, lucky fellows; you see more sun than the rest of us.'

Creeping through the gate, they waited for another Staff motor car and then turned left up a narrow street of houses painted white with blue shutters, the loose bottles protesting on the broken *pavé*, the lieutenant sounding his horn at soldiers deaf to the engine's roar. They crossed a small square where a military band was playing one of the hymn tunes Innes remembered from school, its polished brass instruments glinting in the evening sunshine. It was touching but strange because most of his billets had been in towns that were being reduced to mud and rubble.

Ahead of them stood a church in the middle of a broad street, and running almost its entire length, a plain two-storey building with a grey plaster face, pockmarked by age and neglect. The Crossley drew up in front of its carriage arch with a final chink and its driver stepped down to salute, then shake Innes's hand.

'Captain Innes for Intelligence,' he said, addressing a military police sergeant. 'Show him to the BGI's office, would you?'

Papers again, back-pack in the guard-house, then Innes was led across one courtyard and along a passage to a second that was open to the north. There was a view of the ramparts and the opposite side of the valley where a team of horses was turning the landscape from the stubble yellow of summer to winter brown. In the centre of the courtyard there were the rotting remains of a pergola and on a bench beneath it, two officers in conversation. They stopped and gazed at Innes with what seemed more than polite curiosity.

Intelligence was in the east range, the sun's low rays casting the twisted shadow of the pergola on the tiled floor of the entrance hall. Bright offices with large sash windows

41

overlooked the courtyard on the left of the corridor; the old school classrooms, larger, darker, were on the opposite side. Clerks shuffled between the two, and a subaltern with the red hat band of the Staff was bent over papers he'd let slip to the floor. Innes was very conscious of its institutional echo and that he was keeping step with his guide like one of the schoolboy soldiers who'd occupied the place before the war. The plate on Brigadier General Charteris's door had been buffed so often his name was only just legible. It brought to the front of Innes's mind an image of the rector's study at Edinburgh Academy and the apprehension he'd felt once before a caning. He'd never been comfortable with lies, but he'd learnt the value of expediency there, a lesson made all the more memorable by his stripes. Two academy corridors connected by a thread of time, red-faced Mackenzie swishing away with his birch: 'You'll thank me one day, Innes,' he'd said without irony. Surely it was time to acknowledge the debt, here and now, liar and spy at Charteris's door.

But Brigadier General (Intelligence) wasn't in his office. His adjutant advised Innes to report at eight the following morning, that his billet was on the rue du Paon, and he might join the other intelligence officers for dinner at the club. *Stand down, Innes.* He felt the same sort of shoulder-sagging relief he used to experience in the trenches when an order came up the line to postpone an attack on the enemy. 'I'll find my own way to my billet,' Innes told his guide.

But the shorter of the two officers he'd seen in conversation beneath the pergola was waiting for him in the corridor.

'You're the new boy, aren't you? I should have caught you outside,' he said, advancing the last few yards with his hand outstretched. 'The BGI's on his way back from Amiens.' His grip was firm and his smile engaging. 'Marshall. James Marshall. Section A.' He was a major, a little older than Innes perhaps, but with a round, boyish face and a moustache that was modest by the standards of the Staff. The most remarkable thing about his appearance was his stature; for an officer he was a wee man.

'Been looking forward to meeting you,' he said. 'I read your report. How on earth did you— But look, let me show you this place, introduce you to a few people. Have they arranged a room for you in the town?'

They drifted along the corridor, Marshall interpreting the letters and acronyms on the office doors. 'You're in Section B – intelligence from the occupied territories, and from the new unit you're here to whip into shape. Colonel MacLeod's in charge.' He glanced down, licking his bottom lip as if he were tasting a confidence he must have thought better of sharing. 'I think he's a Scot. There are a good number of us at headquarters.'

'You're a Scot?'

'Edinburgh. Born in India, but yes, family from Edinburgh.' It was impossible to hear more than his class and his school in his voice. 'And you?'

'Edinburgh.'

'Well, it certainly won't hurt you here.'

He stopped at a door with *I (A)* on the plate. 'My part of ship. Operational intelligence – where we piece together the enemy's order of battle, who's in the line, how many, that sort of thing.' He stood back to let Innes enter. The evening sun was streaming through the west-facing windows, striping the room in golden light and shade. In front of an old chalk board there were two large oak tables and the desks used by the section's clerks, arranged in a row as they might have been in schooldays before the war. Three private soldiers were bent over paperwork, and a grey-haired sergeant was standing to the right of the board, stooping to draw on a large wall map of the Front.

43

'Sergeant Ramsey's corner. We tell him he's the class dunce,' Marshall whispered. 'He does a great job of keeping the operational map up to date. I shouldn't say this but . . .' Hand to his ear, he craned to the left, then to the right, like a silent film star searching for an eavesdropper. 'In *my* opinion, the most reliable, the most up-to-date intelligence we receive is from the Secret Service Bureau's network in Belgium – your network. Don't tell anyone I said so.' Forefinger across his lips, he took half a step forward and glanced about the room again.

'Batson in that film *The German Spy Peril.*'

'Ah, you recognised it.' A faint smile and a small bow. 'Do I have a future, when the war's over?'

'Certain of it. And thank you. I'll respect the confidence.' For all the foolery, Innes was quite sure it was meant to be one.

'I'm sure you think it's silly – people here know my opinions, only, they wouldn't take kindly to me repeating them to a new boy, especially someone from the Bureau.'

'I thought we were on the same side.'

'Did you? Well, this is your first day.' He caught Innes's eye and made an effort to smile. 'Rivalries. Jealousies. Didn't Captain Cumming warn you?' He waited to see if Innes would reply. '*Gang warily*, that's all.'

'Thank you for the advice.'

'It's meant well. As I say, your network is our best source. I admire what you've done. Only what I think doesn't really matter.'

The sergeant finished at the map and began weaving between desks towards the door. Innes waited for him to leave. 'Brigadier Charteris, what manner of man—'

Marshall interrupted. 'You're meeting him tomorrow, aren't you?' His gaze dropped from Innes's face to his tie. 'Then you'll be able to form your own opinion soon enough. Please excuse me, but I don't know you well enough to offer mine.'

'No. Of course. Sorry.'

'No need to be. You must be hungry.' He glanced at his watch. 'And we're late.'

The Officers' Club was in an undistinguished courtyard house of the last century. It had served as a home for elderly nuns before the war, Marshall said with a hint of Presbyterian disapproval in his voice. Groups of three and four officers had spilled through the French windows of the mess bar with their glasses. Innes recognised his young driver. He was cutting with an imaginary bat, entertaining his companions with a cricket story, perhaps a memory of his finest innings. A thick-set officer at his side started braying with laughter, drawing for a moment the attention of everyone in the courtyard. Marshall led Innes into the bar, slipping away from familiar faces with a wave and a smile. He was plainly a popular officer. 'Twenty months now at GHQ,' he said, glancing over his shoulder in the crush. 'I'm an old hand, I suppose.'

The mess was dressed like a middle-price restaurant with round dark wood tables for four, starched linen and silver plate. Behind a drape in the corner Innes recognised the thick frame of the nuns' refectory lectern. Young ladies of the Army Auxiliary Corps were serving a first-course consommé. There were a number of tables with empty chairs but Marshall appeared to be searching for one in particular. An arm lifted at the back of the hall and half rising from a seat was his companion beneath the pergola.

'That's lucky,' he said, touching Innes's sleeve. 'Major Graham. Shall we join him?' He didn't wait for a reply but set off across the hall leaving Innes to reflect that their good fortune was not a coincidence. He followed a few paces behind – stopping to let a waitress pass – and there was time before he approached the table for Marshall to bend close and whisper to his friend. Graham was rising to his feet, dabbing his moustache with a napkin.

'Innes, isn't it?' A weak handshake, then he gestured to the chair opposite. 'Not too late for soup,' and catching the eye of a waitress: 'For these gentlemen, if you please.'

'What are we promised today?' Marshall reached for the menu. 'It's usually a choice of one. Ah, fish again. But the club keeps a good cellar.'

'We must order a bottle of something. This has become an occasion.' Graham smiled. 'Do you know about wine, Innes?'

'I'm afraid I don't.'

'Margaux, all right? The 1905, I think.'

'Graham knows about wine,' Marshall said, inspecting his nails. 'Family business. His people are profiteers, they're earning a fortune from our drunkenness.'

'Whisky is no sort of education for wine, Marshall. And if by "our drunkenness" you mean our great and glorious Army, I should remind you that no lesser person than its commander-in-chief is doing very well from the supply of whisky too.'

Marshall laughed. 'Better, I shouldn't wonder. The Haig Dimple bottle – now that's advertising, that's salesmanship.'

'If you're selling to Americans and the working class.'

'Aren't you selling to everybody?'

Graham pulled a face. 'I don't know. Ask our sales people.'

'Such fine sensibilities,' Marshall said, rubbing his hands with pleasure. 'When this is over, I'm sure our commander-in-chief will be able to retire on a comfortable pension from *his* family business. The name sells. Have you ever heard anyone in the line ask by name for a bottle of "Graham's" whisky?'

'I'm afraid, I haven't,' Innes said.

'There you are,' Marshall said. 'And Innes is a proper Scotsman.'

Graham sighed. Turning to Innes, he said: 'Our business is in Edinburgh – the Caledonian Distillery. You've heard of it, I expect?'

'The Cally. Yes, of course.' The wind from the west had brought the smell of malting barley to his nursery window. Some days it crept through the city like the *haar*; strong enough to taste on the steps in the old town, in the wrought-iron squares of the New; and well-to-do strangers stepping from trains at Waverley Station pressed scented hankies to their faces. To Innes, the smell of the Cally was as familiar as wet stone.

'The scent of money,' Marshall said. 'Edinburgh was my first posting. A wind from the east and it would carry to the barracks. My man had a devil of a job brushing it out of my uniform.'

Their soup arrived and Graham ordered a bottle of the claret. Conversation settled in a polite groove. There was to be no talk of war at table, Marshall said, it was a mess rule. Instead a barrage of questions to Innes, about family, school, his universities, his battalion. 'War talk,' he protested, but Graham and Marshall were regular soldiers, and the regiment was home. Graham: Eton and the Life Guards. Marshall: Rugby, Royal Artillery and the new Intelligence Corps. Did they care Innes was a temporary officer? 'Not pukka,' the sergeant major at his battalion's training camp used to say.

Innes tried not to judge on first acquaintance, but he didn't like Graham's manner, his armour – armour because it was an affectation – his lazy arrogance, his clipped aristocratic voice, slouched in his chair like a khaki Pimpernel. He was hiding. The medal ribbons, the way he seemed to have of viewing the room from the corner of his eye, and the suggestion at times of a cynical smile: he wasn't the Army bore he wished Innes to believe him to be. Late twenties? They were close in age. The tired lines, the crow's feet of an older man; perhaps he found sleep difficult too . . .

'So you're joining B,' he said to Innes over coffee. 'MacLeod's new unit.'

'Mess rules.' Marshall chinked a teaspoon against his cup. 'Mess rules.'

Innes said, 'I haven't had an opportunity to meet Colonel MacLeod yet.'

'He's with his volunteers, somewhere near Bethune. Pink Tights is organising their balloon training. Heard tell of Pink Tights?' Graham took a sip of coffee and pulled a face. 'Trench water. I swear it's becoming bitterer by the day.' He reached for the sugar and stirred in a heaped spoonful. 'Old Pink Tights is from the Naval Ballooning School. Pink Tights Pollock. He's teaching these new agents to drop behind the German front line with a crate of carrier pigeons, just in case we don't manage to break through . . .' Graham lifted his coffee back to his lips, careful not to catch Innes's eye. 'Which, I'm sure we will.'

'Major Graham. Mess rules,' Marshall said again.

'Balls,' Graham replied. 'Innes wants to know why he's called Pink Tights Pollock. Don't you?'

'Vital intelligence,' Innes replied.

'Quite right. You're going to be working with the fellow. An elderly chap, a solicitor before the war and a great balloonist. But it seems that early in his service temporary Commander Pollock had a terrible accident, became entangled in the ropes of his balloon. Only managed to save himself by sacrificing his trousers, revealing in the process, yes, you've guessed, a pair of bright pink combinations.'

Innes smiled. 'Let's hope the balloons won't be necessary.'

'Yes.' Graham's gaze flitted across the table to Marshall and then down to his coffee cup. 'Yes. That would be nice.'

Nice. What would Ramble think of them, with their bottles of claret and old boy stories; fencing for some secret advantage, and don't mention the war.

The tables were being cleared without ceremony. Screeching chairs, the clink of china plates, loud voices, a wall of sound that reminded Innes again of his school. What will we all do when the lousy war is over, he thought; how will we organise our lives? Next sitting at the door. The first in the queue, a portly captain of engineers casting hungry looks at the Army Auxiliaries.

'Don't think too badly of him. We live like monks here.' Marshall must have followed Innes's gaze. He dumped his napkin on the table. 'I have some work to do, Graham too, I shouldn't wonder.'

Graham leant forward suddenly and touched Innes's sleeve: 'Surprised? You're surprised we haven't time for billiards or getting drunk – don't deny it. I saw it flicker across your face. Why wouldn't you be?' A sardonic smile. 'That's what they say in the line, isn't it? I used to say the same.'

Marshall shifted uneasily. 'Yes, well, that's as may be.' Consulting his watch: 'Eight o'clock. There's time, Graham – do you think Captain Innes should look at our situation?'

'Yes,' said Graham. 'I think he'd find it . . .' another dry smile . . . 'illuminating.'

Junior members of the intelligence staff were gathered in a loose circle round the map Innes had watched the sergeant marking up so meticulously, smoking, chatting, talk of war permitted once more.

'It's becoming an after dinner custom,' Marshall explained.

A forest of flags with the numbers of the divisions fighting at Ypres was pinned in the centre. 'And this was our position in July before the offensive.' Marshall traced the blue line with his finger, from the high ground at the bottom of the map, looping round the city of Ypres, to the low ground at the top. 'And the second line marks our position at the end of the first day's fighting, best progress here, to the north-east of the city – the Guards and the Welsh – and here in the centre. Your old battalion is with the 15th Scottish?'

Innes said that it was.

'Well the divisions in the centre did well. Took a bit of a battering when the enemy came back at them, but here . . .' His hand swept to the bottom of the map. 'Here on the high ground, the Gheluvelt plateau, well, you can see the story wasn't as good. Two Corps got into trouble, couldn't manage its objectives.' His voice had hardened, staring at his forefinger, the tip across the British line. 'Shame. Now the Germans can enfilade our left and centre.'

Fading voices in the corridor, the heavy clunk of a door, and in Section A there was silence. Marshall was commanding the attention of all the officers in the room, almost a dozen, captain and all ranks below, awkward, avoiding his gaze, as if he was responsible for a blue line that had barely moved in a month's fighting.

'Haven't you chaps got something to do?' he asked. 'This isn't a history lesson. Wilson—' A bookish-looking subaltern straightened his back. 'Have you looked at those interrogation reports?'

Wilson promised to see to it at once, turning, catching his leg at the corner of a table, limping to the door. The rest of Marshall's audience just melted away. When they'd gone, he said: 'Then it began to rain. It began to rain and it hasn't stopped – you can imagine can't you? And this is where we are.' His small hand swept along the last blue line on the map.

'Where should we be?'

'Oh, on the way to the Belgian coast – Ostend. Somewhere

over there.' He gestured to the window. Silence. Innes stepped closer to the map. Yes, there was the flag of the 15th Scottish, cut and coloured with care, the size of his thumbnail. Twenty thousand men. How many flags? Forty? The French and the Germans too. And the sergeant's perfect indigo blue lines. A battlefield of villages and roads, brown wooded slopes and plain white farmland for miles and miles and miles.

'It isn't over, of course. Just beginning, really.' Marshall was at his shoulder. 'There's an attack on the twentieth here, to the north and south of the Menin road. We'll break through, I'm sure.' He sounded apologetic, as if to say anything less would be defeatist. Innes tried to catch his eye but he was squinting evasively at the map.

'Perhaps Pink Tights—I'm sorry . . .' Innes couldn't remember his name.

'Commander Pollock.'

'Perhaps Commander Pollock's balloons are going to be useful after all.'

Marshall looked blank. 'You mean?'

'He means, if we don't break through, this damn fool scheme to drop agents behind enemy lines will go ahead,' Graham said. 'They don't stand a chance either way.'

Marshall frowned. 'I don't know.' He leaned a little to his left to peer round Graham into the room. 'I *do* know it's foolish to say so.'

'One has to be careful, yes. Always,' said Graham. 'But I think we can trust Captain Innes to be discreet.' Again, the suggestion of a cynical smile. 'Goodness, he works for the Secret Service!'

'I used to. Back with the Army now.'

'Yes,' Graham drawled. 'Well, that's as maybe.' Their eyes met briefly. Then: 'I must go. Things to do. An interesting evening for both of us, I think. Innes. Marshall.' Turning for the door, he checked and lifted thumb and forefinger to his thin lips, pinching an almost forgotten thought – or so he wished it to seem – his dark brown eyes searching for Innes. 'You know what some of the Staff are calling Charteris's new unit – it was his idea, by the way, not MacLeod's – they're calling it the "Suicide Club". Thought you should know.'

4

Average Intelligence

INNES WAS AWAKE when the bells of the town's churches struck six o'clock, gazing at a damp stain on a sloping ceiling above his bed that was close enough to touch. A bird was roosting in the eaves inches from his head, a summer visitor perhaps, just a few days from its flight to Africa. Some sticks of oak furniture, an ebony Christ, and on a shelf beneath the window to his right, the books left by the previous occupant, Captain Macrae. He drew back the thin drapes on the deep blue before the sunrise and picked up a copy of *The Thirty-Nine Steps*. A postcard of a naked girl sprawled on a rug dropped to the floor. On a whim he tucked her back in a Protestant prayer book, between pages calling for the baptised to renounce Satan and all his works. Then he washed in the bowl of cold water his hostess had poured for him.

'Are you a religious man, monsieur?' Madame Proust had asked, as she led him up the stairs to the room the night before. 'Please say a prayer for my boys, pray this war will end, pray they will be spared.'

He promised he would, and he had tried to be as good as his word, on his knees, holding the rough cross Ramble had given him between the palms of his hands.

Madame Proust had prepared a breakfast of bread and butter and good coffee. Captain Macrae's coffee, she said, but he wouldn't begrudge a cup to another English officer.

'A Scottish officer, madame.'

She wasn't listening. 'Such a shock, monsieur. Taken ill so suddenly. But these are terrible times. So many dying so young.'

Her bottom lip began to tremble and she bustled out of the parlour before Innes could ask her about Macrae.

Market day in Montreuil – not as it was before the war, perhaps – the square and a few streets lined with carts of vegetables, a little cheese and cheap embroidered cotton, soap and country beer; *les paysans* gathered to smoke and grumble about prices and the wet harvest; the old in black, and some of the young; and at a stall near the École Militaire, a veteran with one arm selling brass souvenirs of war.

'Your father,' Charteris gestured to a chair at his desk, 'met him in India – the hospital at Secunderabad.' He tapped the file in front of him, showering it with ash from the cigarette burning between his fingers. 'Is that why Captain Cumming sent you?'

'I thought GHQ requested me, sir.'

Charteris was staring at him with the detachment of a professional critic before a gallery picture. He had a heavy face, thick grizzled moustache, and the corners of his mouth turned down a little bad-temperedly.

'"Edinburgh Academy": I was educated at Kelvinside Academy in Glasgow.' He spoke with a polite Scots accent. '"Glasgow and Göttingen Universities": I was at Göttingen for two years too.'

'I didn't know, sir.'

'I expect Captain Cumming did.'

'I couldn't say, sir.'

'No.' Slouching behind a desk covered in papers, the ash still drooped unnoticed from his cigarette. 'How did you end up with Cumming?'

'I was unfit for active service – wounded. I was recommended to Captain Cumming. I speak some useful languages.'

'Gaelic?'

'Dutch, French, German,' Innes hesitated, 'I wanted to be of use.'

'Damn it!' The ash had fallen on to Charteris's tunic. 'At Cumming's Bureau? You would have done better service elsewhere,' he muttered, brushing the ash away with inky fingers. 'I read your report. It was useful in confirming information we'd received from our own sources.' His eyes were dancing about Innes's face. 'What do you say to that?'

'I say, I'm glad, sir.'

At last a small smile. 'Yes, well, good work nonetheless. Took courage. I know you have plenty of that.' He tapped the file again.

'No more than the average soldier, sir.'

Another smile. 'I like to have a brandy at this time. My doctor says it will settle my stomach for the rest of the day. I hope you'll join me.'

'Thank you, sir.' He didn't think he could refuse.

'Good.' Charteris was on his feet, dusting the last of the cigarette ash from his trousers. 'You'll fit in quickly here, I'm sure. Lots of us Scots at GHQ. The chief says the Scotch are the best and most patriotic people – and I agree with him.' A heavy-set, broad back turned to Innes at the drinks tray; a solid-looking sapper but with an agile mind, or so people said.

'I met two yesterday, sir.'

'Scotsmen?' Half turning, the bottle in his hand. 'Marshall?'

'And Major Graham.'

'I see.' He frowned. 'They do have some connections, yes. The Charteris family is from the Borders – so are the Haigs.'

There was an engraving of a tower house on the wall between the windows – his ancestral home, perhaps – and on the desk, a photograph of an attractive woman Innes took to be his wife. But for these and a watercolour of a Mogul fort, the office had been furnished by the Army in the style the quartermaster branch deemed appropriate for a Brigadier General (Intelligence).

'Your Gaelic,' he said, handing Innes his brandy. 'You have family?'

'My mother's from the Isles.'

'And your father an Edinburgh man.' He was standing over Innes, cradling his glass in his large hands. 'Well, while you're here I want you to help Colonel MacLeod prepare our agents. When we break the enemy's line they will be with the cavalry.' Pausing to sip his brandy. 'Has Marshall spoken to you about the plan?'

'No, sir.'

'They are to gather as much information as they can to help speed our advance. The Chief's very much in favour.' Charteris turned away. 'The Boche is being beaten, you see. Near the end. It's a matter of keeping up the pressure.' He jogged his desk as he sat down and a pile of papers cascaded on to the floor. 'Damn, damn. Never mind. Later. We attack again in a week's time and we're hopeful of a major success. Your job will be to ensure our agents are ready.'

'Yes, sir.'

'Oh, and Major Graham would like a little of your time . . . some questions about the intelligence returns from your Bureau's network in Belgium.' Rooting on the floor for his papers, he glanced at one, then tossed it casually back on to the desk. 'We have our own sources in the occupied territories, you understand, and we think pretty highly of them. Very highly.'

'Yes, sir.'

'Yes, well . . .' Hands on his knees, he rose to his feet again.

'I usually brief the Chief at this hour. We have a Church of Scotland minister here at GHQ. Do you go to church?'

'Not as often as I ought to.'

'The Chief attends most Sundays. You might have an opportunity to meet him there. Some of our generals are suspicious of clever officers,' he said, shaking Innes's hand. 'But goodness, we work in intelligence, don't we?' Another slight smile. 'The Chief says a good officer need be of only average intelligence, because honour and loyalty are more important. He's right, of course, loyalty does come first, don't you agree?'

Innes agreed, of course. 'I'll teach you not to argue,' his old headmaster used to say, taking the cane from his drawer. Just like the music hall song the men would chorus on the road to the Front: *Hold your hand out, naughty boy.* Everyone had to learn that in the Army. The trench was no place for reason and discourse; university years a distraction. 'Too old at only twenty-five,' he'd complained to a friend in the battalion in his first days. Schoolboy subalterns were best, shaped by simple loyalty, a motto, colours, chapel, and *Play up, play up, and play the game*; that was how the men liked their officers to be, even in the Cameron Highlanders. The necessary 'Yes, sir' of no man's land that drove them over the bags into the filth and a shower of death. A presumption, a place, a view as tightly framed as the few tangled yards that could be reflected in the mirror of a trench periscope. 'Yes, sir,' said with the resignation of one who knows this is how it must and will be. He'd almost forgotten that simple military lesson in Cumming's secret service, in Belgium with Ramble.

Graham came to find him later. 'You look distracted,' he said.

'Do I?' Innes replied.

'Yes, you do. You've spoken to Brigadier Charteris?' He was gazing at Innes from the corner of his eye as before, the same bored expression, the same pride.

'He offered me brandy and soda.'

'Oh? You made a good impression.'

'I'm not sure. His parting shot was "loyalty comes first". Loyalty to him, or Field Marshal Haig, or to the Empire? He didn't say.'

'All three, of course.' Graham half turned to look round the office. The clerks were either bent over their desks or walking between them. 'Perhaps he thinks you're working for Cumming. Are you, by the way?'

Innes touched the red and blue armband he'd been given by the brigadier's adjutant. 'You see. GHQ Staff.'

'I suppose you can take it off as easily as you put it on.'

They spent the morning side by side at a table and Graham's voice took on a livelier tone. He plainly enjoyed his work, secrets, disguises; no more regular Army than Cumming was regular Navy. His questions about the Ramble network were to the point: how reliable were its watchers in Liège? Was it possible to get more intelligence from the enemy's *Operationsgebiet* near the Front? Perhaps they might use pigeons or a wireless set to communicate intelligence faster. There were rumours the Germans were using dummy artillery batteries to draw fire. Would one of the agents in Antwerp be able to confirm a report the enemy was moving reserves from the Eastern to the Western Front?

'What about the Army's networks?' Innes asked. 'I know you have one in Antwerp – one of your people tried to steal one of ours.'

'Does that happen?'

'I'm afraid it does.'

He grunted with amusement. 'Priceless.' Spreading his hands with pleasure on the table: 'Colonel MacLeod handles the Army's networks, I'm afraid. He may have some fresh intelligence on enemy reserves, I wait to be told. Shows the BGI, of course. The Brigadier has to prepare the daily intelligence summary for the Chief.'

'He doesn't seem to think much of the intelligence from our network.'

'I thought you were on *his* Staff now.'

'For a while.'

'Look . . .' He slumped back in his chair impatiently. 'As far as I'm concerned we're all fighting the same enemy.'

'Of course.'

'I don't have time for other ones. My task is to help our commander-in-chief – our men – and I think we're bloody lucky to have the intelligence from your network. Marshall and I agree on that – goodness knows how Marshall would do his job without it. But if you haven't learnt our opinion doesn't count for much here, you haven't learnt anything.' For a moment he was ready to look Innes in the eye.

'I've been here a day.'

Graham looked away again, brushing an imaginary speck of dust from his sleeve. 'Yes, well now you have something to put in your report to Cumming – if you're writing one.'

By lunchtime it was raining and a sheet of water was spilling from the choked gutters at the front of the école. The one-armed veteran had left his table of war souvenirs and was crouching in a doorway opposite. His empty face reminded Innes of hundreds more, the steady drip, drip from tin hats and noses, and mud that gripped like a vice. Some of the Staff were sheltering beneath the carriage arch, waiting for it to ease so they could make lunch at the club. Innes's driver was there too.

'Two hours travelling in this, sir,' he said, the rain splashing on his outstretched hand.

*

The members of the Suicide Club were in huts near Bruay. Innes knew the town a little, his battalion had marched through it in 1915 on its way to the Front for the first time; and after the Battle of Loos what was left had marched back for leave. They drove in silence, Innes gazing out at rain-puddled furrows, a ghost of that time reflected in the glass. Somewhere on the road, a burst of sunlight pricked the window drops, like tiny Very flares falling on a battlefield at night. Then he thought of his old friend, MacCunn, who'd taught history with him at the university and wrote a book on Napoleon: killed at Loos almost two years to the day.

Colonel MacLeod's temporary headquarters was at the edge of an airfield in a naked brick box that may at one time have served as a public convenience. His volunteers slept in a barracks hut next door, and the Royal Flying Corps had lent them a damp shack for 'general instruction'.

'I suppose you've heard what they're calling us?' MacLeod said. 'I don't like it, I discourage it, but the men seem to have adopted the name.'

'Is there an official name?' Innes asked.

'Not really. Brigadier Charteris calls us something different every day,' he said, sweeping his hand from his brow to the nape of his neck as if he were smoothing an honest head of hair. 'In our report for the Field Marshal we called it an Advance Espionage Unit. Bit of a mouthful.'

Innes agreed that Suicide Club was more memorable.

Spying was always a hazardous business, MacLeod said, but agents weren't being asked to throw their lives away. They could ride, read map and compass, they'd learnt codes and to handle pigeons, and they would soon be able to pilot a balloon, although he was confident that wouldn't be necessary. He didn't sound confident. Innes watched him fidgeting, rolling the pen on his desk blotter with two fingers. His tone was defensive, even a little defiant, as if he was struggling with his own doubts. Late forties, short but well built, a heavy face and very bald, but with a moustache so sleek and trim it looked as if it was drawn on with a pen, like a hard-boiled egg at Easter. He wouldn't look Innes in the eye.

'You've spoken to Brigadier Charteris?' he asked. 'He will have told you we're confident of a breakthrough. The Boche is near the end.'

Innes inspected his hands. 'Yes, he did say that.'

'You disagree?'

'London has a different view.'

'You mean Cumming,' he said, rolling his pen faster.

'I was able to gauge something of German morale myself. And our people in Belgium—'

'I was persuaded your experience would be useful, Captain,' MacLeod interrupted. 'We'll see.' He picked up the pen and pointed the nib at Innes. 'Let me tell you now, we hear quite enough pessimism from London. Far too much, in fact. You're back in uniform. You have a job to do.' His military English was slipping, betraying northern vowels, Manchester perhaps. 'Do you understand?'

'Yes, sir. Perfectly.'

The Suicide Club had just returned from a riding lesson with the cavalry and its members were sprawling in battered armchairs, horsehair stuffing spilling on to the floor. A lieutenant of intelligence barked *shun!* and they got slowly to their feet: Belgians, a Frenchman and a few British NCOs. Their clothes were caked in mud after more than one tumble. The cavalry had put them through the wringer, the lieutenant confided in a whisper, the instructors thought it a great joke. Spots of red appeared on MacLeod's cheeks. 'I'll speak to their officer.'

61

He introduced Innes in a booming voice as a special agent, and more surprisingly as a fellow Scotsman. Over the next few days Captain Innes would go through their files and then speak to them individually, he said. Time was short, so they would be called for interview from their balloon training. Later, Captain Innes would address the unit on the subject of 'keeping a step ahead of the enemy'.

Blank faces, bent shoulders, the shuffling of feet, they looked as if the cavalry had kicked the stuffing from them too. No spirit, or so it seemed to Innes. What in hell's name were they doing there?

He read their files on the journey back to Montreuil. Most were in their late twenties and thirties, most spoke good French but little German, and most were in it for a promise of money or promotion. The French talked glibly of freeing their country, but they were probably lying – they weren't the best sort.

When it was too dark to read more he sat and smoked and tried to imagine what Ramble would say. *Don't waste more lives.* That was the trouble with war, especially this one. After the battles of Loos, the Somme, Arras, Ypres, there was an unspoken acceptance of small sacrifices, perhaps any number unworthy of a flag on the GHQ map. To risk a few agents and the Belgian families who would have to hide them was really no risk at all. Flickering dug-out, enemy kicking up a fuss; he used to lie on his wet straw mattress and wonder if 'necessary sacrifice' was senior officer sophistry for what his Dundee sergeant called 'a bluidy cock-up'. Somewhere in the line, men were preparing to raid the trench opposite for a scrap of ribbon or a cap badge that would satisfy intelligence the flags on its map were in the right place. Two or three or more men would be lost and the company commander would have to write to mothers and sweethearts of their necessary sacrifice. He used to silently rage at the waste and curse the nameless desk officer who had sent the order up the line. But now that he was away from the heat and the fury he accepted it as the way of things, just war. Men were sent to their deaths and someone had to give the order. Goodness, he'd done the same, almost the last link in a long chain; no flags, no battalion numbers, names and the faces of men he loved. He'd been glad they knew his order was an echo of someone else, a brass hat who understood how things were supposed to 'map out'. That's what he would have said about sacrifice to Ramble. Of course, it wasn't a moral position: the soldiers who nailed Christ to his cross were just obeying orders.

He touched the driver's shoulder. 'How much further?' It was still raining hard and as dark as the grave.

'Not long, sir. Ten miles.'

His uncle and all the other priests Innes had known had taught that Christ died so mankind might be saved. But if the Son of God's sacrifice was necessary, poor old Pilate was necessary too; trying to keep the Roman peace – he had to do something. He'd acted on the best intelligence available at the time. Commanders made mistakes. They were fortunate, of course, that they had nothing to lose but their reputations.

'You've met the club, then.' Graham caught him in the corridor on the way to dinner. 'Put the cat among the pigeons, I hear.'

'I can't imagine why you say so.'

'Don't worry. Some people are easily offended.'

Innes wondered whether he was fishing or if he'd spoken to MacLeod. 'I won't—worry, I mean.'

Another of Graham's sideways glances. 'Colonel MacLeod won't be joining us this evening, but Brigadier Charteris will be.'

In the École Militaire, a room set aside for a special intelligence mess, BGI presiding at the top table. 'New boy on my right.' He beckoned Innes over. 'Graham, you're on my left.' Their roast beef dinner was brought in cans from the Officers' Club, and there was a skin on the gravy. But Charteris was in good humour, entertaining his staff with amusing stories of the politicians and newspaper proprietors who came to visit 'the Chief'. An impression of Mr Churchill in rhetorical flight was greeted by applause tapped on the table. 'To a tee,' someone said. Innes hadn't heard the Minister of Munitions speak and wasn't able to judge.

'After a few minutes his lisp disappears,' Charteris said, 'and when he makes a clever phrase – and he does all the time – he likes to pause and taste it, as if he's relishing a good brandy. A good brain, but little judgement or practical knowledge of war. He's visiting us next week. So is Mr Asquith. I think him the greatest of politicians. Perfectly straight.' He sucked his teeth. '*That* is more than can be said for most of 'em.' Silence. No one else cared to venture an opinion, but if the BGI noticed, he didn't care. 'If Mr Asquith were still our prime minister, we would not be fighting this war on two fronts,' he said.

Another uncomfortable silence, heads bent, anxious not to catch his eye. Even Graham looked ill at ease, smoothing a fold in the cloth with his forefinger.

'I was wondering, sir,' he said, at last, 'would Captain Innes tell us something about his time in Belgium. This agent of yours, Innes, Ramble isn't it . . . ? What manner of man is Ramble? Brave, of course.'

Charteris touched Innes's sleeve. 'A count, I shouldn't wonder.'

'I'm sorry, sir, I can't say. Only . . .' Innes smiled . . . 'Not a gentleman, no. An ordinary and yet a very extraordinary person.'

After dinner, they gathered at the map and Charteris spoke of the battle to come, his hand swooping back and forth across the enemy line like a plane: Second Army to force the plateau, Fifth

64

Army the Passchendaele ridge; battery and counter-battery the key; a chance for the Australians to show what they can do. He snapped out victory in short emphatic phrases – 'enemy near the end'; 'a question of keeping up the pressure' – just as he'd done with Innes in his office that morning. Again, no one else ventured an opinion. 'Pacifists, cranks and politicians were calling for change'; 'but our duty is clear'; 'Field Marshal Haig, the only man to beat the Boche and save our Empire'. Hand he was counting, it seemed, on everyone in intelligence. When Charteris had finished, Innes stepped out of the École for some air.

The rain had stopped and the cobbles were glistening in the gas light. He walked to the end of the street, the night heavy with a scent of early autumn, of horse chestnuts like the one in his parents' garden. Their boughs reached out over the ramparts, empty conker shells rotting on the gravel path. He bent to pick one up, pushing his thumb into its white flesh. Perfect. Almost luminous. Stooping for another, he was startled by a figure moving beneath the nearest tree.

'Here. Catch.' Marshall threw a conker, warm from his touch. 'You were with Charteris?'

'Yes. I didn't see—'

'I wasn't,' he said, stepping from the shadow of the canopy so Innes could see his face. 'I found something better to do.' He kicked one of the conker shells like a petulant schoolboy, showering the base of the wall with gravel. 'Expect he talked about a breakthrough, didn't he? Enemy close to defeat? Our intelligence is whatever Charteris damn well thinks it should be.' Marshall looked away, a little embarrassed perhaps by his bitter tone. 'I'm sorry. Difficult day. Another difficult conversation.'

'With Brigadier Charteris?'

'Of course. Look, shall we walk a little—were you going too? It will put me in a better mood, it always does.' A short laugh. 'I come here more and more.'

He led the way up steps and on to the broad wall. The grass was slippery and he warned Innes to take care. 'I listened to the bombardment from here when it all kicked off at Ypres in July.'

'I was on the other side,' said Innes.

He nodded. 'I stood and thought of our chaps trying to sleep, counting the hours, the minutes . . . They went over at a little before four o'clock. Still dark – it was supposed to be the dawn – always the promise of the dawn.'

'Yes.'

They ambled towards a bastion, the silence broken only by an army lorry growling up the road below to the town gate, its lights sliding left then right.

'You think Charteris is getting it wrong in some way?'

Marshall stopped and turned abruptly. 'I'm not sure I should say.' Frowning, biting his bottom lip. 'Yes. Damn it, yes. I'm afraid I do think he's wrong. I've told him; others have said so too. The information summaries he prepares for Field Marshal Haig – sometimes I don't recognise—' He took a deep breath. 'There is some good intelligence, but too much is selected to give the impression the enemy is near the end and one more heave will see us through. That's nonsense. Things are bad – food shortages, that sort of thing – but nothing I've seen or heard suggests he's on the point of collapsing. The German Army is still a mighty, mighty machine.'

'Then why—'

'Other sources, he says, MacLeod's networks.'

'In the occupied territories – Belgium?'

'I suppose so – perhaps in Germany too. I don't know.' He was gazing at his feet, grinding gravel with the toe of his boot. 'MacLeod and Charteris are the only ones at GHQ who have access to that intelligence; I suppose Haig – Field Marshal Haig – must see it too.'

'That intelligence comes from the Army's agents?'

'I don't know. It's a sorry situation.' Marshall shook his head. 'Impossible. Day after day intelligence summaries go to the Chief that I think are plain wrong, but when I say so Charteris hides behind his confidential sources, accuses me of being a pessimist, lectures me on the need to offer a clear view to the Chief.'

'Why?'

He shrugged. 'He doesn't like to take the Chief bad news. I think he considers it his job to offer constant encouragement. He understands the Chief, they're close.'

'Or his other sources are very good?'

'I don't know, perhaps. I have to tell the unvarnished truth as I see it, isn't that the job of every intelligence officer?'

'Yes.'

'I don't know about other sources. Ask MacLeod. He won't tell you, of course.'

'No. Angry, isn't he? He doesn't seem to like me.'

Marshall laughed. 'He's probably frightened of you, or jealous. Young hero, Military Cross, spy . . .'

'I'm no different from lots of the officers here – you and Graham.'

'He's probably frightened of us too.' He slapped Innes's upper arm encouragingly. 'Don't take it personally. A prickly character. He's had, well, certain difficulties . . .' He hesitated. 'At home. His wife. But that's none of my business. Suffice to say he hides behind Charteris – he is the BGI's creature – and Charteris is the Field Marshal's man – caught hold of his coat-tails in India. Hindus, Scots, and Hindu-Scots. Charteris is a Hindu-Scot. You and I are Scots.' He leant a little closer to Innes, the reflex from a street light in his dark eyes. 'We've all got friends, connections, haven't we?'

'You?' Innes asked.

'One or two. Not as many as Graham.'

'Is Mr Churchill one of Graham's?'

'Yes. How do you know?'

'Just a look when his name was mentioned at table this evening.'

'Ah.' Marshall stepped back to perch against the stone parapet and gaze through swaying branches at the silhouettes of the town. 'Yes, Graham knows Churchill – and the minister of war, Lord Derby – half the bally government, I shouldn't wonder. He was at Eton with the field marshal's private secretary, Sassoon. The Chief is close to the royal family and so is Graham's stepfather. It won't prevent Graham writing discreet bulletins to his political friends, though. Are you writing to Cumming? I do hope so. That's why you're here, isn't it?'

Innes didn't reply.

'I don't suppose I'm the only one who thinks so,' Marshall said.

'My orders are to do my best for this Suicide Club. Honestly, I wish I wasn't here.'

'I don't doubt it. Actually, I've asked for a transfer more than once.' He glanced at his watch. 'Shall we go? I've a few things I must see to.'

They walked back in companionable silence.

On the steps, Marshall said, 'We have a little dining club, we meet in a private room at a local *estaminet*: Graham, Dunnington-Jefferson, Jack, a couple of other chaps. You must join us.'

'You said you weren't the only one who'd spoken to Charteris?'

He turned to look up the steps at Innes. 'That's right.'

'Graham?'

'Good lord, no. Too clever. Too political. Won't put himself out.'

'Then who?'

'Look, I don't know what you're going to do with this?' Marshall folded his arms tightly, uncertain whether he should say more.

'It would be useful.'

'Ha. Useful. For whom? Me?' He sighed. 'Well, in for a penny, I suppose: the chap who had your billet – Macrae. He was in Section B.'

'Where was he transferred to?'

He smiled. 'Honestly, I don't know whether it was to heaven or hell. He died in the arms of a tart you see, a month ago.' Another flash of anger. 'Charteris kept that intelligence from the Chief too.'

5

With Ramble

M<small>A WAS SITTING</small> with her back against the belfry wall, three large baskets of vegetables at her feet. The low stool she favoured was lost beneath the folds of her skirt and from the window of the draper's shop opposite her white bonnet appeared to bob like a fisherman's float in a pool of fabric. It was almost four o'clock and some of the other women were loading their produce on to barrows and carts to leave, but Ma would be there longer and no one would think it strange. She was as much a part of the little market square at Thielt as the belfry and the old cloth hall, and everyone who passed through it shouted a greeting to her, even the Germans. They called her Canteen Ma because she supplied their mess with fruit and vegetables. She was seventy-three, as thin as a stick and as wrinkled and dry as an autumn leaf. Her toothless grin and wicked sense of humour made her a great favourite with the enemy, and her age and infirmity seemed to place her above suspicion. When the Germans carried out one of their searches of the square, heaving bolts of cloth from the draper's shelves with dirty hands, stealing from the butcher's larder and prodding the baskets of the farmers' wives with their bayonets, Ma sat serenely in the folds of her skirt quite untroubled by their malice.

At the draper's window Madame Maria Simon watched Ma exchange words with an enemy *Unteroffizier*. He was a Bavarian to judge by the silver piping on his greatcoat and the button on his field cap. Some of his comrades were laughing and beckoning to him from Bosmans' café, a short distance away. Leaning forward with both hands, he helped the old woman to her feet. Then he touched the rim of his cap and blew her a cheeky kiss, and there was more good-humoured laughter from the café. A large Staff car with black and white flags flying from the bonnet rumbled across the *pavé* towards the town hall and the guards at the foot of its steps came to attention. No one in the marketplace seemed to notice, because Thielt was the headquarters of the Fourth Army and its generals came and went every day. Ma had watched the kaiser climb the very same steps twice.

'Ah, you're just in time,' she said.

Maria walked up to the baskets. 'You saw me coming.'

'Of course, madame,' she sounded a little aggrieved. 'Of course. You were watching in Monsieur Stevens's window.'

'Nothing passes you by, does it Ma?'

'You left it very late, but I have a few apples. Help me, please.'

They bent together with their hands in the apple basket. 'Ah, madame. You've heard?' the old lady muttered into her lace collar. 'They've arrested the stationmaster, and Monsieur and Madame Timmins – the lawyer, Hubert, too. The others are so frightened.'

'Do you know who betrayed them?'

'There are two new men at the Hôtel de la Plume; Mertens says they're vampires from Antwerp, sent here to spy on us.' Ma reached for Madame Simon's hand and pressed a ball of paper into her palm. 'He's waiting. Tonight at nine o'clock. But watch your step.' Then she rose slowly and said in her usual market voice: 'My back's aching, madame, will you do it?'

They were Belle de Boskoop apples, rough to touch and tart

on the tongue. Madame Simon lifted one to her nose and its fragrance brought to mind an image of her late husband in their grocer's shop, and her two girls dipping into the box they kept beneath the counter. Her younger daughter was still serving at the same counter – when there was something to serve.

'You again!' Ma's voice was raised in warning. 'Have you come to rob an old woman?'

The *Unteroffizier* was walking towards them and this time he was with his friends from the café. 'Give me one of your apples, Ma, and I'll give you a kiss!' He repeated the joke in German for the benefit of his friends.

'A young fellow like you should have more respect for an old woman,' she said.

'Never too old for a kiss, Ma,' he said. 'What about your friend?' He was gazing at Maria.

'Get away with you.' Ma took a step forward, waving her hands at him as if she were shooing farmyard geese. 'If I'm old enough to be your grandmother, madame is old enough to be your mother.'

The *Unteroffizier*'s friends were laughing and shouting encouragement. 'I think Ma's fibbing. You can't be any older than my sister,' he said to Maria. 'Can I see your papers? That will prove it one way or the other.'

'Don't show him,' Ma said, taking a step between them. 'He wants your address – don't trust him with your address.' There was more laughter.

'But I must insist, madame.' The *Unteroffizier* held out his hand. 'It's my duty. You may be a spy like old Ma here.'

Madame Simon reached into her coat for her identity card and handed it to him.

'Your name is Legrand?' he said.

She said that it was.

'You live on the road to Roulers – that's not far. What will your husband say if I drop by to see you?'

'Monsieur Legrand will say, "Come in, Corporal, do you know these gentlemen from your division?" My husband's very friendly with some of your officers, you see.'

'Clever, clever,' he said, holding out her identity card, 'but I don't believe you.'

'Then you should,' said Ma, snatching it from him, 'because Madame is a friend of your Colonel von Petzold.'

'All right, all right.' The *Unteroffizier* held up his hands in a gesture of surrender, then turned to Madame Simon and made a small bow. 'My apologies, madame. A little joke.'

The guards at the town hall came to attention again as a staff officer began to climb the steps. His back was turned to the market but his presence seemed to have a sobering effect on the *Unteroffizier* and his party. When they'd gone, Maria asked: 'Is there a Colonel von Petzold?'

'First Bavarians,' Ma replied. 'Stuck up, they say. He wouldn't have anything to do with the likes of you and me.'

Maria Simon carried her apples to the draper's shop and made a present of them to Monsieur Stevens. Written on Ma's ball of paper were instructions for the rendezvous: *Take the road south and turn left on to Bergstraat. When you come to the second farm on the left-hand side, knock three times at the back door then once more.* It was a kilometre at most but security was as tight in Thielt as anywhere in the occupied territories. There would be patrols on all the roads out of town and anyone caught breaking the curfew would be taken in for questioning at Fourth Army headquarters. Maria Simon's papers were good enough to fool a marketplace corporal but an intelligence officer would be able to prove they were false without rising from his desk. She knew the farm because she had used it as a rendezvous before. This time it felt like more of a risk than she should be taking. Ma had spoken of two German spies from Antwerp. If it was a trap, she would be caught and they would have their grocer's widow.

The draper, Stevens, took her to a house at the edge of town and at dusk she slipped into the lane at the back and walked to a gap in a hawthorn hedge. Across the field to her right was the road to Meulebeke. The flashlights of a patrol were winking through the hedge and she could hear the roar of an approaching motor car. She waited for it to pass, its lamps sweeping across the field towards her as it turned right into the town. For a few seconds the patrol was caught in the beam, and from their silhouettes she was able to judge that it consisted of at least four soldiers and a local gendarme. He would be familiar with the footpaths and bridleways around the town. But she knew how to use the hedge as cover to skirt the field, moving deliberately, pausing to listen for a footfall, the snap and scrape of a twig against a shoulder. On a cold damp night soldiers liked to blow into their hands and stamp their feet, cough and grumble.

She reached the far corner of the field without difficulty and from there she could see the farm, a chink of light at a ground-floor window. The lane called 'Bergstraat' was through the trees to her right. It was unusually still, oppressively so, and she realised she was expecting to hear the rumble of the battle at Ypres. For once, there was only the rattle of autumn leaves. From the cover of the trees a muddy path led across another field to the farmyard wall. It was open ground, and in her hurry to cross it she slipped on to her side and twisted her wrist. Cursing one moment, praying the next, she reached the wall unchallenged and rested her back against it to catch her breath.

The farmer's chickens were making a fuss somewhere. He was fortunate to have some after three years of living with the enemy. His buildings were in need of some care, but that was the war; people were just giving up. The yard was empty and there was still just a single light at the front of the house. She made her way round to the back and knocked three times then once more. It was opened by a man in rough country clothes who reached out to draw her inside.

'Quickly, please,' he whispered. 'You weren't followed?' There was a tremor in his voice.

'You should ask me for my business at this hour, monsieur,' she said, stepping into the dark kitchen. 'If I was a German spy, you'd be done-for already.'

'You're Ramble,' he said, striking a match. 'I'm Lemmens.' By the light of his candle she could see he was a man of about her own age, perhaps just short of fifty. His thick grey moustache was curled at each end like a sow's tail.

He stepped towards the kitchen door. 'This way.'

Mertens was standing at the window, watching the front of the farm through a crack in the shutters. 'I saw you at the corner of the wall,' he said, turning to greet her.

'And I saw the light from your lantern,' she said.

'That was careless of me.' He bent to kiss her on both cheeks. 'I'm afraid the shutter hinge is broken.'

The room was bare and thick with dust. The plaster had fallen from a corner of the ceiling, exposing the timber joists, and the oak panelling covering the walls was cracked and rotten.

'The farm belonged to Monsieur Lemmens' brother. He was shot "by accident", they said.' He glanced back at the window. 'You're sure you weren't followed?'

'I'm sure.'

'You know about the arrests?'

'Yes.'

'The gendarmes are looking for me too. I have to get away. I need a new identity paper and a travel pass. I have to—' He lifted his hands then let them fall back to his sides. 'I don't know—I'm not sure who to trust, madame. I'm frightened for my family.'

She touched his sleeve. 'I will see to things. Be strong.'

He nodded and tried to smile. 'First in Roulers, then this . . .'

'Yes. It's unfortunate. People make mistakes, but we have to consider the other possibility.'

'I have . . . for days. That's why I asked you to come. I thought at first that someone had broken under interrogation – farmers and their wives, station-masters, bakers like me – of course it will happen. But when they started arresting people here.' He pushed at a piece of plaster with the toe of his boot. 'I think we have a traitor, only, I don't know who. You've heard about these spies from Antwerp at the Hôtel de la Plume?'

Maria frowned. 'A few months ago we took in some people who had been working for one of the British Army's networks.'

'Yes, the clerk at the hospital in Roulers and his friends.'

'Yes, the clerk.'

'De Wilde. I saw him the day Captain Innes and I gave the enemy the slip at Moere.'

'Have the Germans arrested him?'

Mertens shook his head. 'I don't know.'

'And the people he brought with him, some of them live here in Thielt?'

'The man with the fabric shop in the square, Stevens, he came to us through the clerk.'

'The draper was with the Army network?'

Mertens heard the anxiety in her voice and turned quickly. 'You think he's working for the enemy?'

'I can't tell.'

'But he knows you were meeting someone here?'

'Not here, but we should leave all the same. Monsieur,' she said to Lemmens, 'we need somewhere else. A barn, even a wood close by . . . until morning.'

Mertens was moving towards her. 'No, you should stay.' His gaze shifted to the door in the panelling to the left of the fireplace. 'Lemmens, help me . . .' The wood was damp and swollen and Mertens had to tug with both hands, his foot against the chimney-piece.

'Joos, we must go, all of us—' She reached for his arm. 'They may have seen your light at the window.'

With a crack of splintering wood the door flew open to reveal a shallow cupboard with empty shelves.

'Safer for you here,' Mertens said, picking himself up from the floor. Lemmens was on his knees inside the cupboard, pushing at the bottom shelf. The back was pivoting out and sideways and by the light of the lantern she could see a recess in the walls, a brick box less than six feet square.

Mertens said: 'There are bolts inside the door – use them. Stay here until morning then open the trap-door – there's a ring in the floor and a rope down to the cellar. The cellar door faces the trees to the right of the farm. Take this,' and he held out the lantern.

'You're coming.'

'I can't leave Lemmens, and we'll be able to move quicker without you.'

'No. All of us must stay,' she said. 'We leave together or hide together.'

Lemmens grunted impatiently. 'Just make up your mind!'

'I have. Together,' she said.

Mertens opened his mouth to protest when there was a thump at the back of the house. A second later, there was another, and she knew that the door was being forced with boots and the butt of a rifle.

Mertens shoved her so hard she hit her head on the edge of a shelf. Turning quickly she hissed, 'Now you!' Their enemy would be in the room in a matter of seconds. 'Please, Joos.'

He leant forward with the lantern. 'Take it. You must be quiet. Remember the bolts—' Their eyes met and he smiled weakly. 'And my family . . .'

The back of the cupboard swung into place and a second later she heard the enemy's boots in the room and shouted orders. She drew the bolts and stepped back into the recess. The Germans would open the cupboard door, but would they notice footprints in the dust? The shouting was over and she could hear someone speaking in Flemish. He was moving about the room, his voice fading, then rising. She thought she caught her cover name, Legrand, and she could hear more banging and the clump of boots as they widened the search upstairs. But now the cupboard door was opening and the enemy was only the thickness of a piece of wood away.

'Nothing here, sir,' she heard a soldier say in German.

'Nor from the front of the house . . .' said someone else. He had a deeper, more cultured voice – perhaps an officer or one of the Antwerp spies. 'Is there an open window?' Then in perfect Flemish: 'Where is she?' – and she was sure he must be a spy. 'Where is she?' he said again.

Mertens said, 'Who?'

The footsteps were back in the cupboard and she heard the same man say, 'You were in here? Someone has been here.' And then she heard him knocking, rap, rap, rap at the sides of the cupboard with his knuckles. There was only a little time. Dropping quietly to her haunches she felt about the floor for the ring. Rap, rap, rap, at the back of the cupboard now, and she heard him say, 'She's here. Break it down!'

Her heart was pounding but her mind was clear. Holding the ring with both hands she pulled as hard as she could and it came away. At the same time she was aware of shouting on the other side of the cupboard, and as she was lifting the timber trap, the crash of a rifle shot.

'Hold him down,' she heard the spy shout. A few seconds later, the spy was in the cupboard again. Once, twice, banging the back with the meat of his fist. 'Come out! Come out or we'll shoot.'

But she had hitched up her dress and was lowering herself through the hole, her shoes slipping along the rope.

'Fire once,' he shouted. Splinters flew over her head and she must have knocked over the lantern because the recess was plunged into darkness. Her arms were aching and she wondered if she had the strength to climb down the rope. The next thing she knew she was falling. It couldn't have been far, but for a few seconds she could only sit there shaken and breathless. Above her they were breaking down the back of the cupboard. Somehow she managed to rise and stagger to the cellar door. There wasn't time to creep and hide, there wasn't time to be careful, only to trust to the night and run for the trees; run and run, and keep running, and pray for God to guide her to a ditch and a pile of autumn leaves.

6

The Chief

MACLEOD STEPPED INTO the hut with the signal held aloft. 'You see,' he said, 'you see!'

The members of the Suicide Club got slowly to their feet. They didn't see, and they didn't care. That didn't matter because MacLeod was there to impress Innes.

'From Agent Le Nusse. A pigeon this morning.' MacLeod was excited and that told its own story. Perhaps he realised because his face was a barometer and red spots were appearing on his cheeks. 'We can talk about it later,' he said, crisply, 'when you've finished with the men.'

Check points on bridges and roads, curfews in the *Operationsgebiet* near the Front, etiquette when confronted by the enemy – what more was there to say? Learn your story men, listen to your local contacts, don't touch their women, and pray. Questions? No. They'd heard it before. Back now to the cavalry, to a waterlogged field and short rations, the ridicule and the snobbery, waiting for the big breakthrough. There would be another attack on the twenty-sixth. All the club's members were to return to the Front but one. An agent called Petit was attempting to fly over enemy lines that evening: a Frenchman but with a little Dutch, twenty-two, a patriot, not fit for the Army but fit enough for membership of the Suicide Club. He'd volunteered for the flight, or so MacLeod said. Pink Tights was at Armentières preparing a balloon.

MacLeod was still holding the signal when Innes walked into his office. 'It's the first we've received from an agent of this unit, and with Petit on his way, well, it couldn't have come at a better time. I've informed the BGI. He'll want to say something to the Chief.'

Innes offered his congratulations. Timely, yes. Very.

'I confess I'd given up on Agent Le Nusse – Remy, that's his real name. He's been there a while. Seems to be living just outside the *Operationsgebiet*.'

'And the signal, sir? Was it useful information?'

MacLeod didn't want to say. 'Can you see to Petit? Last-minute advice, encouragement, that sort of thing. Tell him about the signal. I would do it myself but there are things I have to do.' The colour had risen to his face again. 'Expect he'll be nervous, but he's ready, I think. Commander Pollock seems to think so.'

Enemy artillery had ploughed Armentières. Innes had passed through the town in 1915 and again in '16; he'd eaten frites and eggs in one of its many *estaminets*, slept in a splintered orchard, and been woken by drunken men singing of sergeant majors and eunuchs and women of easy virtue. The town hall clock was still stuck at eleven. The place was just knocked about a little more, a good billet even harder to come by. Rooms beneath roofs were for officers and the occasional madame, although most had taken their trade to somewhere they could be sure that the only risk they were running was from the usual diseases. Petit was in a ruined house not far from the pockmarked field Pink Tights had selected for the flight.

He was sitting in plaster dust, his back against a stone chimney-piece, gazing up through a frayed hole in the ceiling at the dusky blue of the sky. On any other day in September it would have been something to treasure. 'Conditions are good,' he said, his voice trembling a little.

'No, no, please don't get up,' said Innes, 'and we should speak Flemish. How are you feeling?' A foolish question. The right side of the man's face was jumping. He was trying to disguise it, rubbing his eye with his forefinger.

'Look, I thought I would go through a few things with you.' Innes picked up an empty ammunition crate – 'This will do' – and set it on its end. 'What is the first thing you'll do when you land?'

'Destroy or hide the balloon,' Petit replied, mechanically. He had resumed his place at the hearth, knees up to his chin.

'And if your contact isn't there, or you land in the wrong place?'

'Find cover. If necessary, approach someone for help, perhaps a priest.'

'And make your contact as soon as possible.'

They worked through checks but stopped when the Frenchman's attention began to wander.

'You know enough.' Innes leant forward to give his arm a squeeze. 'You'll be fine.'

'Do you think so?' Petit began to crumple. 'I'm sorry.' To save some face he pressed his forehead against his knees. Perhaps it was Innes's gesture, reaching across the dusty floor, sweeping rank, class, nationality aside. It didn't seem strange to Innes because he'd offered the same small comfort to his men countless times in the line. MacLeod and Pollock may not have thought to. But what did they know of those hours before action, the kaleidoscope of memories and fears to which the imagination was always prey: Must I? I must. Then God give me courage to do my duty; but oh, the things I wish I'd done; the things I should have said to those who love me.

Lifting his head at last, Petit asked: 'Would you send this

for me, Captain?' His thin face was very white. 'To my mother.' Slipping a hand inside his jacket he produced a small white envelope. 'I wasn't sure what to say to her . . .' His eyes were suddenly wide with concern. 'But I didn't tell her about my mission. Please believe me.'

'I do. Of course, I do.' Innes took the letter. 'Don't worry. Try to be calm.'

Petit sat back, still hugging his knees. 'She thinks I'm working in a hospital.'

'Where is she?'

'With my aunt in Orleans. But our village is only thirty kilometres from here. That's where I'm going tonight if I can land the balloon.'

'When you land the balloon.' Innes glanced at his watch. Seven o'clock. 'I must speak to Commander Pollock, and you must eat. Is there anything else I can do for you?'

'A priest. Do you think it's possible?'

Innes said he would try.

Pollock was very excited. 'Perfect conditions. Favourable wind, slightly north-east. Upper wind speed fifteen knots. Start filling our balloon at ten, I think.' He was a fussy little man, with a shock of white hair and a fat moustache waxed like the late Lord Kitchener's into a handlebar.

'Petit isn't very good, you know. I did warn Colonel MacLeod. No! Not like that,' he shouted. 'On its side.' The balloon was laid out in the field and his assistants were attaching ropes to the basket. It was large enough for only one man, its wicker sides no more than waist height.

'What did Colonel MacLeod say?'

'Not to fuss, that Petit only needed to do it properly once.' His gaze fixed on his men, he took half a step closer. 'It's twisted, Osborne, unhook it and start again.'

'When do you want him here?' Innes asked.

'No. Start again, man!' Turning back to Innes, he said, 'At ten. I'll take him over everything one last time.'

The church in the main square had been reduced to a shell, the floor of the nave choked with burnt timber. Someone had rescued a plaster head of Jesus and placed it in a niche at the west end, dark brown eyes turned up to heaven. The priest's house had gone too, a pile of smoke-stained brick in its place. Innes visited the office of the town major. Try the hospital on the Ypres road, he said, an army padre was ministering to the wounded there. But it was too late for that and only a Catholic priest would do.

Petit was still sitting in the dust by the fireplace, candle in one hand, his rosary in the other. He didn't open his eyes and acknowledge Innes until he'd finished his silent prayer.

'I'm sorry. I tried,' Innes said, lamely.

Petit didn't reply. The light of the dancing flame on his face reminded Innes of the old priest who'd knelt with a candle in warning and was knocked unconscious by the butt of a German rifle. Just when he was ready to give up on God, someone else's faith helped to rekindle his own anew. People not prayer, he'd observed to Ramble once. God working through people, came the reply, because her faith was unshakeable.

'I think you should eat. There's a cook-house in the next street.'

'I'm not hungry,' he said. 'How much time . . . ?'

'If you're sure.' Innes peered at his watch. 'Ten minutes to be on the safe side.'

He nodded.

'Compass? Papers?'

'Yes.'

'Good.'

The ammunition crate was still standing on its end. 'Do you mind if I sit with you?'

'Will you pray with me?'

Surprised and a little embarrassed, Innes said: 'I don't pray often.'

'Don't you believe?'

'Sometimes, yes.' He hesitated. 'Yes, I do.'

Petit smiled. 'I wanted to confess.' Closing his eyes, he began to whisper the act of contrition from the Mass – 'Deus meus, ex toto corde pænitet me ómnium meórum peccatórum' – and Innes whispered it with him. Then an Ave Maria, but louder, and the Pater Noster. After that they sat for a while in silence, Innes with his eyes shut too, but conscious of the time and the rumble of gunfire to the north at Ypres.

'We must go,' he said at last.

Walking from the motor car towards the circle of light, the balloon billowing towards them like the black sail of a ship, straining at its mooring ropes. Pollock grumbling, 'Hold that basket down, will you!'

Ready monsieur? Remember it's three thousand feet. Check compass. Check map. North-north-east and the wind will take you there. High over the Front, as far as the canal, then down to a thousand to search for a field to land. Out of the basket at once, let the balloon go, and the rest is your business monsieur, not mine. And on the bonnet of Pollock's motor car, a gramophone. Strike up the band, Sergeant Osborne, if you please, 'La Marseillaise'. A salute and manly British handshakes. Step back, step back, *au revoir*. And the balloon was away with Petit crouching in the basket, rising so quickly, in seconds it was gone.

'That's that, then,' said Pollock, 'job well done.'

How could he tell?

'Whisky?' he asked, as they tramped through the mud to the motor cars.

'I don't know his name,' said Innes.

'Petit.'

'His first name.'

Pollock shrugged. 'Does it matter?'

Innes's driver took the car off the road twice on the journey back to Montreuil and by the time they'd ground up the hill to the gate it was almost dawn. Inside its walls there was a perfect stillness, the careful order of centuries. Birds roosting, clocks chiming, rampart trees swaying in the gentle breeze that had carried Petit across the line. Armentières seemed more than hours away – it belonged to a different age. There, soldiers of both sides were standing to, checking their rifles, fixing fresh belts to the machine-guns, climbing on to the fire-step to let fly – just in case. To greet first light, a new ritual for this new age: the Hour of Hate. Innes concentrated on putting it from his thoughts but it was difficult when the mind was weary. There was always a memory then to fill an empty street with noise.

Madame Proust was not happy to be seen in her brown wool dressing-gown and her hair-net.

'Sorry to wake you,' he said, as he followed her down the hall.

'They said you were away,' she grumbled.

'Who? My man, Phillips?'

'Not your servant. An officer. He came here with two soldiers. He wanted Captain Macrae's things.'

The books had gone from the bedroom. The mattress had been lifted too. Someone had searched Innes's clothes, checked his shaving kit, sniffing perhaps the invisible ink he kept in the cologne bottle; and on top of the secretaire a letter he was writing to his sister had been picked up and put back carelessly. There was nothing to be done until the morning, so he took off his boots and jacket, loosened his tie and fell back on the bed to sleep.

He woke sweating from his dream with a start. It was the one he always had, of burial and resurrection. Half past seven, Saturday market noise rising from the street and a gentle knocking at the door. That would be Phillips, rapping with a knuckle, and again, just a little louder.

'Hot water, Phillips,' he shouted.

'Right you are, sir,' came the muffled reply. He spoke with the same jaunty air he would have used with customers to his barber's shop before his call-up.

Clean again – as much as he ever felt he could be – and seated in Madame's parlour with bread and a little coffee.

'I've spoken to your Philippe about more,' Madame Proust said, hands on her narrow hips, 'but he says your field marshal has given an order – officers are to have no more coffee than an ordinary soldier. What can I do, Captain?'

Innes nodded. 'The officer who came yesterday, can you describe him to me?'

She closed her eyes. 'He spoke good French. Brown hair. Brown eyes. Tired eyes. Perhaps the same age as you. A gentleman.' She opened them again and pointed a bony finger at his chest. 'Medal like yours.'

'The Military Cross?'

She shrugged. 'And another. Blue and red.'

Innes sipped his coffee.

'You know this officer?' she asked.

'Yes.'

At the École Militaire, the talk was of the next battle. Charteris had returned from his morning conference with the Chief and spoken to his officers of the plans for the attack on the twenty-sixth.

'But you haven't heard, have you?' Marshall said, pulling a chair close to Innes's desk. 'It will be carried out on as wide a front as possible to ensure – and as a clever university chap you will be impressed by this military logic – to ensure "the tactical advantage of attacking on a wide front". So, professor . . .' He opened his hands and brought them together with an emphatic clap. 'What do you say to that?'

'I don't understand?'

'You don't? Well, nor do I. But it must be obvious because no one has made any effort to explain why attacking on a wide front will be more successful this time than it has been all the other times we've tried it.' He closed his eyes and shook his head. 'This is where it begins, here – intelligence. Do I sound disloyal? I've been here too long.' He glanced over his shoulder. MacLeod had stepped into Section B and was speaking to one of his clerks. 'But this isn't the time,' Marshall muttered. 'Do you ride?'

'Like a sack of potatoes.'

He laughed. 'It's good for my self-esteem to see taller men make perfect fools of themselves. And it's important to take exercise, don't you think? Shall we say four 'o'clock? The stables are to the south of the town, beyond the Post Office and the ramparts . . . rue de la Tour.'

Everyone seemed busier than Innes. To what purpose, he wondered? He sat at his desk with a cigarette and watched the couriers come and go. More air reconnaissance, another interrogation report – a prisoner plucked from the enemy line; how many men lost their lives for that piece of paper? – and the secret intelligence from Army agents in occupied territories he wasn't trusted to see. Straight to MacLeod's office, no doubt.

The Colonel showed no interest in Petit and his flight and barely acknowledged Innes.

Late in the morning Charteris was driven back to the Château de Beaurepaire for lunch with Haig and a newspaper editor who could be relied upon to see things 'our way'. Major Graham was out of the office too. For a while Innes read the daily information summaries he'd missed, noting the many pieces pointing to a collapse in enemy morale. In one summary, a letter found on a dead German described 'blood in Berlin's streets' and 'people driven by hunger to resist'; in another, enemy soldiers were deserting and there'd been a cut in their rations. A cook-house report on a captured loaf made Innes smile, because it 'proved' the enemy was fighting on sawdust and 'a high proportion of cinders'.

'You see. Drip, drip, drip,' Marshall said when they met at the stable. 'That's what I mean – that's why it starts with intelligence.' He sighed wearily. 'You don't have spurs? I'll see what I can do. I've borrowed a horse for you. Not too lively.'

A chestnut mare with a white blaze on her head and a cunning eye, or so she seemed to Innes as he hopped round the yard trying to mount her.

'Come on, sir. Shorten your reins,' the groom said, with the stable note of disdain horse people reserve for a rider of any rank who has a poor seat. Marshall was smirking too. 'Dear me, Innes. Perhaps Hawkins here can find you a pony. Ah, there, you've managed it; thought you never would. Back straight, old boy.'

Trotting south-west, they were between hedgerows in less than a mile. It was a careful countryside cultivated for hundreds of years, some fields ploughed, some gold and striped with stubble stalks, open as far as the eye could see, the sky shifting shades of grey and rolling slowly like a broad river. The warm breeze caught the horses' manes, and at an open gate Marshall said: 'Are you up to it?' He spurred his mount to a gallop, and yes, Innes was ready; touching her sides with his heels – but too hard because she shied before finding her stride – from canter to a gallop, heart in mouth and his legs shaking, the horse pulling, eating up the field, stubble and dirt flying, and so damned exhilarating.

'I can see you enjoyed that too,' Marshall said, bent over his horse's neck. His face glowed with well-being. 'Doesn't it make one glad to be alive?' Their horses were blowing and pawing a restless circle.

'Yes. The eternal yes.'

'Did someone very clever say that?'

'Nietzsche.'

'Sounds like a Hun.' He grinned boyishly. 'Come on.' Through a gap in the hedge, plodding diagonally across the next field towards a belt of trees. 'There, Innes . . .' He gestured with his stick. 'On the other side of the road; the Field Marshal's chateau, Beaurepaire. We'll stay on this side.'

'Do you think Charteris is still with the Chief?'

Marshall frowned. 'Let's not speak of him . . . or the war.'

'As you wish.'

'Isn't it your wish too?'

'To escape?'

'You don't think it's possible?'

'For a short time,' Innes said, 'on an afternoon like this, at full gallop.'

'You must find it difficult.' Their eyes met for a second before Marshall turned his head away. 'I hear you were given up for dead.' He waited for a response but there was none. 'Sorry,' he said, 'no war I said, didn't I?'

Innes leant forward to pat his horse's neck. 'I was lucky. There isn't anything more to say. Lucky.'

For a while they didn't speak, the horses ambling on, loose stones cracking against their hooves like rifle shots, and high above the fluting of a skylark.

'Do you know that poem by Rupert Brooke?' Marshall said at last. 'You write, don't you? I forget the title, but the first line is, "God be thanked who has matched us with His Hour"'

'Who told you I write? A hobby . . . once.'

'Doesn't matter,' said Marshall. 'What I want to say is, that's how I felt – still feel about the war – that there is something noble in being a British soldier; selfless, brave. In spite of everything, the terrible casualties . . . oh, and the nonsense sometimes at headquarters.'

Silence.

'I was at school with Brooke,' Marshall continued. 'His father was my housemaster.' Reining his horse to standstill, he swung in the saddle so he could look Innes in the eye. 'Do you think it's peculiar that I feel that way, after what you've been through?'

Innes frowned. 'What have I been through? I'm here.'

'That isn't what I mean.'

'I know what you mean. Why are you asking?'

An embarrassed laugh. 'You've read Nietzsche.'

'Are you testing me?'

Marshall protested. 'Really, Innes. If you'd rather not . . .'

Innes lifted a gloved hand – sorry, he'd spoken sharply. 'I don't know. Was it right to go to war?' He gazed at the ground to gather his thoughts. 'Yes. Of course. Yes. But I can't think of soldiering as noble. My men were brave, I loved them for . . . their decency. To fight in such places and find love, humanity, perhaps there is something noble in that. They were fighting for *their* country. I don't suppose they cared much about anyone else's. I'm not sure I did. But now I've seen with my own eyes what the Germans have done to Belgium.' His

91

horse was shifting, chomping her bit impatiently, and he tried to soothe her. 'There girl, there. What can you see from a trench? The routine, the killing, always feeling tired. It muddies the mind, and only the love you feel for your men matters. Yet you still send them out to die. And for a time you hate the brass hats for their senseless orders . . .' He sighed. 'But perhaps they aren't senseless, it is just that you can't see the larger picture.' He lifted his head to look at Marshall. 'Trust. I *want* to believe in our commander-in-chief and his generals.'

Marshall considered this for a moment. 'This is the worst time. I admit my faith is being tested too. You know, the Chief has asked the Navy to place its forces in a state of readiness for our next attack; we're going to be at the coast for Guy Fawkes Night, it seems. That's what? Thirty miles in six weeks. We've been fighting for seven weeks already, given it our best shot some might say, ninety thousand casualties, and in that time we've managed only three and a half miles.' He closed his eyes and shook his head. 'Of course, Charteris would tell you, "the night is always darkest just before the dawn".'

Silence.

'Enough.' Marshall tried to smile. 'I don't want to belly-ache about Charteris. Generals have to be optimistic, but honest, too – above all honest.' He shortened his reins. 'Let's stop this. Look, here's something else to think about . . .' He spurred his horse forward . . . 'Catch me, if you're up to it. *Ha!*'

And Innes following, his mare quickly into her stride, but pushing her harder to make up the yards between them, stretching out, hands steady and low, conscious suddenly that Marshall was set full tilt at a hedge. Battling with her head, just in control, breathless as she rose to meet it, and she seemed to hang there, then over, and he slumped over her neck, struggling to keep his seat. Damn it, Marshall was laughing. A show of insincere applause. 'Well done, you're still there.'

'Of course, I am. Are you disappointed?'

But Marshall was gazing beyond him now to the corner of the field. 'We have company.' A party of horsemen was trotting along the line of the hedge towards them. To judge from their hats, there were two officers with an escort of two troopers, red and white pennants streaming from their lances as if they'd just ridden off the field at Balaklava. 'I suppose there was always a possibility,' Marshall said.

Innes asked if it was the field marshal, although he was sure it must be.

'He rides every day, but not here usually.' Marshall paused, biting his bottom lip. 'I don't think he'll stop. I hope not. Peculiar. Now I feel guilty . . . our conversation. I always feel guilty in his company.'

Closer, over a small rise, and Innes was surprised to see three hounds following the horses. It was impossible to imagine; surely they were not hunting before the next battle? Except, after three years of war almost nothing was unthinkable. Haig, on a large chestnut horse, was straight back and steady, and plainly in good shape – a cavalryman, of course. His companion was a less accomplished rider – a thin and saturnine officer whom Innes took for the field marshal's private secretary, Sassoon. Three hundred yards, two, and Innes was conscious of Marshall fidgeting beside him, and of his own nerves. Why, for God's sake? He'd seen Haig before, although it was only at a distance. The 'eyes right' figure, almost alone in the late afternoon sunshine, his long shadow sweeping over the stubble towards them; the commander of at least a million men and the painted china face of as many mugs and parlour plates; cursed and reviled and praised as the architect of small victories and terrible defeats, and battles that were neither one thing nor the other; the man who gave an order that sent a university historian called Francis MacCunn to his death; the author

93

of many orders, and many deaths . . . but wasn't that the story of every field marshal who ever held a baton?

'Here we go,' Marshall muttered.

Haig brought his horse to a high-stepping walk. He was intending to stop. Marshall's arm rose, and Innes followed, with a smart salute. The field marshal, lifting his chin a little, his eyes a very light shade of blue – the sky just after sunrise – strikingly handsome for a man in his fifties. Clearing his throat, he said: 'A little exercise, Marshall?'

'Yes, sir.'

He nodded but said nothing. It was a toe-curling silence.

'May I introduce Captain Innes, sir?' Marshall said at last. 'He's joined us in Intelligence.'

Haig's gaze settled on Innes. 'A Cameron, I see. Your battalion, Captain?'

'The Sixth, sir,' Innes heard himself say.

'The Sixth?' His fat grey moustache arched as he pursed his lips in concentration. A commander-in-chief's moustache. 'With the 15th Scottish?'

'Yes, sir.'

'A good division.'

'Thank you, sir,' said Innes.

Another disconcerting silence, broken at last by the field marshal's secretary, Sassoon. 'Captain Innes was sent to us by the War Office – Captain Cumming's Bureau,' he said, leaning from the saddle to be closer to Haig's ear. 'Helping to train the agents of the Advance Espionage Unit we've posted with the cavalry.'

Again there was a long pause before Haig spoke. 'Brave fellows. Are they ready, Innes?'

'Yes, sir.'

'We'll have work for them soon.' Clearing his throat once more, he turned to Sassoon and back, deliberate in even

94

small movements and gestures, in his speech too – or so it seemed to Innes. 'You must excuse me, gentlemen. Enjoy your ride. Excellent for the spirits.' He pricked his horse into a walk, then a slow trot. They saluted his back and watched him cross the field with his entourage, and they said nothing until long after he was out of earshot.

'The responsibility he carries.' Innes was surprised by the tremor in Marshall's voice. 'Reserved, yes, and yet noble. Yes, noble.'

That word again. 'Like the war itself?' he asked.

'In a way. He represents our determination to see it through.' Marshall sounded defensive. 'I don't know him, not really, not at all, but there is something remarkable . . . one can't say *charisma* . . . honourable, lofty. A moral force. He is like a great cathedral. Do you see that?'

What did Innes see? He saw men from his battalion climbing the ladders at Loos and a strip of tartan blowing from German wire; he saw a fisherman from the Hebrides floating face down in a shell hole, and in the summer heat on the Somme he saw flies rising from the corpses in a seething cloud.

'Like a cathedral, you say?' He offered Marshall a weak smile. 'I don't know. Like the Edinburgh barn the Presbyterians still call St Giles, perhaps.' He paused. 'But weren't you surprised by his hounds?'

'We should ride back . . .' Marshall was urging his horse about . . . 'By the road, it's quicker. As for the dogs, I expect they were Sassoon's. Would it matter if they weren't?'

'On the eve of battle? Yes.'

'He must take exercise, Innes. Goodness, we were just speaking of how important it is to escape for a time.'

Innes didn't want to argue. 'This much occurs to me,' he said, 'if he weren't an optimist he would be crushed by his responsibilities – that, or he is chiselled from stone, like your cathedral.'

But Innes was troubled most of the way back to town by his failure to speak honestly. Haig had asked him if the members of the Suicide Club were ready, and he'd offered 'Yes, sir.' Nothing noble in that reply. Trust. Trust again, because an officer owed it to his men to speak the truth, and it was a commander's duty to listen. He wanted to speak of it but Marshall looked preoccupied, perhaps troubled by something too.

'You'll ache in the morning,' he observed at the stables.

'I do already.' Innes hadn't been on a horse since he was wounded in the leg.

An Angelus bell was tolling in one of the town's churches. Somewhere, old women were bending before a chapel altar to chant the 'Ave Maria' and perhaps pray for peace. Innes could imagine his mother in Edinburgh, a splash of blue headscarf almost lost among the benches at the Sacred Heart Church, too arthritic to kneel for long, although sometimes she would forget and struggled to rise. 'Na cur cùl rium, ach dian tròcair,' she would pray: 'turn not from me, but have mercy'. 'God won't listen to me if I don't ask him in Gaelic,' she said.

Walking slowly back to the École Militaire, Innes said: 'Someone collected Macrae's things.'

Marshall glanced sideways at him. 'Poor old Macrae, I hope his family didn't hear about the tart.'

'Do you know who was responsible for investigating his death?'

'Why do you ask?'

'Simply because I want to know what happened.'

'That is simple. He was overweight and his heart couldn't stand the excitement. But if you don't want to take my word for it, a chap called Saunders came to speak to us. Military

96

Police in Étaples.' He pulled a face. 'Earthy sort. Bad attitude. Used to be a sergeant in the Metropolitan Police.'

Innes limped the last quarter of a mile, the pain from the old wound too much to disguise. 'Overdid it a little,' he said, when Marshall expressed concern. 'I'll be fine in the morning.'

A Staff car was parked outside the école, a grey-haired corporal at the wheel. 'Charteris's driver,' Marshall whispered, 'I really don't want to . . .'

But the guard-house door was opening and a second later the broad silhouette of the BGI appeared beneath the carriage arch. Head down, lost somewhere in thought, he came towards them like a front row forward with an eye for the try line. He was almost upon them before he noticed.

'Innes. Marshall.' Ash stain on his tunic, his tie knot slipping, and there was ink on the fingers of his right hand as he answered their salute. 'Riding, I hear? Glad you managed to find time.'

Marshall stiffened. 'A little exercise.'

'Yes, of course. I must make time too. And you met the Chief.' Perhaps Innes showed some surprise because he gave a short laugh. 'You see, gentlemen – spies everywhere. But that's what you would wish from your BGI, isn't it? And you made a good impression, Innes. The Chief is pleased the Advance Espionage Unit is ready for action. I might take you to dinner at the chateau, but not until we've seen the back of Mr Lloyd George.'

'Bad luck,' said Marshall, as Charteris's motor car pulled away. 'Dinner there is a grim affair.' He frowned. 'Does that sound disloyal, too?'

'No. It sounds honest, and I thought we'd agreed that honesty is more important in our work than loyalty.'

He shook his head. 'Oh, professor, professor. You look for some deeper meaning in everything don't you?'

'We met the Field Marshal only an hour ago. How did Brigadier Charteris know?'

'Sassoon. I expect he rang Charteris, or he may have spoken to Graham – they're on good terms – they were at Eton together.'

Innes nodded. 'I see.'

'Now what do you mean by that, I wonder?' Marshall's blue eyes were sparkling with amusement.

Innes wasn't sure what he meant. More connections, more loyalties perhaps. He wasn't concerned with that now. Walking through the school, across one courtyard and the next, his thoughts were still of his failure to give an honest answer to his commander-in-chief whether he wanted to hear it or no. He'd made a good impression with a lie. He wasn't sure if he'd meant to – they'd exchanged just a few words – but the irony! He'd been sent to GHQ because 'important people' suspected Army intelligence of varnishing the truth.

'Are you listening?' They were at the door to Section A, and Marshall was speaking. 'Dinner at the *estaminet*, at eight . . . if you're not too tired.'

Innes said he thought he would be.

Of course, he knew spies were expected to ingratiate themselves with lies. But my duty is to the truth, he thought, whatever Cumming might say. And loyalty? That he owed to those who were really fighting the war, the ordinary folk who couldn't tell the truth because no one important cared to ask; men like the little Frenchman, Petit, flying to nowhere in his balloon.

Madame Simon watched the priest sweep the bench dry with the sleeve of his coat. The park was a poor choice for a rendezvous but he knew nothing of such things. It was just across the road from the military prison and passers-by were bound to wonder why its chaplain was meeting a woman at dusk in the rain.

She had watched him walk away from its gates and through the park to the canal, and she was satisfied no one was following him, but she was going to wait a little longer in the trees just to be sure. The bench was across a gravel path, a dozen or so yards away. Father Georges was crouching over his knees, trying to shrink beneath the broad brim of his clerical hat. His gaze seemed to be fixed on the concentric circles that were ruffling the water of the canal. She didn't know him but Lux had sent word he was trustworthy and willing.

Lux was sending her fresh identity papers too. She had escaped from Thielt with only the muddy clothes on her back and a terrible cold that she had picked up in a ditch. A week later, it was still with her. She had followed the prisoners to Ghent in a farm cart and found shelter with the ironmonger who ran the network in the city. The local lawyer they found to represent Mertens and Lemmens at the military court wasn't expecting to win, and the German prosecutor was going to press for the death penalty. Cut all contact with the network in Thielt and Roulers, she had told the ironmonger; they would rebuild with the help of their contacts in the church. Lux had promised to send someone to the area.

It was after six o'clock now and Father Georges was fidgeting impatiently. Stepping back from the tree-line, she checked the paths through the park and could see no one. A couple of workmen were hurrying home along the opposite bank of the canal, and in the gloom beyond she could see the lamps of a passing motor car. Her footsteps on the gravel made the priest start, and he was plainly very relieved to see only a middle-aged woman in a country scarf and dress.

'The Abbé sent you?' he said.

'Call him Lux, Father,' she replied.

'Then you must be Ramble.' He sounded a little disappointed.

'Yes, I'm Ramble.'

He was shorter and at least fifteen years younger than she was, but that wouldn't concern him because Monday to Friday his congregation was made up of widows and middle-aged housewives like her.

'Do you have my papers?' she asked. 'I will take those now, in case we have to leave in a hurry.'

'You think—'

'A precaution, Father, that's all. It will be safer if we walk.'

Reaching into his coat pocket he produced an envelope and presented it to her.

'You haven't opened it?'

'No, of course not.'

He was piqued by her question but she didn't have time for his feelings. 'Have you seen Mertens?'

'I heard his confession. He seems resigned to . . . well, whatever may befall.'

'He is a brave, a fine man.' The words stuck in her throat and for a few seconds she felt too much to say more.

'He was beaten in Thielt and in the prison here,' the priest said, 'but he wanted Ramble to know he's told them nothing.' He smiled. 'And now she does know. I'm not sure if it's useful but he said—'

'A minute, Father. We have company.'

A man was striding along the gravel path towards them. He was well dressed in a heavy overcoat and the plain clothes policeman's Homburg hat, but he was carrying a leather case like a banker. She sensed the priest tense beside her. The stranger slipped a hand inside his coat and she held her breath too, but he was only fumbling for his cigarettes. He smiled and tipped the hat as he walked by.

'I thought . . .'

'Yes. It's always like this,' she said. 'We should finish our business and leave. There was something more you wanted to say?'

'Mertens was surprised how much his interrogator seemed to know about your organization – a churchman called Lux; a soldier called Lazarus; and you, a woman with the code-name *Ramble*. She even mentioned the British Secret Service.'

She frowned. 'Anything else?'

The priest gave a little shrug. 'She was so clever, it frightened him. German, of course. One of his guards called her the *Fräulein Doktor.*'

'The interrogator? A woman?'

'Fräulein Doktor. That's what Monsieur Mertens said, yes. A woman, like you.'

She stopped and turned so abruptly she kicked gravel against his shiny black shoes. 'Not like me, Father.'

7

Report

'SORRY TO DRAG you to Downing Street,' Hankey said, 'but I have the War Policy Committee, then the Prime Minister wants me to drive down to his house in Surrey. Coffee?' He opened the door and spoke to someone in the outer office. Standing on a Turkish rug in front of the fire, Cumming, in his uniform. A small smile for the chancellor of the exchequer in the corridor, a polite inclination of the head as he passed Mrs Lloyd George in the hall; a grey-haired captain with monocle and stick worthy of no more notice than any of the other elderly naval gentlemen who visited Number 10 to talk of their ships and munitions and harbour defences.

'Terrible mess in here.' Hankey stepped back to the fireplace. 'I don't have an office at Number 10 because L.G. would be in and out all the time. This one belongs to his secretary, Jones.'

Cumming lifted his chin to the picture above the chimney-piece. 'William Pitt?'

'Lord Liverpool. He used to be the first prime minister you saw when you stepped into Number 10, but L.G. wanted him out of sight. He said he could think of some other Tories he would like to hang in a dark room – and one field marshal.' Hankey lifted the poker from a brass tree and leant over the guard to stir the coals in the grate. 'You'd think a Welsh chap like Jones would know how to keep a fire.'

Cumming said: 'I have a report from Innes, may I read it to you?'

'You know, I think I've made the fire worse.' The embers were pulsing slowly. Hankey gestured to the armchair by the window. 'There's more light there.'

The view was of the muddy Downing Street garden and the suburb of huts built for staff brought in to support the administration of war.

'It's changed a good deal since Mr Asquith's time,' Cumming observed.

'Someone woke up and remembered we were fighting a war and the sooner we won it the better.' Hankey ran a hand over his bald head as if he were trying to smooth the cares of government. 'Perhaps Captain Innes can offer us some assurance we're making progress.'

'The latest attack seems to have met with some success.' Cumming dropped into the chair – 'there' – and hung his stick on the arm. 'But what does success mean after three years? Innes says the weather was heavy in the hours before the attack but we advanced about a mile and held eleven enemy counter-attacks. That sounds like a small victory. Casualties were high – I expect you know that. I'm sorry there wasn't time to have this typed,' he said, peering at it through his eyeglass. 'I'll have it sent over this afternoon. Innes says his espionage unit was with the cavalry in readiness for the big breakthrough. It's expected at any time, according to Charteris, and one supposes Field Marshal Haig thinks the same.'

'I'm sure he does.'

'Is this all very familiar?'

'Yes, but a fresh perspective is always useful.' Hankey glanced at his watch. 'Go on.'

'There are a few general observations that are, well, very Innes. He writes of *a strange air of detachment at GHQ, as if the battle at Ypres is part of a great exercise.* And that *Charteris claims the preliminary operation at Messines was a great victory and that our casualties were negligible.* And he asks, *when did ten thousand become a small number? A General cannot be paralysed by fear of casualties, I am sure, I am only thankful my part in this war is a small one.'*

Cumming looked up from the paper. 'He's a university chap, if you remember, a prof or something of the sort. There is a little more about the atmosphere at GHQ, but I don't think it's necessary . . .'

'Messines was June,' said Hankey. 'It's now the end of September. Ten thousand casualties has become a hundred thousand.' His gaze drifted down to his small hands, resting in his lap. 'The Prime Minister was sceptical from the start, now he's becoming very fractious. No faith in Field Marshal Haig, I'm sorry to say. Does Haig have a grasp of the situation? Really, I wonder.'

'Isn't that's what we sent Innes to find out? He does have something to say about the politics . . . may I? *Politics often arouses more passion at GHQ than the state of the battle. The BGI sets the tone. He enjoys company, is a great raconteur and is very free with his opinions of politicians and news-papermen. I do not think he trusts me entirely, but he seems to like me, and for all his bluster and Presbyterian prejudice, I like him.'*

Cumming lifted the letter closer to his eye-glass. 'He says Charteris speaks of politicians in the most disparaging terms . . . *ignorant, meddling, untrustworthy, cowardly* – and, not to put to fine a point on it, he hates Mr Lloyd George.'

'The man must have been drunk to say so to a junior officer.'

'Perhaps. You know, he gives the impression it's impossible to put a cigarette paper between him and the Field Marshal on anything. Innes says, *Charteris told me that soldiers could always afford to be "clean and honest, not like politicians and parsons". Perhaps that is why he is forthright in his opinions, because to do anything else would be unworthy of a soldier – even a head of intelligence. "Politicians and parsons"; better say, "politicians and newspaper proprietors", and the sniping at both may be evidence of a great fear that someone will be held to account for failure if we do not break the Germans at Ypres soon. Charteris believes the enemy is teetering, and when he falls the war will be over quickly, and Staff officers and politicians who demur are dismissed as "pessimists" or worse, "defeatists'" "Good fellows" at headquarters are all optimists. One assumes we fight all our battles in the hope of winning and stop when there is no evidence that we are. But fresh pieces of intelligence supporting the case for "one more heave" appear in the GHQ information summary almost every day. Charteris produces this intelligence like a conjurer pulling white rabbits from a top hat. Some pieces are from the usual sources, dressed up a little by the BGI. The best intelligence must come from the Army's spy networks in the occupied territories. It is sent via its office in the Netherlands and is processed here by Section B. I see nothing of it, of course. My duties are simple: offer advice on reports from the Ramble network and wet-nurse the new espionage unit, and nothing more.'*

Cumming paused again. 'The wags at GHQ are calling it the Suicide Club, and its members seem to like the name.'

'Like moths at a flame . . .' Hankey lifted his hands from his knees in a big fist and touched them to his lips 'Like moths, they seek refuge in death.'

'Poetry?'

'R.L. Stevenson, man. The Suicide Club stories.'

Cumming frowned and cleared his throat. 'I'm not much of a one for stories, Sir Maurice. May I? Innes doesn't seem to have made a good impression on the officer in charge of this Suicide Club. *I try to ingratiate myself with Colonel MacLeod,* he writes, *oh how I try, but he does not appreciate my "we Scots" banter and talk of "hame".'*

Cumming looked up. 'MacLeod was disgraced. His wife was caught with stolen jewellery, he took the blame and went to prison for her.'

'I remember reading something of the sort.'

Hankey pointed to the letter. 'Is there much more? War Policy at ten.'

'Just a little,' Cumming said. '*I have touched upon the siege mentality at headquarters, the sense among those close to their "Chief" that the war is being won in spite of our elected representatives, that enemies at home must be seen off – the Ps – politicians, pacifists, poets and pessimists, oh, and appeasers. This defensive thinking is apparent in everything Colonel MacLeod says and does. For all the talk of the honest soldier, is there anyone at headquarters with influence who is allowed to stand outside the circle of wagons surrounding Field Marshal Haig? Major Marshall speaks his mind and is ignored.*

'*The newspapers are here, of course, and are well looked after in their own chateau outside the town. Two press warlords are expected on the morning of the 25th and the Prime Minister in the evening.* Are you travelling with him?' Cumming asked.

'Yes. Perhaps you should come too.' Hankey had risen from his chair again and was standing with his nose almost pressed to the window, gazing out to the garden. A dark sky was building above the wall, the breeze shaking petals from the roses beneath the terrace. 'The War Office still wants your bureau for the Army, you know.' He turned to look at Cumming. 'Someone is sure to raise the matter while we're in France. Besides, if you come you can speak to Innes.'

'GHQ is lobbying politicians already . . . Haig has received Mr Churchill and Mr Asquith. Let me find it—' Cumming turned to the second page of Innes's report and ran his finger down to a passage he'd marked in green pen.

'Here: *Haig sees most of the first-rank politicians and a good number of the second too, in fact for one who is reported to consider them to be no better than parsons, he spends a good deal of time in their company, even while he is commanding a battle. "Another awful day of MPs", Charteris said to me yesterday, and for an hour or so our école was as busy as the lobby of the House of Commons. We must hold our nerve, he told them, the Field Marshal will beat the Boche, who is near collapse anyway. If only Mr Lloyd George could be persuaded not to "tie our hands". I am sure the MPs were flattered to be shown the "true picture". They left with their lines from Charteris and I expect they will use them in Parliament to play merry hell at home.*

'*Mr Churchill was less malleable, and his visit was most instructive. He joined our intelligence mess for dinner. Charteris had to deal with some small matter. If he had stayed he could not have failed to notice that Major Stewart Graham is on the best of terms with the Minister. Old friends, I would say. Do you know Graham? He is head of counter-espionage in Section B. Fought at Ypres in '14 and again in '15 and was badly injured in a gas attack there. Distant with me. But I am reminded of something Marshall said on one of our night walks: "most of us at headquarters have friends". Is Marshall one of yours? He has gone out of his way to be helpful. Naturally, he assumes I am working for you. Marshall, Graham, Jack of the topographical section, Faunthorpe in censorship; I expect all of them are writing to their "friends". There are so many politicians in khaki. While men fight at Ypres we intrigue. Charteris says the war is being waged on two fronts;*

here in France and in Downing Street. I think he must be right.

'Was Captain Macrae another of your sources, by the way, or did he belong to someone else? If he was your man, you will know he was concerned about the reliability of some of the Army's intelligence sources and that he raised the matter with the BGI and then the War Office. You will also know that he died in the arms of a prostitute in Paris-Plage – that is what the police say. To be sure, the Bureau should make enquiries in London. I will see what I can turn up in Paris-Plage. I want to know more about these sources in the occupied territories, but I have no idea where to begin. Army networks are MacLeod's responsibility. There are files in MacLeod's office, I think: that will present a challenge. I must say, I do feel like a sneak. I want someone to persuade me this is for the men going over at Ypres, and that it is honest.'

Cumming folded the letter. 'And he asks for news of the Ramble network in Belgium. Did you know this Macrae?'

The Secretary to the War Cabinet was gazing distractedly out of the window at the new garden suburb. 'Innes has a colourful imagination, doesn't he?'

'He writes poetry. But not the whingeing sort,' Cumming said. 'He writes in Gaelic, so I don't suppose it matters what he writes.'

'You won't make friends in Downing Street with that sort of talk, Captain. The Prime Minister is a great lover of the Welsh language.' Hankey pressed his finger-tips to his brow. 'A poet but also an astute fellow: Innes understands the difficulty we have. But can he be trusted to keep his counsel if he's caught doing something he shouldn't? Perhaps with one of those files he mentioned in his report . . .'

'I think so. He knows nothing of your interest, of course.'

'Good.' Hankey's gaze dropped to the floor, then to the door. 'My dear fellow, forgive me . . . the War Policy Committee . . .'

'Of course.' Cumming rose on the arms of the chair and stood breathing heavily. 'You know I haven't asked, Sir Maurice, but if you *do* have – how does Innes put it – "friends" at headquarters, perhaps now is the time . . .'

Hankey inclined his head a little. Was it a gesture of acknowledgement? Cumming couldn't be sure.

8

September 23

THEY SANG 'FIGHT the Good Fight'. Perhaps they sang it
every Sunday. Then they sang 'Love Divine, All Loves
Excelling' as the sun poured through the windows of the hut
on to the makeshift altar with its Christless cross. Haig was at
the front of the congregation, Charteris was by his side, and
Innes was watching as they bowed their heads to pray,
pretending to do the same, but only for a moment because he
was there to observe the field marshal before his maker. 'Call
on the Lord for inner strength and resolve to complete your
task,' the earnest young Church of Scotland chaplain urged in
his sermon. And later: 'Nothing can withstand the prayers of
a great united people.' Strange, Innes thought, because a lot of
men had prayed very hard on the Somme. Haig's back was so
very straight, because it wasn't necessary to kneel before the
Presbyterian God. Faith and hope and optimism before a bare
cross in a simple whitewashed church, where victory was
ordained and the Philistines were vanquished by a man wielding
the jawbone of an ass. Innes couldn't remember praying for
victory before. It seemed to him that God was in the small
things – if he was there at all – the kindnesses of men.

At the end of the service the field marshal was the first to
rise, with a reticent smile and a nod to familiar faces. His blue
gaze rested on Innes, and although it was only for a second
it was enough to make Innes feel guilty, as if he were telling

another lie – which he was, in a way. There was something in Haig's eyes, the set of his face, a stiffness that was shyness, or determination, or both. He was so very scrupulous about his appearance – that moustache, clipped proud and imperial – turning his head deliberately as he walked between the church benches. It wasn't charisma, Marshall was right about that, but an inner strength, perhaps the force Nietzsche called man's will to power: *Der Wille zur Macht*.

Innes joined the queue to return his prayer book and by the time he'd shaken the chaplain's hand Haig had gone. But Charteris was still there, well groomed for church and full of bonhomie. He was driving to the press chateau to brief the correspondents on the state of the battle. 'Something we can let them print,' he said. Innes watched him leave, then limped down the hill to the garage for his own motor car.

His driver's name was Jenkins, a South Wales Borderer and miner from the Rhondda. He was in his thirties, stout, balding, and a Bolshie. How he'd come by such a cushy billet was a mystery. 'My good looks,' he'd said on one of their journeys, which was amusing because his squashed features reminded Innes of his father's Chinese bulldog.

'Bruay again, sir?'

'No, Jenkins. Étaples.'

He sucked his teeth. 'There's trouble there, sir. It'll be difficult getting into the camp.'

'What sort of trouble?' Innes caught his eye in the side mirror before he looked away.

'I wouldn't like to say, sir.' It was plain from the excitement in his voice that he wanted to very much.

'Come on, man.'

'I'm surprised you haven't heard, sir, with you being in intelligence,' he said with just the suggestion of a smirk. 'They're calling it a mutiny. The Aussies and some Jocks—oh, sorry, sir.'

'Go on.'

'Trouble with the canaries who do the training there. They can be rough, see, and, well, things got out of hand. Someone was shot, and the whole camp's in uproar. They chased the Military Police out, and some of the men broke into the town – wanted what the officers get, I shouldn't wonder.'

Innes could imagine the resentment of soldiers, bullied by sergeants who'd done none of the fighting, and Paris-Plage just across the river, with bars and women out of reach to all but their officers.

Jenkins didn't know how many men were involved or if it was over, because no one wanted to be caught talking about a mutiny. 'Quickest way to get shot, see. You won't say anything, will you, sir?' Jenkins's wide-set eyes sought his in the mirror. 'I wouldn't have spoken, only you were talking about going there . . . and you being such a gentleman.'

Innes thanked him for the compliment but that was still his intention.

As they drove into Étaples the heavens opened again, the rain drumming on the bonnet of the motor car and Jenkins cursing under his breath. At the first security check a sergeant from the Honourable Artillery Company stepped out of a sentry-box to inform them of a 'spot of bother'. They should drive without stopping, first along Infantry Road, then left on to Tipperary, follow the railway along Supply, and the police station was opposite General Hospital Number 24. If they reached the cemetery they'd gone too far. Jenkins said he knew to keep clear of the cemetery.

Wet white bell tents sprawled over the hillside above the beaches of the Canche estuary. The hospitals were at the bottom of the slope in long wooden huts, and beyond the railway at a safe distance from the men, a nurses' hostel, the administration and a guard-house. Trenches and a no man's land were cut in the wind-blasted dunes to the north, and the cemetery at the edge of the camp could be seen from almost everywhere, the rows of weather-beaten crosses creeping up the slope to a copse of pines. Since Innes's one and only visit for training on the eve of the Somme, it had grown by many battalions.

They drove slowly through acres of shivering canvas with barely a soul to be seen, wet soot from the camp incinerator speckling the windscreen, a snatch of distant bugle. There was a stillness that was more than Sunday quiet. Through a gap in the wire dividing the camp into compounds, Innes caught a glimpse of the hospital train in the sidings below; round a corner another glimpse, of a cemetery procession, nurses, a few soldiers, a coffin draped in the Union flag. There were no senior officers hanging from trees, no red flags, if there'd been a mutiny it was over and the men were back in the proving ground they called the bullring – even on a Sunday.

At the intersection of Infantry Road and Tipperary, a posse of troopers from the Honourable Artillery Company was forcing three men into the back of a lorry at bayonet point.

'A Scotsman, sir,' said Jenkins, eyes flicking to the side mirror and away. He was trying not to smile.

Innes wiped the condensation from the passenger window with his glove. One of the prisoners was wearing a kilt and the green glengarry of the Gordon Highlanders. 'A British soldier like you, Jenkins.' What had the Highlander done? Was it a mutiny, or were men who risked mutilation or death for their country driven to distraction by the shouting and petty rules of those who ran the Base Camp?

'It can't come to an end quick enough, can it sir?' Jenkins was watching him in the mirror.

'No, boyo, it can't.'

Slopping through the mud on Supply Road, they came across

two Voluntary Aid Detachment nurses and Innes offered them a lift. One was a debutante from Berkshire, the other a fitter's daughter from Liverpool with red hair and a bright smile that reminded him of his sister. Trouble in the town, they said. Annie, the nurse from Liverpool, thought it had started with a fight over a girl, but Rosemary, the debutante, said a police Red Cap had fired on some soldiers: everyone was confined to camp, and no one was to use the word 'mutiny' or mention it in a letter home, on pain of something.

For five minutes Innes shared their laughter, their sideways glances, the scent of lavender soap and the rustling of their starched uniforms beneath their capes; Annie lifting her arms to tidy a strand of loose hair into her cap, Rosemary's big green eyes; and when they enquired shyly if he would be staying in camp he was aching to say yes. Watching them scurry for shelter, he reflected again that the war was a long series of goodbyes.

The picket on the railway bridge directed them to a sturdy green two-storey long-house. Jenkins parked in a space marked by a row of perfectly white washed stones. In the dunes to the right of the police station, there were a dozen wood and canvas shanties, some with small gardens, although most of their flowers were dying.

'The Red Caps,' said Jenkins, catching Innes's eye again. 'Away from everyone else.'

There was pandemonium inside the hut, feet and voices bouncing off the wooden walls, a bullet-headed sergeant at the front desk berating one of his men, and on a bench beneath a rain-lashed window facing the sea, two Australian prisoners in wrist manacles. It seemed to Innes that everyone in the station was either frightened or cross.

'Sergeant.' He plonked his stick on the front desk. 'The Assistant Provost Marshal. Captain Saunders.'

The sergeant turned with his mouth open to shout, but snapped it shut comically the second he saw he was being addressed by a Staff officer.

Beyond the partition, clerical orderlies were typing and answering phones – doing the things clerks do – and a police corporal with a black eye was flicking through some files. The room was painted a gloomy military green and papered along one wall with orders and regulations. Most of the desks were empty and Innes wondered whether their usual occupants were hiding or busy snuffing out the revolution. The sergeant led him to a door with a large brass nameplate of the sort more commonly fixed to mahogany than pine. Knocking tentatively, the sergeant was instructed to enter.

'Sir. Captain Innes from GHQ.'

Innes was peering over the sergeant's shoulder and caught Saunders rolling his eyes to the ceiling. 'Sorry to arrive unannounced,' he said. 'It's urgent, I'm afraid.'

'Isn't it always?' Saunders leant forward and ground his cigarette into an ashtray. 'What *more* can I do for GHQ? The buggers are back in the bullring, their leaders in the guardhouse. The Anzacs are off to Ypres . . . the camp's quiet . . .' He opened his arms and offered his palms like a hot gospeller at prayer. 'Nothing more to say.'

Innes stepped into his tiny office and sat down. 'The mutiny isn't my concern.'

'It wasn't a mutiny.'

'Captain Macrae . . . you investigated his death?'

Saunders stared at him belligerently. 'This isn't about the riot?'

'I told you, that isn't my concern.'

He sucked his teeth. 'Look, Captain—'

'Innes.'

'Look, Innes, the politicians are about to descend upon us

here.' He shook his head incredulously. 'We're trying to put things in some sort of order. Now if you don't mind . . .'

Perhaps it was the old dug-out jaundice, but Innes stared at him and thought: goodness, how the war throws up these men, with their doorplates and large desks, and King's Regulations to the letter, all of them bald and jowly like Saunders, with small eyes and toothbrush moustaches; men who called you 'old boy' and spoke too correctly to be the real thing; men of the QM Branch and the ASC, the MMP and MFP, and all the rest pocketing a good day's pay with a very respectable chance of being able to spend it; men who didn't care if the war went on for ever.

'If you don't mind!' Saunders repeated, losing his temper and pushing his chair away to rise.

'Actually, I do,' Innes said. 'This is an intelligence matter. If you aren't going to help me you better ring Brigadier Charteris and tell him why.'

Saunders looked down at his desk, picked up a pen and put it back again. 'Intelligence,' he muttered, dragging his chair back to the desk. 'Of course, if it's for Brigadier Charteris.'

'I want to know about Macrae, how he died, where, and with whom.'

'In the arms of one of la Duchesse's tarts . . .'

'And if anything struck you as unusual about his death.'

'Unusual?' Saunders offered something between a leer and a smile. 'He didn't have time to pay. Oh, and he was circumcised.'

Innes frowned and shook his head.

'All right, all right,' said Saunders, defensively. He slid out from behind his desk. 'Wait here. I'll get the file.'

Innes stood on the steps of the police hut, hat and stick under his arm, a sea breeze ruffling his hair, free at last of cigarette smoke and stale innuendo, of Saunders' quiet malevolence. There were threads of sunshine on the camp, its hard lines, its filth and wire, lost for a moment in a dazzling white glow, then the break in the clouds closed and the hillside slipped into shadow again. Jenkins was calling to him, turning to open the door of the motor car.

'Behind the Continental Hotel, sir,' he said, as they drove towards the bridge. 'I'll have you there in a jiffy. I often bring *gentlemen* here.' He paused for chapel emphasis, so Innes was in no doubt what he thought of those gentlemen. 'They call it Paris-Plaging.'

'Did you take Captain Macrae Paris-Plaging, Jenkins?'

'No, sir. I did hear from the boys at the garage that he came here. Easy in intelligence, see, you can go anywhere.' Glancing in the mirror at Innes. 'Mind, the gentlemen from the Quartermaster's Branch, they're the worst.'

Innes interrupted. 'Thank you, Jenkins.'

One of his maiden aunts had spent a few weeks recuperating from a chest complaint in Paris-Plage. It would have been gentile and respectable then – Janet Innes was very particular – but the war ran through towns, through all their lives, like a great fault line. There was before and there was after. The ladies and gentlemen and the children with buckets and spades had gone, and the old seaside resort had learnt how to paint its face and hitch up its skirts. Gazing from the car to the other side of the river, Innes wondered if in his last hours Macrae had managed to find some peace there. There was nothing of significance in the police file; no mysterious sign on a scrap of paper; no dog that did or didn't bark – Innes couldn't remember which was correct – no incriminating marks on the body, other than some light scratches on the shoulders – oh, but how Saunders had enjoyed talking about those. And for once Innes had lost his temper. Macrae was worthy of some respect, trousers on or no. 'He did *his* bit,' Innes had said, pointedly shaking the cardboard file at Saunders: 'at Ypres, at Festubert and Loos.' Saunders had taken it very personally, which was fine.

From the file Innes had learnt that Captain Macrae was thirty-two, a bachelor and a regular soldier who transferred to the new Intelligence Corps at the beginning of the war. Place of birth: Inverness. Closest family: his parents in Dingwall. On the night of his death (Sunday, August the twenty-third) he dined at the Continental Hotel with another officer (unnamed) and ordered two bottles of wine. According to the waiter, he was florid of face and plainly agitated, and 'like almost every Englishman' he drank too much too quickly. His companion was calmer and 'behaved like a proper gentleman'. At 21.00 they left the hotel and parted company, Macrae arriving at the brothel fifteen minutes later. He spoke to its keeper, la Duchesse, and then he was shown to an upstairs bedroom. In the course of sexual congress with the prostitute, Agnes Bourgeois, he suffered a seizure. At 23.00 the Military Police and a local doctor discovered Captain Macrae lying dead on the floor in only his socks. No documents of a confidential nature were found near his body. No autopsy was authorised. Circumstances of death were not to be disclosed to his family.

They were now in Paris-Plage, driving along a parade with the beach to the right, the tide out and the wind swirling sand like a river to the sea. It was deserted but for seven or eight pale young men in striped bathing costumes who were racing towards the waves, splashing through the shallows, falling, picking themselves up before they could feel the cold, then diving for deep water. *Les officiers en Anglais.* The sort of healthy exercise GHQ would approve of, but Innes turned away, his eyes tightly closed. In their dash to the sea he saw a grotesque reflection of battle; soldiers rising, running, and diving for cover, so real, so acute that for a moment he could taste the dirt and cordite.

'All right, sir?' Jenkins sounded concerned. 'The one on the corner with the blue shutters, that's the Continental.'

He turned left beyond it into a Sunday-quiet street and parked the motor car opposite a small shop. 'This is the place. The women are usually on display, dressed like shop assistants.' He muttered something in Welsh that sounded very rude. An elderly face at a lace curtain two doors down, a little boy on a door step opposite; the big Staff car was already attracting unwelcome attention. 'Don't worry about my door,' Innes said, opening it himself. 'I'll meet you later. Wait at the Continental.'

A few flimsy articles of ladies' underwear were on display in the window but the shop behind was bare. Innes wondered if they were for sale or merely there to promote la Duchesse's service, but with so many young gentlemen across the river there was surely no need to advertise. A young woman dressed as a maid answered the door. Madame was still in bed and not used to visitors at this hour on a Sunday. Innes explained that he'd come on urgent business rather than for pleasure, and was shown into a small dark parlour furnished with cheap gilt and lace, an unhealthy fern struggling for light on a table beneath the window. Madame's place of money in the evening, it was lit to compliment women wearing cosmetics and not much else. Once or twice he'd been tempted in his cups to pay, in those bad times when he was sure there was no God or Order, and no reason to hope he would survive. In the cold light of day, he was relieved he hadn't done something he knew he would always be ashamed of.

There were voices in the hall and a moment later la Duchesse swept into the room.

'Ah, *monsieur le capitaine,* so early,' she said, offering her

119

hand, 'and a Sunday. But perhaps you are going back to the Front?'

Tall and shapely, late forties or early fifties, her fine features and dark complexion suggested to Innes a connection with the Maghreb. She was simply but expensively dressed in a black satin skirt and a white satin blouse, a large bloodstone on a silver chain hanging at her chest.

'We've seen so few English officers since the trouble at your camp . . . it is all over, Capitaine?' She had a delightfully husky voice.

'Yes, but most of the officers are still confined to Étaples.'

'Not for long I hope, my girls miss them so much. But you are a Staff officer, no? So you come and go as you please.' She smiled coyly. 'Is there someone in particular you've come to see, Capitaine?'

Innes explained why he was there. 'Loose ends,' he said, just a few points GHQ wished to clarify. If she was disappointed she didn't show it. For British headquarters, for 'Sir Dug-less 'aig, anything,' she said with a teasing smile. 'You understand French? Captain Macrae, il était très gentil, un vrai gentleman anglais – veree sweet, an English gentleman.' Macrae had visited her house four, perhaps five times and always asked for Agnes. His death was a terrible shock. To die so young and not on the battlefield, one could hardly credit such a thing. 'What could I say to poor Agnes? I said to the other officer, the major . . .'

'Captain Saunders. The policeman?'

'No, not your policeman. A major.' Another mischievous smile, and she reached across to tap Innes's shoulder. 'A crown, yes? Not three pips, like you.'

He returned her smile, excited for a moment by her perfume and her large brown eyes. 'Yes,' he said in almost a whisper. Then more forcefully: 'Yes. A major. Do you remember his—'

'He had a ribbon like yours.' She pointed at his chest. 'Purple and white.'

'The Military Cross? Was it Major Graham?'

Her lashes fluttered. 'Gray-ham, yes. He wanted to be sure Captain Macrae hadn't left any letters here.'

'Did he?'

'No. He came to make love to Agnes.' Her lashes fluttered again.

'Did Major Graham say why he thought there might be letters here?'

She gave a little shake of her head.

Agnes Bourgeois was not a beautiful woman. She had an old face, although she was probably in her twenties, and she was painfully thin and angular. Innes wondered if her rougher clients made her rattle. She was dressed demurely in black, like a village widow, perhaps for Sunday, the day of rest.

'Captain Macrae talked a lot,' she said, gazing down at the bed where he had died *in flagrante*. Brassy, it almost filled her room, and there was an uncomfortable-looking dip in the middle of the mattress.

'What did you talk about?' he asked.

She shrugged. 'He talked.'

'About?'

'I don't know . . . Scotland, his family, lots of things . . . I can't remember.' Shrugging again: 'I didn't mind, if that was what he wanted.'

'He always asked for you?'

'He said I reminded him of someone.'

Innes tried to catch her eye but she looked away. Head and bony shoulders bent, arms folded tightly across her small chest, it was difficult to imagine her arousing passion or joy. She seemed so fragile, so vulnerable. Perhaps Macrae had taken that

121

for innocence and wanted to protect her. Perhaps he'd thought to find tenderness and a deeper intimacy that was more than the moment they shared in her old cotton sheets. Perhaps.

'Did he talk about his work, his duties?'

'Not about the war.' She shook her head vigorously. 'Only about what he wanted to do when it was over.'

'And what was that?'

Another shrug. She couldn't remember or she didn't care.

'Did he leave anything with you?'

'No. I told the other officer.'

'He didn't believe you, Agnes. He sent me to ask again. He knows Macrae left some papers here.'

'No, monsieur. No.' Hugging herself tighter. 'I swear, only this book and a photograph.'

'Show me.' He watched her step quickly across the room to a plain oak chest of drawers and extract them from her lingerie.

'Here,' she said, thrusting them at him.

'Sorry, I have to check,' he said. Her brown eyes flitted to his face and away. He was taking what he wanted without even a by-your-leave, like the men who tumbled her in the brass bed.

The ink-stained photograph was of an officer in trews and a glengarry, full of face and figure. 'Captain Macrae?' She nodded. It had been taken at a studio in Bethune – Innes had visited the same place – and written on the back in floral letters a dedication from *Your affectionate, Donald. July 1917*. The book was a collection of Tennyson's poems in English. It seemed like a strange gift to give a French prostitute. Leafing through its pages, he found two lines bracketed in pencil: *But O for the touch of a vanished hand, And the sound of a voice that is still!* The sentiment was obvious and didn't suggest a hidden message or code, but he couldn't be sure.

'Did he read poems to you in English?'

'I don't understand.'

'I'd like to keep it a few days,' he said. 'You'll get it back. I promise.'

Not a flicker of emotion: she gazed at Innes as if she didn't have feelings. It irritated him. 'Why did he die on the floor?'

'When he had his seizure, he rolled off the bed.'

'Where—which side?'

She pointed to the floorboards at her feet.

'Did you care?'

'I don't understand.'

'Did you care?'

'I was sorry.'

'Did you care for him?'

This time her silence made him feel ashamed. He was still behaving like a customer, assuming he could insist on anything he wanted from her. No, he was behaving worse, because her thoughts and feelings were not for sale. Why did it matter what she felt for Macrae? He had no right to judge.

Jenkins put out his cigarette with the toe of his boot and walked round the front of the motor car to open the passenger door. 'Find what you wanted, sir?'

'None of your damn business, Jenkins,' he said, climbing inside. In truth, he would have struggled to answer. He was returning to Montreuil with no more than the vague sense of unease he'd left with that morning; that and two lines of Tennyson he'd bullied from a prostitute. So much more satisfying to have taken them from a femme fatale. Instead, he'd found sallow, silent Agnes, a small brown flightless bird, as scarred by the war as the man who'd died in her bed searching for finer feelings. 'In the line of duty' the telegram to Dingwall would say, and that was probably the end of his story, but if there was more, Innes was quite sure he knew who to ask.

*

Major Stewart Graham wasn't in the mess for dinner. 'With Second Army,' Marshall said. Charteris was there, and in great spirits. He'd spent the afternoon showing the Chief some of the prisoners taken in the recent fighting. 'A poor-looking lot,' he declared – another proof that the Germans were on their last legs. Marshall caught Innes's eye and frowned. Later that evening he sought Innes in the Section B office to explain: 'He arranged it all, you know. He put the worst-looking prisoners together, the thin ones, the young ones, the ones in threadbare uniforms, then invited Haig to inspect them.'

'Charteris?'

'Yes, of course, Charteris.' He was fuming. 'Who else?'

'How do you—'

'I just do. And that's not the only thing. One of MacLeod's sources claims the enemy is preparing to withdraw to a new defensive line. Charteris has varnished that nicely for the Chief.'

'You don't agree?'

Marshall closed his eyes, fingertips pressed to his forehead. 'I don't know. It's part of the malaise here in intelligence – a lack of proper procedure.' He opened his eyes. 'No. Actually, no, I don't believe it's genuine. A single unsubstantiated source from inside the occupied territories. I haven't seen anything else to suggest it's true – nothing from your Bureau. Your Agent Ramble, wouldn't he know?'

'Not necessarily. But the train watchers may have noticed something, more traffic . . . do you have the returns from our network?'

The September files were delivered to Innes's desk by the grizzled sergeant who marked the map. There were six in number – thick brown cardboard covers stamped *Secret*, with the handwritten instruction that they should be returned to Cabinet 6 (c) in MacLeod's office. In each were pages of fine tissue covered in tiny letters: *w* for cattle trucks and wagons, *v* for passenger coaches (*les voitures*), *w.plats* for flat trucks, *w hausettes* for the high open trucks. The trains were meticulously counted and recorded as they rattled from station to station and through junctions too small to appear on anything but the largest-scale maps of the occupied territories. Liege, Brussels, east to west, the 10.15 through Ghent on the eighteenth: ten wagons of soldiers and a coach of officers, eight trucks of ammunition, and twenty of horse. Innes remembered an old lady at Fourmies who used to count with her knitting needles, pearl one, knit one, pearl three more. He turned the flimsies, checking them against logs made by the clerks. Divisions in and out of the line at Ypres – that was to be expected, of course – but there was nothing to suggest a withdrawal or the strengthening of a new position.

By half past eleven, his eyes swimming, out of cigarettes, out of patience, he was ready to admit defeat. The office was empty but for a duty clerk and the map sergeant, who seemed to haunt the place day and night. Innes got up slowly and stretched. The old wound in his leg was aching.

'Take these back will you?' he said, summoning one of the clerks, but a second later he checked him with a raised hand. 'No, I'll do it.'

He wasn't sure why. It wasn't a job for an officer. An impulse. An idea that was still no more than a feeling. Files against his chest, he stepped into the corridor and across to MacLeod's office. He listened – somewhere someone was typing a steady two-finger rhythm – knocked lightly for form's sake, then opened the door and closed it carefully behind him. It was a narrow room with oak filing cabinets on the right and a desk at the end beneath the window; functional, tidy, Army. Innes walked over to the desk and picked up the only personal object he could see, a studio portrait of a handsome woman of middle years standing with her arms folded on the back of a chair. Marshall said the colonel loved his wife immoderately but she cared nothing for him. There'd been some sort of scandal. Innes wiped his fingerprints from the silver frame and put her back where he'd found her.

Careless of MacLeod to leave his cabinets unlocked. Cabinet 6 (c) Occupied Territories and Agents: Section Red for intelligence sent by the Bureau and Ramble's network; Section Green for GHQ's own organization. Innes took a file from Green and opened it on top of the cabinet. The first report was from an 'Agent Q' on enemy troop movements in the Bruges area; the second on German morale in a place called Axel – a village west of Antwerp? Innes couldn't remember. But there was nothing remarkable, as far as he could tell, just small pieces to slot into the picture of the whole. Putting the file back, he was on the point of lifting a second when he heard someone at the door. Time only to close the drawer and turn, but too quickly, like a bloody thief. Graham – Major Stewart Graham MC DSO – was watching him with lazy eyes and a supercilious smile that suggested he was not in the least surprised to find the new boy in the colonel's office in the small hours.

'Find what you were looking for?'

'Hello, Graham. Returning some files – the Ramble network reports – our train spotters. I'm doing a favour for Marshall.'

Graham raised an eyebrow. 'Oh, come on Innes.' He shut the door quietly and stepped a little closer. 'I know what you're doing. I hear you've been Paris-Plaging.'

'Jenkins told you, I suppose.'

'Jenkins? No. Captain Saunders. Fortunately, he rang me.' Graham settled his shoulder against a cabinet. 'What would the BGI say if he knew you'd visited that notorious old tart, la Duchesse – and the Chief – God forbid!'

'I wanted to know . . .'

'About Macrae.'

'But you were there before me.'

'What do you think he saw in that prostitute? I really can't imagine.'

'And you collected his belongings from my lodging, and went through mine.'

Graham inspected his finger-nails. 'The thing is Innes, you're barking up the wrong tree.'

'You had dinner with Macrae the night he died.'

He laughed. 'Are you accusing me, old boy? Your tone . . . Graham, the German spy, done in dear old Macrae, is that it?' Laughing again. 'The truth is so disappointing almost always, don't you think? The poor chap died of a heart attack brought on by over-exertion. Unless you discovered something else, a tell-tale clue, Dr Watson – something I missed?'

Innes shook his head. 'You saw him that evening. Dinner at the Continental.'

'He wanted my help. I have connections. Marshall's told you? Yes. Well, Macrae was worried about things at GHQ.'

'In intelligence?'

'He wanted to know who he might speak to in London.'

'What "things"?'

Graham's gaze slipped away for a moment as he considered his answer. 'You won't find anything useful in those.' A lazy wave at the filing cabinets. 'Have a word with Hoyland, Fifth Army Intelligence. Macrae went to see him just before he died. They were thick as thieves. Now if you'll excuse me, I really don't want MacLeod to find me here . . . with you.'

But at the door Graham turned back with his thumb and forefinger to his lips. 'Some important people in London want to replace our Chief – drag him down, Innes – did you know that? But he is the only man capable of leading us to victory – he *will* win the war, and I for one will do all I can to help him.' Again the supercilious smile, then he was gone.

9

24 September

THE GREY MAP sergeant was marking up the weather when Innes stepped into the Section A office the following morning. *Glass steady. Cold morning with slight haze.*

'And the forecast?' Innes asked.

He turned with the chalk in his hand and white dust on his sleeve. 'Quite good, sir.' Over the next few days he would be asked the same question many times. 'Only—' He frowned, opening and closing his mouth, caught in two minds whether to say more.

'Go on, man.'

'They say the ground's cut up bad.'

'They do say that.'

'Will two days be enough to dry it, sir, before the next push, I mean?'

'I don't know.'

They stood in silence before the map, Innes's gaze racing over contours and names that after weeks of intense fighting would be with them both for ever. Anzacs to lead the next attack through the shattered stumps of a wood to the east of Ypres. Were their chaplains praying for sunshine? Innes remembered as a boy stepping from his uncle's house on Eriskay and standing with his arms out, enjoying the splash of rain on his skin, sometimes blinding on his face.

The sergeant said something he didn't hear.

'Sorry, Ramsey, what was it?'

'Colonel MacLeod, he wanted to speak to you, sir.'

MacLeod was at his desk. 'I've received a signal from Agent Petit.' The portrait of the colonel's wife was in its proper place and Cabinet 6 (C) was firmly shut: Graham had kept his counsel.

'You see, he's alive.' The red spots were rising to MacLeod's cheeks again. 'Obviously. He's sent some grid references – an enemy artillery position – I thought you'd like to know.' His eyes flitted to Innes and away, fidgeting with his pen, always so ill at ease and always a little defensive.

'But that isn't why I wanted to speak to you. Major Graham says he's asked you to visit Fifth Army – evaluate some papers they've taken from a German prisoner – something to do with the Moere gun – you know about that, don't you?'

'Yes, sir.'

MacLeod ran his palm over his bald head. 'Major Graham has made the arrangements.'

Jenkins was on the street outside the école with the engine of his motor car running. Graham had organised that too.

Fifth Army headquarters was in a chateau ten miles to the west of Ypres. It was a stone box of windows and pilasters, with all the pretensions of the neoclassical style but with none of its elegance and joy. A Red Cap held Jenkins in the gravel drive as the Fifth's commander and his entourage pulled away from the front.

'See that, sir,' Jenkins pointed through the passenger door window, 'just in front of the trees, there.' Across the lawn, at the edge of an autumn wood, Army Auxiliaries were clipping a box hedge into a perfect ornamental dome.

'Keep-ing up stand-ards,' Jenkins observed, drawing out his syllables in disgust.

But if the topiary, the raked gravel and mown lawns presented one impression of Fifth Army HQ, then the traffic to and from the chateau, the motorbike messengers and Red Cap marshals shouting and gesturing, the staff from Corps and Division on the steps offered another. Innes sensed in their frantic activity the air of apprehension before a big attack, when every second is counted and every second is precious.

In the entrance hall he was directed up a grand but vulgar orange varnished-wood stair to the first floor, then left into a corridor dividing the front and back of the west wing of the house. Intelligence was in the old drawing room at the front, its doors open for a posse of clerks who were leaving with map canisters and files. A conference had just finished and the Fifth Army's intelligence officers were talking in small groups, smoking, collecting their papers and their hats and sticks. Between the windows at the far end of the room, a major was leaning against an ornate white marble chimney-piece, gazing intently at the fire like a khaki Sybil who sees days of trouble in its flames.

'Major Hoyland?' Innes saluted. 'Major Graham sent me. Innes. Intelligence at GHQ.'

'Graham?' Hoyland frowned. 'What does he want?'

'It's about Captain Macrae. I believe he came to see you just before he died.'

Hoyland stood up straight and turned to Innes. He was middle aged, stout, with the rheumy brown eyes of a drinker.

'Look Captain—'

'Innes.'

'We're about to attack again. Macrae was a good fellow, but he's dead.' He peered pointedly over Innes's shoulder. 'If you'll excuse me, General Gough is expecting me.'

'Macrae was unhappy with intelligence at GHQ. Did he tell you why, sir?'

Hoyland's gaze flitted to his face and away. 'Graham sent you, you say?'

'Yes.'

'Didn't think he had any time for Macrae. And Brigadier Charteris?'

Behind Innes, laughter and receding voices as the Divisional intelligence officers drifted from the room. 'Brigadier Charteris doesn't know.'

Hoyland looked uneasy. 'General Gough is with Field Marshal Haig at Doullens; Brigadier Charteris too, I shouldn't wonder. I'm expected there.'

'Major Graham isn't acting alone. Important people are concerned.'

'Important people? So you say.' Hoyland shook his head cynically. 'You know if Graham wants something, he should damn well speak to me himself.'

'Major Graham thought it would be more discreet if I visited you.'

'Oh, did he? Well, I don't know you, I've never met you.' He glared at Innes for a few seconds, then his shoulders dropped a little and he took half a step to his right to view the room: three officers were talking near the door, an orderly was clearing cups and ashtrays. 'It is a matter of honour. Loyalty, to the Army, our commander-in-chief,' he said.

'I'm sure we're all loyal.'

He touched the corners of his mouth with thumb and forefinger, then nodded slowly. 'Macrae wanted to look at some of our files. Prisoner interrogations mainly. Something didn't make sense, he said.'

'Why didn't he use the files at GHQ? You copy everything, don't you?'

'Of course.' Hoyland took a deep breath. 'Didn't want Brigadier Charteris or Colonel MacLeod to know. He wasn't happy with the way they were presenting intelligence: too optimistic, too much weight given to unverifiable sources, not enough to our bread-and-butter work. He said he wanted to take it to the War Office but he needed evidence. I told him to talk to one of the generals, keep it in the family . . . He was trying to put together a file.'

'Did he manage to?'

Hoyland shook his head. 'I don't know. I don't think so.'

'The unverifiable sources?'

'I don't know. He didn't think much of MacLeod.'

'And you don't know if he found what he was looking for?'

'I don't even know what he was looking for.' Hoyland shifted his weight on to his right leg, hands in pockets, gazing at the floor. 'He was unhappy with the way our intelligence is presented to Field Marshal Haig. He isn't the only one. He thought it was his duty to do something but died before he could, and that is the end of the matter.'

Innes wanted to slap him. 'Others feel the same? But they aren't prepared to do anything.'

Hoyland flushed with anger. 'Perhaps we're waiting for Graham and his important friends, Captain.' He looked at his watch. 'And now I have more pressing concerns.' The conversation was over. He wanted to return to the simpler business of war.

Innes watched him walk over to his officers, issue an instruction and leave. Another wild goose chase, or so it seemed, and he wondered if Graham had known it would be and was playing with Cumming's little spy.

But half-way down the stair someone called his name, and looking up he saw Hoyland leaning over the bannister. He disappeared for a second, then reappeared, walking quickly down to stand on the step above Innes. 'One thing – I don't

133

know if it's important. Faust. It was something to do with Faust, that's what Macrae said.'

'Are you sure it was Faust?'

'Yes, Faust.'

'Not Tennyson.'

Hoyland sighed, ostentatiously. 'Faust. A German play. Faust.'

'Goethe.'

'Is it?'

'And you don't know what he meant?'

'Haven't a clue.'

Innes reached into his tunic pocket for a piece of paper. 'So these lines from Tennyson don't mean anything to you? *But O for the touch of a vanished hand, And the sound of a voice that is still.*'

Hoyland sighed again. 'Nothing. Just Faust.' He stared at Innes for a moment, then shrugged and turning, trotted back up the stair.

'You're waking the whole town with your knocking.' Standing in the doorway in a grubby nightcap and old fisherman's coat, an old man with a white beard lifting his oil lamp to see Innes clearly. 'I thought the Germans were here,' he complained in French.

'Is Major Graham at home?' Innes heard his voice at a great distance, like whispering at the bottom of a deep well.

'Asleep. It's after three o'clock.' The old man's gaze wandered over Innes's filthy uniform. 'After three.'

'Then wake him up!'

Lights were appearing in windows on the opposite side of the rue de Saint-Wulphy. The old man let out an oath and told him to wait. Innes barely noticed the incivility, his thoughts strung along a line to the west of Ypres, with the

134

men of his old battalion. He had met an acquaintance on the steps at Fifth Army headquarters. They've been in it since the beginning of 'this show', he'd said, and in the few yards it had taken Innes to walk to the motor car, a wish to know how they fared had become a compulsion. He'd rattled out of Ypres in an empty ambulance, and although it was his first visit to the salient, the view through the dirty rectangle of glass was of autumn on the Somme and other fields; of pitted earth and low ruins; of stumps and putrefying horses – some still between shattered shafts; of men with weary faces straggling out of the line, and soldiers clean and silent marching into it; the centuries man made and cultivated, the distinguishing features of landscape wiped away, until all that was left to mark one place from another were contours and a grid reference. The new geography – almost subterranean – trenches and tunnels and dug-outs, like the home of the brutal and brutalised in H.G. Wells's story of the future, *The Time Machine*. And in keeping with this new reality, new names: at a casualty clearing station just off the road, Innes had been directed north-west along Dud Street to Dirty Bucket Corner and thence to Cameron Copse. Aircraft high above and dusty pink shrapnel puffs, the rumble of shell-fire a mile or two to the south; after so many weeks of fighting it was almost peaceful. Then out of the blue, a blinding flash. He closed his eyes, flinching at the memory – blown off his feet and against the back of the trench as a shell burst a few yards from the parapet, and another and another, the chunks of shrapnel flying past his head; splintering, gouging shrapnel in a shower of earth that left him trembling on his hands and his knees, just conscious of screaming and shouts for a 'stretcher bearer' as a corporal machine-gunner's life pumped away, splashing the sandbag wall and swirling lazily in the greasy sump at the bottom of the trench. Someone had picked Innes up – reduced in his own eyes, perhaps in theirs too – and then, what? Brushing shoulders with men leaving the line, moving in a blur, awkwardly, as a swimmer treads water. How he'd found his old battalion he couldn't recall. C Company, Bowman in command now. 'What a sight, Lazarus,' he'd said: 'You look as if you've been pulled from another grave.'

'Innes! Wake up. For God's sake, man.' Graham had him by the shoulder, searching his face. 'What is it?' He drew him over the threshold by his sleeve and instructed the old man to bring coffee. At the top of the stairs they passed someone in a nightshirt. Was it Wilkinson from Section C? Graham sent him back to his bed.

'Sit there.' He pushed Innes into a chair and adjusted the oil lamp. The circle of light climbed the walls of his room, which was small but comfortable, furnished with pieces he must have found for himself; a carved oak armoire, cheval mirror, a British brass bed and a bookshelf with just six titles.

'Here.' He handed Innes a whisky, then pulled a chair closer, balancing his own glass on the arm. 'You've been to the Front. Your old battalion?'

'Yes.' Innes's voice cracked. He cleared his throat and said it firmly. 'Yes.' Graham nodded thoughtfully. His nightshirt was tucked into his trousers, his braces hanging round his hips.

'Did you take Jenkins?'

'Jenkins? No. You know Jenkins?'

Graham's glass was hovering at his lips, light jumping in the crystal. 'It's a mistake to go back.' He took a drink and Innes did the same, suffused for a moment in the peat and warmth of the whisky.

'I don't mean to the Front – to your battalion.' For once

Graham was looking him in the eye. 'How long has it been? A year? You know how things change.'

'You've seen what it's like?'

'Of course.'

'A wilderness, a dreary bloody wilderness of mud and metal and decomposing bodies and . . . you know . . .' It was plain from his face he did know. 'Bowman says—'

Graham raised his chin. 'Who?'

'C Company CO. He says they lose the wounded, they slide into shell holes and drown.' C Company's commanding officer had said a lot of things: that the battalion was reduced to half-strength, that company sergeants White and Urquhart were dead, Corporal Fryer too, lieutenants Wilson, MacNeil and Dickson-Smith. A shell had burst at Dickson-Smith's feet. 'Peculiar, but it didn't kill him outright – must have been the mud,' Bowman had recalled, slumped against the wall of his dug-out. 'Thought he was dead – just a heap of flesh – then he said something. He'd lost both feet and an arm – stomach torn to ribbons. The look in his eyes – I'll never forget it. Thankfully, he died a few minutes later and we consigned his body to a shell hole.' Poor Bowman, trembling as he recalled Dickson-Smith's terror at his mutilation, at the pros- pect of death, or perhaps of something worse – of life, broken, pitiful, useless. God they'd all been terrified of that. But lucky old Lazarus had got a Blighty one and now a GHQ armband – he was just a tourist. Bowman didn't say so, none of C Company's officers had said so, no, that was Innes. 'To see how you all are,' he'd said. He hadn't even brought them a bottle of whisky.

'Innes?' Graham was shifting in his chair. 'It's like the 1915 winter. The trenches at Givenchy.' He looked down, perhaps picturing that time, up to his waist in slime. 'We've all lost friends. Soldiering on to the end, that's what it's about now.'

'I met a lieutenant on the boat here, a Cameron called Boyd – a Surrey Scot like you. Nice young fellow. He was sick on his tunic. Six days in the line – he didn't have time to learn – brains all over the parados.' Innes took a sip of his whisky. Someone was on the landing outside the room, stepping lightly so as not to disturb the house again. Perhaps it was the old man.

'Fifth Army, what did you—Innes, are you listening!' Graham reached forward as if to touch his arm.

'You're at GHQ, they said, tell us, when is the war going to be over? I said we were wearing the enemy down, we thought he was ready to break. But Bowman, or one of the others, said the Hun opposite C Company seemed to have plenty of fight, and if he was going to break, he'd better damn well do it quickly before the British Army ran out of men.'

Graham sighed a tell-it-to-the-padre sort of sigh and glanced at his watch. 'Advanced headquarters tomorrow. Lloyd George is visiting the Chief.' He drained his glass, hands on knees to rise. 'I don't know why you came, but you should go to bed now . . . and see the doctor in the morning.'

Innes felt a surge of anger. 'What did Macrae tell you?'

'What did Hoyland say?'

'I told him you'd sent me . . .'

'Trying to destroy my reputation.'

'And that you had the confidence of important people . . .'

'Did you now.'

'And they trust you to get to the bottom of this.'

Graham laughed. 'I wasn't sure you were up to that sort of dirty trick. That's the real Lazarus. Another drink?'

Innes shook his head. He didn't know whether he was angrier with himself or Graham, or just angry with the whole business. Sitting in the C Company dug-out, almost ashamed to be alive, he'd felt beneath his tunic for Ramble's jagged cross and pressed it against his chest, drawing strange comfort from the pain.

'That's what you told Hoyland,' said Graham. 'What did he say to you?'

'That Macrae was unhappy with the intelligence presented to Field Marshal Haig and went through prisoner interrogations and some captured documents looking for discrepancies – but you know that. He wasn't much help. I'm not sure you expected him to be.'

Graham tilted his head, the way he had of looking sideways. 'Really, I'm sorry you don't trust me. Cumming put you here to spy on us, I might have reported you but I've chosen to help you. You should be more grateful.'

'Why have you chosen to help me?'

'Isn't it obvious? I have concerns too. Goodness, you've spoken to Marshall, and Macrae sought me out, remember? Actually, I told him to leave alone, forget it. That was a mistake.'

Silence. Innes was too tired to know whether to believe him.

'You better go to bed,' said Graham.

'Does Faust mean anything to you?'

A small frown on Graham's brow. 'Why?'

Innes didn't reply, trying and failing to catch his eye.

'Faust.' Graham made a sucking noise as if tasting the word. 'Hoyland did tell you something.' He was tempting Innes to say more. When he didn't, he said: 'Faust is a network in Belgium. One of MacLeod's networks.'

Another silence. Graham crossed then uncrossed his legs.

'Go on,' said Innes.

'I can't. The intelligence comes through the Army's agents in the Netherlands straight to MacLeod and Charteris. I don't know whether Faust is a good source or a bad one . . . good, I suppose, because its product is tightly restricted, although the same could be said for the security of all our networks – yours too, I shouldn't wonder.'

'Macrae didn't mention it to you?'

'No.'

'What sort of intelligence does the network—'

'Your guess is as good as mine.'

'There's no way of identifying it as the source of—'

'No. None . . . oh, short of asking MacLeod and Charteris, or the Army's agents in Rotterdam.'

'And a written record?'

'Somewhere. I expect the office in Rotterdam keeps one.'

'And you haven't wondered—'

'Of course, I have. Marshall too, but he knows even less about our operations in occupied territories than me. Proof, Innes, more than a gut feeling, more than Macrae's suspicions.' Graham looked pointedly at his watch again. 'You're not going to find it here – now.'

Innes got to his feet. 'I asked Hoyland about the Tennyson, but it didn't mean anything to him.'

'A gift. Macrae was a sentimental man. I expect he gave it to his tart—'

'Agnes.'

'Because she knew what he wanted; she made him feel he was loved.' Graham smiled. 'Do you remember? *Half a league, half a league, half a league onwards, All in the valley of Death rode the six hundred.* Every schoolboy's Tennyson. We know about that now don't we: the valley of Death.' He stepped over to the door. 'Do you need someone to help you home?'

Innes answered curtly that he did not.

'I was at school with the poet Grenfell, you know. We were—' Graham paused. 'Yes, friends . . . of sorts . . . Julian was a clever fellow. Have you read his poem "Into Battle"?'

Innes said that he had.

'He enjoyed the war. Said he loved his fellow man so much more looking down the barrel of a sniper's rifle at him. Some of us still do . . . love the war, I mean – in a way.'

Graham bent a little in thought. 'Poor Grenfell,' he said at last. 'Stopped a Jack Johnson with his head, and that was that.' He lifted his gaze slowly up Innes's muddy tunic. 'You can see yourself out, can't you? Quietly, please. Oh, and Innes – the quack – go and see him, for God's sake. Go tomorrow.'

10

25–26 September

Poor Phillips had the devil of a job brushing the mud from his uniform. He set about it with infinite care and the easy bonhomie of a man of service. Keeping the home fires burning, he said. He'd brought a letter from Innes's mother. She had begun writing to Innes in English, to help the censor, she said. He'd assured her no one would read her letters, but she did it all the same, perhaps for a war effort that seemed to touch everyone's lives in so many ways. Innes's father was unwell, she wrote, too old to be working so hard at the hospital, and she worried about his sister, always. He put her letter aside to read again later, then he wrote a note of thanks to the prostitute for her Tennyson and wrapped it in brown paper. Phillips would take the package to the GHQ post office at the southern gate.

At the École Militaire, Charteris was briefing press barons from London, the proprietors of half a dozen newspaper titles. MacLeod was preparing a note on the strength of German reserves for the conference with the prime minister.

'All about hearts and minds,' Marshall observed, dryly. 'They want to be sure we're beating the Boche, and the BGI will tell them that we are.'

Innes thought of the wilderness he'd visited the day before, the crack and black curl of shrapnel, the trench line of half-drowned shell holes with soldiers clinging to the slime at the lip, the bodies, scraps of tartan and German grey, and he asked: 'Is Lloyd George visiting the Front?'

'What would be the point of that?' Marshall replied.

Then, at 08.00, GHQ learnt of an attack by the German 50th Reserve Division between Tower Hamlets and Polygon Wood. Sergeant Ramsey began drawing a new black line west of Ypres. Midday, a second assault north of the Menin Road, and the penetration of British front and support lines. Confusion. MacLeod ordered Innes to visit members of the Suicide Club but changed his mind; Charteris requested facts for the conference and left to attend it without indicating what he would require. In the late afternoon the situation was restored by a counter-punch, and Ramsey was able to move his flags back to where they were at the beginning of the day. Charteris returned. He had forgotten his facts. Mr Lloyd George was dining with Haig, the conference would resume in the morning, he said, and so would the next phase of the great British push. Captain Cumming was with the PM's party because the conference was expected to place his Secret Service Bureau under the Army. 'Damn silly to duplicate effort,' he said. 'I'll tell him we're keeping you as part of the new arrangement, Innes.' Then he was away to take his place at the field marshal's table. Perhaps Graham was there too.

Innes worked late, ate with Marshall, and walked the ramparts. They spoke for a while of the battle and the weight of expectation. In a few hours the guns would open up on German strong points again and tanks would try to find a way. The men would rise along five miles of line and advance a thousand yards because it wasn't possible to offer artillery support for more. Innes asked, how many yards to Ostend, how many to Berlin? Marshall said he was expecting to gallop there; it took only a leap of faith.

'You believe in miracles, don't you? I thought all you Romans believed in miracles.'

Innes was taken aback. 'Did I say I was Catholic?'

Marshall looked uncomfortable. 'You must have.'

But Innes was sure he hadn't.

In the early hours he woke shaking and sweating. It was a while before he could accept everything, but his heart was still. Of course, it was coming – he fumbled on the bedside table for his watch – in thirty-eight minutes. Thirty-seven. Thirty-six. The creak of old bed springs as he shifted his position. Lloyd George at the chateau, was he sleeping? And Haig? Thirty-five. Bowman of C Company with last letters and valuables, waiting for the dawn. But Innes was too exhausted to wait with him. He was woken for a second time by Phillips at the door. 'We're at it again, sir,' he said, brushing Innes's tunic. 'Zero Hour, five-fifty, one of the gentlemen told me. Used to wake me up. Not now. You can get used to anything, can't you?'

Innes said nothing because he used to offer the same glib comfort to new men. It was nonsense. There were so many things . . . rats licking the brilliantine from his hair as he slept, the blind terror of being blown to ragged pieces, and the thick, cloying sweetness of the dead – a taste like no other – some things it was only possible to endure.

Into battle, then. Sergeant Ramsey was busy all morning at the map, bobbing between the lines with his pen, enjoying his role at the centre of attention. Officers from the other departments in the école drifted in to gaze over his shoulder and ask questions. 'Any word on the 3rd?' 'Lost their way in the mist, sir.' 'And what about the 5th Australian?' 'Making good progress.' And so it went on.

144

At midday Graham returned from the Château de Beaurepaire to announce the conference was over and the prime minister was motoring to Fifth Army to look at prisoners. He raised a quizzical eyebrow to Innes but made no effort to speak to him alone, and after a few minutes he scooped some papers from his desk and left. Innes was ready to follow him. There were things to discuss. Faust. What should he say to Cumming? Tennyson, Faust: it was all a bit ridiculous. He pushed his chair away in frustration, because so were the orders he was writing for MacLeod. A delivery of carrier pigeons to the Suicide Club's agents behind enemy lines: waste of time. He got up and wandered over to the map, then to the door. Too late to catch Graham, he'd glided in, and now he'd glided out. MacLeod seemed to let him do as he pleased, intimidated by his 'connections' perhaps, or by his old school show that some might take for shyness, but Innes knew to be arrogance, plain and simple. Damn the man, what about Faust?

Innes needed air. He sat with his eyes closed beneath the rotten pergola where he'd first seen Graham, left hand to his temple, his right feeling for Ramble's cross.

'Are you all right, sir?' the messenger asked.

'Day-dreaming,' he said, which was a lie. Inside the offered envelope there was a scrap of paper with a time, the name of a village on the road to Étaples and a single letter: *C*.

A one-street village in the gloaming, camouflage-green Rolls-Royce outside a *tabac*, and the captain in a tattered leather armchair on the pavement, coffee and a cigarette, stick against the table. He was in naval uniform but bare-headed, although there was a nip in the air, his trench-coat over the arm of the chair. A light glinting gold in his eye-glass made him look sinister, like an enemy villain in one of Mr John Buchan's shockers.

'Why are you smiling?' he asked, half rising from his chair, as solid and British as Hearts of Oak. 'Did you have some difficulty?'

Innes apologised for being late, but securing a Staff motor car without a driver wasn't easy. They shook hands and Cumming summoned the aged *patron* in clumsy French and ordered more coffee and a chair for Innes.

'Are we winning?' he asked. 'We seemed to be at lunch.'

'You mean today? The day's objectives were taken.'

'And Field Marshal Haig is very confident.'

Innes nodded slowly. 'You were at the conference, of course.'

'But not in the conference room. Those who were say he is preparing for another decisive breakthrough.'

'The members of our little club are with the cavalry again.'

'Your club?'

'Brigadier Charteris's club, MacLeod's club, the Suicide Club, the agents we're going to throw at the enemy.'

'Ah, yes. That club.' He craned forward to peer at Innes through his monocle, all chin and nose and curiosity, like a marsh bird in the shallows. 'You sound weary and rather cynical, it's not like you, Innes. Not you,' he said.

'Sorry.' Innes sighed heavily. 'I'm pleased it's going well, of course. Honestly, there seems little point in my staying here. I think I would be of more use with our people in Belgium.'

'Charteris doesn't think so. Wants you at GHQ.'

'I understand we'll all be working for the Army soon. You too.'

C grunted. 'Is that what he said?' Two fat fingers drumming on the chair arm. 'I bet that's what he said. Over my dead body.'

'Because important people will protect us?'

'Know the value of what we do, Innes.' He reached for his coffee cup. 'But of course, you're being facetious.'

A motorbike came grumbling along the street towards them. Innes watched C fidgeting, waiting for it to pass, his thin lips tight with impatience. 'Apart from ingratiating yourself with Brigadier Charteris, what have you managed?' he said at last, chinking his cup and saucer down carelessly. 'That fellow in intelligence . . . the one who died *in flagrante?*'

Innes told him what he knew of Macrae, of his dinner with Graham in the Continental, of Agnes and his conventional taste in poetry, and, by the by, of a mutiny in the British Army – did C know? Well, no one was to talk about it. Then, of dipping into MacLeod's files, and that he was caught by Graham. Graham again: stepson of an equerry to the king, old school chum of Haig's secretary, fiercely loyal to his commander-in-chief. Graham, the head of counter-espionage at GHQ, who'd guessed Innes was a spy but was prepared to help – a little; nudging Innes towards Fifth Army and to MacLeod's secret source: Faust. An agent or a network or both.

'I see. So it's not Tennyson, it's Goethe.' Cumming took out his monocle, closed his eyes and pinched the bridge of his nose. 'And what, pray, does all that amount to?'

'Perhaps nothing. I'm sure there are other Army agents and networks in the occupied territories. Graham says Charteris thinks particularly highly of this one. Perhaps he's right to.'

'Hmm.' Cumming reached into his pocket for his cigarettes.

The *patron* of the *tabac* was calling across the street to an old woman, and in another doorway, the silhouettes of two small boys gazing at the Rolls-Royce, glancing furtively at C, perhaps working up to a dare.

'Did Macrae have clearance for Faust material?'

'Graham says no.' Innes paused. 'But Graham knows more than he says.'

'You're right not to trust him.' C offered his cigarette case and Innes took one.

'You mean his important friends might not be the same as ours?' he said.

'That's right. You *are* becoming cynical, Innes, must be GHQ.'

'I'm learning.'

At the corner of his eye he saw one of the boys darting forward to touch the motor car. Not quick enough. 'Allez-vous-en!' the *patron* bellowed.

Cumming winced. 'Today we're winning,' he said. 'What about tomorrow?' He paused to draw on his cigarette. 'Do you trust your new comrades to know? If I recall, you suggested in your report that Charteris was conjuring up evidence to support his case for one more heave.'

'The Field Marshal's case. I said it was a possibility, that's all.'

'Yes. But you were unsure of Charteris's sources. Faust may be one of 'em. Too good to trust to his own Staff: that's very convenient, isn't it?' C flicked his cigarette into the street, the tired springs of his armchair creaking as he shifted his weight. 'Damn it, we're nowhere near the Belgian coast, are we? And winter's just around the corner.'

Innes looked away. Beyond the *tabac* the white road climbed the valley side into darkness. 'What you mean is, you want me to stay at GHQ.'

'For now. Find out more.'

'Graham thinks your important people want to use Charteris to undermine Field Marshal Haig – replace him as commander-in-chief, if they can.'

'Your concern is Army intelligence, can we trust it? Concentrate on that.'

Cumming shuffled to the edge of his chair. 'I'm meeting the Prime Minister's party in Boulogne. I think we're visiting Fifth

Army tomorrow – almost close enough to be killed.' He gave a wry smile. 'Don't tell anyone but someone who knows says our prime minister becomes very fidgety near the Front. He's a bit of a coward . . . not politically, of course. Anyway, GHQ wants to show him some Boche prisoners. More proof we're winning, I suppose.' Picking up his stick, he levered himself out of the chair. 'See if you can find out more about Faust. I'll ask Tinsley to do some digging in Rotterdam – he'll know all the Army's agents there. Ah monsieur—' The owner of the tabac, was hovering, hands in his apron. 'Pay him would you, Innes? I haven't any change.'

Innes walked with Cumming to the Rolls-Royce and pretended to listen as he spoke with small-boy passion about its engine.

'And the network? Ramble?' Innes asked at last.

Cumming looked away, running his hand round the back of his neck as if feeling for an aching muscle. 'Ramble's safe, but there have been some difficulties. Ramble says our Army is proving a problem there too. Some of your watchers in Thielt and Roulers were arrested, and a courier – *promeneurs* you call them, don't you? Most unfortunate. Tinsley says he was one of your best.'

'Can you remember his name?'

'Not sure I was told.'

'Well, you don't need to know, do you?'

'No.'

'But the Army—

'We took over its network in the enemy's forbidden zone . . .'

'The *Operationsgebiet.*'

'Just so. Well, the Army's network was compromised by one, possibly two spies, and now the enemy has rolled up all the old Army watchers and ours too. Yes – before you say anything – it was a mighty cock-up, and to anticipate your next question, I don't know if it has anything to do with your Faust – I don't – but it doesn't fill one with confidence, does it?'

Silence. Cumming was pushing a stone with the end of his stick. 'I know what you think of this operation,' he said at last. 'Some of this *is* politics, yes. But you can see what is at stake now. And I won't leave you at GHQ for ever. If Faust is a problem, you will have to go back to find out more.'

Innes nodded, then leant forward to open the driver's door. 'Perhaps Charteris and Haig are right. Let's hope there won't be any need for the Americans or our little Suicide Club or Faust. Perhaps we'll all be home for Christmas.'

C offered a stiff smile and hoisted himself up into the motor car. 'I'll make enquiries about your Major Graham.'

11

27–28 September

THERE WAS PIGEON shit on the seat, a grey tongue on the window and the sleeve of Pollock's trench-coat too. He said it was lucky. They were bouncing across a field with crates of cooing birds, a noise that reminded Innes of wind shaking the heather. Commander Pollock had moved his balloons closer to Ypres and the Suicide Club had followed him. Most of its members were with the cavalry, where shiny boots and buttons counted for a great deal and foreigners in workmen's clothes for nothing. A few judged capable of landing a balloon alive were still with the club and flying.

'Your Colonel MacLeod wants a pigeon run into the occupied territories tonight,' Pollock shouted over the noise of the birds and the engine. 'One of my pilots is to rendezvous with one of your agents.'

'They're not my agents,' said Innes.

'You train them.'

'I do my best.'

'I'm sure you do, old boy, as do we all. Anyway, my pilot's to drop the pigeons, then return. Only, I'm not confident he will, not in this weight of wind. Madness to try.'

Innes nodded. 'Well, you'll have to be firm.'

Pollock looked aggrieved. 'I tried, but you know what he's like; wouldn't listen. Rather rude, actually. Goodness, there must be an easier way of gathering intelligence . . . what about a wireless?'

The lorry dropped into a rut, the crates jumped, and Pollock fell across Innes's lap. Profuse apologies. He was struggling to rise, one side of his grey waxed moustache drooping disconsolately. 'For God's sake, careful man,' he shouted to the driver. 'You'll frighten these poor birds to death.'

The new clubhouse was on a farm in the Second Army sector to the south of the city. It had been used as a British billet since the beginning and bore many scars. MacLeod was in the yard, his arms crossed impatiently on his broad chest. 'They look healthy, don't you think?' he said, pushing a finger through the bars of a cage. 'Some chaps from Barnsley have them. They let them loose on training flights all over France.'

Pollock bit his lip. Country solicitor careful, he was in two minds whether to speak, glancing at Innes for guidance. 'The wind's rather strong, Colonel,' he observed. 'It might be better to postpone tonight's flight. The surface speed is close to nine knots. I want to be sure—'

'Sure of what, commander?' Red spots had risen to MacLeod's cheeks.

'Well, we haven't tried the balloon in that sort of wind – it would be wrong to send an inexperienced pilot.'

'You trained him, didn't you? It's my decision.'

Pollock hesitated, but he was angry too. 'With respect, Colonel, I don't think you're qualified to make one.'

MacLeod exploded. 'Do as I say, damn it!' Did he stamp his foot? Innes thought that he had. Pollock was shocked. The corporal-driver at the door of the pigeon lorry was staring blankly into the distance. MacLeod glared at them all and then turned and walked stiffly away.

'Well, I never,' said Pollock, pulling anxiously at his moustache.

Innes turned to the driver. 'You better back this up to the barn.' The birds had to come off the lorry. 'They need seed and water,' Innes explained. 'I'll speak to the pilot – Smet?' He was certain to go on his mission now, after the colonel's public display. Pollock seemed to understand.

The pilot was supposed to be sleeping upstairs in the farm-house but his room was empty. The club's training sergeant said he'd gone for a walk along the track behind the barn – just follow the poplar stumps to the dyke. Innes was ready to – content to walk away from an atmosphere he could cut with a knife. But MacLeod had heard his voice and stepped from the old parlour bareheaded, his gaze flitting from brick floor to window, avoiding Innes's eye.

'I'd like a word, Captain.' He sounded calmer, even a little sheepish.

The old parlour was damp and smelt of urine, and the names of those who'd come and gone were scrawled on its flaking plaster walls. There were two kitchen chairs and MacLeod had spread his papers on a rough oak table.

'Sit down, please.'

Innes did as he was bidden.

'What I'm about to tell you mustn't leave this room,' MacLeod said portentously. 'The Commander-in-Chief is bringing the next phase of the attack forward to October the fourth. The entire Cavalry Corps will be waiting behind the Yser Canal, and once we've driven the enemy from Passchendaele, we – that is to say, Field Marshal Haig – anticipates a rapid advance to the coast.' He leant forward earnestly, his chin inches from the table. 'You can see how important it is to obtain fresh intelligence from our agents in the occupied territories.'

Innes took a deep breath. 'I don't understand, sir?'

'The carrier pigeons.' He picked up a pen, put it down, then picked it up again. 'The weather may not improve. If the pilot—Smet? If he fails we will have time for more flights.' He paused, lifting the top of the pen, then clicking it back again. 'We have the balloons.'

'I see. Do we have the pigeons?'

'I'm not sure I like your tone, Innes. You have rather a high opinion of yourself, don't you?' He shook his head vigorously, a roll of flesh quivering beneath his chin. 'It's a difficult decision, a risk, but we have to take them every day.'

Innes inspected his hands. He didn't know what to say. Valuable intelligence might be waiting to wing its way to GHQ. Was it fair to doubt MacLeod? Nothing was as simple at headquarters as he'd thought it would be . . . from that first evening with the majors Graham and Marshall. It was becoming harder to accept things as a simple military necessity. In MacLeod's order to fly he saw small *p* politics and pride. Success or failure, the pigeon run would appear in the field marshal's daily intelligence summary as paper proof that the colonel's little club was doing its bit. That would be a comfort for a man at war with almost everyone and himself, stung by real and imagined slights, by the whispers of a scandal in his wife's past, by the patronage of an unpopular BGI, even by his name and the short vowels he let slip when he was angry.

'Innes! Wake up man.' MacLeod tapped the edge of the table. 'If you haven't anything to say . . .'

'Only that Commander Pollock seems to think it's unwise to attempt the flight today, sir.'

'Commander Pollock will do his duty.'

'You asked me to speak, sir.'

'I know your opinion, Captain, and the matter's closed.'

'It will affect the morale of the others, sir.'

MacLeod's chair screeched as he pushed it from the table. 'The matter's closed. That's an order.'

Innes lifted his hands in exasperation. 'It's madness, worse than suicide.'

Bang like a gunshot: MacLeod's fat hand on the table. 'Go back to GHQ!'

Eyes front, Innes got to his feet. A crisp salute and he was turning to leave when he remembered the pilot. 'I should speak to Smet, take him through procedure one last time . . . in case he doesn't make it back.'

Silence. MacLeod licked his lips. 'You show me no respect,' he said quietly. 'Go before I put you on a charge.'

A charge? Innes didn't think MacLeod had the courage. He'd look a fool. But he wasn't big enough to change his mind, so there was nothing more to say. *Base wallah*, that's what the men in Innes's old company used to call his sort; *Base rat*.

Innes with Jenkins driving south from Ypres, slowing for munitions lorries, then a column of soldiers. So many hours on the road in September. Sleep wasn't easy on a stop–start journey, afraid to dream. Too much reflection was worse, the conversation with MacLeod spinning and hissing like an old gramophone disc. He'd handled it badly and he was afraid that Smet was going to pay. The colonel's rank deserved respect, if not the man. What had happened to the old Edinburgh Academy 'Yes, sir'? He'd spoken to MacLeod as if he were a lone sinner. Pride? Politics? Naive to presume generals responsible for the lives of many thousands of men were any freer of both. No one Innes had met at GHQ was ever ready to criticise the field marshal's great battle plan, only the failure to implement it properly. Fault was found in the line, in the trenches, in a failure to follow orders, a failure to secure objectives. Failure was a front-line word. Wasn't that the trouble? If the plan was deemed by everyone on the field marshal's staff to be a 'sound' one, what reason did his generals have to change it or to bring the battle at Ypres to an early end; to say *'Enough!'*? That was pride too, that was small *p* politics.

'Sir,' Jenkins called to him, 'looks as if there's a road block.' A military policeman was flagging down their motor car. Half past four of the clock, stuck in a jam at a crossroads outside Cassel. The war, it seemed, had stopped for the prime minister's motorcade. Was Cumming still with him? Innes closed his eyes and waited for it to pass. Perhaps the great plan to win the battle at Ypres was a good one – he couldn't say – perhaps it was the extravagant claims made for it that were bad, the talk of distant objectives and the collapse of the German Army. That was Graham's view, Marshall's also. They blamed Charteris and MacLeod, and they'd been ready from day one to communicate the same to Innes. Were they honest brokers? Marshall, perhaps, but Graham was too small *p* politics clever, cleverer than Charteris, cleverer than MacLeod. He was like Cumming. Innes wanted things to be simple. Clean. That's how it had been in the occupied territories with Ramble.

Into the corridors of the École Militaire, neatly typed from Corps and Division, the latest intelligence from the air, prisoner snippets and patrols, paper, paper, paper. But the section clerks were half a yard slower after the intense activity of the last attack; the new line on the wall map an inch or two closer to Passchendaele. Why did everyone care so much about that line? Innes had heard generals say they were grinding down the enemy. Did it matter where, if the object was simply to kill and maim as many German soldiers as possible? And yet everyone at GHQ was in thrall to the map. Some days it was supposed to be a battle of attrition, on others it was a battle to advance that black line, and the cavalry was on standby for the breakthrough. Only remember we're supposed to be winning, Innes said to himself as he settled in his seat. He would watch, wait, shuffle papers round the desk, and when it was quiet pay another visit to MacLeod's office.

But the clock to the left of the great wall map seemed to advance at the pace of the flowers he'd tried to grow once on a trench parapet. Marshall came to speak to him, and he was chipper for a change. There was more paper. A cigarette. And he stepped outside for a few minutes to enjoy the fresh sweet smell of autumn decay after rain. Back at his desk with train returns from the network, eleven o'clock and the section almost empty at last; he was on the point of rising for his attempt on MacLeod's files when Charteris put his head around the door.

'Ah, Innes. Good. A word,' he said, 'in my office, if you don't mind.'

In the short time it took Innes to walk the length of the corridor, the BGI had poured them both a whisky.

'Medicinal in the morning,' he said, brandishing his bottle of Haig, 'but in the evening it's a pleasure.'

Innes accepted his glass with relief. Plainly MacLeod had not had an opportunity to speak his piece about the morning.

The BGI flumped into a chair and waved his drink at another. Did Innes talk to Captain Cumming? Downing Street was proving 'sticky' about new arrangements, but he was confident the Army would bring the Secret Service Bureau to heel. Sipping his whisky – was it his first? His face was florid and there were smudges of shadow beneath his eyes. The top of his tunic was undone and a tuft of dark hair was showing at the collar. He was a little grubby, and that made him appear more human. His voice and manner were middle-class Scotland with a whisky, and Innes sensed a presumption of fellow feeling and that he wished to share confidences.

'You see, it's like the Somme,' he said. 'The Germans were near breaking point then, but the weather was against us . . .

157

this is the same.' He finished his drink quickly and poured a second, too tired or wrapped in his thoughts to offer another to Innes. The casualties were awful to think on, the temptation to stop fighting so great. He knew men in the line were saying it was hopeless, but GHQ had to draw up a balance sheet of gains and losses and count the cost coldly. The correct thing was to press on because 'we're winning', he said, and there was no doubting either his conviction or his sympathy. He didn't ask for an opinion, and Innes would have struggled to offer one, only, at the tip of his tongue a question: how can you be sure?

But Charteris was on his feet again, drifting round the office with his glass, lifting a paper from his desk and letting it drop, ridges of concern on his brow. He had noticed it was only possible to push the horror of what was happening in the field to one side when he was sure they were winning, he said. Did Innes pray? Without hope, without faith, who could go on in this war? He knew Field Marshal Haig felt the same way – just imagine the burden he had to bear, the weight of expectation, the sniping of the politicians, the prime minister. If only it were possible to believe Mr Lloyd George was acting sincerely, purely in the best interests of our nation.

Settling at his desk, he pinched the bridge of his nose, lost for a moment in private thought. 'I enjoyed our conversation,' he said, at last, 'but I won't detain you longer. There is just one matter. Colonel MacLeod is with the Advanced Espionage Unit, so I'd like you to run over to the chateau tomorrow and speak to the field marshal's secretary. You've met Sir Philip Sassoon? He's requested some information from you on the activities of the unit – just headlines, ready for action, that sort of thing – at eight o'clock. All right?' Charteris offered a farewell smile and his gaze dropped to his papers.

Innes was at a bit of a loss to know what to say. After a

few seconds he settled upon 'I'm quite sure Colonel MacLeod would wish to brief Sir Philip himself, sir.'

Charteris didn't look up. 'I don't doubt it,' he said, 'but he isn't able to.' Then sliding his forefinger down the paper in front of him: 'Is that all?'

Innes rose and walked away from the whisky fumes, pausing at the door to glance back at the brigadier, his head still bent, yellow in the light of his desk lamp, his large hands clasped now, like the man of prayer he claimed to be. There was no one in his outer office, the corridor was deserted too, silence in the sections for once, only the echo of Innes's footsteps. In the courtyard he realised he'd forgotten to try MacLeod's door. He didn't have the heart to go back. He was too preoccupied by his failure to do his duty as a staff officer to give more than a passing thought to his mission as a spy. First Haig, then a lack of candour with Charteris: the purple and white ribbon he wore in recognition of courage in battle, the respect ordinary soldiers showed him; he'd betrayed them both. The easy excuse was that he was caught between the roles of honest staff officer on the one hand and emollient spy on the other, but it wouldn't do, because men's lives depended in war on telling the truth to authority. Once, twice, but not three times. In the few minutes it took to walk to his lodging he resolved to speak frankly to the field marshal's secretary, come what may.

Cumming felt at ease on the open bridge of the destroyer. The wind was light from the north-west and warm enough for a sailor to be comfortable without a coat. A landsman? That was a different matter. Mr Lloyd George was somewhere below, entertaining the ship's officers perhaps. There was no doubting his popularity. The people's champion, Cumming had heard a petty officer say. Of course, if you taxed the rich you could always count on the votes of the great unwashed. Cumming hadn't voted Liberal at the last election and he wouldn't be voting for the prime minister's party at the next. Still, cometh the hour, cometh the man. He was an inspiring speaker, a great leader in time of war.

'Are we nearly home?' Hankey was at Cumming's shoulder, wrapped in a thick black coat, a hand to his Fedora hat.

'Fifteen minutes,' Cumming replied. The lights of Dover were already twinkling on the portside.

'You have a steam yacht, don't you?'

Cumming said that he did, although he had precious little time to enjoy her.

'You know, Captain, it's months since I spent any proper time at home.' Hankey took a step forward to join him at the rail. 'First the Prime Minister's visit to Wales, then France. Did you hear about our escape? We were at a crossroads near Poperinghe when the Hun lobbed an eleven-inch shell at us – whistled over our heads and burst a hundred yards away. L.G. was very shaken, convinced it was meant for him, which is ridiculous, of course. But if you haven't experienced anything like it before . . .' He reached into his coat pocket for his gloves. 'Brigadier Charteris laid on a show for us: a cage of prisoners, a very sorry-looking bunch. Hand-picked by his staff, I shouldn't wonder.'

Cumming glanced round the bridge. The officer of the watch and his men were gathered about the binnacle a few feet away, gazing through night-glasses at one of the escort ships on the starboard side. Her course would take her too close and a signalman was readying the Morse lamp to say so.

'I spoke to my man, Innes, by the way.'

'Oh?'

'He's concerned about one of the Army's sources in the occupied territories.'

'Only one? We sent him to unravel them all.'

Cumming frowned. 'I don't think we were specific about sources, Sir Maurice, I mentioned a general problem with intelligence.'

'Is it something I should mention to the Prime Minister?'

'Not yet. But I'm bound to say I share his concern.'

Hankey turned to face him. 'Go on.'

'Our Ramble network has had some problems. The Germans arrested some of our watchers – good men and women, experienced, careful – and the trouble began when we took some people from the Army.'

'I see. You think—'

'I don't know, Sir Maurice. Not without my own man in the occupied territories.'

'Innes.'

'He's close to Ramble, he knows the network. It's a setback at an important time.'

From somewhere in the box of sea about them, the distant wail of an escort's siren, answered a moment later by a deafening blast from their own ship. Hankey shrank into his coat, his face lost in his collar and the shadow beneath his hat. On the foredeck below them sailors were moving quickly to ready the mooring ropes.

'You know, Cumming, the Prime Minister was firm on the independence of your Bureau, he's in favour of co-operation, of course . . . it isn't a competition.'

Cumming stiffened. 'I can assure you, Sir Maurice, this has nothing to do with the future of the Secret Service Bureau. It may be coincidence, but I think we must investigate.'

Hankey nodded, then looked away. 'Haig's still promising decisive results. If he fails, and I pray he doesn't, well, there will be changes at GHQ. The Prime Minister will insist upon them.'

The ship gave a little shudder and began to lose headway. Five cables off the port bow, the Admiralty Pier, like a stone arm thrown about the harbour. Beyond it the dim glow of the town's veiled blackout lights and the chalk cliff. The captain was on the bridge speaking into a voice pipe, and from the darkness astern they heard a ragged chorus of sirens as the escorts began to peel away. Hankey slapped the rail with his leather glove.

'I must join the Prime Minister.' Turning towards the bulkhead door he checked, lifting his right hand to his brow. 'Perhaps Innes should continue at GHQ a little longer . . . that would be wise, I think. Just until we know how things will turn out at Ypres.' He offered a small smile. 'But it's your decision, Cumming, of course.'

12

Beaurepaire and After

W ALKING BRISKLY UP the gravel drive, Innes reflected
that the Château de Beaurepaire wasn't as grand as its
name suggested or trench rumour claimed it to be. It was a
modest brick *manoir* for a field marshal who was reputed to
have quite simple tastes. A party of his soldiers was raking the
gravel at the front, a thankless task on a blustery day, with
yellow and brown sycamore leaves tumbling up to its steps.

Innes was greeted at the top of them by an aide-de-camp
and shown into a small room off the entrance hall. Its white
walls and hard chairs reminded him of a doctor's surgery and
the anxiety one always feels in such places. He stood at the
mirror over the fireplace to adjust his tie, grimacing again at
the thread of grey in his hair and the old man lines at the
corners of his eyes. Somewhere, a clock chimed eight. Deep
breath, back straight, he was determined to present a confident
face to Sassoon. It was all about show in the Army. In the
trenches he'd learnt to pretend he knew what he was doing
at all times.

The door was opening, and he turned to greet the field
marshal's secretary. 'Sir Philip.'

'Innes.' Sir Philip Sassoon looked immaculate in a uniform
cut to complement his slight frame perfectly. 'Welcome to
Beaurepaire.'

'Colonel MacLeod is with the unit at the Front, I'm afraid.'

'You'll do very well, I'm sure.' Sassoon smiled, his face long and white, with lazy brown almond-shaped eyes – was he the only British officer in France without a moustache? Jewish, because Marshall had said so, and well connected, a Member of Parliament and one of the richest young men in England. 'I understand, Captain, that some people at GHQ refer to your unit as the Suicide Club?'

'Most people.'

'You should call it the Espionage Unit in your briefing.'

Innes was taken aback. 'Yes, of course, Sir Philip.'

Sassoon's office was only a few steps down the hall. 'You won't have long,' he said, standing aside for Innes to enter. 'Field Marshal Haig is leaving for his advanced headquarters at half past eight.'

Innes felt a frisson of anxiety. 'I thought I was here to brief you, Sir Philip?'

Sassoon's attention had switched to a large food hamper at the feet of one of his clerks. 'Is that from Fortnum's? Not here, Blair, not here. Find someone to take it to the kitchen.' His gaze lifted to Innes's face again. 'I'm sorry, what did you say?'

'You wish me to speak to Field Marshal Haig?'

'Of course.' Sassoon raised an eyebrow. 'The Chief doesn't want to hear about your unit's activities from me.' Again the slight smile. Polite or provocative? Innes sensed he was relishing the moment.

'Ready?' Walking to the double doors in the wall opposite, he glanced over his shoulder at Innes. 'Wait until I announce you.'

Inside, the field marshal cleared his throat. 'Enter.'

Sassoon did as he was bidden, leaving the door ajar. Innes heard his name and took another deep breath. Then the door swung open and he was marching stiffly into the room, three, four, five steps across the polished parquet, concentrating his

164

gaze on a crack in the panelling to the right of the field marshal's head. A salute then silence.

'*Ahem.*' Haig cleared his throat again. Then he said, 'Sit down, Captain Innes.'

Two hard dining chairs; Innes took the nearest. The field marshal was leaning forward a little, a pen in his right hand, his left on some papers. His face was a little heavier than Innes remembered, his lips and his jaw set the same, as if chiselled from Edinburgh sandstone. As before, Innes was struck by the milky blue of his eyes.

'You've found time to ride, I hope, Captain?'

Innes said he hadn't been able to. Another silence, in which he tried to meet the field marshal's gaze.

'Sassoon tells me you were in Belgium,' Haig said at last. 'How did you find the people?'

'Ready to do all they can to liberate their country, sir. Grocers, railway porters, priests, farmers – but they think of themselves as soldiers fighting for freedom.' Innes swallowed hard, because this was his chance to speak for Ramble and all the brave ordinary people who risked their lives every day, unseen, unsung. 'They take great risks to provide us with information . . . they're grateful to us . . . very grateful.'

Haig looked uncomfortable. '*Ahem.*' The fingertips of his left hand were tracing small circles on the cover of a red leather file. Innes heard Sassoon take a step closer. 'Captain Innes's experience behind enemy lines has been invaluable in training our new agents, sir. I believe some of them have been deployed by balloon, Captain?'

'Five agents, sir,' said Innes, directing his answer to Haig. 'I believe it is Colonel MacLeod's intention to send more.'

Another pause. 'Yes.' Haig nodded deliberately and opened the file. 'Brigadier Charteris says they are already providing useful intelligence on the enemy's movements.'

'I believe Colonel MacLeod has heard from two, sir. The quality of the intelligence, I can't judge.'

'Why not?'

'Colonel MacLeod handles that side of things personally, sir.'

'I see.' Haig stared at him for a few seconds and then looked down at the open file. 'Thirty agents,' he muttered, his gaze lifting slowly, deliberate in his movement and his speech. 'We have thirty agents with the cavalry.'

'Yes, sir.'

'*Ahem.* The speed of our advance will depend on accurate intelligence.'

'Yes, sir.'

'You trained these men?'

'I've spoken to most of them, sir.'

Again, the steady penetrating gaze. Innes realised he was holding his breath. He knew he should speak, only how to begin? It felt sacrilegious to express doubt, like a cymbal clashing on a stone floor, resounding in lofty arches.

'If I may say, sir, I'm not confident our agents have the necessary experience or guile to provide valuable intelligence – not without assistance from the local population.' He paused to invite a response. None came so he pressed on. 'I relied on local people for intelligence, sir. It takes time to build a network – safe houses, letterboxes for information drops – and time to learn how to—to stay alive. Even simple things . . . You know, the Germans shoot anyone keeping carrier pigeons?'

Silence. Haig was staring at him intently. After what seemed like a minute, he said, 'I'm sure Brigadier Charteris has taken these matters into consideration,' and he looked over Innes's shoulder for confirmation.

'Yes, sir,' said Sassoon, although he couldn't possibly know.

'Yes.' Haig repeated, his gaze dropping back to Innes.

'It's my duty to say, sir . . .' Innes hesitated because Haig had closed the red file and was reaching across his desk to slide it neatly into a tray. 'Sir, my experience tells me we have nothing to gain from this operation . . . that is my opinion. The balloon flights will come to nothing. In fact, we're wasting these men's lives. Sir, the Secret Service Bureau has the necessary contacts. It has local people on the ground; let them handle this . . . We might give them a shopping list and offer them the means to deliver up-to-date intelligence – perhaps a wireless . . .'

Another long silence, the field marshal's eyes were still fixed upon him. Innes tried to imagine what he was thinking. His face was a little stiffer and his hands had shifted to the edge of the desk.

'Thank you for your report, Captain.' Pushing his chair away. 'This is a matter for Brigadier Charteris.' He got slowly to his feet. Innes was dismissed.

'Sir.' He stood quickly and to attention and Sassoon took half a step forward to shepherd him from the room. It might have ended there. Later, he wondered why it didn't. But there was no single reason, only feelings that rose from the pit of his stomach; the resentment of trench years, the muddy ghosts that were with him always, anger, despair, the anger that used to carry him into no man's land, bending without thought to help a wounded man under fire – for that feeling they'd decorated him for courage. 'I think you should know, sir,' he said, 'we – the Staff – call the new espionage unit the Suicide Club, because no one gives those men a chance.'

Haig didn't speak but continued to stare at him impassively; not a flicker of emotion; a recruitment poster; a porcelain plate; a bronze statue. In the tense silence the clock seemed to tick louder, Sassoon coughed, and his leather boots squeaked as he stepped closer to the desk. At last the field marshal spoke a firm, 'That will be all, Captain Innes.'

And that was all. Sassoon was holding his elbow but he managed a salute, and the door closed quietly behind them.

'Well. Innes.' Sassoon smiled wryly. 'One should applaud your honesty, I suppose.' Then glancing pointedly at his clerks, he said: 'Follow me, please.'

Innes knew it was time to do as he was told.

On the steps at the front of the house he breathed deeply and felt calmer, his feelings untangling in the cool breeze, carried away like the threads of an old cobweb.

'Better?' Sassoon enquired. 'There will be repercussions, I'm afraid. I must say, you went further than I expected you to.' He placed his hand lightly on Innes's sleeve for a moment, so smooth and so very clever.

'This was meant to happen in some way.'

On the breeze now the roar of an engine, and a few seconds later a large and shiny black Staff motor car passed the trees and came up the drive towards the house.

'General Gough,' Sassoon said, dropping down a step. 'My dear fellow, you will have to excuse me.'

'Why, Sir Philip?'

Sassoon turned to look up at him. 'Oh, do I have to explain? You were presented with an opportunity to speak your mind and you chose to.' Their eyes met for a moment. Five inches shorter, two steps down, and yet he still contrived to look down his nose. 'Take my advice old boy, speak to a doctor,' he said. 'Tell him you've been working too hard, you're over-wrought, nerves, that sort of thing. Believe me, it will help.'

The Staff car was creeping slowly round the gravel circle to the bottom of the steps. Sassoon wished him *au revoir* with a weak smile, but he was too politic to offer his hand.

*

Innes expected his situation to unravel quickly, and he used the first hour at his desk to write and code a short note to Cumming. But the morning rolled on as always, and by lunchtime he was ready to destroy his note. Wasn't it vanity to assume the commander-in-chief would give him a second thought when his armies were preparing for their next push? In any case, Innes had told the truth in a place where too little of it was spoken, or was that vanity too? How long had he been in Haig's office – four, five minutes? – no more than ten, too short a time to remember its decor. The pouchy skin beneath the field marshal's eyes, the threads of gold in his grey moustache, Innes could recall his face with perfect clarity, most of all his steady gaze. There *was* something in the man's silence, Marshall was right, a certain lofty sympathy that could inspire faith and confidence he would do the right thing. Pray, that it was so.

And Charteris? Innes decided the honourable thing would be to speak to him before someone else had a chance to. It was bound to be unpleasant and waiting would only make it worse. Rising from his desk he walked out of Section and along the corridor to the BGI's office. Too late. The brigadier was on his way to advanced headquarters.

Innes was too tense to settle to his work, so he left the école and climbed up to the ramparts. Smoke was spiralling from the woods across the valley, west into the flat grey sky. The Army's labour gangs were taking more timber. For what? Duckboards to cross the battlefield, perhaps, trench props, or for the fires of winter. Innes tried to imagine the field marshal's suave secretary up to his knees in freezing water. That would be something he would pay to see. *You went further than I expected*, Sassoon had observed on the steps at Beaurepaire. What did he mean? It would be easy to make too much of a careless remark. What was it Ramble liked to say? A spy is never free from suspicion, it grows like a cancer until one day it kills the man and there is only the spy. Fine, but what would Ramble say to the seething politics of GHQ? Innes bent to pick a rotting conker shell from the path, rolling it in his hands, then bowling it over the wall like a grenade. Is it me or Charteris, or are both of us targets, he wondered. And if it wasn't a flight of his fancy, who else was involved – Major Graham? Bound to be Graham.

From the town below there came the sudden sonorous note of a heavy hand-bell trapped in a narrow street; urgent, unfriendly, impossible to ignore. Innes walked to the top of the steps. Was it in the rue du Paon? The sound was muddier, moving in the direction of the Officers' Club. It was taken up as he stood there by another bell in the abbey tower of Saint-Saulve, a deeper echo that lifted the cawing rooks from the horse chestnuts opposite, reaching out from the town to the country, as it must have done in the centuries of war with England.

As Innes hurried down the steps a flare broke in a golden shower over the wall. The rue Porte Becquerelle was full of people and noise. The staff, from colonel to private, was trailing from the École Militaire to the nearest town gate. A fresh-faced officer of the town guard was encouraging them at the top of his voice to move quicker, while from the pavement opposite some of the older residents of the street laughed and jeered in French: 'Where are the English soldiers going? The English are running to the woods.'

Innes saw the young lieutenant quartermaster who'd driven him to Montreuil on his first day. 'What's happening?'

'Air raid,' he replied cheerily, 'or so they say . . . a practice, I expect.'

Innes let him go, almost skipping to catch up with his comrades. They were like excited children released by a school

170

fire drill. An old woman was watching the procession from the step of her home a few feet away, chewing and sucking her toothless gums, and two doors down, a mother with a crying infant in her arms. The ordinary folk. In the great GHQ scheme of things they were left to burn.

'Lost, sir?' a military policeman asked, 'Plenty of shelter in the walls.' He stepped back to avoid a motor car that was pushing on to the gate, its French driver cursing and honking its horn. 'All right, all right,' he shouted pointlessly in English, 'mind how you go!' Through grey exhaust fumes, Innes noticed the one-armed veteran who sold his war souvenirs outside the école. 'English soldier run, English run,' he was shouting. When he stopped his bottom lip began to tremble and he wiped his right eye with a knuckle. Above the din of the street, a bang Innes took without thought for a second Very flare. A moment later there was another, closer, and his heart beat faster because this time it was more like the rumble of an explosion. He could see the apprehension in the faces about him. For a second there was a peculiar stillness, as if they were praying they were mistaken, a breathless second, broken by the tolling bell and the wailing of the infant.

'Go, go,' Innes heard himself shouting in French. He tried to cross the narrow street to the mother and child, but soldiers and some of the townsfolk were running. He was knocked sideways and staggered to keep his feet. When he looked again the mother had gone. He allowed himself to be carried by the crowd to the gate. Stepping clear there, he looked back up the street to where members of the guard were marshalling stragglers, and he could hear the hornet drone of approaching aircraft, then an explosion west of the town. The next made him flinch, although it was at least a mile away. Then a series of detonations, creeping closer, a tongue of flame rising from somewhere near the old citadel. Against the sky, the rigid silhouette of a large bi-plane, two planes, three. Gotha bombers. Someone had Innes by the arm and was trying to draw him away. 'No. Look to yourself,' he said. The street was almost empty now, and his gaze was drawn to two figures – one a man in uniform, the other a small boy of five or six. They seemed oblivious to the noise and destruction the enemy was reeking at their back. With a start, Innes recognised Graham. He was carrying a stick in his right hand and his left was resting in a fatherly way on the boy's shoulder. The wee boy's face was lost beneath a cap many sizes too large, his chin planted on his chest, studying his tackety boots. A few yards from the gate he lifted the cap and his cheeks were streaked with tears.

'Glad I've found you, Innes,' Graham said, breezily. 'This is Louis. He says he lives near the Citadel, so he's keeping me company for now.'

Another detonation, like the growl of a large beast, and Louis shrank beneath his cap.

'They're not very good – miss everything – up to now, anyway,' Graham observed. 'All the same, we should find some shelter.'

From the gate, he led them along the muddy leaf-strewn path at the foot of the ramparts. Members of the Staff were chatting and smoking on the tree-lined slopes below, their vivid red tabs and hat bands conspicuous amongst the decaying greens and browns of autumn. The explosions seemed more distant at the white stone base of the wall. Clutching it for support as he slid along the path, it seemed to Innes to be one more measure of war and a world turned upside down, in which the defenders sought refuge beneath the medieval walls rather than atop them as soldiers once used to, and the civilians were left to fend for themselves. An officer of the town guard tried to persuade them to hide in the woods, but Graham assured him he knew of better shelter, and after a few more yards he directed Innes down rough steps into the trees. Almost hidden at the bottom of the slope was a stone and half-timbered cottage. Graham knocked sharply at its door and tried the handle without waiting for a reply.

'Monsieur le Forestier's home,' he said, as if his name was explanation enough. The house was empty, no soldiers, no townsfolk, no Forestier, but a large cellar with shelves of dusty bottles.

'All very good,' Graham assured Innes as he bent over a table to light two candles. 'Shall we open one? Yes, I think we will.' He took a bottle from a shelf and placed it on the table. 'Sit down, Louis,' he said in French. 'You're safe here.' The little boy did as he was told and perched on a stool, his boots dangling a few inches from the flagged floor.

'Corkscrew,' Graham muttered, stepping away from the candlelight. 'Were you ever in Arras?' He began rooting around in the darkness at the end of the cellar. 'Dozens of old tunnels there – our men use them as shelters. This one is mine. Ah, here.' A second later he was back in the light with the corkscrew and two glasses. 'I bought the wine and I'm not inclined to share it. You won't give away my secret, will you?' He paused, the corkscrew poised over the bottle. 'You know, I don't think you'll have time to.' Then he began turning it into the cork.

Innes dragged a stool to the table. 'At the gate . . . you said you were glad you'd found me?'

'Yes, that's right,' Graham said. Pouring the wine with one hand, he reached into a pocket with the other. 'Here.'

A square of yellow signal paper: Innes took it slowly, pinching it between thumb and forefinger.

'Suspicious?' Graham was amused. 'Dear, dear . . . when I've trusted you with the secret of my cellar.'

Innes gazed at him impassively for a moment, then

unfolded the paper, lifting it closer to the candle. The signal read: *Heavy batteries at 3967 7844. 38th Division moving to trenches between S23 and T54. 20th, 9th and 221st Divisions all reported dangerous weakening of fighting strength. Trouble in 1st Bavarian Reserve near Zandvoorde with two regiments taken from the line.*

Typed at the top of the signal was *SECRET FX/3.161.*

Graham had taken a stool opposite, the candlelight playing on his face as he considered the tears of wine in his glass.

'The *FX* is Faust?' Innes asked.

Graham lifted his glass in affirmation.

'You took it from MacLeod's office?'

'No.'

'It's from London? The War Office?'

Graham raised an eyebrow. 'Really, Innes.' He didn't want to be pressed on the matter. 'It's the quality and tenor of the intelligence that's important – it might be very good, it's certainly specific. But is it cross-checked with another source? I doubt it, because it's too specific, too perfect. Is it trustworthy?'

'And your opinion is . . . ?'

He gave a little shrug. 'We don't know enough, do we? I have my doubts, but it seems to me that it's your job to find out, and you should tell Cumming so.'

Innes stared at him for a moment, conscious in the silence of someone moving about the kitchen at the top of the stairs. Graham lifted his eyes to the ceiling. 'Well, what do you think?'

'How can I tell?'

He laughed and gestured: 'Not Faust, the wine, old boy.'

Innes picked up his glass, swilled the wine round the bowl and took a sip, gazing over the rim at Graham as he considered its palate, which was complex, very tannic, and too chill to really appreciate. A rare burgundy that would be at its best in an hour or two, Graham said, if only they had time together to drink it properly. His teasing tone seemed to imply Innes didn't have much to spare.

'You know about the meeting with Field Marshal Haig, then?' Innes asked, quietly. 'Pleased?'

Graham avoided his gaze. 'You mean?'

'I mean, you arranged things with Sassoon, didn't you?'

Leaning across the rough table, Graham pressed his forefinger into the hot wax at the top of a candle, then raised it to show Innes a perfect white wax fingerprint. 'Guilty, as charged.'

Innes raised his glass to his lips but lowered it without drinking. 'Are you going to tell me why?'

'You told the Chief the truth didn't you . . . we both know that is in short supply at GHQ.'

Innes snorted sceptically. 'Please, Graham.' Sitting in his private cellar, with shadows dancing about the walls and his face; to hear him talk of a need for candour at GHQ was ridiculous.

'You misunderstand me, Innes.' For once, he sounded needled. 'I don't care a fig for your Suicide Club, my concern is for the Chief – to protect the Chief.'

'You can't think anything I say is likely to—'

'Not just from Charteris.'

'You mean me?'

Graham laughed. 'He doesn't need protecting from you.'

'Then why do you want rid of me?'

'From Cumming, from those he serves, from Downing Street, from those who use the Staff to attack the Chief. I've told you: Field Marshal Haig will win this war, he's the only one who can.'

'*Floreat Etona*, is that it?' Innes was losing his temper. 'Major Graham and Captain Sassoon have decided who will win the war for us all?'

'No.'

'At the behest of *your* political masters?'

Graham tut-tutted crossly. 'Don't raise your voice, you're frightening the boy.' Louis was shaking with apprehension, or the cold, or both, his shoulders bent, his hands wedged between his thighs.

'Are you all right?' Innes asked in French.

'I expect the air raid's over, Louis,' Graham said, 'we can leave now.' He made to move and the little boy followed his example, slipping from his stool.

'Oh, not quite yet,' Innes said, touching Louis' shoulder. 'No, I don't think it's safe quite yet, Major Graham.'

Graham closed his eyes for a moment and sighed heavily like a teacher struggling with a dull-witted pupil. 'Look, Innes, you're a fish out of water here. There's nothing more for you to do. Tell Cumming about Faust; I'm sure you have already. Goodness, isn't that enough? Go back to Belgium and leave things at GHQ to . . . well, to me, actually.'

Innes felt a surge of anger. 'You're very anxious to be rid of me.'

'Graham the spy again?'

'Faust may be cover for—'

'Don't be a bloody fool.'

Graham's *fool* echoed to every corner of the cellar.

'Leave things to you, you say. And what is your intention?'

'Now?' said Graham, rising quickly to his feet. 'I intend to leave. There's nothing more to say. Things will take their course. Come on Louis, time to go home.' Catching Innes's eye, he nodded to the bottle: 'Take it if you like.'

'It isn't to my taste.'

Graham shrugged. 'I don't imagine it is.'

In the kitchen they were greeted by the elderly and obsequious Monsieur le Forestier. He knew Louis' parents and promised to take him home, a service for which he was well rewarded by Graham. The enemy had flown away, and Innes could hear English voices on the path above the cottage. The staff of the British Army was emerging from the trees, from cellars and recesses in the rampart walls. It would be business as usual at the école within the hour.

'You know, we attack again in four days,' Graham said. 'If we don't break through in the next two to three weeks, I don't think we will . . . not this year.' He tilted his head back, gazing at the grey sky. 'The Chief is confident we will, but if we don't, the politicians will remember the promises, and they will want to know why we made them. They'll look to intelligence.' He raised his arm, holding his palm flat. 'You see? More rain.' It was speckling their uniforms, pattering through what was left of the leaf canopy. 'Discover all you can about Faust. I'll do what I can here'. He glanced sideways at Innes, trying perhaps to gauge his expression. Then he asked, 'You're going to see the BGI?'

Innes said that was his intention, yes.

Graham nodded. 'Tell him you're suffering from battle stress. Something came over you when you were speaking to the Chief. Did Sassoon tell you to do that? Goodness, you've reason enough to say so.' He offered Innes his hand and his smile, which was always just a little supercilious. 'I know what you think of me. It may surprise you to learn that the longer I serve on the Staff, the more I hate the word *gentleman*. In the British Army it's used to compliment officers with no power of thought, no imagination, no initiative. But you' – his lips were twitching with amusement – 'you, sir, you are no gentleman.'

Innes was ambushed as he was crossing the courtyard of the école. 'Brigadier General Charteris is expecting you,' his aide-de-camp said, rising from the bench beneath the pergola. A cigarette was burning in a saucer, and there was ash on Charteris's sleeve, as always. One of these days he was going to set fire to the mountain of paper on his desk and on the floor and on every other surface in his office. He ignored Innes's salute and carried on writing, back and forth in a neat hand that seemed strangely at odds with his slovenly appearance. He was trying not to show he was angry, but it was plain enough in his face.

'Explain yourself,' he said at last.

'You're referring to my briefing with the commander-in-chief, sir?'

'Of course I am, man.'

'I thought it was my duty to inform Field Marshal Haig that the espionage unit wasn't ready and never would be, and that we are throwing these men's lives away on a wild goose chase.'

'I know what you said, Captain Innes. What I want to know is, why?'

'Sir, it was my duty to offer an honest opinion.'

'Were you asked for one? A junior officer, with no experience of the Staff . . . You were to report on the work of your unit.' Charteris leant forward to grind his cigarette butt in the ashtray. 'I don't know how Captain Cumming conducts affairs at his Bureau, but in the Army . . . well, you remember we spoke of loyalty? You have betrayed my trust. A personal betrayal . . .' For a moment he was almost speechless with outrage. 'The discourtesy . . .'

Was Innes making things worse? He knew he didn't look very contrite. He felt what his father liked to call a 'do the right thing' calmness, and the cussedness he was famous for in the family. 'But I would like say to say in my defence, sir, that I believe I was acting in the interests of the Army and the members of the Suicide Club.'

'Captain Innes!' Charteris was rising from his chair. 'I will thank you not to speak of the espionage unit in that disparaging way. I have spoken to Colonel MacLeod . . . You clearly think you know better than senior officers, than me.' He was leaning across his desk now, his large head so close Innes could see the pulse in his temple and the broken capillaries over his cheek-bones. A boxer in his youth, no doubt. 'I can only think you were sent to GHQ to cause trouble,' he said.

'I thought I was—'

'No, I don't want to hear your—because your loyalty was clearly in question from the start.'

'If I may, sir—'

'You may not! There is no place at GHQ for men with divided loyalties. I understand from Sassoon that you're a Roman . . . a man who already puts his church before his country . . .'

'That, sir, is an insult to Catholic soldiers, to our Irish soldiers.'

'Half-hearted in their country's cause at best. The right attitude, the right spirit . . . Captain Innes, you have shown precious little of either. Your time on the Staff is over.' His voice was rising. 'Get out, Captain. You are dismissed.'

Innes stared at him calmly for a second, then saluted and turned to the door. So that was that: Cumming wasn't going to be happy. Well, fuck Cumming.

October 1917

We go on again tomorrow. With a great success, and good weather for a few more weeks, we may still clear the coast and win the war before Christmas. It is not impossible, but it is pouring again today.

Diary of the Director of Military Intelligence, Brigadier General John Charteris, 8 October 1917

13

Chequers

T HE ENVELOPE HAD been burning a hole in Hankey's pocket for hours, but now he was free to open it he was reluctant to do so. He had carried it to a bench in the formal garden below the house. Beguiled by the evening sunshine, he sat for a few precious minutes and listened to the cawing of the rooks, in the parkland trees at his back, and the lazy snipping of a gardener, on his knees between the low box hedges. After the talk of war, the planning for tomorrow and next year, he was touched by the sense of a centuries-old order, by the symmetry of the Tudor house, its tall brick chimneys and mullioned windows, its square garden beds of rose and lavender and lichen-yellow flags.

It was late on their second day at Chequers, and this was the only waking moment of peace he'd been able to enjoy. Men with great decisions to make should spend time sitting and reflecting in places such as this, he thought, and listen for a still small voice. This prime minister loved the open air, he loved to walk, but his mind never seemed to be at rest. They had followed a path into the Chiltern hills the day before and argued about war policy every step of the way, so absorbed in their differences they missed the turn back to the house. Mr Lloyd George was a subtle man, devious when he wanted to be – which was quite often – but he trusted too much in heat to generate great light. Soon he would notice that his Cabinet secretary was missing from the conference and summon him back to the sounding seat on his right.

Contemplating the envelope and tilting it to and fro in the late evening sun like a mirror, Hankey could make his titles and the honours for his service march across the paper. With a sigh he ran his nail under the leaf and drew out a single sheet of paper. Captain Cumming had a remarkably fine hand for an old sailor with thick knuckles and a passion for engines and ropes. The Whitehall Court address of his Secret Service Bureau was embossed at the top, and it was dated yesterday, the twelfth of October.

My Dear Sir Maurice,

I understand from your people that you are spending the weekend at the Prime Minister's new country residence. In your absence a couple of matters have arisen, the first concerns the future of the Secret Service Bureau, the second, that of my agent, Lazarus. You have your ear to the ground always, I know, so it is entirely possible you have heard a little of both already. If that is the case, let me begin by reassuring you that nothing is known of Downing Street's interest in Innes's activities.

To deal briefly with the first matter: the War Office has begun a review of military intelligence. All well and good you might think, room for improvement there, but I am reliably informed its recommendation is written already. Put simply, the Army is going to swallow us up. To that end, it will offer to pay for the Bureau. No need to remind you, I'm sure, but he who pays the piper calls the tune. Remarkable, when the Foreign Office has expressed its continuing support for our work and our _independence!_ We look to Downing Street to save us again. I must say, it is a great pity GHQ is not concentrating all of its fire on the enemy, but I suspect this *fresh attack on our integrity is not unconnected with the second matter I must raise with you: the Lazarus affair.*

Let me begin with an apology and acknowledge Captain Innes has let us both down badly. I have heard his account of the meeting with Field Marshal Haig now, and the damn fool says he felt he owed it to his commander-in-chief and the members of the Suicide Club to offer honest counsel. Did he expect to be thanked, I asked? He said no, but I think yes, he hoped he would be. Perhaps it is something to do with his religion. I know you have a strong Christian faith, Sir Maurice, but you will forgive me observing, I hope, that Roman Catholics are always looking for saints and saviours when there are rather more of us sinners in the world.

Brigadier Charteris was furious, of course. He views Innes's attack of honesty as a breach of his trust, and for once he and I are in agreement. The irony of this was not lost on our Captain Innes. The brigadier blames the Roman Church too, but in a different way. He is full of Scotch prejudice, it seems. Apparently, it was the Field Marshal's secretary, Sassoon, who told him Innes was Catholic. I am quite sure that man Sassoon considers everything he says very, very carefully.

Hankey lifted his eyes from the letter to the upper terrace. He could hear voices, laughter, the translator speaking French, and the prime minister attempting and failing to do the same. If they came down the steps to the lower terrace they would see him in the garden. Mr Lloyd George was telling his guests the story of his recent visit to the Front and the shell that had whistled over his head and burst just a hundred yards away. Hankey had heard him speak of it three or four times, and always with new colour. Now his French counterpart, Monsieur Painlevé, was admonishing him for not taking more care. The 'English' needed their people's champion to lead them to victory, he said. It might have been a politician's platitude but it was spoken with a passion Hankey found quite moving. Pray God it would be so. He was on the point of rising when the party on the terrace began to move away. When he was satisfied he would be left alone, he opened Cumming's letter again.

I am quite sure that man Sassoon considers everything he says very, very carefully.

Sassoon, the door-keeper, chosen for the very political skills the field marshal affected to despise.

One Scotchman's prejudice towards another would be of no significance were it not that Innes is convinced Graham and Sassoon orchestrated the whole thing. Time Innes took some leave, you might think – he certainly has a bee in his bonnet about Graham – but now I have heard his account of how things stand at GHQ I am inclined to believe he's right.

Graham and his friends have no time for Charteris but they are loyal to Haig and wish to protect him from 'political interference', in particular from Downing Street. Who are these friends? After careful enquiry I have a list of politicians, two newspaper proprietors, soldiers and royal equerries, past and present. You may have your own names. No one on my list is of the Prime Minister's Party. In fact, one might say, they are of 'the Soldier's Party' or 'Haig's Party'. If there is another failure, if the battle at Ypres is lost in the mud and there is blame to apportion, they will want to make sure it stops short of the top of the Army.

There's nothing more that can be done at GHQ at this stage. Charteris will endeavour to keep the Bureau at arm's length until the Army swallows us whole. So, what to do about Faust? Graham seems to think Faust is a problem, and he is

better placed than Innes to judge. Of course, he may just be
using Faust as an excuse to fob off the Bureau, but Innes
doesn't think so. He says Graham is genuinely concerned
about the reliability of GHQ's intelligence and the weight
given to this source. On the one hand Graham wants rid of
us, on the other, he needs our help. As you know, we have our
own concerns about the security of the Army's networks in the
occupied territories (we are still picking up the pieces in
Thielt and Roulers!). I have sent Innes to the Netherlands with
authority to dig up all he can, which was what he wanted to
do anyway. He was so anxious to return to his old job I had
half a mind to ask him if he'd engineered his own dismissal
from GHQ, but I think he's too honest to do that, as we now
know to our cost.

The Army's operations in the occupied territories are run
out of Rotterdam. My head of station, Tinsley claims to know
all about them – the rogue. He has his means, none of them
honest, but you will not wish to know the details.

'This is where you're hiding.' Mr Lloyd George was coming
down the steps from the upper terrace, his hands stuffed in
the pockets of his grey wool jacket.

'I'm sorry, Prime Minister.' Hankey got to his feet and walked
towards him. 'A letter from Cumming of the Secret Service.'
He waved the evidence, then slipped it back in his jacket.

'Cumming, I see.' His head was bowed and there were deep
frown lines between his eyes that disappeared when he smiled,
which was not often of late.

'I have spoken to Painlevé. I said, "Monsieur Prime Minister,
we cannot have another year of terrific losses like this year."'

They were side by side now with only a corner of the box
hedge between them, and they were almost the same height,
which was rather on the short side. But Mr Lloyd George

was fourteen years older and in the short time Hankey had known him well his moustache and the mane of hair he swept from his forehead and behind his ears had turned completely white.

'I suppose you've heard the news from Flanders?' he said.

'Very discouraging, Prime Minister. I understand things have, for want of a better description, bogged down.'

'Bogged down will do very well. Bogged down – as I predicted – and I'd like to say this . . .' He paused to reflect for a moment and Hankey sensed he was working himself into one of his holy passions, preacher's finger pointing to the evening sky. 'Human life is very precious. It takes twenty-one years to make a man. The country can face losses, but not without some successes, and if we permit Haig to carry on like this he'll break the Army.'

He was staring at Hankey like a cantankerous goat: disagree and I'll charge.

'If it is your intention to remove Field Marshal Haig, I think it is my duty as the Secretary of your War Cabinet to remind you that its members—'

'—will fight me to the last, yes.'

'And the government will fall.'

'Then perhaps it should, Hankey.' He turned towards the park and lifted his head a little to gaze beyond it at shadows on the hill and a line of trees traced against the sky. 'What did Cumming have to say?'

'Regrettably, his man at GHQ has blotted his copybook. He's been expelled. Not before he raised fresh concerns about Charteris and his whole operation.'

'So, he's off the hook!'

'No, Prime Minister, I wouldn't say so. Cumming's Bureau is continuing with its investigation into his sources – one in particular. I'm confident he'll turn something up.'

Someone on the upper terrace was calling the prime minister. After a few seconds there was a second voice, and soon an anxious chorus.

He sighed and turned to face Hankey. 'You know Haig's preparing another attack? It will be just like the others. When it's over I will see how things stand with the Cabinet. It's only a pity so many of our people will lay down their lives before I do.'

After dinner, after favourite Welsh hymns at the piano, and only after the prime minister had said goodbye to their French guests, Hankey retired to his room and replied to C's letter: *Approved. Hankey.*

14

Rotterdam

TINSLEY PARKED HIS motor car on the opposite side of the street. Beyond the canal and the poplar trees, ahead and to the left, number 207A Heemraadssingel was a terraced house in the traditional style with flat, reddish-brown bricks pointed in white, stone steps, and a stone balcony. Just one room wide but four storeys high and a cellar, Tinsley said. Comfortable in the Dutch way. It was a new district, a broad green finger of land in the east of the city where two young Englishmen of military bearing might arouse less suspicion, but only a little less. They may have convinced their immediate neighbours they were shipping brokers, but everyone else in the game knew they were spies. Rotterdam was alive with spies, with the Allies and with their enemies, and the neutral Dutch police watching them all. Innes gazed from the motor car at number 207A and wondered if the air of intrigue in the city owed something to the centuries-old gloss of Dutch life, to the God-fearing folk who built their churches and homes and paid for their portraits and fine china with profits earned in the slave trade; to the show of tolerance but secret antipathy they felt for the foreigners who sailed into their port; to neighbour peering through curtains at neighbour, searching for cracks in the finish of prosperous and publicly perfect lives. In a way, Innes was there to do the same, because the residents of number 207A were representatives of British Army GHQ. Absurd, really, that his business was with his own, when the enemy's intelligence office was only a few streets away.

'That's one of 'em.' Tinsley nudged him. 'At the door. Here,' and he thrust some field-glasses at Innes. 'Lieutenant Blackwood. He's new. The other fella – Bennett – he's been here a while.'

Blackwood had large anxious rabbit eyes. He was standing outside the house, pretending to adjust his scarf while he checked the street.

'He looks so young,' said Innes.

'You all look young to me.'

'I expect we do, Tinsley, I expect we do. So there's just two of them in the house?'

'And the servants. Mesman acts as butler and valet and message boy, his wife as housekeeper, cook, and maid – a good cook, I hear.'

Blackwood was on his way now, walking south along Heemraadssingel towards the docks.

'And this Mesman . . . ?'

'He's mine.' Tinsley pushed back his hat and scratched his broad forehead. 'An ex-sailor. He wouldn't sell secrets to just anyone, but he knows me, knows we're on the same side – and I've helped him out of a spot of bother.'

'Oh, what sort of bother?'

Tinsley had an expressive face, a baggy weather-beaten face, a fifty going on sixty hard-knocks face, and now it was full of disdain. 'Look Innes, a nice clean chap like you don't need to know any details.'

That was how it worked in Rotterdam. Tinsley was one of C's 'scallywags'. He ran the Bureau's operation as a private enterprise, lining his pockets in a number of different illegal ways and sometimes in the king's name. He'd sailed beneath the red duster, a merchant mariner through and through, foredeck to bridge, rough West Country manners. His Dutch was poor and his religion was of a superstitious sailor's sort, but after more than a decade in the city of ship receipts, of weigh bills and dock returns, he knew the people, he knew who to grease and who was unimpeachable, and if he had almost as many enemies as he had friends, his friends were placed well enough to keep him at least a step ahead of his enemies.

A rogue but a useful one, and a patriot of sorts, because his duty to the old country presented many new business opportunities. Competition from the other British intelligence services, the Army and the Navy, he took personally, and that was why he had been happy to help Mesman with his 'spot of bother'. He'd probably dressed it up as a simple act of kindness, but now it was a debt and it was time to exact payment.

'Mesman knows nothing of Faust?'

'Nothing.' Tinsley turned to the open window, flicking his cigarette butt on to the pavement. 'Not a thing. Nor do our *passeurs*, and that's strange because some of our people do work for the Army too. Are you sure about this Faust?' He sounded impatient. It was four o'clock in the afternoon and if there was more talking to be done he would probably prefer to do it in the bar of the Hotel Weimar. 'Let's go.' He reached down beside his seat for the crank handle.

'Just a minute. Where do they keep their papers?'

Tinsley sighed heavily and lowered the handle to the floor. 'It isn't going to be easy.'

The filing cabinets were in a first-floor office, he said. Bennett slept in the room above, and Blackwood in the room below, and one of them was in the house at all times. *Passeurs* visited with intelligence from the other side of the wire and left with fresh instructions for the Army's networks – perhaps for Faust. An English girl called Dawson helped with typing and the accounts, and three times a week a teacher from Berlitz visited the house to chat to them in Dutch. Evenings they spent working or playing piquet. Once a fortnight, Bennett visited contacts outside the city and spent the night away, and on most Thursdays he reported to the British military attaché at The Hague.

Innes said: 'I see what you mean.' He could also see a twinkle in Tinsley's eye and a suppressed smile, creased and white-whiskered like a great walrus. The old rogue had thought about the problem and was biding his time. 'Well come on,' Innes prompted him, 'what do you suggest?'

Tinsley sucked his teeth. 'We might be able to have a few hours inside their house on Sunday.'

'You said one of them was always in the house.'

'Well, not quite all the time. Mesman and his wife have Sunday evenings off, you see. The British Army can't cook, so Bennett and Blackwood eat at a restaurant in the old town.'

Innes smiled. 'Sunday it is, then.'

'I'll see to things.' He reached down to his right for the crank handle and offered it to Innes again. 'Now make yourself useful.'

Tinsley was making the arrangements, so Saturday was time to lose. Innes spent it wandering the old town, gazing in shop windows for something he might buy his sister. He ate lunch at a brasserie with a view of the Willemsbrug and the docks on the opposite bank of the river. Then, reluctant to return to the dingy little room Tinsley had rented for him near the railway station, and with no appetite for culture, he walked a few miles more. By four o'clock the light was falling and it was beginning to rain. He found a small church dedicated to a Dutch martyr he'd never heard of and sat before a bank of flickering candles to rest a while and listen. Somewhere in its arches there was a beat of pigeon's wings, and he could hear the women of the lady chapel clicking their rosary beads, the young priest shuffling round his altar. Old churches were alive with noise, sparks of sound that seemed to echo and flow in a current, the air vibrating, electric, like the seconds felt after the last note of a mighty fugue.

When his thoughts began to get in the way he paid for a candle and tried to focus them on the faces of the people he would have prayed for if he was able to pray. Pressing the candle into the top of the stand, he burnt his wrist on the one below, which was something he always seemed to do and something that always felt like an act of penance. Ramble said he was determined to find ways to punish himself. That thought reminded him of another: his final meeting with Marshall at GHQ. He had carried Innes's bag to the motor car and stood in silence by the passenger door gazing at his boots. 'You know, I applaud your bravery,' he'd said at last. 'Kicking your football out into no man's land to chase – it was in the true spirit of the Suicide Club. You're like a chap with shell shock I saw running about in full view of the enemy. They teased him for a while, firing at his feet, then they got bored and shot him through the head.' Innes had tried to laugh for some reason, perhaps to be polite.

'Is it possible to live again?' he'd asked Ramble once. 'Lazarus, Lazarus, how can you doubt it? Don't you dare,' came the reply. That was Ramble.

Innes dropped a few more cents in the box for another candle just for her, and without thinking this time, spoke a simple prayer.

On the following day they met at Tinsley's office. Tinsley's thief was there, small and spry, softly spoken, shifty, ingratiating. 'But with good references,' Tinsley joked. He said his name was Reitz and that he hated the Germans, but when they told him he would be stealing from the British he just shrugged and muttered he was a professional. They drove to Heemraadssingel and parked on the opposite side of the canal as before. The thief dozed under his cap while Tinsley smoked and talked about the import–export business he would run after the war. 'Might be a job for a good Dutch speaker like you,' he said, 'someone I can trust.' Innes listened to be polite and when that duty was done he stepped from the motor car for some air. A stiff north-westerly wind was stripping the last yellow leaves from the poplars and birches and ruffling the waters of the canal. Undaunted, families in church clothes were promenading the gravel path, as they did every Sunday.

Innes chose a bench beneath a weeping willow, turned up his collar, pulled down the brim of his hat and closed his eyes. The clear air, the soporific of distant voices . . . He woke with a start after only a few minutes, quite sure he was in a trench and he was sleeping on duty.

Tinsley was waiting on the pavement beside the car. 'Blackwood's left already.'

'It's half past five.'

'So he's early.' He sounded tense.

'What's the matter?'

'Nothing. Just wondering where you were.'

The lights were still on in the first-floor office. Innes said: 'We should wait in the car. Bennett might see us here.'

'That's rich,' Tinsley grunted, 'you wandering off and all.' He opened the driver's door. 'Oh, look here we go.' The light had gone out in the office. 'He's on his way.'

Tinsley stepped on to the running-board and swung his large frame into the driver's seat. Two minutes, three, four, and someone switched on the hall light, then the door began to open. Innes bobbed behind the black-painted body of the Mercedes.

'That's Bennett,' Tinsley muttered. 'All right, let's go.'

Walking quickly across the garden, across the canal bridge; three men, tall, large, and the small one carrying a bag of tools. They were conspicuous even in the gloom, a strange party on Heemraadssingel on a Sunday evening when families were preparing for dinner or the last church service of the day. Mesman was waiting on the step and he ushered them into the hall. His wife was standing at the parlour door. 'Get back, woman,' he snapped in Dutch.

Innes said, 'You expect them back at eleven?'

'Not before, not usually.'

'Not usually? Someone should have followed Bennett to make sure.'

'Well, it's too late now,' said Tinsley, 'unless you want to wait another week.'

The office door was locked with a simple pin tumbler.

'Careful,' said Mesman, 'the British check it for scratches.'

'Don't teach me my business,' said Reitz, rummaging in his bag for a skeleton key. It took him only a matter of seconds to open. Innes caught Tinsley's arm as he was reaching for the light switch: 'Curtains first.'

Bennett wasn't on top of his paperwork. In the first drawer of his desk Innes found dozens of unpaid bills, personal expenditure on suits from Jermyn Street, on shoes and wine and flowers – perhaps for the young lady in the second drawer, elegant in a white summer dress and barefoot, a lock of her blonde hair across the frame.

'Well I never,' said Tinsley, lifting a file above his head, 'this is me. They've got one on me. You know what the bastards say . . . *untrustworthy . . . lining his own pockets . . . with the expected reorganization of operations in occupied territories . . . can be cut loose . . .* What does he mean about a reorganization?'

'Not now,' said Innes, 'I can tell you—' He was interrupted

by the shrill trilling of the telephone on the desk in front of him.

Mesman stumbled back from the curtains. 'Don't, please.'

Tinsley shook his head in disbelief. 'What do you take us for, man?'

'Anything in the cabinets?' Innes asked, raising his voice above the bell.

'Files on the enemy, files on Dutch policemen – greedy bastards – two of my best contacts are taking money from this shower too. I'll have to see about that. There are some train-watching reports from Antwerp, Brussels, Liege . . . nothing in the forbidden zone, and no FX signals – that's your Faust, isn't it? No FX signals I can see . . . not yet.'

The telephone stopped and they all breathed a little more easily. In the bottom drawer of Bennett's desk there was a service revolver wrapped in a cloth and two leather-bound ledgers. They were written in a bold hand, names on the left and payments on the right. 'Come across any accounts books, Tinsley?'

'Only for clothing, paper, food, that sort of thing.'

'Show me, would you?'

He sighed heavily and dropped a book on the desk. Innes glanced through the first pages. It was a routine balance sheet of income and expenditure on everyday items.

'A girl comes in to do the accounts?'

'That's right. Miss Dawson.'

'She's meticulous.' Innes shut the ledger and pushed it back to Tinsley. 'So, these two are Bennett's books. He takes more care with the Army's money than he does with his own, but he isn't a book-keeper. He doesn't seem to trust Miss Dawson with these. Payments to agents?' The entries were very particular, just a name and a code reference in letters and numbers. There were about twenty regular payments, small sums for the most part, just a few florins. Only, once a fortnight

. . . Turning back then forward, running his finger through July and August and September, he could see something like a pattern. The largest payment in the ledger was 500 florins made twice monthly on a Tuesday, and the name in the ledger was 'De Foor'. On the Monday before, a sum of 200 florins was paid to an agent called 'Lippman', and another 200 on the Wednesday after to a 'Brinkerhoff'.

'Does the name De Foor mean anything to you?'

'No,' said Tinsley over his shoulder.

'Brinkerhoff? Lippman?'

'No.' He turned to look at Innes. 'I can ask our *passeurs*. What have you got?'

'Shit!' Mesman stepped away from the curtains. 'It's Captain Bennett!'

'All right, everyone shut up.' Innes turned to Reitz. 'Lock the door and turn off the light. Quickly now.'

'Knock him out in the dark,' said Tinsley, 'he knows my face.'

'Shush.'

The light went out and there was just a slither of blue through the curtains. Innes heard a voice in the hall, a baritone and well-educated English: Bennett was speaking to Mesman's wife. Then his footsteps, hurrying up the stairs. What now? Reitz was a faint silhouette at the door lifting a hand to scratch his nose; Mesman was still standing stiffly at the curtains; and why couldn't Tinsley breathe more quietly? Bennett would be through the door before they could stop him, unless Reitz . . . But he was a small man. Innes reached across the desk for the ink-well. It was made of smooth thick glass, solid enough to knock a man senseless. Captain Bennett was at the top of the stairs, turning left on to the landing, two steps, three steps, then the rattle of the handle as he opened his bedroom door. Innes moved slowly forward, gesturing to the others to stay still. Then they heard his footsteps approaching and Innes knew they were going to have to deal with him, and that everything was going to pot. He transferred the ink-well to his left hand while he dried his right on his trousers in readiness to strike: could he? Bennett twisted the handle once. He twisted it twice. Then they heard him turn away, and a moment later he was drumming down the stairs. Innes closed his eyes and ran his fingers through his hair.

Bennett was in the hall now, apologising to Mesman's wife for interrupting her supper. He wouldn't be late, he had an early start tomorrow, he said. So would she be good enough to ask her husband to prepare the motor car for seven? Goodbyes, the front door closing, and Mesman was watching at the window: 'He's gone, and please, you must go too. Please.'

Innes, switched on the light. 'We won't be much longer.'

'You might have killed 'im with that.' Tinsley was gazing at the ink-well.

'Protecting your good name, Tinsley.' Innes wiped the ink-well with his handkerchief and placed it back carefully on the desk. 'Look, these names in Bennett's book – twice a month on a Monday.' He pulled the ledger across the desk, spinning it round to show Tinsley. 'You heard Bennett? He wants his motor car tomorrow.'

'I told you, he leaves the city every fortnight, just for a night.'

'Well, this must be who he sees.' Innes tapped the ledger entry for Lippman with his forefinger. 'There's another payment due tomorrow. First Lippman on Monday, then De Foor on Tuesday, and Brinkerhoff on Wednesday. The best part of a thousand florins in two days.'

Tinsley picked up the ledger and peered at the names. 'A thousand florins. Every fortnight? Wish we had that sort of money to splash around.' He shook his head regretfully. 'What has this to do with your Faust?'

'I don't know. Maybe nothing. But if Faust is GHQ's best source . . . don't you pay your best the most?'

Tinsley grunted. 'On what Cumming lets us have?'

'We have something here.' Innes took the ledger from him and put it back in the drawer. 'Wouldn't you like to know what Bennett buys with a thousand florins?'

15

To the Border

BENNETT WAS AHEAD of them, ramrod straight, gripping
the wheel too tightly, plainly more used to travelling in
the passenger seat of his Peugeot. It was a fine motor car,
gleaming navy blue and chrome. The small business folk and
shoppers in the city's Hoogstraat stopped to stare.

'Bloody fool,' Tinsley shouted over the engine of his own
car. 'No common sense. Army officer class.'

'You're talking like a Bolshevik,' Innes teased, but he was
right about the Peugeot, it was too flashy for a ship broker
living on the Heemraadssingel.

From the city, they drove south across the river Waal. There
was very little traffic on the roads and Tinsley was obliged to
keep his distance. Bennett must have driven the route many
times, because he didn't need to consult a map. They lost him
for a while in Gorinchem and stopped to ask an old lady if
she had seen a motor car fit for a member of the royal family.
Racing through morning mist in the countryside beyond the
town, they came upon him again without warning. 'Fuckin'
hell.' Tinsley stamped on the brake and dropped quickly from
his vision. 'If he turns off the road in this we'll never find
him. So, what now, clever clogs?'

'He can't go much further,' Innes said peering at his map,
'we're only a few miles from the border.'

The mist cleared a little as they drove into the outskirts of

Breda, but by then Bennett had pulled away. They followed the road past the railway station, across an old moat, the green tip of the town's Gothic bell tower their beacon. There was a small market in the main square, countrywomen in white bonnets and black dresses were selling their bread and root vegetables, the pastries the locals called *Moorkop,* and big yellow cheeses. Innes stopped one woman and asked if she'd seen Bennett's car. She looked at him suspiciously. His Dutch was good but she could tell from his accent he was a foreigner. 'You would have noticed,' Innes prompted her, 'large, navy blue? A friend of mine. We were supposed to meet here.' She considered him for a moment and then pointed to the other side of the square.

'He's probably on his way out of town by now,' Tinsley said. It was stop-start through the market, the locals reluctant to make way for a big city motor. Tinsley clipped a table and incurred the wrath of an old farmer in Bible black with a voice like a Dutch Moses. 'Just fuck off,' Tinsley muttered under his breath; and turning to Innes, he said, 'Hoping to surprise Bennett, were you?'

Clear of the market at last, they drove past the east end of the church and turned left on to a street of shops. The Peugeot was parked half-way down in front of what was – to judge from the Turk's head above the door – the local pharmacy.

'Let me out here,' Innes said, 'then pull up at the next corner.'

He was dressed in a worn brown suit, black hat, and black bow-tie, and he slouched along the pavement with a hand in his trouser pocket like a poor tradesman with too much time to spare. Bennett had parked badly, and passers-by were struggling to squeeze between his car and the pharmacy. A large and prosperous-looking man, perhaps a banker or a lawyer, rapped on the window – 'Hey!' – then stepped off the pavement to roll round the other side.

Innes noted the handsome shop-front and the name on the sign: Lippman. Bennett was there for more than a headache cure. He was standing at the counter with his hat in his hands and his back to the window. Where was the pharmacist? The shop was furnished in a traditional way with shelves of white and brown bottles, a porcelain phrenologist's head, a silver cash register, a set of scales, and a mortar and pestle. All this Innes took in at a glance as he waited his turn to squeeze past the motor car. When it came, he walked on a little way, then stopped to gaze in an ironmonger's window. Bennett wasn't going to be long or he would have made a better fist of parking. One of his contacts was probably using the pharmacy as a letterbox, a *passeur* from the occupied territories perhaps; the border was so close. But Innes was just guessing. The whole thing seemed a bit ridiculous, with the enemy only a few miles away.

He counted a minute and then turned back to the pharmacy. This time there was no one close to the car and Innes was able to crouch at the window and pretend to tie his bootlace. A man in a white coat he took for the pharmacist was standing at the counter, his face hidden by Bennett's shoulder. Bennett was counting out money and the pharmacist slid a brown paper bag towards him. It was barely more than an impression, but Innes caught a glimpse of a grey-looking man with a pinched, elderly face and spectacles. Then Bennett was offering his hand, half turning to leave, and Innes was conscious of someone trying to squeeze past him and of a coat brushing the side of his face. He rose quickly but not quickly enough because Bennett was stepping out of the pharmacy. Their eyes met and his were full of suspicion.

'Hey. Is that your car?' Innes demanded in Dutch. 'No, don't walk away, I'm talking to you,' and he tried to grab Bennett's sleeve.

'I don't understand,' Bennett replied in Dutch.

'Your car. You can't park it like that.'

'Sorry. I don't understand.' He opened the passenger door and slid the brown paper bag across the seat.

'Who do you think you are?'

Bennett stopped and gazed at him coolly. 'Get lost,' he said in English. Innes tried to look uncomprehending and defiant. He watched Bennett walk round the front of the car, then he turned away, rocking and muttering like a resentful local.

The engine roared because Bennett was too heavy on the throttle, then the motor car rolled by. Thirty yards further on it passed Tinsley bent low in his Mercedes.

'You were taking a chance, weren't you?' he said as Innes climbed in beside him.

They followed Bennett south out of town and along the bank of the river. After about five miles he turned west on to a roughly metalled lane and slowed to almost walking pace. Tinsley waited until his Peugeot disappeared in the mist. They would have to take it in stages, he said. Innes didn't think Bennett was going far, the lane was badly rutted, the border only a mile away.

Cursing and wincing, Tinsley coaxed his Mercedes into a wood where the surface began to improve. In among the mature beech and pine, there were stands of saplings protected from the deer by fencing, and after about a hundred yards small white posts appeared on both sides of the lane. Innes found the wood on his map but there was nothing to indicate it belonged to a private estate. Through the trees ahead of them, wispy mist like old man's beard was floating above a broad stretch of open water, perhaps an ornamental lake.

Innes said, 'Slow down. Look, we have to hide the car. There.'

The lane ahead curved left round the lake, and a logging

track met the bend from the right. Fifty feet was all the car could safely manage along the track, but fifty was probably enough. Innes left Tinsley at the wheel and walked the last short way. Rising from the mist like something in a fairy tale was a fine brick house with an octagonal tower at one corner, large windows, and a pitched slate roof. It was seventeenth-century elegant but thick and square like the keep of a medieval fortress, and it must once have been one because it was surrounded on all sides by the still water of the lake, the vivid yellows and browns of autumn reflected in its surface. The only way into the house was across a stone bridge that was wide enough for a small cart but not a motor car. It was easy walking through oak and beech and sycamore and Innes covered the ground in only a few minutes. From the cover of the tree-line he could see a cobblestone drive to the gates of the estate and through the mist the chimneys and gables of a lodge and stables; he could see Captain Bennett's Peugeot on the bank at the end of the bridge and another motor car, something large, something American; and he could see the entrance of the house, eight windows and one over the door, a hall perhaps or an estate office.

He glanced at his wristwatch: almost half past twelve. The servants were probably busy preparing lunch for the owner's English guest. It was a risk but nothing compared to going over the top. Best to be shameless, stroll out of the trees like a tripper or a motor car enthusiast. Bennett had left the brown paper bag on the passenger seat. Something about its shape suggested the curve of the small bottles in the pharmacy window. Round the Peugeot, trailing his fingers over the lamps and the silver lion like the car fanatic he was supposed to be, then over to the swaggering American motor with its white leather seats and white wood running-boards. A box was strapped to the board on the driver's side and a name was painted on the lid: De Foor. And that, Innes reflected, was enough.

Tinsley was stamping his feet to keep warm. 'You're sure no one saw you?'

'No, I'm not sure. I don't think so.'

'And this De Foor?'

'According to Bennett's ledger, he gets a thousand a month.'

'Must be expensive keeping a house like that, with servants and gardens and . . . well, horses.' He clapped his driving gloves together. 'What now? We should move the car before dark.'

Innes reached into his coat for his cigarettes. 'The border must run through the estate, perhaps a mile, half a mile away . . .'

'A lot of these landowners have farms on both sides of the fence.'

'Yes, they do, don't they,' he said, tapping a cigarette on the back of his case. 'Well, I've found somewhere you can park your car closer to the house.'

In the end they were there for the rest of the day. Tinsley wrapped himself in a blanket and dozed on the back seat of the car. Innes found a raised bank in the trees where he could sit and watch the house and the falling leaves. He thought about Faust and GHQ, he thought about the battle at Ypres and home and Ramble, he thought about a lot of things, and when he was tired of thinking he got up and walked and smoked and hummed songs and jigs and most of a symphony. The lights came on in the entrance hall and the landing and in most of the windows in the west wing. One of the servants drove away in the big American car, there was a delivery for the kitchen, and another servant arrived on a bicycle. At about eight o'clock he heard Tinsley stumbling through the wood towards him. He'd fallen over a root in the dark and torn his trousers. Cursing, he sank in the leaves beside Innes. He was hungry and fed up and what if Bennett was staying the night? They should find a room in Breda.

Innes rolled back on to his stomach to look at the house. 'Perhaps in an hour,' he whispered, 'or two hours.'

'Fuck.' Tinsley slapped his knee.

The awkward silence was broken at last by the sound of an approaching motor car. A minute later its headlamps swept the trees to their right as it turned from the lane on to the cobbled drive. It was De Foor's American seven-seater.

'See what you mean,' said Tinsley, 'a Stoddard Knight. That's a long way from home.'

The chauffeur parked in front of the house as before but with the engine running. He was half-way across the bridge when the door opened and a servant came out with instructions.

Tinsley had taken out his field-glasses and was gazing at the lighted doorway. 'Four men putting on coats. No, one's a servant. I can see Bennett.'

'Perhaps you should get our engine started.'

Tinsley ignored him. 'Here we go.' Three men were walking across the bridge to the waiting car. 'But I can't see their faces. Bennett's getting in the back . . . and someone in a cloak . . . De Foor? The other fellow's well dressed . . . bowler hat, and I say, mustard-yellow boots. He has a beard.'

Innes gave him a shove: 'Come on, we must go.'

Tinsley caught his foot in a bramble cord and fell again, this time scratching his hands and his face. The Stoddard turned right off the drive into the roughly metalled lane they'd come along, but it was five minutes before they were ready to follow.

'Can you see without lights?' There was only a sliver of moon.

'If we're slow,' said Tinsley.

'Do you have a gun?'

'Christ. Do you think we'll need it? It is Captain Bennett!'

Innes felt embarrassed. 'Well, not for Bennett. Just a precaution.'

Tinsley glanced across at him: 'Steady on, Innes.'

They drove through the wood to a fork in the lane. Tinsley stopped the Mercedes and switched on its lamps. Innes found a tyre track in the broken surface. 'I think, right.' That was south towards the border.

'You know, if they stop their car, they'll hear our engine?' said Tinsley.

'They're bound to stop, they can't go much further. We'll have to hide your car here.'

But the ground was too soft and there were trees on either side of the lane.

'Then here.' Tinsley reached under his seat for his revolver. 'Just be careful who you point it at.'

Innes smiled. 'You're right. You keep it.'

Bennett would probably take him for a German spy and shoot him, and what a story that would make. But everyone said he was lucky, so perhaps he would get away with it. Lucky Lazarus, more lives than a cat. He walked on quickly, conscious of his footsteps and the distant roar of the retreating Mercedes. Round the next bend and there was the Stoddard, big and brassy, filling the lane, and because he was lucky there was no one there, not even the driver. The border was a ten-acre field away. He could see the fence and the lantern lights of the guards, he could see the moon glinting on the wet roofs of a village on the other side, the silhouette of its church. Three years ago Bennett's friend could have driven across his estate to say his Sunday prayers there. Some of his farm buildings were only a few feet from the fence. There was a light at the door of a hay barn. That was where Bennett and his pals would be.

The field was open grassland with a few mature trees, parkland once perhaps. Innes followed the skirt of the wood, then cut across to a low outbuilding close to the barn, bent double through the long grass, a nerve tripping in his bad leg, his trousers soaked with dew. The border fence was forty feet away. It didn't look that much on the Dutch side, there was just the matter of two thousand volts. Because he was lucky the enemy was patrolling another section of the wire. At the back of the outbuilding he paused to catch his breath and listen, then he edged his way along the wall to the front. Peering round the angle of the building, he could see a crew-yard overgrown with weeds and the hay barn, its double doors ajar. Someone was speaking English, there was laughter and a loud bang like a door slamming shut. He was weighing up the risk of moving closer when the light went out in the barn. A moment later the door creaked open and he heard Bennett say, 'Very satisfactory. I always say so, I know, but he's a brave fellow.' He stepped outside with his hat in his hands and was joined by the man Innes took to be De Foor. His driver closed the barn doors and secured them with a timber batten. They were a man short. Tinsley had followed a fourth through his glasses at the house, a tall man dressed in a bowler and mustard-yellow boots. They may have dropped him in the woods, but more likely he was still inside.

'Shall we?' De Foor touched Bennett's sleeve. 'Home and a glass of the whisky you've brought me.' Turning to his driver he said in Dutch: 'You can turn the motor car round, Gerrit.'

Quickly, lightly, Innes retreated round the angle of the building and dropped to his belly on a pile of rubble and broken earth.

Seconds later he heard Gerrit swishing through the long grass, too intent on hurrying to the car to notice the outline of a man a few yards from the path. Then Bennett and De Foor walked past in silence, conscious perhaps of the enemy on the other side of the fence. The sensible thing would be to wait until they were away in their big car, but by then the missing man in the bowler and the boots would have gone.

Innes lifted the batten from its housing as quietly as he could and opened the barn doors just wide enough to slip inside. He stood with his back to them while his eyes adjusted to the darkness. He felt calm even though his mind was racing with possibilities. The only thin blue light was from a high window he couldn't see. Bennett must have used a lantern, so that would be somewhere. He heard rustling to his right and it reminded him fleetingly of a company dug-out and MacCunn chasing rats with a spade. The lantern was hanging beside the door. By its light he could see a wagon, its axle supported by a timber horse, and he could see a mound of hay and some farm implements against a wall. Inside, the barn was remarkable for a general air of neglect; outside, there was a field of long grass waiting to be mown. It was very slovenly and most unlike the Dutch – they were such fastidious people.

Innes tied the lantern to a timber brace and picked up a pitchfork. A few forkfuls from the bottom of the pile were enough to expose a trap-door of black sheet metal, the width of a man's broad shoulders. Lifting it open by the edge, he could see the top of a brick shaft with a ladder fixed to the side. He didn't wait to consider whether he should stay or go, because he knew the longer he thought about it the harder it would be to find the courage. The shaft was fifteen feet deep and a tight fit with the lantern, and he was bathed in sweat before his feet touched the bottom. There was a tunnel – as he knew there would be – square like the end of a coffin and pitch black like his dug-out on the Somme. Just gazing at it made him feel sick. Go now. Don't stop for a second. Forward knee, forward elbow, forward knee. The lamp toppled over. He was terrified it would go out. He must have struck his forehead against the planking because blood was running into his eye and he could taste its salt on his lips. Later, he remembered chanting a prayer over and over and over in his head until he rose trembling in the shaft on the other side.

He climbed the ladder with no thought for what he would find when he reached the top. He tried to lift the trap-door a few inches with his right hand but was only able to force it open with both, the ring of the lantern in his teeth, its glass burning his neck. All he could see through the gap was a patch of night sky, but instantly he felt calmer. Bloody fool. Bloody fool because he couldn't go back in the tunnel . . . not yet. He hooked the lantern on the ladder and extinguished the flame. There was only one thing he could do.

A deep breath, count of three, and he lifted the trap-door out with his arms and his shoulders. Up and rolling out on the wet grass, he was just a dozen yards from the barbed-wire belt in front of the border fence. He could see a stand of trees, a ploughed field, houses on the outskirts of the village he'd noticed from the other side. Where were the guards? They must have gone to sleep. On to his hands and knees, dropping the door back, and he scrabbled to replace the covering of turf and leaves. Then stooping low he made his way lightly into the trees. A lot of things flitted through his mind as he searched for somewhere to hide: that he was across the border with no contacts close by, no map, no papers, and no idea where Bennett's man in the bowler hat was going; that if he waited an hour or two he might find the strength to go back along the tunnel – but if he did, what next, because he would have wasted an opportunity and there wouldn't be another for at least a fortnight. He wondered why it hadn't occurred to him before that Bennett's man was probably the third payment in the ledger. Was Brinkerhoff an alias, or did people know him by that name in the village? He thought of Tinsley stumbling over to the barn and cursing him for a 'bloody fool'; that Ramble would say the same but more delicately. He touched the cut above his eye that he'd picked up in the tunnel, then he touched the rough cross beneath his shirt. Would he make it as far as the village? He remembered Marshall's story of the shell-shock case wandering no man's land with a death wish, and he remembered he'd pretended to laugh.

16

Sanctuary

INNES STEPPED OUT of the trees with the sense of elation felt by those just glad to have taken a decision come what may.

In the first days at the Front his company had walked into battle in a line. Some were still doing the same two years later on the Somme. Innes had encouraged his men to use cover until they made their last dash for the wire. Sometimes it ended there, sometimes they didn't make it that far, sometimes they fought their way into an enemy trench, shooting and stabbing and shouting like savages. But first there was the dash for the wire. He'd done it half a dozen times – more – but he could only recall a few hazy images, like the flickering pictures in an end of pier peep-show box.

Out from the trees then, into open ground turned by the plough, with only a scrappy hawthorn hedge for cover. Later, he would remember the bone-weary weight of the mud on his boots and the old pain in his thigh. On the other side of the hedge the enemy was speaking in the Bavarian dialect, and that reminded him momentarily of a woman from Munich, a student he'd fallen in love with for a few hours. He would remember lying on his side with his head in a furrow – the mud liquid grey and smelling like shit – and feeling an urge to laugh when he realised he'd run to the hedge for cover but the lane was crawling with Germans – it was their service route from the village to the border.

Of the last dash across a gap in the hedge to the wall he would remember nothing more than the pounding of his heart and relief at the feeling of rough brick against his cheek. He would forget that he lost his hat.

He heard more German before he could think. Flat in the shadow between two houses he waited for three members of the *Landsturm* militia to stroll by. No Brinkerhoff, which was to be expected, but either he lived in the village or he had a regular contact there. The village was under curfew, shut tight for the night and no one would answer the door. It wasn't much of a place, just one main street to a small market square and some darker side streets. The leather and hobnail patrols didn't concern Innes greatly; always his fear in these places was the other man in the shadows. A light step from a doorway and the click of a secret policeman's revolver in the back.

There was a bar on the main street with soldiers drinking coffee and beer, and he could hear the echo of boots and orders shouted in the square. He glanced at his watch. It was almost ten o'clock. They were preparing to change the guard at the border. He would have to lose the watch because it was too smart for a man in shop-keeper's clothes. Pity – it was a present from his father.

The village church was an ugly brick affair on the square. A light was shining in the ground-floor window of the guest house opposite. The Germans were probably using the place as a billet. He found the parochial house at the corner of a narrow street facing the east end of the church: close neighbours, no lights visible, no possibility of forcing entry through the front door. But there was a back-yard door to the left of the house. Innes lifted the latch slowly with his thumb. The hinges of the door needed oiling – perhaps that was deliberate. The windows on the ground floor of the house were shuttered but there was one a little higher he could reach from the roof of the coal-shed, and casting around the yard he found a poker. Careless priest, his window-frame was rotten and the catch lifted from the wood with only a little pressure. Head first on to a half-landing, he turned to lower the window back in place. Then he heard footsteps and the arc of an oil lamp began creeping round the stair towards him.

Someone said in Flemish, 'Who is it?' There was a slight tremor in his voice. He was an elderly man.

'Father? Don't be afraid,' said Innes. 'I need your help.'

The priest stopped climbing at the curve of the stair but Innes could see his smoky shadow on the wall opposite, the lamp in his right hand, lifting the bottom of his cassock a little with his left.

'Who are you? Tell me what you want, there's nothing valuable here.'

'Can I talk to you, Father? Please be careful, your light will be seen at the window. If I come down . . .'

The priest didn't reply at first, his shadow shimmering in the heat from the lamp, then he turned and walked back down the stairs.

He was waiting for Innes in the parlour. The lantern was on the table near the door and he had walked round it to stand in the shadow on the other side. He was a thin grey man of more than sixty, with striking blue exophthalmic eyes. His cassock was too big and worn shiny in places, loose threads hanging from the buttons. Thirty-three buttons, Innes remembered, for the years of Christ's life, only, two years were missing. He was gazing intently at Innes.

'I'm a British spy.' Innes paused, inviting the priest to say something. He didn't so Innes said, 'You know, if the Germans find me I'll be shot.'

Another silence, then a simple 'Yes.'

'I need your help, I need somewhere to hide.'

The priest dropped his gaze for a moment. 'You may be lying. Perhaps you're working for the Germans.'

'I'm a British officer, Father.'

'Spies, secret policemen, how can one tell?' he asked, coolly. 'And what is there to choose?'

'Do you believe that, Father?'

'I believe in—' He stopped with the name of Jesus frozen on his lips. Someone was thumping the front door lightly with the meat of a fist, but firmly enough to rattle the chain and the bolts.

Innes asked, 'Are you expecting a visitor?'

'There's a curfew,' he said, 'do you think it's the Germans?'

'I don't know.' In Innes's experience, German soldiers liked to hammer, kick, and shout. 'May be one of those secret policemen. My life's in your hands, Father. I put my trust in you, if you're—'

The priest cut across him: 'Put your trust in God.'

Standing at the parlour door, shivering a little in his wet clothes and with tension too, he remembered for a moment the chaplain at GHQ and his version of the 'put your trust in' sermon. Trust in God, trust in Haig, trust in the next life, trust this priest, when trust was a very fine thread that could be snapped so easily. Was the priest a good liar? Innes could hear him reassuring someone. If there was a strange noise, it was probably a fox scavenging in the yard, he said, but he would make sure the house was secure, and thank you neighbour for your concern. The bolts slid back into place and Innes heard his footsteps approaching along the hall. Pushing the parlour door open, he said, 'It was one of my neighbours. He shouldn't have come out at this hour, it's too dangerous.'

'Thank you, Father.'

He didn't reply, he just stared, as one who sees more than

mud and blood and workman's clothes, more than skin. His protruding eyes were unblinking, confessional eyes.

'What is your name?'

'My friends here call me Lazarus.'

'What is your real name?'

Innes hesitated. 'Innes. Captain Alexander Innes.'

The priest considered this for a moment, then said, 'My name is Father Albert Claes. You say you have friends – in Dreef? Then why don't you go to them?'

'Not here, Father. Antwerp, and elsewhere. As you can see . . .' Innes touched the front of his jacket. 'I came across the border tonight.'

Father Albert nodded. 'I see.' But it wasn't clear from his voice that he believed. 'You better get dry. You were lucky, there are always lots of Germans in this village.'

He led Innes down the back stair to the kitchen, directing him to an old armchair by the range. He must have been sitting there when he was disturbed by Innes because his breviary was balanced on the arm. Innes watched him light another lamp, then shuffle to the sink to fill the kettle.

The dreariness of the decor, the yellow laundry hanging on the pulley maid and the ebony cross hanging on the wall, the bare oak and cheap bone china, the damp and the cabbage and the incense, were like every parochial house he'd ever known, like his uncle's home on Eriskay. It was familiar, it was ordinary, it was a life of duty and sacrifice.

Father Albert offered him a cup of tea, and he took it with a smile of gratitude. It was very weak and served without milk, and Innes wondered how many times the priest had used the same tea leaves. Tea, coffee, food, fuel, everything was hard to come by.

Father Albert lifted his cup to blow away the steam, then lowered it without taking a sip. 'Where in England are you from?'

Innes said he was from Scotland, from Edinburgh. He said he used to be a university teacher and that he'd studied in Germany and Amsterdam. He had volunteered for the Army and now he was a soldier-spy, but only for the duration. He said as much as he thought he needed to say to convince the priest he was who he claimed to be. Albert listened with a face schooled by a generation of parish secrets to betray no emotion.

'And what are your intentions now?' he said, at last.

'I followed someone here, Father. Do you know of a man called Brinkerhoff?'

The priest considered this for a moment; 'What do you want with this man?'

'He's a *passeur* – smuggling information, people perhaps, food . . . tea – he may not be using that name here. He may not be from this village but he would need a contact, somewhere to hide.'

Father Albert's gaze didn't waver even with the cup to his lips. Surely his tea was cold by now; Innes wondered if he liked it that way. Those eyes, the desert silence, perhaps he wore a hair shirt. If he sought his God in hardship, he lived in the best of times.

Innes felt very weary suddenly. He looked down at his hands, caked in mud and a crust of blood. 'Are you a patriot, Father?'

'Yes.'

'So many good people are fighting – priests. You know what the Germans are doing to this country? I ask a lot, I know – a leap of faith – but if I can't ask it of you Father, who else in this village?'

He nodded slowly. Then he rose and reached up to the shelf above the range. 'My sister's only son.' He offered Innes the photograph. 'Peter. He died in the first weeks.' He cleared his throat to disguise the tremor in his voice. 'A good boy. We were close. I hoped—well—' What he'd hoped for was gone, his sister's hopes too, the hopes of many mothers and fathers, and uncles. They were left with studio memories of downy boys in new uniforms – chest out, chin up, that's the spirit for the camera.

'I'm sorry, Father.' Innes handed back the photograph.

'You fought? Then you've known loss.'

'Yes.'

'Would you like something stronger than tea?'

From a kitchen cupboard he produced a bottle of wine without a label. 'I care for about a thousand souls in this village, Captain Innes, but no one by the name of Brinkerhoff . . .' Wiping a glass on a dirty towel: 'But I have heard of someone – a *passeur*, you say? – he may go by that name – from Antwerp. My housekeeper says he has money, sometimes a motor car. Goodness knows where he finds the fuel.' He poured Innes some wine. 'I'll speak to someone in the village, someone I trust to be discreet.'

Innes took a sip, then inspected his glass because it was communion wine.

Father Albert noticed: 'You have communion in your church?' He probably noticed everything.

'I'm not a good Christian, Father, but my church is your church.'

He nodded, perhaps approvingly. 'Then you know it's just wine, before the Mass.'

Innes had drunk it as wine once before, as an altar boy. He remembered how afraid he was that its warmth in his throat and stomach was something to do with hell. He was beaten for that and was almost grateful to accept it as a penance. But it used to confuse him that the blood of Christ tasted just the same.

'My uncle was a priest,' he said.

'Oh?' Father Albert didn't sound interested. 'Captain, this Brinkerhoff, he's working for the Germans?'

'I don't know. No.'

He frowned. 'For you . . . the British?'

'I can't say. It's confusing, I know. I'm sorry, Father,' he said, balancing the glass on his knee. 'It is important he doesn't know I'm here.'

They didn't discuss how long he would stay. Father Albert led him up to a room in the attic, closed the shutters, lit a candle, and presented him with a chamber pot. Innes wasn't to leave the room until he was invited to do so by the priest in person. The sheets were cold and the blankets smelt of camphor: Innes fell asleep at once. He woke before dawn, shaking, sweating, Father Albert at his bedside with a glass of water. 'You were shouting,' he said. 'A nightmare? Here, drink.'

Innes did as he was bidden. 'If it happens again, will anyone hear me?'

'No. My housekeeper comes at eight o'clock. I'll send her away.'

'Is that wise? Won't she be suspicious?'

His face stiffened a little. 'Leave that to me.'

The next time Innes woke there was light at the cracks in the shutters. His watch said almost eleven o'clock. The priest had visited a second time and left soap and water, a tarnished mirror and three books. He'd emptied the chamber pot. Innes opened the shutters just a few inches so he could wash and inspect the cut above his eye. The books were religious in character. He spent some minutes flicking through a martyrology with delicate watercolour illustrations of saints suffering in imaginatively gruesome ways. It was such silly stuff he lost his temper and tossed the book against a wall. No one was capable of that sort of smile with their guts hanging about their knees; not Peter, not Christ himself.

He lay down on the bed and listened to the rumbling of his stomach and for footfalls on the stairs. It was cold enough to see his breath. That reminded him of his uncle's parochial house too, the wind rattling the glass and whistling into the bedroom in the eaves. When it was too much to bear, when the windows were opaque with frost, he would creek down the stair to sit at the peat fire, so close the nerves in his face and hands would ache. Uncle Allan would appear with a tartan rug about his shoulders and a drip at the end of his nose, and he would ask the housekeeper to make them both a hot toddy – but no whisky for the boy.

He'd picked up the book of martyrs and folded back its creased pages before the priest came to see him with food and the story of his day.

'I asked a man I trust,' Father Albert said. 'There is a *passeur* who visits the village every few weeks. He's about forty, of medium height, dark brown hair and beard. Is that your Brinkerhoff?'

'With respect, Father, from that description . . . Does he wear a bowler hat?'

'He dresses in workman's clothes, but my parishioner says he has money. He drives a motor car, he wears a velvet waist-coat under his jacket, and boots, he wears very fine boots.'

'Tan colour, perhaps mustard yellow?'

'Yes. He must be a vain man. His name's Joseph Springer. He has things you can't buy anywhere else – food from Holland, chocolate, beer, petrol – but my parishioner says people are afraid of him.' Father Albert scratched his brow with his forefinger, and Innes noticed that his nails were dirty and needed cutting. 'He stays with Kalff, the butcher here in the village. I don't know this Kalff, he doesn't come to our church.'

'Is Springer still here, Father?'

'He left for Antwerp this morning. I have an address, do you want it?'

Innes said that he did.

'So you will go to Antwerp?'

'Yes, I think so . . . if I can.'

Father Albert leant over folded arms to stare at him inquisitorially. 'You don't sound sure it's the right thing to do, Captain.'

Sure? What could one ever be sure of in life? He needed help, he needed papers, he needed a disguise; he needed someone to deliver a letter to the cathedral in Antwerp. There were friends who would help him there, he said, but the courier would have to be careful because the Germans had their spies. No names, no faces, a collection box on the pillar at the entrance to the chapel of St Luke in the ambulatory. It had to be someone with their wits about them, someone who wouldn't panic if they were searched and could write *Lux Aeterna* on the envelope without being seen, just before they dropped it in the box.

Father Albert listened with the patience of one of his watercolour saints. It would take a couple of days, he said, but he would deliver the letter in person. He couldn't ask one of his parishioners to take such a risk.

When he left, Innes began the first of many idle hours wondering whether Springer or Brinkerhoff or Faust was worth anyone's life. From a jumble of doubts and fears he settled with the thought that no man can ever be entirely confident he acts for the best and purely out of reason.

He remembered Petit and the other members of the Suicide Club, and his anger at the waste of their lives. How much did he care? He cared some, but the anger was for his pain too; killing, almost being killed, lost friends, lost hope. They were all members of the same Club, really. He thought of Graham at GHQ, so keen for him to pursue the truth about Faust, but somewhere else. And of Cumming's one-man war to preserve the independence of his intelligence service by casting doubt on the reliability of everyone else's. He considered the motive of those 'important people', the politicians who were quick to blame Haig but didn't have the guts to replace him. And as always, he thought about Ramble and felt for the cross beneath his shirt. Ramble would try to laugh at him, shake him and then order him to 'stop thinking', because sometimes it was a curse. She believed in simple good, in the power of conscience, in sinners and in martyrs, and she would be in Antwerp.

17

Paris-Plage again

UMMING LOST HIS bowler hat between the motor car and
the entrance to the hotel. He limped in pursuit and almost
managed to pin it to the pavement with his stick before the
wind lifted it away, tumbling it along the esplanade. One of
the Continental's boy porters gave chase but it was surely a
lost cause. His wife had bought the hat in Jermyn Street only
a few weeks before. It was unforgivably careless and she would
tell him so, and because he was an old sailor he was superstitious and he wondered if it was an omen.

The dining room was as depressingly cold and gloomy as the
evening. The Staff had lit a few candles but one end of the room
was in complete darkness and so were the walls above the picture
rail and the plaster ceiling. The gilt furniture and the carpet had
seen better days: that was the story of Paris-Plage. A couple of
nurses and their army beaux from the base camp across the river
were whispering and giggling at one table; an elderly man dressed
like an undertaker's mute in an old frock-coat was bending low
over his soup at another. One of the nurses caught Cumming's
eye and gave him a tipsy smile. She was about twenty with a
bundle of red hair and china-white skin, and he wondered how
it would be to spend the evening with her. No fool like an old
fool, Shakespeare or some other clever fellow said.

The only other guest was sitting in a corner by the window
with a bottle of wine and two glasses. He was in uniform too,

late twenties, thin face, slight of stature, with the purple and white ribbon of the Military Cross on his tunic. He rose from the table with a certain lazy confidence and came forward to offer his hand.

'Stewart Graham.' His grip was disconcertingly limp. 'You've come straight from Boulogne?'

Cumming said that he had.

'And are you returning to Boulogne tonight?' Graham pulled a chair away from the table. 'There are rooms here at the Continental if you decide to stay, Captain. I can't vouch for the mattresses.' He smiled with just a corner of his mouth. 'Expect they take a pounding in this place. Perhaps you were wondering . . .' Nodding to the nurses' table: 'This is a favourite watering hole for base camp officers with girls, at least, it used to be . . .' Lowering his voice a little more: 'Before last month's trouble; the mutiny we're to pretend didn't take place.'

'I am catching a lift on a destroyer from Boulogne,' said C. 'I'm afraid I don't have a great deal of time.'

'But you'll join me in a glass of wine.' Graham offered him the bottle. 'Your chap, Innes, is no connoisseur. We drank a very good burgundy but . . .' Another slight, perhaps slighting smile. 'Do you enjoy wine, Captain?'

Cumming grunted impatiently. The chair was narrow and low and he was struggling to position his wooden leg under the table.

Graham lifted his glass in salute, then took a sip. 'Have you heard from Innes?'

'Why do you ask?'

'Oh, interest. Concern. Clever chap, admirable – you do know he's crocked, don't you? I don't mean his leg – his nerves. They're shot. Well, who wouldn't be a little jumpy after what he went through? But I saw him fall apart in my room. Thought you should know.'

Cumming pulled a pocket-watch from his waistcoat. 'You said you had something important to discuss with me?' He clicked the watch case shut. 'I must leave at nine.'

'My business is simple to state really.' Again the lopsided smile. 'I helped Innes with a certain matter . . . you know that, of course.' He paused. There was a commotion at the nurses' table. 'Hello, what's wrong with her?' The nurse with the red hair was choking and her junior officer was on his feet patting her back firmly. 'Oh dear, too much wine, I expect.' Graham inspected his glass and put it back on the table without drinking. 'The war's corrupting us, even in small ways, don't you agree?'

'You were saying,' said Cumming.

'I was saying that I helped Innes. As you know, some of us are unhappy with the way things are at GHQ. Not to put too fine a point on it, Brigadier Charteris has to go . . . and some of the others too.'

On the other side of the room the nurse was crying. The lieutenant – an Australian, to judge from his uniform – had taken the opportunity to slip an arm round her shoulders.

'Go on,' said Cumming.

'Some in the government would like to go further, I know, but in the Army, we see it differently. Ah, you smile. Perhaps you think Major Stewart Graham is taking too much upon himself?'

'I know of your connections, Major.'

'And I know you are trying to save your Secret Service Bureau.' Raising his hand: 'Please, Captain, we're both trying to do what is best for the country. I can be of use to you.' He put his elbows on the table and leant closer still. 'The fighting at Ypres will end in the next few weeks. All the talk of reaching the coast and knocking Germany out of the war – that's been forgotten. We will be lucky if we secure the Passchendaele ridge – and we were supposed to have taken that in the first few weeks of the battle. But Charteris is still predicting the imminent collapse of the German Army. Any sign the enemy is beaten, any small piece of prisoner gossip, is seized upon and circulated as proof that one last push will do it.' His gaze strayed beyond Cumming to the body of the dining room. Satisfied no one was paying them any attention, he said: 'Ypres won't be the last of the fighting this year; there will be more. I can't say—'

'No, of course.'

'The thing is our intelligence – the Staff at GHQ – has no credibility in the Army or with the War Office any more. No one believes any of it. So, you see, he has to go.' He considered his next words carefully. 'There are some influential people in government and the press who see the need for change – for a BGI who will tell the Chief the truth.'

'Does Sir Philip Sassoon speak to these influential people?'

'Sassoon? No . . .' He brushed the question aside with a gesture. 'They have complete faith in the Chief, and so does the Army. No one believes there is anyone better.' His gaze wandered past Cumming to the waiter, who was approaching their table with a menu. The old man in the frock-coat had gone and the couples were on their feet ready to leave. Cumming wondered if the nurse with the red hair was going to stay the night at the hotel. She was giggling uncontrollably again as she struggled to walk in a straight line. Did she know what she was doing and what might happen next? The Australian was going to make love to her for the price of a boiled chicken and potatoes.

'The recriminations have begun, of course . . .' Graham was speaking again. 'Charteris blames the weather, the politicians, the French. He thinks if he is forced out it will be the Chief next, and I rather think Field Marshal Haig feels the same way.'

Cumming nodded slowly. 'I see. Your friends are worried that if Field Marshal Haig doesn't make changes to his Staff—'

'Downing Street will get its way, yes. Although God knows who they'll find to put in Sir Douglas's place.'

Cumming took his monocle out and wiped his eye with his forefinger. 'I have no idea what Downing Street thinks. But I will certainly inform those that need to know, of what you and your *influential* friends in government think – if that is the purpose of this meeting?'

'I'm a great admirer of the Bureau, Captain. I am confident we will be able to help each other in this matter.'

'You're offering to keep me informed?'

'To do what's best for the Army.'

'I see.' Cumming slipped his monocle back and gazed at him intently. 'Your friends know of your intentions?'

'No.'

He didn't believe Graham but he nodded slightly all the same. 'Perhaps I will join you in a little.' Pouring half a glass of wine he lifted it to the candle to consider its colour, then its nose. 'Very good, I'm sure.'

'Do you think so?'

Cumming ignored his smile. 'And in your opinion, this network or agent – Faust – GHQ is placing too much trust in this source? It occurred to Innes – and to me, actually – that you were sending us on a wild goose chase.'

'No. I'm sure Faust is genuine. Captain Macrae came to me with his concerns – we met here – this table.' He paused. 'I admit, Faust isn't our first concern. Faust is just one source. If it wasn't Faust it would be something else, because Charteris is the problem. More than that, the problem, one might say, is the way things are done in intelligence at GHQ.'

Cumming watched him pick up his glass and sip his wine. He wasn't as easy as he pretended to be. 'You asked about Innes? He's chasing your Faust. No one knows where.'

He frowned. 'I didn't make Faust up, Captain.'

Cumming wasn't sure. Faust was such a convenient distraction. He might have said that Graham's influential friends wanted rid of Innes and they'd got their way; and he might have said, they'll do all in their power to hold the prime minister at bay. He might have said those things, but he didn't because it wasn't the Secret Service Bureau's battle. Poor Innes.

The boy porter he'd sent in search of his bowler hat was waiting at the cloakroom door. He'd found it floating upside down in a puddle. Cumming felt obliged to tip the lad, although it went against the grain.

18

Antwerp

THEY WERE TWO priests on their way to Antwerp to confer with their bishop. Lux made the necessary arrangements. He sent an identity card in the name of Father Vincent van Linden, a travel pass, a cassock, a white collar and a cape. Father Albert borrowed a horse and trap from a farmer. 'Do I look like a priest?' Innes asked at the door of the parochial house.

Father Albert considered him for a moment. 'You look like a man who carries a heavy burden,' and reaching inside his cassock he produced a rosary of ebony beads. 'That you shall keep,' he said.

They took the road to Hoogstraten, hard rain soaking through their capes, splashing on their hands and the seat. Father Albert sat with his eyes closed and his chin on his chest, drops dripping from the broad brim of his hat on to his knees. Innes held the reins and showed the whip to their mare, relieved to be away after three days in the attic room with only his thoughts and the priest for company. His gaze fixed on the bobbing head of the horse, the rain, the rhythm of her hoofs and of the wheels lulled him into something like a stupor.

They left the trap at a stable in the village and bought tickets for the next steam tram to Antwerp. Father Albert introduced him to the clerk in the booking office as a priest from Brussels. 'They'll check your identity cards on the tram and at the station in Antwerp,' the clerk said, with knowing eyes. 'I'm afraid they don't make exceptions for priests, Father.'

The seats at the front were occupied by soldiers of the *Landstrum* militia, their black oilskin caps arranged neatly in the rack. The rest of the carriage listened to their shouts and laughter in hostile silence. A young woman insisted on giving up her place for Innes as a mark of respect for the cloth. Father Albert sat in front of him staring out at the soot-stained countryside, the heathland, the spoil heaps, the scrappy villages. Innes wondered if he should have gone on alone. He took it for granted he could put people's lives in danger, that it was their duty to help a spy. One day he would take that leap and fall. He took out his torn brown identity card, five inches by four; he didn't look much like the priest in the photograph. Most of the network's documents were prepared by the owner of a print shop in Rotterdam, then tossed over the border fence in a weighted bag, but someone must have cobbled Innes's together from an old one in Antwerp. The stamp and signature of the district commandant were genuine, and the forger had tried to cover the face with a stain, but if the Germans took the trouble to investigate they would discover the card wasn't registered with the police.

Their first German policeman was in a hurry. He boarded in Oostmalle and walked between the seats, his eyes flitting from card to face. Innes smiled and said something in German but he didn't reply. He left them at the last stop in the village, ready to catch a tram going back the other way. The second policeman merely glanced round the carriage, shouting a few words of greeting to the militia men at the front. The tram passed beneath one of the forts in the ring round the city, its wall tumbled by the enemy's artillery in the first weeks of fighting. Soldiers of the new garrison clattered up the steps at the next stop, veterans of real fighting to judge by their wound stripes and their faces. Innes caught snatches of their conversation; the things soldiers like to speak of always, everywhere. Their *Unteroffizier* was from the east of his country's empire and he didn't care much for priests, because who could trust a man who wasn't interested in a woman. Priests were cunts, especially young ones, he said, catching Innes's eye.

No one in the carriage was surprised he was disrespectful because he was the occupier, the bully who knew he was hated and wanted to be feared, too. *Schrecklichkeit* or terror, the enemy called it, and it was a cold policy of shooting, looting, reprisals, and forced labour in the Reich. All propaganda, the peace party in Britain liked to say; Innes would like them to take a tram ride with him into Antwerp and see.

By one o'clock they were approaching the remnants of the inner ring of forts they used to call the last arsenal of the kingdom: banks and moats and brick and stone redoubts that had no place in the new age of long-range guns. The tram rattled to a halt in a cloud of soot and steam in front of the Turnhout Gate. Local workmen were being held in a queue at the stop for a security check and soldiers and another plain-clothes policeman were the first into the carriage. He stood at the top of the steps, commanding attention, in no hurry to do his duty. His gaze drifted back and forth across the aisle. In his late forties, Innes would say, with a chipped and angry face. A dark-corners policeman of a sort the locals were calling Berlin vampires. He started examining identity papers on the other side of the tram. Innes felt the prickle of fear on his skin and pinched his knuckles. He had to be calm and he had to concentrate. There were soldiers on the pavement and more in the carriage, and he wouldn't get far in a cassock if he tried to run. Besides, there was Father Albert to consider.

The policeman was questioning the woman who'd surrendered her seat to Innes. His voice was quiet and firm, his Flemish quite poor and interlaced with German. Fräulein's papers were in order and he was handing them back to turn across the aisle. Innes gripped the seat in front to rise. A diversion: he would try to deflect the policeman, make a fuss, protest about the *Unteroffizier* who'd called him a cunt, stand up, point, demand an apology. He was so tense he didn't hear footsteps until they were just behind him and someone was barging past his shoulder, someone in a cloth cap and blue worsted workman's jacket, so slight he was surely only just a man. But he shoved the policeman so hard he fell sideways and cracked his head on the steel bar at the top of the seat.

The workman was at the entrance before the members of the *Landstrum* thought to move. He almost fell down the steps, stumbling on to one knee at the feet of an old woman in the queue at the stop. In the seconds it took him to rise, the alarm was raised in the carriage, with shouting, the clatter of boots and guns, and the policeman hammering on the carriage window. He was so close Innes could smell his cheap scent. His escort was pushing through the queue, but the workman was on his feet and away. The soldiers must have shouted a challenge because people were parting like a wave in panic. There he was again, twenty yards and running, but running too straight. He seemed to hesitate, then he turned left to run along the wall. But he was too close to the Germans, and they were kneeling, taking aim from the pavement. It was the veteran sergeant who put him down, the sergeant who hated priests.

Innes watched the soldiers gathering round the body, and the policeman walking to where it lay. 'We must go,' he whispered in Father Albert's ear. The old priest glanced back at Innes. 'I have to see to him.' ·

The workman was sprawled face down, arms and legs bent in an unnatural shape. Blood was seeping into the cracks between the stone setts near the dead man's head, but the bullet hole was in the middle of his chest. The shot would have carried bone and muscle to his heart. The policeman gave the order to turn him over, and Innes followed Father Albert to his knees.

He must have known the prayer because he could hear his voice in unison with the priest. He was conscious of the vampire standing above him too, of the perfect crease in his brown trousers, of his feet shuffling impatiently and the toecaps of his boots. Just a boy of about fifteen, shock and fear frozen on his face. Innes reached forward to close his eyes but a soldier brushed his arm aside. They searched his body and found his identity card, a family photograph, and something the policeman seemed to think might be a message.

Innes touched Father Albert's arm, and he inclined his head a fraction in acknowledgement. With a great sweep of his right hand he made the sign of the cross over the boy, and slowly, stiffly got back to his feet. No one thought to prevent them slipping away. Local men who'd seen them kneeling by the body touched their hats, and an old lady asked Father Albert for a blessing.

They walked through the gate into the city and turned off the busy rue des Champs into the back streets north of the zoological garden. The lantern spire of the Cathedral of Our Lady was their landmark, glimpsed at the angle of buildings, across squares, white against shelves of deep grey sky that promised more rain or even snow. They walked in silence, shaken by the death of a boy in a street, at a tram stop, with ordinary people going about their ordinary Saturday business, shopping for the little they could buy. Innes was as used to death as the priest. He was used to the taste and smell of that place where men lived only to take life, and fought their great war for a civilisation that was somewhere else. At the Front, civilisation was memory, sometimes of a wild mountainous place, sometimes of a city with fine buildings and statues and paintings and little shops and pavement cafés; a city like Antwerp or Edinburgh. Except, in Antwerp people were shot in the street. Was Father Albert able to make sense of the boy's death as a sacrifice, like the stories in his book of martyrs? There wasn't the paper and ink in the world to tell of so many sacrifices.

There were German soldiers in the cathedral too. They'd come to wonder at Gothic beauty, arches and aisles, the paintings by Flemish masters in the ambulatory. Some were there to pray. Centuries of invaders had prayed in the Cathedral of Our Lady. Puritanical zealots and republicans had visited their hate on the place, smashing wood and stone. The sanctuary lamps were still burning and Christ was still hanging on his cross in the windows, the light pouring through his many colours, his image fading and forming on the stone flags of the nave like a vision of the resurrection.

Innes's instructions were to meet Lux in the south transept where he would be hearing confessions between two and three. They were a little early, but Father Albert needed to rest.

'Then perhaps you should leave me,' Innes said, 'it would be best, Father.' Father Albert knew Lux was a churchman but no more, and that was how it should be. They sat in a side chapel until he was ready. Innes asked if there was somewhere in the city he might stay, but he wanted to return to his village to take the Sunday Masses. He listened to Innes's thank-you and did his best to smile.

'I pray it will all be over soon and I will pray for you,' he said in his cool way.

They shook hands and Innes watched from the chapel arch
as he walked slowly along an aisle towards the west door, his
shoulders a little hunched as he stepped aside for a German
soldier. When he'd gone, Innes lit a candle for him, and the
boy, and for everyone else. He was still contemplating its flame
when he heard the swish of a robe, and before he could turn
someone touched his shoulder.

'Father Vincent.'

'Abbé, how are you?' He looked thinner than the last time,
wearier, closer to fifty years than forty, a black stork in his
cassock and biretta. 'Is it six months?'

'Easter, with Ramble,' he said. 'I wasn't expecting you.'

'I wasn't expecting to come. Is she in the city?'

'You must tell me why you have come, but not now. There
were no difficulties?'

'Just this,' he said, taking his identity card from his pocket.

The abbé nodded. 'I'm arranging something better.'

'And a boy . . .' Innes paused for a smartly dressed man
passing the entrance to the chapel. 'He was on the tram, about
fifteen – they shot him by the Turnhout Gate. Do you think
he was one of ours?'

The abbé didn't know and his immediate concern was for
the living. 'Tell them you come from Lux,' he said, and he
handed Innes the address of a safe house near the Church of
St Andrew. 'Go now. I'll visit when I can.'

It was ten minutes from the cathedral, just off the rue Nationale.
Madame answered the door because monsieur was in the park
with their children. Innes tried to thank her and compliment
her upon her house but she wanted to hurry him up to the
draughty space beneath her roof tiles. She was frightened and
snippy, because it was her husband's decision to shelter a spy.
She gave Innes a candle stub, matches, and two blankets, and

he found somewhere between the tangle of crossbeams and frames to stretch out. But he wasn't comfortable and when he closed his eyes and drifted, he was back at the gate with the upturned face of the boy. At six o'clock madame brought him a bowl of thin soup, a bundle of ill-fitting workman's clothes and the news that he was to move again. The abbé had arranged a safer house closer to the river, she said, and his guide was waiting downstairs. That night he slept in a tailor's roof.

Early Sunday morning he was on the move again, walking along the river towards the docks in the north of the city, past the offices of the shipping lines and the old castle they call 'the Stone', the bells of the cathedral summoning the faithful to the first Mass of the day. Another house, another attic room, a window with a view across the Scheldt to Fort Isabelle, and to the south he could see the top masts of the ships in the Bonaparte Basin, idle and rusting. His protector was an old lady called Madame Thomas, a doctor's widow and a Walloon from the south who spoke to Innes in French. Her home was a fine Flemish house in a terrace of fine houses, but Madame struggled to climb her steep stairs, and she'd sold her best furniture to pay for food and coal.

'I've arranged for new papers,' the Abbé Buelens said when he visited on Monday morning. 'It will be a few days, but they're coming from the usual place this time.'

They were sitting in the attic room, sharing Innes's single mattress. The abbé's knees were drawn up to his chin, and his bony hands were smoothing the creases from his cassock. 'You're warm enough? I will bring you more clothes when I can.'

'Thank you, Father.'

'It must be important to bring you here unannounced.'

'Yes. I think so.'

The abbé raised his eyebrows in a show of surprise. They were bushy, and black like his hair, and they were the first thing anyone noticed about his face. 'You don't sound very sure.'

'I'm looking for a man called Springer. He may use the name Brinkerhoff. He may use other names.'

'And this Springer or Brinkerhoff . . . ?'

'A spy. A British Army spy.'

Buelens closed his eyes and pinched the bridge of his nose. 'I see,' he said, although it was plain enough that he didn't.

'Have you heard of an agent called Faust, Father?'

'British too?'

'Springer may be this Faust. I need to know.'

'And Lazarus . . .' The abbé opened his eyes and reached out to touch his arm. 'This is more important than our work?'

'It *is* important, Father.'

He inclined his head thoughtfully for a moment. 'If I appear reluctant, well things are difficult. We have had our troubles with your British Army . . . but I have faith in you,' he said, turning open hands over as if he were celebrating the sacrifice of the Mass.

Innes had written down everything he knew about Springer, and it didn't amount to more than half a dozen lines. 'He's something on the black market,' he said, sheepishly. 'There won't be many men with the petrol to run a private motor car.'

The abbé looked up from the paper. 'And yellow boots, you say.'

'Tan, actually, but he may not be wearing those.'

'No, I suppose not.' The abbé chuckled, then he began to laugh. It was infectious laughter of a sort that must run its course. But Innes could see even through tears that he was worn out by secrets and responsibilities. Trench laughter they called it in the line, where men would often go off at the slightest thing.

'That's better,' the priest said, wiping his eyes with a small lace handkerchief. 'I feel better.'

There was silence between them for a while. Then Innes asked: 'You said there were difficulties?'

'Our networks near the Front . . . we've lost some brave people, good people. It was my fault.' He closed his eyes for a second and passed a hand over his brow. 'We took on people we didn't know from one of your Army's networks and one of them was an informer. We're trying to start again from scratch in Thielt. You know, they've arrested one of our priests there.' He frowned his Old Testament frown. 'Things are hard enough for the church, the Cardinal is virtually a prisoner in his own palace.'

'But you're safe? And Ramble?'

He gave a little shrug. 'None of us are safe, we're all in God's hands.'

Innes was sorry to lose the abbé's company, and he regretted not being entirely honest with him about the troubles at GHQ. Priests did know something of politics as a rule. Was the half-truth Innes told the abbé any better than a lie? Rising from the mattress, he walked over to the window to gaze at the shifting sky and for just a minute a burst of sunshine on the river. He would have hours to spend considering the stain on his soul (if he possessed one), and the time he would have to pay for it in purgatory (if there was such a place). The abbé had promised to send him some books. He couldn't leave the attic during the day, or the house at any time before his new papers were ready. 'You'll have plenty of time for contemplation,' the abbé had said, enviously. He was a prayerful man. Innes wished he could paint the moods of the North Sea sky, listen to music on a phonograph or the market-day stories of Madame Thomas. He didn't enjoy his own company, because like most people with something to forget or regret, he needed to be busy. In hours of idleness he heard whispers: Faust was an excuse to run and hide from the war in an attic, one voice said; he was risking the lives of others because he was afraid of the tunnel, whispered another; and a third said, he should be dead, because it had been impossible to escape that dug-out. Dawn to dusk for four days, and at night when Madame gave him a candle and he trudged back up the stairs.

On the last day of October she brought him a book by Charles Dickens and a note from the abbé. The book was an edition of *Great Expectations* in Flemish. The note said the network had traced Springer. He owned a nightclub in the south of the city, one of only a few permitted by the German military, and much frequented by the same. The abbé wrote of its *low reputation* and at the bottom of the page he'd scrawled a line in quotation marks: '*I am the spirit that negates.*' Innes guessed it was from Goethe's play *Faust*.

'No need. He says he's going to visit you,' Madame Thomas said when Innes asked her to deliver his reply.

He was lying on the mattress in the fading light of the late afternoon with the book open at his side when he heard voices and then the footsteps of the abbé on the stairs.

'You thought I'd forgotten you, I hear.' The abbé looked at him a little reprovingly. 'You should know we've been busy on your behalf.'

Innes said he did know and he was grateful.

'Your papers.' The priest handed them to him. 'Madame Thomas's nephew from Namur, in the city to work.'

The network's forger had used a file photograph of Innes in a cloth cap and simple suit. The travel stamps seemed in good order. 'I'd like to visit Springer's club,' he said.

'It will be difficult.' The priest's black brow met in a single intimidating line. 'The Germans use the place.'

'Yes, you said in your letter, Father. All the same, I must. I can't be sure this Springer is Faust, but he may—'

'Oh, he knows something about Faust. Have you read Goethe, Captain? Springer's club is called The Mephistopheles – it's too much of a coincidence, don't you think? Mephistopheles is the devil who does Faust's bidding in return for his soul when he dies.'

Innes nodded. 'Do you know when Springer bought the club?'

'There's someone downstairs who might know.' Glancing pointedly at his watch. 'The Cardinal wishes to speak to me. I must go. Are you coming?'

Innes followed the priest to the ground floor where Madame Thomas was waiting with his coat and his biretta.

'Your name is Olivier.' He offered Innes his hand. 'I know I don't need to say so, but be careful, Olivier. As for the club, my friend will help you with that. I'll try and visit you tomorrow. Now madame, you will see me to your door?' he said, turning to the old lady.

Innes watched them walk along the hall. At the front of his mind he heard the priest say, 'Your nephew's name, madame?', and he heard her voice, self-deprecating, unsure: 'Olivier from Namur.' But at the back of his mind he was considering the smile the abbé had tried to disguise as he turned away. It was the sort of knowing smile he used to imagine on the face of the priest in the confessional when he ran through his sins as a teenage boy. The sort of smile that made him realise some things should always remain between a man and his maker.

'The parlour. In the parlour,' Madame said, shooing him to the door. He was shivering, but not so Madame might see. It was foolish to be apprehensive of what he most devoutly wished for, and troubling because he hadn't imagined he would feel that way. Stop thinking, Ramble would say, because some feelings are beyond sense, beyond your reason, they are just how it is to be human.

He took a deep breath and opened the door. There was a small coal fire opposite and an oil lamp on a table by the hearth. Then he saw her standing in the shadow of the room by the drapes. The shutters were closed but the drapes were open. She was holding one, her left arm raised above her head, watching him watching her. He couldn't see her face.

'You shouldn't have come to Antwerp,' she said, coolly. 'Will you leave us please, Madame Thomas.'

The door closed and they stood staring at each other. She looked like the middle-aged grocer's widow that she was and he wanted to say so: that was his injured pride. But she would laugh or worse, she would feel sorry for him.

'I came for Faust,' he said. 'Lux has told you?'

'Yes, of course,' she said, taking a step out of the shadow. Her dark brown hair was arranged in an unruly bun – he knew it was tinged with grey. Her scarf was on the back of a chair and she was wearing her black wool coat over her charcoal grey skirt and her blue and white striped blouse. They were her Sunday clothes.

'You're sure it was for this Faust?' Plain from her tone that she didn't believe him.

'For goodness sake, Maria . . .' He lifted his hands in exasperation: 'I followed him – Brinkerhoff, Springer whatever his name is – there wasn't time to warn you.'

She took another step towards the light. Now he could see her face. It was a strong face. As always, she was wearing too much rouge. Her eyes were dark brown, set wide and large, her lips a full and perfect bow, her nose too broad for classical taste. She would only admit to forty; he knew she was closer to fifty. No amount of powder and rouge could mask those years, her care, her responsibilities. Pretty once, perhaps, Innes thought her handsome still, and decent and determined and wise. He loved her.

'It wasn't for me?' The firelight was flickering in her eyes. 'You didn't come back because of me?'

He laughed and it sounded false. 'I'm not going to pretend I'm not pleased to see you . . . or do you want me to?'

'You put people in danger – Father Albert, and some others.' She wasn't reproaching him, she was stating the facts, but he was angry all the same.

'It's a war, isn't it – here in Antwerp too – I've heard you say so enough times.'

She frowned and closed her eyes for a moment. 'Well, you're here now,' she said, opening them again.

'Faust is important,' he said, lamely. 'I didn't tell Lux, but Faust is one of the Army's chief sources of intelligence.'

She reached for the grey scarf she'd left on the back of the chair. 'I'm tired, Alexander . . .' She walked round the furniture to the fire. 'You can tell me tomorrow.'

He watched her stir the embers, then put the guard in place. Then she picked up the lamp.

'Madame Thomas has let me have a room.'

'I thought we might talk, it isn't late.'

She sighed. 'I'm tired, Alexander.' She turned to look at him, her back to the fire. 'I just want to go to bed.'

'Yes.' His voice sounded distant because he was upset. Most of all he was disappointed she'd forgotten the things he'd said to her. He wanted to shake her, he wanted to kiss her hard, he wanted her to need him too, but he knew he should behave in a proper way – proper for a soldier. She had more to think about than his feelings and the ones she used to say she had for him. But the silence between them was oppressive.

'I'm in the attic,' he said, turning to the door. 'You have the lamp.' He indicated with a gesture that she should lead the way upstairs. As she passed her skirt brushed his legs, and he caught the scent of her cologne. Why the perfume, those clothes, if she didn't care?

At the first landing she stopped and held the lamp between them. Then lifting her large brown eyes to his: 'My bedroom's here.'

'Yes,' he said, weakly. A lot of things came to mind as he repeated it more firmly: what now, and why was she behaving like this? And, he wondered if she was right, that he had come back to Belgium for her; and she was shorter than he'd remembered her, but he liked that; and no one in his brief life had made him feel so deeply; but he wasn't ashamed to desire her, because they were fighting a war, and what people might say about her age didn't matter. He swallowed hard. 'I have the cross you gave me. It's been—' He couldn't think how to describe just what it had meant to him. 'It's been with me—everywhere.'

Her expression softened and she smiled – a little coyly, he thought. Then she reached out, feeling with fingertips for the cross beneath his shirt. 'I prayed for you every day.' Her voice sounded deeper. 'I said I would, didn't I?'

He pressed her hand to his chest, her old wedding ring hard beneath the knuckle of his index finger. 'I've missed you.'

'Have you?'

Pinching her sleeve he pulled her closer, tilting her chin so he could look into her eyes. She tried to turn away. She was shaking, biting her lip. She was trying not to laugh aloud.

'What?' he said.

'So, you still want to have me?' she replied.

'Ramble, I hate you,' he said.

19

The Mephistopheles

S HE LIKED HIM to undress her. It took a little time – she liked
that. They made love with the light up because she liked that
too. Sometimes when they made love she would catch his wrists
and say 'slower' or 'harder' or 'kiss me there'. She didn't like him
to whisper, not even 'you're beautiful' or 'I love you'. 'Shut up.
Stop thinking,' she said, with a finger to his lips. He liked her to
sit wet on his stomach, her scented hair in his face. If she didn't
come before him, she would say, 'finish me off' and pull his hand
down there. She knew her own mind in all things, or she seemed
to. She liked to be in charge, she liked certainty. Perhaps that was
some sort of insecurity. She was clever and would listen to reason,
but most of her decisions were intuitive. Once she'd made up her
mind something felt right it was hard to shake her. That was a
strength and a great weakness, or so it seemed to him. But in
bed she was passionate and without inhibition.

'Do you love me?' he asked when they finished.

A short laugh and she turned on her side, hand to his cheek,
craning forward to kiss him.

'Say it,' he said.

She smiled and stroked his face with her fingertips.

'Go on,' he demanded.

She kissed him again, so suspicious of words. Spies were
liars; she was a soldier.

*

Later, he watched her while she was sleeping, his arm beneath her pillow, her head against his chest. She wasn't vain. The powder and rouge were the habit of years at a grocer's counter. She wouldn't care that he could trace those years at the corners of her eyes, in deep lines above her lip. 'What would your mother say if she knew you went with me?' she'd asked him once. He'd made light of it: 'That Madame Simon was very lucky.' But his mother would be horrified: that was Edinburgh, where even Catholics were Puritans. His mother was from an island in the west but she'd lived in the cold east a long time. Speak to me in Scottish, Ramble sometimes said – she meant Gaelic. She liked to think he came from an island with mountains where people spoke a language that didn't sound German or French. She wasn't interested in Edinburgh.

Turning on to her back now, the sheet slipped from her shoulder. He reached beneath it to touch her breast, running his hand lightly down to her belly. They'd lived together for a month, travelled together, and she'd helped to arrange his arrest and sentence to labour in the enemy's forbidden zone. Lux was important but it was Ramble's network, the watchers were her people. They trusted her because she was the grocer's widow from Louvain, an ordinary working woman – and yet extraordinary. Madame Maria Simon used to make the customers smile – the men at least. Remember how she would sing at her counter? And on market days she liked to haggle for the fun of it. Then she had slipped away from Louvain. To the Netherlands, her daughter said. Who could blame her? Things were almost unbearable. Enemy soldiers were punishing her city. They shot the mayor and the police officers, they burnt thousands of homes and one of the finest old university libraries in the world; they had raped her neighbours, beaten her local priest, and deported young men to work in their Reich.

247

Innes was fascinated and jealous of her past. He could see and feel it in her body. But she didn't like to talk about the past or the future. He knew she was the mother of two grown-up daughters. When he'd tried to press her to say more, she'd grabbed him below and squeezed him so hard he cried out. She had laughed and said something in Flemish like 'that'll learn you'. He'd laughed too, through his tears.

Rolling on his side, he kissed her dark eyebrows, then her cheek, then her neck.

'No,' she mumbled sleepily, and she tried to shove him away.

But beneath the sheet he was fondling and kissing her breasts. Eyes still closed, she pushed his head again. 'I'm tired Alexander,' she said. But he kissed her tummy then down to her thighs. He knew he would be able to arouse her because she'd shown him how to.

She woke him at about five o'clock. 'You were shouting' – her hand on his brow – 'one of your dreams.' She stroked his forehead, then bent to kiss him tenderly.

'This is like a dream,' he said when she finished.

'Don't be silly.' Swinging her legs out from under the covers, she reached over to the table to turn up the lamp. 'I need the loo, and we should talk about this Faust of yours.'

He watched her walk across the room, broad-hipped and sensuous. Taking a dressing-gown from the hook on the door, she turned to smile at him, lifting her hair over the collar. It was an old blue modesty gown, ankle to chin, but it was open and he could see her large breasts and the dark triangle of her pubic hair between her plump thighs. She was on parade. Perhaps she wanted to remind him that after all the kissing and the caressing, this was his lover, old enough to be his mother.

'When we've talked you must go upstairs before Madame Thomas is awake,' she said, turning back to the door.

He told her about his time at GHQ, about the Suicide Club and Brigadier General Charteris, and he could see from her face that she disapproved of one British intelligence officer spying on another. But she said he was right to speak his mind to Field Marshal Haig, that there was nothing the Army's Suicide Club could manage better than her people.

'So, you think this Faust is a German spy?' she said.

'It's possible,' he replied.

She frowned. 'You've followed him here, you must think so.'

'Faust may be a network. It's such an important source.' He bent down to pick his pants off the floor. 'My orders were to find out more.'

She clucked disapprovingly.

'Well?' he said, rising from the bed to pull them up. 'What is it?'

'It seems to me, if you're wrong you'll do more harm than good. Did your C tell you to come here?' Before he could answer she flapped a hand at him. 'No. Don't tell me. Don't.'

'I hope he trusts me to make the right decision.'

She gazed at him for a moment, then leant forward to touch the scar on his thigh. Her fingers were long and thin and she took great care of her nails: that was one small vanity. 'I have someone who can take you to the Mephistopheles, a good comrade. He's met your Brinkerhoff – everyone here calls him Springer, by the way.'

He bent to kiss the top of her head. 'Thank you.'

'I don't want the abbé to worry about this matter,' she said. 'We've lost friends in Brussels and in Mons, and the Germans are watching all the priests who are close to the cardinal.'

She was looking up at him with her big brown eyes and her gown had fallen open at the neck again. He wanted her a third time. Perhaps she could see it in his face.

'You must wash yourself and go upstairs,' she said.

'And later?'

'I must organise things.' She picked up her towel. 'Now go.'

Vincent Luyten was a middle-aged family man, solid and sober as bank managers everywhere seem to be. He had a big bald head, he wore small round tortoiseshell glasses, and he blinked behind them like an anxious owl. Not the sort of man anyone would associate with rule breaking or resistance, but Jesus and the abbé had called him to the service of the network. He met Innes at a house near the club and insisted on the correct procedure, turning back the lapel of his jacket to reveal three straight safety pins. Innes did the same.

'Springer's a good customer of the bank,' he explained, 'a valuable one, I mean. But I don't think respectable people go to his club.' He pursed his lips disapprovingly. 'There will be prostitutes.'

'They make very good spies,' Innes observed. 'Listen, are you sure you're ready for this?'

The club was in a large house near the city's southern train terminus and there was a girls' school at the end of the street. 'Mephistopheles' was flaking red from the sign above the door. The shutters were closed and the only visible light was through a chink in curtains at a top-floor window: it was a word-of-mouth sort of business. Innes knocked and the door was opened by a muscular young man in an ill-fitting suit. 'You have an invitation?'

'Do we need one?' Innes replied. 'My friend here knows Monsieur Springer.'

He peered at them suspiciously. 'You've been here before?'

'Don't you want our business?'

He hesitated. 'You know the boss, you say? Let me see your papers.'

*

250

The doorman introduced Lily, who showed them to a couch and offered to serve glasses of wine. Innes asked for a bottle. The couch was deep and soft enough for a man to sink in and lose his soul. It was the old drawing room, a place for the family, for polite conversation, singing, charades. Monsieur Springer had made some changes. At one end he'd built a small stage, at the other a bar, and he'd painted and furnished the room in burgundy and gold. In the flickering light of the large fire it looked like a cheap theatre set, almost too seedy to be truly sinful. It reminded Innes of the haze and the taste of ash the morning after.

About a dozen customers were lost in the couches or lolling on their arms, whispering in German and Flemish and French to their girls. At the chimney-piece, three junior officers in the uniform of the enemy were laughing and bantering about a comrade's comic liaison with the wife of a local shopkeeper. Lily brought the bottle of wine. Bending low to pour two glasses, her loose-fitting gown fell open, and to be sure they noticed she lifted her hand slowly to the notch at the base of her neck. She spoke nicely in Flemish: her pals Sophie and Eve were anxious to meet local gentlemen, they were so pretty and lively . . . look, standing at the bar with Monsieur Springer. Not now, Innes said. She sighed and smiled her brittle smile, touching his arm like a dear friend. Then she gathered her gown together and glided back to the bar.

From the corner of his eye Innes watched her reporting to the man she called Springer. He wasn't wearing mustard boots tonight, but was ready to greet the kaiser in white tie and tails.

'That's your Springer?'

'That's him,' said Luyten. He was blinking furiously.

'Stay calm.' Innes picked up his wine. 'You remember our story? Then smile. Be confident. We're enjoying ourselves.'

Springer was whispering to his Lily, watching them too. Tall and spare, casting a long shadow on the wall behind the bar, he was only a few paces away but his face was hidden by the pile of Lily's hair. Touching her shoulder, kissing her cheek, he drifted away, first to the boisterous young men at the fire. After a few words, he moved on to someone else, circling, casually working his way round to Luyten, his intention quite clear. A moment later he was presenting his hand to the banker.

'What a pleasant surprise, monsieur. I had no idea . . .'

Luyten shifted uncomfortably. 'A favour for my young friend here.'

Springer looked at Innes. 'Monsieur, my name is Springer. This . . .' He lifted his arms as if to embrace the room. 'This is mine.'

Innes raised his glass. 'You're Mephistopheles.'

'An old name. Monsieur . . . ?'

'Thomas. Olivier Thomas.'

Springer shook his hand. 'There are still opportunities for a little wickedness here,' he said, turning back to the banker, 'to escape our troubled times.'

'My friend here is more troubled by the times than me,' Luyten replied, defensively.

'I understand, monsieur. I didn't expect a man of your reputation . . . well, perhaps you are here to protect the bank's interest. Let me say, business is good, although a little quiet tonight.'

Springer was still smiling. It was a slight smile that meant nothing, his gaze restless, his hands too. Thin and in his forties, Innes's first impression was of an unremarkable face and an unremarkable voice with an accent hard to place. His manner was obsequious, clinging, like a patina of rust or a film of oil on water.

'You're from Antwerp, Monsieur Thomas?' he said, catching Innes's eye and holding his gaze for only a moment.

'Excuse me, Monsieur Springer, but you've seen my papers?'

'One can tell so little.'

'But monsieur, you said your club was a place where we might forget our troubled lives.'

His smile tightened. 'Yes, of course.' He lifted his gaze from Innes to one of his soldier guests. 'If there's anything . . . these drinks . . .' waving his hand over the table . . . 'it would be a pleasure. Important to please my banker.' The soldier was trying to tip the pianist from her stool. 'I think it's time for a soldier's song.'

He made a stiff little bow – 'Please excuse me' – and he moved on, weaving round chairs and outstretched legs to the piano.

Luyten put down his glass with a sigh and shuffled to the edge of the couch. 'Shall we?' He was ready to leave and Innes was ready to let him, but there wasn't time to say so because Lily was shepherding another one of the girls over.

'I would like to introduce Eve,' she said.

'Hello Eve.' Innes smiled at her. How old was she? Older than she should be, thinner, paler. He offered her something to drink and a place on the couch. Lily perched on the arm.

'Do you sing, Eve?'

'A little, monsieur.'

'And you Mademoiselle Lily?'

Mademoiselle Lily said that she did – a little. Conversation wasn't going to be easy. Springer was still coaxing the soldier from the piano. Some of his comrades were jeering and calling the names of their favourite songs.

Innes wasn't sure how it was done. Was it by the hour? He sat patiently sipping his wine. One of the other girls was leading a stout soldier to the door. Worse the wear for drink, he caught his leg on the corner of a table and fell sideways over the back of a chair. Thin arm round his shoulders, with soothing words his slight companion hauled him back to his feet with practised ease. Did the girls prefer clients to drink a skinful before the walk to the bedroom? On the couch beside Innes, Luyten, ill at ease, thinking perhaps of his dear lady wife as Lily nuzzled his shoulder like a hungry mare. Now Eve's bony hand was creeping between Innes's thighs, her breath hot on his neck and in his ear. 'Do you like?' she whispered.

'Oh, yes,' he whispered back, 'is there somewhere?'

Of course there was somewhere.

Eve's room was on the second floor, at the end of a corridor, dingy as everything seemed to be since the war. She drifted, silent, no taller than his chin, and so fragile a strong wind might catch her up and carry her away. Opening her door, turning on the light, drawing him in by his sleeve. Like old Adam, he thought.

'I have wine.' She bent beside the bed. 'But you have to pay.'

'That's understood,' he said.

She said Monsieur Springer preferred payment in marks. The room reminded Innes of Paris-Plage and poor grey Agnes with her *Collected Tennyson*: how many men had she wiped from her thighs since Macrae?

'You are very handsome,' Eve said as she offered him the wine. Her voice was expressionless, her eyes too, gazing up at Innes, inviting a kiss. 'You are nervous.'

'Yes,' he said, truthful in a way.

'Your first time?' A small distant smile. 'I will get ready.'

She lit a candle and placed it on the bedside table. Sliding her gown from her shoulders she hung it over the bed end, her back to Innes.

'Get undressed,' she said.

'Yes.' He didn't move, watching her peel off her stockings, sickly white even in the candlelight, her bony shoulders bent over a bony knee and a green-black bruise at the top of her thigh. He felt sorry for her. She was no more than twenty.

Glancing back at him she said, 'Is something wrong?'

'No.' He bent down, pretending to unlace his boots. She was in nothing but her underwear.

'Just a minute.' She stepped behind a small screen. Rising quietly he took a step closer so he could see her in the cracked reflection of a cheval mirror. Opening her chest of drawers, she took out a tin and a light blue chiffon scarf. She tied the scarf tightly above the elbow of her right arm, then turned back to the tin: surely it could be for one thing only. He'd never seen it done before and he felt a frisson of disgust. What could have brought her to such a place? Stupid to ask when she was standing in her underwear, waiting to fuck a stranger. Nothing belonged to her.

She was too busy with the needle to hear him approach. Loose hair falling round her face, the point a few inches from her vein. He caught her wrist in one hand and pinned her left arm firmly back with the other. She didn't struggle.

'Let me go. You want some, you must pay,' she said, trying to face him.

'Your other customers like it?'

'I don't let them.'

'But you're willing to make an exception for me?'

'It's mine. Let me go,' her voice was defiant but she was trembling like a bird in winter.

'When you give me the needle.'

'You're going to steal it.'

'No. I want to talk, that's all.'

She let him take the syringe and place it in the tin with the rest of her drugs paraphernalia.

'All right?'

She nodded, her gaze flitting to his face and away. She was

rubbing her wrist, shivering a little, or was she experiencing some withdrawal from the drug?

'I'm sorry about your wrist.' He picked up the bottle. It was the Bayer Company's Heroin – a type of morphine, he'd heard. They sold it over the counter in Germany, or they used to when Innes was a student.

'You're cold,' he said, lifting her gown from the bed and holding it up for her. 'Are we going to be disturbed?'

She looked at him suspiciously. 'Who are you?'

'Sit down and I'll tell you.'

He told her he was a patriot, working to liberate their country, and he needed her help. He would pay her and she would come to no harm. But he could see she was afraid, her back to the bedhead, knees drawn up to her chin. She wouldn't look him in the eye.

'You might be one of Berlin's vampires,' she said. 'You might be trying to trap us.'

'Us? You mean the other girls? Springer?'

She nodded.

'Why would the Germans want to trap you?' He turned and pointed to two postcards slipped into the frame of the mirror, one of the Alps in winter, the other of a city, Heidelberg, perhaps. 'From admirers?'

'Customers,' she said.

'Aren't they your best customers? Why would they want to trap you?'

'Because they do.' Hugging her knees tighter: 'That's what Monsieur Springer says.'

'What else does Monsieur Springer tell you?'

But she refused to say.

'So I told her I was a British spy,' he explained to Ramble later. 'I wanted her to trust me.'

'A prostitute?' she replied. 'A drug addict? You're a fool.'

She was right to be angry, but he was right too, because Eve had told him all she knew. 'You see, we're on the same side,' she'd said. German soldiers told her bits and pieces and she offered them up to Springer. The other girls were doing the same, and in return he was supplying them with heroin. It came across the border once a fortnight. A prostitute called Lucy had found a label with the address of a pharmacy in Breda. 'How do you pick up these bits and pieces of information?' he'd asked. 'Sometimes we go through their pockets,' she told him, 'if they're in the Army, Monsieur Springer wants to know their units. It's on their passes. And anything about other units and guns. I don't get much of that because I don't understand it. Also, where they've been, where they're going, how they're feeling. Even bits about their families. And if I've got a policeman, well, his station, where he lives, that sort of thing. And any gossip about other officers.'

'And what does Springer do with the information you give him?'

'I'm hot,' she said, flapping her face, then loosening her gown. She kept glancing at the tin: 'Can I? Please.'

'Does the name Faust mean anything to you?'

She frowned. Faust did mean something. When he pressed her she began to cry.

Sitting at the end of her bed, touching her thin foot, he'd said: 'I need to know, Eve.'

And she'd whispered : 'Why don't you ask *him*? Ask Springer.'

'Is Springer Faust?'

She had sniffed and drawn her foot away. Only touch me if you're paying for that too, he had taken her gesture to mean, and he felt embarrassed by his presumption. 'I don't understand,' she said; 'We're on the same side.'

'Yes, it is difficult to understand.'

Eve had told him in the end because she wanted her heroin. Faust was a German with round wire spectacles, and he always wore a blue suit and a black Homburg hat. He visited the Mephistopheles a day or two before its proprietor drove out of Antwerp to the border. Faust didn't drink and he didn't touch the girls. One of Lily's German soldiers said he was a vampire because he worked at the General Government Building for the Fräulein Doktor. But he'd regretted saying that much, pinching Lily, making her cry out and promise not to tell.

'You see, Alexander,' Ramble said. 'Who can trust the word of a prostitute? Your Eve will tell this Springer next time she needs this drug.'

Innes reached beneath the sheet to caress her bottom. 'I don't think so.'

It was some time after three o'clock in the morning in the bedroom at Madame Thomas's house. He'd woken Ramble and she was still angry because he'd walked back across the city after curfew.

'But don't you think a prostitute can love her country?' he said.

Turning from him and on to her back, she replied: 'She's letting the enemy have intercourse not for her country, but for money, for her drug.'

'Perhaps that makes her hate the enemy more. That's enough.'

She pursed her lips thoughtfully. 'I don't think you can hate someone if you allow them to do that to you.'

'You say that because you can't imagine sharing that sort of intimacy without feeling.'

'Can you?' He leant forward to kiss her chest but she pushed him away. 'Besides, hate is a feeling,' she said, 'and so is fear.'

Innes remembered the look on Eve's face. 'We'll find some way.' He'd persuaded her to help him identify Faust. 'He won't see you. People come and go from the General Government all the time.' But she was frightened. 'Does Springer beat you?' He had grabbed her thin arm, forcing her to show him the puncture marks. 'Did he make you like this?' Yes, she was frightened of Springer, she was frightened of him too, but she was brave. Perhaps you had to be to give yourself to strangers. Innes had let her take her drug. He'd watched as she prepared the vein, drawing a drop of blood, shooting the drug back. She'd begged him to stay a while: 'Or people will say I didn't please you.' So he'd paid for her services and waited for her to fall into her drug sleep, covering her pale body with a sheet.

'Don't you ever feel afraid, Maria?' he asked Ramble. 'Soldiers live with fear, and some it breaks. You know what it can do.'

'You mean, to you?' She brushed his cheek with her fingertips. 'You do well enough, Alexander.'

'I try.'

Ramble turned to look him in the eye, their heads close. 'I *do* worry you fight so hard against your feelings you aren't sensible, that's all. It's as if you can't be cautious or . . . I don't know, that if you tried you'd just . . . stop.'

'Fall apart, you mean?'

She kissed him tenderly. 'Perhaps I'm a foolish woman to let you go on.'

'Do you think you can find a place where we can watch the General Government Building?'

Drawing quickly away, she said, 'That's what I mean.' Her dark eyebrows gathered in a frown. 'I've heard of this Fräulein Doktor, she's something in their military intelligence – one of their spy-catchers. You remember, Mertens?'

'Of course. He helped me in the *Operationsgebiet.*'

'He was interrogated by her. She must have had something to do with the arrests in Thielt. She knows my code-name and yours and she asked about the priest called Lux.'

'And Mertens . . . ?'

'He's dead.'

'Oh God, I'm sorry . . .'

'Listen.' She placed her hand over his mouth. 'He's gone, but she's still with us and she's dangerous. You don't know this Faust, but if he's working as a spy for your Army . . . Alexander, you must think about this, because you're risking his life.'

'I have. We can be careful. Look, it's a feeling – isn't that what you always say? Perhaps Springer is working for us; perhaps he's working for them too. Who the hell is Faust working for? How can I tell? But you've had your own troubles with our Army . . . isn't that why things fell apart in Thielt?'

She stared at him for a moment then leant forward slowly, her lips brushing the top of his arm. Then she bit him – hard. Innes pushed her head away as she sighed loudly with exasperation. 'Serves you right.'

'That's what I would expect from a prostitute, not a soldier.'

'How do you know what to expect from a prostitute? Are you telling me the truth?'

'That's it.' He tried to roll on top of her but she struggled, pushing his chest away, raising her knees.

'I'm not that easy,' she said, 'not just any old woman.'

'All right, all right.' He stopped, falling back on to his side. Ramble snorted. 'Is that the best you can do?'

'I'm a gentleman.'

'A gentleman?' she said. 'And what about all those other gentlemen? What do you think your Field Marshal Haig would say if he knew his officers were paying heroin to prostitutes?'

This time when he moved on to her she didn't resist him. 'Perhaps I'm not a gentleman. But to answer your question, I'm sure my field marshal would be disgusted.' He bent to kiss her and she closed her eyes and lifted her chin to meet him, but he stopped a couple of inches from her lips. 'There's nothing more obscene than metal tearing flesh and smashing bone. Is my field marshal offended by that?'

'Shut up, shut up, shut up,' she said.

November 1917

We have won great victories. When I look at the appalling casualty lists I sometimes wish it had not been necessary to win so many . . . When we advance a kilometre into the enemy's lines, snatch a small shattered village [Passchendaele] out of his cruel grip, capture a few hundred of his soldiers, we shout with unfeigned joy.

Prime minister, David Lloyd George, in a speech
to French government representatives in Paris,
12 November 1917

20

Intelligence Mess

'TOO AWFUL, GRAHAM, really, I can't begin to describe it to you,' Marshall said, but he tried nonetheless. 'Imagine a lead sky with cold drizzle falling, and mile after mile of blasted earth from which every decency has disappeared, only, here and there a stump, a ruined pillbox, a shattered wagon, a gun buried to the muzzle. Mud sticks like treacle, slip and you're lost; so many of our wounded drown. Imagine picking your way from crater to crater – the lips of the craters join to form a narrow isthmus, you see – but you're under fire, sometimes on your belly, advancing a few feet at a time. Run and you lose your footing – you're down, and the filth has you, and the water is many feet deep. Imagine the corruption in that water, because there are torn bodies everywhere. Then imagine what is left of a man who endures such a place.'

'Allow me, sir.' Marshall's batman stepped forward to adjust his tie. 'I'll get the mud out of the tunic in a jiffy.'

'Thank you, Seymour. The trouble is, I feel the mud here . . .' He pinched the back of his hand: 'Under my skin.'

Graham said, 'I know.'

'Do you?' Marshall turned to him from the mirror.

'I was there yesterday.'

'The thing is, I don't think we do *know*, Graham. The stink, the feel, it's a slough of despond. Here, listen . . .' Half a step to his bedside table and he picked up a worn black leather-bound book, thumbing for the place. 'You know I'm not a religious man, but this is from *The Pilgrim's Progress*: "This miry slough is such a place as cannot be mended; it is the descent whither the scum and filth that attends conviction for sin doth continually run."' He lowered the book slowly. 'And *we* are dressing for dinner.'

'You're feeling guilty for what?'

'I think we have a share in the scum and filth. Don't you?'

'I'm thankful the battle's over.' Graham leant forward to put out his cigarette. 'Our penance will be to listen to all the usual excuses offered for failure.'

Marshall dropped the book on the bed and struggled into the tunic his batman was holding to his back.

'Getting a bit tight this one, sir.'

'Thank you, Seymour.'

For the first time in a while it was a full intelligence mess at the École Militaire, with Brigadier General Charteris presiding. Fish would be run from the Officers' Club. The orderlies would do their best of course, but they were never quick enough to stop the sauce congealing. Marshall sat and watched the others with no appetite for conversation. Charteris was playing with his food too. A clever man, he knew what people were saying: a quarter of a million casualties, for what? A quagmire; a desolation; a place called Passchendaele; a God-damn mess – and why wasn't it stopped weeks ago? The stink of it seemed to hang in the dining room.

Coffee was served in the Section A office, the brigadier slouching in front of the great wall map with its sergeant keeper at his side. Marshall remembered talk in August of a larger one to show the entire coast, Brussels, Antwerp, and the German border. Charteris cleared his throat, demanding their attention.

'We attacked again on the 6th, I'm sure you know, and the whole of the Passchendaele ridge is now in our hands. We have beaten the Germans to breaking point.' He paused to draw on his cigarette, turning from the room to the map. His shoulders were so broad they filled the front from Poelcappelle in the north to Zonnebeke in the south, and his large head was covering the new bulge in the line at Passchendaele.

Staff stood staring at his back, chinking their china cups and shuffling their feet, and from an office somewhere along the corridor, the rhythm of a typewriter like the distant echo of an enemy machine-gun.

'Some will call it a barren victory, too many lives thrown away.' He turned back to gaze at them a little defiantly. 'The Chief *says*, if we keep fighting here we must win next year, so the offensive will begin again next spring.' His eyes were tired and there was the usual dusting of ash on his tunic. 'There has been some negative comment about GHQ Staff. I don't want this to concern you. If we have a big success the whole thing will blow over. There is one more battle to fight this year. Third Army at Cambrai is ready – everything is well for the attack.'

Some of the others were nodding politely. Graham was disguising a yawn. More time ticked away with talk of fresh intelligence, the parlous state of the enemy, and MacLeod may have said something about his agents in the occupied territories. Marshall wasn't listening. 'Stand down', over at last, and he was left alone at the map, staring at its light and dark shades. Ringing in his ears, his own voice calling 'Stretcher-bearer!' And they had come, in a series of spurts and dives, bullets following them all the way. A corporal was holding the front poles. 'Too late, sir, can't you see?' He had been angry with Marshall for putting his life in danger for no good purpose. The dead man was a Canadian called Jimmy from Ottawa and there was a ragged star-shaped hole in his forehead through which a small pouch of his brains was hanging. Minutes before he'd been speaking to Marshall of the battle for Passchendaele village. 'Our boys were falling like ninepins,' he'd said, 'but it was worse for Jerry because when he stood up to surrender he was mown down by his own machine-guns firing from the rear at us.' For some reason he'd laughed – a tired, hysterical little laugh. Then, the crack of bone and he'd slid from his mud chair, done-for by a sniper. Most bodies were twisted in unnatural shapes by the force of death, half buried or sprawling in shell holes. The Germans were old and black. Not Jimmy; there was almost a smile on his face; he looked at rest, quite peaceful. Then Jerry had opened up with a sharp barrage, sending steel and mud flying over Marshall's head. He'd crawled his way out, and if the men took pleasure at the sight of a Staff officer on his belly, good luck to 'em. From the far side he'd glanced back across the crater to where Jimmy the Canadian was lying on his side, waiting for the next rain and his long slide into oblivion.

'Are you fighting the last battle or the next one?' Stewart Graham was at his shoulder.

'I was thinking of the Canadian I met this afternoon.'

'Crawling about in no man's land? Don't you have enough to do here.' Graham took out his cigarette case. 'You?'

'Does anyone pay any attention to what I do here?'

Graham glanced sideways to be sure no one was paying them any attention. 'Charteris didn't say, but you've noticed, I'm sure,' he said, stepping up to the map. 'Look, the line at Passchendaele sticks out like a sore thumb.' He traced it with the side of his hand. 'The Germans will pinch it off the first serious attack they make. Only a matter of time.'

He paused to draw on his cigarette. 'But cheer up: you heard the Brigadier.'

'Actually, I wasn't listening.'

'We have *fresh* intelligence proving the Germans are going to collapse.' He raised an eyebrow, smiling his corner smile. 'Faust, I shouldn't wonder. Isn't it always when the source is too secret to share with the rest of us . . . But that must make you feel better?'

'You know, Graham, I think I would be more use crawling about in no man's land.'

'Defeatist talk.' Graham laughed, and clapped him on the arm. 'Keep right on to the end of the road and all that.' He dragged his finger slowly back across the map and away. 'I'm meeting Sassoon.' Then with another half-smile, he said, 'When we've won our battle here, we can set about helping to win the war again.'

Marshall needed to escape, to climb to the battlements, to breathe. Gazing across the valley at the hills in silhouette to the north, his thoughts turned again to Jimmy the Canadian, his blond hair caked in mud, his brains turning black. What colour were his eyes? They were still open. Their light faded the moment he surrendered his life with a gasp. That's how it seemed to be. A religious man would say that small gasp was Jimmy delivering his soul to his maker. Marshall wasn't sure. He shook his head vigorously, because he didn't want to dwell on the whys and wherefores. Above the hills, the moon was in the third quarter. Imagine it floating like a boat in a crater. But it was raining and he could hear drops pattering on his hat. They would be falling in the crater water like the shock waves of an explosion, smearing the moon's reflection across the surface. Perhaps there were star shells too. The men would be crouching in their capes. Some would have found shelter in the ruins of the enemy's concrete. Impossible to sleep for long, but they would try because there would be another morning, perhaps a sunrise.

He made his way back down the steps, the last of the horse chestnut leaves slippery underfoot. It was almost two months since he'd stepped out from beneath a tree to surprise Innes. He had been angry that evening. The trees were bare and he was still angry. The Army was his life, but of late he'd begun to wonder whether he should change his life.

Trailing back to his billet, flinging his tunic on a chair, he was contemplating a glass of whisky before bed when there was a knock at his door.

'Me,' said Graham, pushing past him into the room. 'Thought you should hear this.' For once, he was forgetting to play the bored cynic. 'I've been with Philip Sassoon, and Charteris has offered to go.' Sinking into the only armchair: 'That's the good news.'

'Field Marshal Haig refused to let him?'

He gazed pointedly at Marshall's glass. 'Yes, the Chief has refused to accept his resignation. Can you believe it? Allowing a little for loyalty, and our Chief's—' He paused. 'Well, his idiosyncrasies, one can just about understand why he would refuse. For me? Thank you,' he said, accepting his whisky. 'You heard Charteris this evening, of course?'

Marshall sat at the end of his bed. 'Some of it.'

'The bit where he mentioned criticism of the Staff? The Chief is under pressure to get rid of him. Sassoon says it isn't just Lloyd George who wants to force changes, there are influential voices in Parliament and the press – *The Times* – and one or two of the Chief's Army commanders have spoken in confidence to the Secretary of State for War.'

Marshall sipped his drink and said nothing.

'I must send you something better,' said Graham, turning

his whisky against the light. 'Anyway, Sassoon says Lloyd George has begun sounding out members of the Cabinet. He wants rid of Haig. That's the difficulty: the Chief won't let Charteris go because he thinks he'll be next in the firing line. But Sassoon is of my view: the Chief has to be persuaded to cut Charteris loose. If he doesn't, well, he's going to make it easy for the Prime Minister to push him aside too. Charteris will drag us all down, I dare say. Sassoon is going to speak to our friends in government. Something will turn up, perhaps Faust . . . anything. So you see—'

'See what?'

Graham rolled his eyes. 'I must say, Marshall, you're slow tonight. That things are coming to a head.'

What do I see, Marshall wondered? He lifted the whisky to his lips and breathed its fumes. Men on their bellies in mud he could see, and a pouch of brains he could see, and when men were dying in the filth he could see there was something shameful in the rivalries and the intrigue and the misplaced loyalties of those charged with responsibility for the direction of the war. He'd had a bellyful of GHQ. 'We've lost our way here,' he said at last. 'Stuck in our own mire.'

Graham put his glass down and got to his feet. 'I can see you're tired and a little fraught, old fellow . . . An exhausting day.'

'I've decided to apply for a transfer,' Marshall said, rising too. 'I don't know, back to Division, perhaps the War Office.'

Graham caught his eye. 'Charteris will turn you down. Can't afford to lose you. Goodness, there are so many idiots and halfwits here, even he can see you're a good thing. You know MacLeod has sent more of his Suicide Club off in balloons this week – just for something to say to the Chief, I shouldn't wonder – bloody fool. No, Marshall, you're too valuable.' Reaching for the door handle, he offered his cynical old half-smile. 'Perhaps we are in a mire . . . I'm going to fight for every bloody yard of it and if you don't want to hand the conduct of the war over to that little Welsh goat, Lloyd George, you will do the same. We need to save the Chief from himself, and we will.'

21

Ramble and Eve again

'**M**ADAME THOMAS HEARD you shouting.' Ramble was kneeling over him, touching his forehead with a damp cloth. 'Do you want a drink of water?'

'No.' Innes reached for her hand. 'It was just –'

'I know,' she said. 'Another of your dreams.'

'You know everything about me, Maria.'

'You are a clever man, Alexander, but sometimes you talk such rubbish.' She tugged his sheet – 'It's eight o'clock' – and exposed him to a blast of freezing air. He protested it wasn't fair and curled into a ball to cover his nakedness.

'Life isn't fair,' she said. 'Didn't your mother tell you?' She looked fierce in her Sunday widow weeds, a little matronly too. He hadn't seen her for two days and in her absence he was back in the attic.

'Up!' she said, pushing his shoulder. 'We're going to church. I'll wait for you downstairs.' She left him shivering. There was ice inside the window. Rising from the bed, he reached for his vest and his woollen long johns, and took a pee in the chamber pot. A trench shave in cold water, scraping at a piece of broken mirror, and the thought as he gazed into his own dark blue eyes that Lazarus may have left something of himself in his tomb. The Gospel didn't say, because the Evangelist really had nothing much to say about the living Lazarus. Was it possible he was besmirched by the hours he had spent in his grave clothes? Ramble had implied such a thing was possible. 'You fight so hard against your feelings, sometimes you aren't sensible,' she'd said.

He walked arm in arm with her through the old town, the yellow sun glinting in lead-paned guild house windows, the comforting dissonance of many city bells summoning the faithful to church to pray for family, for food, for freedom, the strength to endure another winter and to resist in small ways. In the Grande Place the enemy's military band was competing for attention with a jaunty march tune that offered plenty to the trumpets, the instrument of the invader always. 'Go pray, if you must,' they seemed to say, 'but when you leave your churches remember there is a new German order.' But for all their huff and their puff, they were afraid of Sunday. They'd made an enemy of the church. There was a strong military presence at the town hall and at the general post office, and the black eagle was draped round the plinth of Reubens in the place Verte.

At the west door of the cathedral the local gendarmes were checking the identity papers of their neighbours beneath a new relief of the Last Judgement. Ramble and Innes shuffled to the front of the queue and handed theirs to a young policeman in a dark blue uniform and a helmet like a British bobby's. Two veteran soldiers of the *Landstrum* were watching at his shoulder, the elder, a sergeant with a hard bloodshot face. Ramble caught his eye with a sideways glance and the suggestion of a smile. She could always arouse the interest of a soldier. Innes had seen her deploy that smile many times. 'Like this,' she'd said when he'd mentioned it to her once: 'lower my eyes and my chin – my "buy something from my shop" smile – for the gentlemen. Are you jealous?' He'd protested that it was the sort of smile a proper gentleman would ignore, and she'd laughed and said he was a liar. But while the veteran sergeant followed her with his eyes, Innes offered his identity paper to the young gendarme.

Solemn Mass was under way and the nave of the cathedral was full, the congregation at the west end restless, straining to hear the celebrant almost two hundred feet away. Ramble led Innes into a side aisle where they found seats behind a pillar, close enough to hear the tinkle of the bell as the priest held the body of Christ up over the altar. Ramble knelt with her rosary to her lips and mumbled a prayer. Her face was severely framed by her blue scarf and in the shifting chiaroscuro of the cathedral she looked her age. Innes felt a surge of tenderness. On her knees here she was a different Ramble, the mother, the prayerful patriot, a woman the sergeant at the door wouldn't recognise.

He knelt beside her, conscious of the rows of worshippers in the nave to his right. Between mothers and children, the bakers and tailors, lawyers and honest labourers, there were spies who didn't care a fig for Jesus. They were the Berlin vampires, watching and listening. Innes glanced at the faces of the men close by, careful not to catch anyone's eye. Most were in their forties or older, because the young men were being forced into labour battalions in the German Reich.

Ramble touched his sleeve. 'It's time.' She rose to take Communion. They'd agreed Innes should slip away. She would meet him when Mass was over in the second chapel on the south side of the ambulatory, beside the confessionals. 'Say a prayer,' she said, squeezing his hand. The cathedral was full of communicants queuing or leaving or seeking a quiet place. No one seemed to notice Innes but to be sure he stopped beyond the choir screen to light a votive candle and ask for all the things Ramble would wish for. Satisfied no one was following him, he walked round to the chapel and sat on the penitents' bench to wait for her.

'I hope you'll go to confession,' she whispered when she found him. 'I'm sure you need to.'

'And tell a priest about the sins I've committed with you?' he replied.

She frowned. 'Do you think that's a sin?'

'I'm teasing you.'

'I don't think we're committing a sin,' she said, not entirely with conviction. She didn't like to disobey the church in anything.

'Don't you think Lux knows anyway?' he said.

'No!' she whispered, indignantly.

'Is it a sin if he does?'

She frowned and turned away. She didn't like him to be clever about the church. 'You told me your uncle was a priest,' she'd complained once, as if that simple fact alone required a special loyalty from him.

The Abbé Buelens was late and looked very distracted. 'We must be quick, we aren't safe here. Has Maria told you?'

She shook her head.

'There have been more arrests in Brussels, Lazarus, and the network in Ghent . . . Monsieur Bouts and his two sons, he's a farmer with land by the railway.' Buelens passed a hand over his brow. 'And I'm afraid the priest who helped you here, Father Albert. Of course it may be a coincidence.' It was plain from the tone of his voice he didn't think so.

An image flitted through Innes's mind of the old man's bulging blue eyes floating in a dark police cell, eyes that might strip the conscience of an enemy interrogator bare. 'Springer uses the village. He has something to do with this.' He felt a pang of guilt. 'I'm sorry.'

'Father Albert may have confided in someone – he didn't

276

have experience of such things.' The abbé laid a hand on Innes's sleeve. 'I know he was glad to help.' He tried to smile. 'He is in God's hands now. Pray for him.' Innes nodded because he knew the abbé meant it to be more than a platitude. But Father Albert was now in the hands of secret policemen who would care nothing for his age or his cloth, and the abbé knew that too.

'Maria has told me about this prostitute,' he said. 'I think it is a bad idea.'

Ramble was avoiding Innes's eye.

'I know that's how Maria feels,' he said, 'but I'm sure this is important – I must—we must know the truth. So much is at stake, and—'

Ramble lifted her hand. There were footsteps, and a second later a crow-black member of the clergy passed the chapel screen with a small smile for the abbé.

He sighed. 'It's all right.'

'Perhaps you should sit between us, Father.' She shuffled along the bench to make room for him. 'It will look as if you're counselling us.'

'Yes, I will,' he said, 'and if you'll listen to my counsel Lazarus, leave this matter, this Faust. Look.' Reaching into his cassock, he took out a tightly folded square of paper. 'This is from the young priest who has organised the train watchers in Hirson, across the border in France. The line's a busy one, I'm sure you remember, it runs along the Front through Fourmies, and up to Valenciennes and Cambrai.'

'I *do* remember, Father.'

'He says the Germans are bringing in new divisions. The stationmaster at Fourmies says three: the 107th, the 123rd, and the 98th. They've come from the Eastern Front, from Russia.'

'To Ypres?'

'No. They are to act as a reserve in the Cambrai sector. Here.' He offered the paper to Innes. 'This is important, yes?'

Innes nodded.

'Then you must take it back to Rotterdam, Alexander,' Ramble said.

'You want to get rid of me?'

She flushed a little. 'No. The intelligence—it's best.' Her gaze drifted momentarily to the priest and she flushed a little more. 'It's important. You said so.'

'Yes. But it doesn't have to be me. One of our *passeurs* will do.'

The abbé was fidgeting. 'You can ignore our advice, of course,' he said, stiffly. 'We are bound to help a British officer.'

'I'm sorry, Father. It's my duty to see this Faust thing through.'

'Is it?' He stared at Innes for a while, his eyes almost lost beneath his brow. 'Then it's settled. I will deal with this,' he said, slipping the paper back in his chest pocket. 'If Faust is your only concern, there is no need for us to meet again.'

'I will see to everything,' Ramble said.

'Father, we all owe you so much.' Innes felt large and clumsy beside him. 'I will be careful.'

The abbé tried to smile. 'Be careful and be wise, Lazarus. Listen to Ramble,' and lifting his right hand he gave them both his blessing.

They left the cathedral by the south transport. Innes wanted to amble in the sunshine through the place Verte or catch a tram to the park, but Ramble said it wasn't safe.

'It has never been safe,' he protested. 'It hasn't stopped us before.' But she was determined to hurry him back to the attic. He smiled ruefully. 'I'm your madman in the room at the top.' She didn't understand it was a joke.

He reached for her hand but she pulled it away.

278

'Not here,' she whispered sharply. 'Can't you see how people look at us? They think I'm your mother.'

'It's your clever disguise.'

'Lux said "careful". Remember your Father Albert? Come.' She took his arm as a mother might and lengthened her stride.

'Do you know where they're keeping Father Albert?'

'Perhaps the prison on the rue St Roche, perhaps the gendarmerie in the place St André, or at the General Government if the Germans are still interrogating him.'

'I liked him.'

'There's nothing we can do.'

They turned on to the embankment and walked for a while in silence, conscious of the field-grey uniforms among the families promenading by the river in the sunshine. Innes's spirits were lifted by the dancing light and the view of the open fields on the bank opposite, caught – or so it seemed – in a thick slow moving coil of the river. Above the land, above the Scheldt, brilliant blue as high as heaven, a sky they would have prayed for at Ypres.

'Don't you think Father Albert's arrest is suspicious?' he asked, when it was safe to.

'I agree with Lux, you should go back with the intelligence of the new German divisions, because that is more important.'

'You persuaded Lux against me,' he said, although he'd been trying not to.

'I gave Lux my opinion,' she hesitated, 'but he knows you better than you think.'

He asked her to explain but she shrugged and said they should talk about something else.

Madame Thomas had left a note on the kitchen table. She was at church, but there was some bread for breakfast, a little watery butter and a few spoons of ersatz coffee. He pleaded with Ramble to make love but she resisted because it was a Sunday. In the end she allowed him to lead her upstairs because she was as hungry as him for intimacy. But she was angry with herself when it was over. She lay naked, propped on her elbow.

He reached over and touched her flat nipple with the pad of his thumb. 'Don't be cross. We share so little time.'

She smiled and stroked his face. 'It's a mistake, really. We're soldiers.'

'We're people.' He bent to kiss her neck, then her chest, and she reached down to run her fingers through his hair.

'What will we do when the war ends?' he asked, his cheek warm against her tummy.

'It won't for us,' she said. 'Don't spoil it, Alexander.'

He watched her wash and climb into undergarments, her corset and her black church dress, and he watched as she tidied her hair at the little vanity mirror, like something from a painting by the late Monsieur Degas. 'Don't let Madame Thomas see you like that,' she said, nodding with an earthy smile to his nakedness, 'they're mine – for now.'

He laughed. 'Of course . . . always.'

The following evening she took him back to the Mephistopheles and waited at the home of a baker on the other side of the street. Innes had tried to persuade her not to come, but she insisted on being his guide through the curfew. No need to show the doorman his identity card a second time, and Lily smothered him with smiles like a regular.

'You've come for Eve? But she's busy Monsieur Thomas,' she said, 'perhaps you would like to meet one of the other girls?'

But Monsieur Thomas was ready to wait. The lights in the

club seemed lower, the drawing room busier and noisier, with more German officers, some quite senior. A colonel's birthday, Lily said. There would be music and singing and even a bottle or two of champagne. Springer was sliding between couches, pausing here and there to ooze false bonhomie. Innes knew he'd been noticed, and sure enough, he wasn't able to taste his wine before Springer sidled up with his 'how nice to see you'.

'But where is my banker friend, Monsieur Luyten?' he said.

'Busy being a pillar of the community,' Innes replied.

'I was surprised to see him here, he has such a nice reputation.' There was the suggestion of a smirk. 'A friend of the cardinal's, I believe.'

Innes really couldn't say.

'And you, Monsieur Thomas? You are . . . ?'

'A businessman with a range of interests, rather like yourself Monsieur Springer.'

'In Namur?'

'And elsewhere.'

'I see. Well, there may be something for you here in Antwerp.'

Innes said, 'I'm sure there must be.'

Cheering, applause, a full-figured lady in black frills and little else was tripping on to the stage, bowing and twirling so her audience could appreciate her red wings. 'I'm a little devil,' she lisped in bad German, 'and I'm going to sing for you.' More wild cheering and laughter, and Innes was suddenly conscious of cheap gentleman's scent. Springer was leaning closer to be heard.

'It isn't the time, monsieur, but, please . . .' Reaching inside his tailcoat he took out his business card. 'At your convenience. You're waiting for Miss Eve? She won't be long.'

Innes wondered how he knew. Another smile and he was away, and in the course of their short exchange his gaze had barely flickered above Innes's necktie.

So he waited and watched the little devil sing and prance, strutting in her stockings and her wings to the out-of-tune piano and the clapping and whooping of the colonel and his guests. *Enjoy, enjoy, if you must*, he thought. Sin was supposed to be out of fashion, even in Paris. Unpatriotic, he'd heard it said. The sin that never seemed to pall was killing one's neighbour.

Eve came for him before the devil could begin her second song. 'A German officer from Hamburg,' she explained, 'but Monsieur Springer arranged things because you were waiting.' She seemed pleased to see Innes, a little frightened too. 'He was asking about you,' she said, 'and he wants me to find out more.'

They sat on the bed in her room as before. It smelt of the sex she'd just had with the German officer. She didn't seem to notice, or she didn't mind. He asked her if she was still willing to help her country. She said that she would if her country was still willing to pay. Brave girl, he said, because a girl was what she seemed to be, even though she was just a little younger than him. Brave and naive and sly – like most addicts – and a patriot only for a price – was that so bad? A prostitute, yes, but not such a veteran she was without hope.

'Do you have a mother alive?' he asked.

'In Brussels.'

'Tomorrow you will receive a letter from a friend of your mother's. It will say she's very ill. You must persuade Springer that you have to go to her for a few days. I will meet you in front of the Southern Terminus.'

'I won't be able to. He's too clever.' She clasped the neck of her gown, drawing her knees to her chin.

'It's your mother, she's dying – you'll manage.' He smiled. 'I trust you, Eve.'

She listened and fidgeted as he explained that his friends

had organised an apartment with a view of the entrance to the German General Government.

'We'll keep you safe. All you need to do is look for the man you know as Faust. Springer will never know.'

He had to let her pick up her needle before she would agree. 'And you will stay with me now, won't you? You must. I want him to believe I please you.'

He sat and watched her fall into her drugged sleep and he only left when he judged she would be able to boast of giving him all the pleasure an ordinary man is capable of experiencing in a short evening. Lily was patrolling the stair, and she showed him out of a servant's entrance at the back of the house. She must have presumed that he was content with his service because she didn't bother to ask.

22

Faust

R AMBLE SAID EVE wouldn't come, and if she did it would
be with Springer or a policeman in tow. Ten minutes late,
conspicuous in a large hat with a pink feather, she strutted
across the station concourse towards them, raising a white
gloved hand in greeting. She wanted to look fashionable, she
wanted to create a stir. She moved her hips in a way that
demanded attention and she was receiving it from every enemy
soldier in the station. She didn't look like the sort of young
lady a respectable young man would dare take home to his
mother.

'I'm here,' she said, without any of the anxiety she'd shown
the night before.

'I'm glad,' said Ramble, sarcastically.

Eve was too happy to notice. 'I persuaded Springer – I did
it, monsieur.' Her pleasure was quite enchanting.

The apartment was no more than a bare room at the top of a
Flemish brick shop in the Shoe Market.

'This is where you stay, mademoiselle,' Ramble said, 'a bed
there, you see, and you'll have to make do with this,' and she
held out a chamber pot. 'Ask the men to step outside if you
like.'

Eve blushed but looked at her defiantly. 'I will.'

'Don't tell anyone your name. They know not to tell you

theirs.' Ramble indicated two chairs by the window. 'You can see the General Government Building from here. No one should notice you, but be careful. Use these.' She lifted some eyeglasses from the back of the chair and offered them to Eve.

'Monsieur, will you stay?' Her eyes were pleading with Innes.

'As often as I can,' he said.

They left her curled in a chair, an old policeman called Van Delden at her side.

Half-way down the stair, Ramble stopped Innes and said, 'She'll do for you and for herself, you know.'

Innes reached for her hand but she drew away. 'What do you want me to do?' he said. 'Tell her I made a mistake and we don't need her? We do. Give her a chance.'

She snorted with disgust. 'Don't be stupid. I know people, and you're so . . .' She lifted her hands in exasperation. 'Stupid.'

'That's unfair – and not like you.'

'I'm angry and I feel sorry for her. I do. Don't you see? If she betrays us – and she may not be able to stop herself – you know what will happen to her.'

'I'll make sure she doesn't betray us – you can help by being nice to her.'

Ramble closed her eyes with a small sad smile, and when he tried to touch her she brushed past with a determined step, her footfall on the bare stair echoing to the top and the bottom of the house.

He didn't see her for a while. She sent him food and clean clothes and from time to time someone from the network to relieve him for a few hours. But Eve preferred him to be there and he was glad to be of use at last. He missed Ramble. Sometimes he dared to close his eyes and imagine her broad assured smile and her body shaking with suppressed laughter; to imagine whole pillow conversations, their love-making, her slow firm caress. Her country, her people, and when he left, as one day he would have to, she would carry on as before, obliged perhaps to pick up his pieces. A disturbing notion came to him that he was only willing to see and hear what he wanted to – like Charteris and Haig. His family liked to joke that once his jaws were clamped round something he would shake and worry it, he wouldn't let go. Charitably, his mother called it fixity of purpose. It went deeper than reason. His old CO said 'bloody obsessive', and the Army had decorated him for it with a Military Cross.

That was the sense of his day dreams. Eve woke him from another at night, her face very white in the light of the star-lit room. She said he was shouting, but she wasn't afraid because some of her Germans did the same. 'Sleep,' she said, placing her thin arms lightly round him and her head on his shoulder, 'and I will sleep beside you.' But he couldn't sleep for worrying what Ramble would say if she found them lying on the mattress together. Later, he let her take some of her drug.

The crowd began to gather outside the General Government at sunrise. Three days at the window and Innes was able to recognise some of the faces. At half past seven the military commandant of the city stepped very carefully from his large motor car to avoid catching his cloak on his spurs. His cavalry boots were quite dazzling. Soldiers and the token gendarmes kept petitioners away as he swept up the steps and through the open doors with what looked even from four floors up like the arrogance of a conqueror. The grey stone municipal building he'd chosen for his headquarters was so out of place in a street of Flemish brick it might have been built for him. From November dawn until after dusk a stream of officials and ordinary folk would pass in and out for instructions, permissions, pieces of stamped paper – that was the German way.

Innes remembered it was like that in the Reich even before the war, before the military took charge of everything.

On the first and second days Eve had recognised some of the regulars from the Mephistopheles. 'I'm bored,' she complained, 'are you sure he comes here?' At a little before nine on the third she squealed, jumped up with a hand to her mouth and kicked her tea across the floor as she did so. 'That's Faust!'

'Who?' he asked, snatching the field-glasses from the hook by the window.

'It's him, it's him.' She was jumping as if the war was won.

'Calm down, someone will see you,' he said, sharply. 'Which one?'

Three German officers were chatting on the pavement; a motor car drew up and a liveried driver got out to open the passenger door; locals were passing by, mostly women; and four members of the *Landsturm* were turning into the building. 'For goodness sake, Eve, who, *who*?'

'There!' She grabbed his arm 'Can't you see? The old man on the steps – talking to that funny-looking woman. He's got a grey moustache, and, and – a hat, but everybody has a hat – a Homburg, on the steps.'

Innes adjusted the focus and had him at last. He didn't look like a master spy, he looked like the owner of an antiquarian bookshop. 'Are you sure it's him?'

'Yes, yes, I'm sure,' she panted.

He wasn't old, but Innes understood why a woman not yet twenty might think so, because he was whiskered and grey and wore thick round glasses. Was he Jewish? He had the sort of face it was easy to forget, and that was dangerous. Faust, yes, the code-name *Faust* made sense. He was listening attentively to his companion. Her back was turned and she was wearing a large blue hat. Petite, expensively dressed, and yet soberly, for the office. Her conversational gestures were slow and graceful. Peculiar: just watching her, he knew she was someone out of the ordinary.

'I've done it, haven't I?' Eve was still wriggling with excitement at his side.

'Eve, the woman— One of the Germans told you Faust worked for a Fräulein Doktor – do you remember?'

'A soldier, a captain called Siebert – a beast, really. But not me – he told Lily. He threatened her, made her promise not to tell anyone.'

Was she a doctor? The woman turned a little and he caught a glimpse of her pale face beneath the brim of the hat. It was just an impression of an interesting face, small, round, with a full bottom lip and a weak chin. Blonde perhaps, but he couldn't be sure. In her late twenties. If she were an intelligence officer, it was careless of her to be talking in the street. But their business was now over. She was edging down the steps towards the Mercedes that had drawn up a few minutes before, the liveried driver still holding the passenger door. Faust was moving too.

'Don't leave,' he shouted to Eve.

Thumping down the stairs two at a time, he clattered into Ramble's ex-policeman.

'Something's wrong – is it the prostitute?'

Innes grabbed his arm: 'Never mind her. Faust – he's here. You can help me.'

The noise brought one of the lads from the shoe shop to the bottom of the stair. Innes pushed him roughly aside and stepped out on to the pavement, the policeman at his shoulder. 'Van Delden, isn't it? Follow me, but not too closely.'

The Shoe Market seemed much busier from the street. Burghers' wives were shopping for clothes and the small luxuries most of the city could no longer afford, like tea and coffee and cheese and meat you might eat without boiling it from the bone. Innes waited for a tram to pass and then hurried to the other side. Faust had turned towards the city's main commercial district along the street known as the Meir. He was two or three minutes ahead by now, or he may have stepped into a shop. Stride out and hope was all Innes could do. Hope he wasn't inviting unwelcome attention, that he hadn't overdone it on the stair, that the bloody little corporal who'd shot him in the leg was up to his eyes in mud and crawling with lice.

He was expecting to walk most of the length of the Meir, and almost hurried past Faust without noticing. He was gazing in the window of a tobacconist, just a hundred yards or so from the door of the apartment, hands in pockets, pulling his brown tweed coat tightly round him. The coat was a little long for a short man. Perhaps he was using the shop reflection to see if he was being followed – it was a routine precaution – if so, he'd chosen unwisely. There was quite a queue at the tram stop opposite, and two countrywomen were hawking their vegetables from a barrow. A few yards further on, a delivery boy had been knocked from his bicycle and was being helped back to his feet by the culprit – that was causing a stir too. Innes strolled over to the queue to consult a timetable. He could still see the shop at the corner of his eye. Faust was edging towards the door. Perhaps he wanted to buy tobacco but wasn't sure he could afford to. He must have decided he wanted it at any price because he was going inside. Someone touched Innes's shoulder.

'That was Faust, at the shop window?' It was Van Delden. 'You want me to go into the shop?' His face was so close Innes could smell garlic on his breath.

'No, too risky. We'll follow him, and if we can, see where he's staying. You take that side of the street and I'll take this side.'

The tram came and went and the countrywomen sold the last of their *rutabagas*. A German soldier was helping to lift their barrow into the street while three of his friends stood idly by, laughing and poking fun at him. Faust emerged with his tobacco at last. He consulted his pocket-watch and after a moment's reflection he carried on walking along the Meir. Innes did the same. He tried to keep a distance of about twenty yards but it wasn't easy because Faust's pace was quickening, and the further they walked the busier the street seemed to be.

Innes lost sight of him for a few seconds, then for more than a minute. That was how it happened – a momentary lapse of concentration – that was how it always happened. His leg was hurting, he was craning over the heads of passers-by for a glimpse of a brown felt hat, and they knocked him clean off his feet. A gendarme and a German on an ordinary street patrol. He cracked his shoulder and elbow and it was a few seconds before he was able to rise. When he did he had the presence of mind to address them in German.

'What the hell are you doing? I'm chasing a suspect – a spy.' He thought that might be enough and he tried to move away, but the German sergeant planted a large hand in the middle of his chest: '*Soldbuch*'. He wanted to see Innes's Army papers. Innes protested he was a captain in intelligence, his suspect was getting away and if he did they would both be held responsible. But the sergeant insisted: '*Soldbuch*'. He was a Prussian, so he would know the rules and regulations by heart.

They wanted to take him to a gendarmerie. He said it was an intelligence matter, so only military headquarters would do, and goodness, they were going to catch it there. They didn't let him go, but they took less care than they should have done. He was free to walk without restraint and at his own pace, and he walked quickly in spite of the ache in his leg. He walked like an officer sorely affronted, and the last thing he said to them was 'For God's sake, keep up'. A few seconds later he cut in front of an approaching tram and ran for his life.

He ran through a blur of faces, bouncing off one man, knocking a child who tangled with his legs to the ground; into a side street that was too straight and too empty; breathless, his nerves strung as tightly as a concert violin, and angry because he'd made such a hash of things. Turning right into a cul-de-sac, left down a closed passage between shops into another street, hurrying now but walking because it was dangerous to run anywhere for long in the occupied territories. After about ten minutes he was confident he was clear of the sergeant and his lackey. They might alert the Army and cordon the area. They might forget the whole thing to avoid the humiliation of admitting he gave them the slip. To be sure he would keep walking in busy places. Walk until it was safe to stop.

It was early afternoon when he climbed back to the room in the Shoe Market. Eve was lying on the mattress. She was wearing one shoe and her hat and her coat were lying in a heap on the floor. A thread of saliva hung from the corner of her mouth. Innes shook her gently and spoke her name, and she opened lazy-lidded eyes just long enough to mumble something he wasn't able to catch. He wiped her chin and stroked her hair from her brow, then he covered her with the coat, put the syringe back in its box, and sat at the window to wait for her to emerge from her stupor. It felt like the fag end of the day already. Blue-grey cloud was rolling in from the sea and the first flurries of rain were chasing people from the market. The sentries had retreated from the steps of the General Government to new positions beneath its entrance arch. Still the Staff cars and the motorcycles came and went, officers and plain-clothes policemen, and the locals seeking the permissions they needed to do almost anything. Ah, but what a mess he'd made of things. He was going to have to tell Ramble. It was too much to hope the old policeman had managed to do what he'd so spectacularly failed to. But if Van Delden wasn't in custody there would be more opportunities, and if he was, well, the enemy would probably beat the truth from him, then come thundering up the stairs to capture a British spy and his prostitute.

Eve was stirring, uncurling beneath the coat, drawing it away with her feet. 'It's you,' she said, blinking the sleep from her eyes. 'Was I asleep for long? I must have been, it's dark.'

Rising to her elbow, then on to all fours like a sleek cat, she pretended to stifle a yawn as her gaze flitted furtively about the floor.

'It's here,' he said, pushing her box with the toe of his boot: 'the syringe too.'

She smiled, shyly. 'What do I do now?'

First money, he would pay her, then he would give her a ticket from Brussels and her travel pass with the correct stamp – the network had seen to it all. But before they left for the station, he would remind her not to breathe a word of the truth to anyone, not even to Lily. Don't be tempted into a confidence, Eve, he would say, upon your frail shoulders rest the lives of good people. He would say she was a fine and brave person too, he would thank her, and kiss her cheek, and promise to remember her.

Innes followed Eve home from the station to be sure she was safe. Strange that she thought of the Mephistopheles in that way. He reproached himself a little for not caring enough to ask her about her real home. From the shadows of the street he watched her step into the light of the club's lamp to greet the doorman. The curfew bell was calling the new evening rite of the city: *to your fireside, to your fireside.* No one was supposed to be on the street without good reason or authority from the new order. It would be safer and therefore wiser for Innes to return to the Shoe Market – how many lives do you think you have, Lazarus? Twice he was forced to hide from enemy patrols, and it took him twice as long to walk to Madame Thomas's home as it would have taken in the free city. He watched the street for a while before approaching her door. Satisfied no one else was doing the same, he knocked three dots lightly with a knuckle then a dash.

Madame was in her dressing-gown and slippers. She let him into her dark hall without a word but when the door was closed she gave him quite a few. It was late and she was frightened and she had seen nothing of Ramble for days, was she safe? Madame Simon had promised her more food and fuel. Then Madame Simon would bring her both, he said. He sat at the embers of the parlour fire for a while and listened to her troubles, and when she had spoken of them all she gave him an oil lamp and he climbed up the stairs to the attic.

In the small circle of its light he could see his cardboard suitcase open on the floor, Father Albert's black bead rosary on top of a white shirt Ramble had found him. He extinguished the light to save Madame's oil, lay down on the lumpy horse-hair mattress, and rolled himself into a cocoon of blankets. Turning his head slightly he could see a square of night sky, the cold panhandle of the Great Bear and the North Star. There would be ice on the glass again in the morning, just as there used to be in the attic bedroom at his uncle's house. Stirred by the memory, he reached over to the case for Father Albert's rosary. He tried to pray as the priest would wish, and even if the words were wrong or jumbled, the simple act of trying made things seem better. His thoughts returned to Ramble and he struggled with the senselessness of his disappointment that she was not there. When he stopped blaming her and just missed her he fell into an exhausted sleep.

He woke with his heart trying to leap from his chest. It took a moment to realise someone was hurrying up the stairs. He was still rolling free of the blankets when the intruder burst into the room. Ramble was standing stock still in the door. It was too dark to see her expression, but her silence made him feel sick.

'What is it?' He was on his knees. 'Tell me, for God's sake.'

She inclined her head to the side, almost to her shoulder. Then she made a noise that sounded like a sob, but he knew it couldn't be: not Ramble.

'Please—' He rose and took half a step towards her. 'Maria—' Holding out his hand: 'Tell me.' He was surprised by his voice because he sounded so impatient. 'Are you hurt? Come here.' He was holding his right hand open but he didn't reach out to her. 'Please.'

She lifted her eyes from his hand to his face, then she looked away. Her whole body was shaking.

'Sorry,' she said, clearing the phlegm from her throat. 'Sorry.' She wiped her nose with the back of her hand. 'Do you have a handkerchief?'

'Yes. Yes, of course.' He bent to take one from his cardboard case. 'Here.'

She wiped her nose properly then she dabbed her eyes and tried to smile, but she was still biting back tears. 'Sorry,' she said again. 'You're safe, thank God.'

'Is that it?' he said. 'You were worried about me?' He should hold her. She wanted him to hug her, but he couldn't bring himself to, and that made him feel confused and angry. What's more his bad leg was trembling uncontrollably. 'There's more isn't there? It's someone else.'

She nodded because she couldn't speak, the pain so plain in her face. This time he stepped forward to grasp her by the elbow. 'Tell me, Maria. Tell me now.'

'They've arrested the Abbé,' she said in a small voice. 'The Germans have taken Lux.'

23

The Grand Hotel Weber

R AMBLE SAID, 'YOU'RE pinching, Alexander.'
His fingers must have tightened round her arm. 'When?'
'Two days ago.'
'They may let him go.'
'No.' She shook her head. 'Not just Lux, I don't know how many yet.' She sniffed and wiped her nose with her knuckles even though she was holding his handkerchief, but when she spoke her voice was stronger. 'They arrested Monsieur Luyten, – the banker who took you to the Club.'
Innes let go of her and turned away. 'Do you think Father Albert told them about Lux?'
'Not the priest,' she said, reaching up to unpin her headscarf. 'No, he was strong, and they wouldn't torture a priest.'
'Then Luyten?'
'Perhaps. He has a family. They arrested him three nights ago. His wife should have told us.'
Ramble was so close to Lux, they'd built the network together, trusted, respected, loved each other in a no nonsense way.
'I'm sorry, truly I am.'
'All who know and loved him are sorry,' she said, quietly. 'We must pray for him and we must go on.'
'Yes, I know,' he said, stepping closer to her. 'What I mean is, I'm sorry I was so weak when you told me. I wanted to hold you.' How to explain? He couldn't. 'Can I hold you now?'

Her large brown eyes were searching his face. 'Not yet,' she said. 'I don't want to hear about your feelings – not yet.'

He nodded slowly. 'I'm sorry.'

'Stop apologising.' She pushed his suitcase away with her foot and settled on the mattress, her knees drawn up to her chin. 'Tomorrow we move to another house.'

'Did Luyten know about this place?'

'Just a precaution.'

'But he will have told them about you.'

'He doesn't know my real name,' she said. 'But now we must talk about you. Our comrade, Monsieur Van Delden, says you were very careless.'

'Yes, I was careless. It won't happen again,' he said. 'And Van Delden?'

'Your Faust is living in the Grand Hotel Weber near the Central Station. It's one of the ones the Germans have taken for themselves. The best, Van Delden says. They've kept on some local people – he knows one of the assistant managers. Help me up.' She held out her hands. 'I think I need a cup of tea.'

She'd brought some in her bag, and the food she'd promised to Madame Thomas. Innes made the tea while she sat close to the range, her eyes closed, a hand to her brow.

'You're exhausted,' he said, placing a cup and saucer beside her on the range.

'Not her best china!' She picked it up and balanced it on her knee.

'Sorry.'

'You British – always apologising.'

He had no idea how she knew that to be true, but he was glad to see her smile.

She lifted the cup to her lips. 'I know the name of your Faust.' She paused to take a sip of tea, the bone china handle

pinched between her perfectly manicured thumb and forefinger like something from a guide to English etiquette.

'Well?'

She took another sip. 'His name is Herr Engelmann and he
lives in room 306.'

'Engelmann?'

She was trying not to laugh, but it just seemed to spill out
of her.

'What is it?'

She raised her hand and reached across to appeal for help,
because she was laughing too hard to speak, so hard there
were tears on her cheeks again. He smiled and looked away,
and the storm passed after only a minute.

'Better?' he said.

She sighed. 'It was nothing – the expression on your face.'
But he knew that was just an excuse. She let him pick up her
hand and kiss it, and he bowed to kiss her wet face. 'I was so
worried about you,' she said.

'I know.' He pulled a chair to the range and sat beside her.
'Do you think Van Delden's assistant manger can get me into
room 306?'

The Grand Hotel Weber occupied an elegant corner of the
avenue de Keyser. It was a new hotel and as fine as its name
suggested it should be, with all the luxuries a first class trav-
eller or officer of a foreign army might wish for, and at a very
reasonable price. Once it had welcomed guests from all corners,
but the city's commandant had taken a great shine to the place,
and now they came from only one: Germany. Served the owner
right, some of the locals said, wasn't Herr Weber German too?
Others said it was breaking his heart, that the hotel was his
pride and joy. He'd built it in the style of *la belle époque*, with
a facade of pilasters and friezes, with bronze statues of

298

beautiful women representing the continents, and to crown the building a copper cupola.

'And now his German friends won't let him near the place.' The old policeman smiled with unmistakable *Schadenfreude*. 'Here we go,' he said, nudging Innes's arm, 'this one.' A tram was trundling along the boulevard towards them, its battered green body framed perfectly by the domed railway palace of the Central Station. 'Ticket to the Opera. Sit behind me and don't speak.' Van Delden was giving the orders now. 'And don't get up to leave before I do.'

Suicide, Ramble had said. If Innes was so sure Faust was working for the enemy, well, she could arrange for him to receive a visit from one of their safety-pin men.

'Would you?'

'Are you sure?' She knew he wasn't sure.

'There's another way.'

'Suicide,' she said again. But he talked her round, because she was preoccupied with the collapse of the network in Antwerp. 'What will be left?' she asked him. 'Why don't you worry about that?'

There was one condition: Van Delden would have to agree. His life would be in the greatest danger.

He was sitting two seats in front of Innes now, his head bent over a newspaper. There were another six passengers and the driver. Impossible to be certain, but Innes didn't think any of them were secret policemen. Van Delden was making a great fuss of turning a page of his paper, drawing the gaze of everyone on the tram. He'd agreed to help with alacrity, but he had his conditions too. 'My city, my contact, my show,' was what it amounted to. Plainly, he didn't entirely trust Innes, and why should he? He'd witnessed Innes's ignominious display in the Meir. He trusted Ramble and hated the Germans, and that was enough.

The bell rang, brakes screeched, and the tram shuddered to a stop. Van Delden waited for an elderly lady to negotiate the steps. Innes followed them both on to the pavement. Beyond the street limes that lined both sides of the boulevard was the red and white awning of the Grand Hotel Weber, and through the top branches of the nearest tree Innes could see the naked continent of Africa and the wrought-iron balconies of the third-floor windows. According to their assistant manager, 306 was at the front of the hotel. They were to meet him at the kiosk beyond the entrance, because that was closed to all but the military and their guests. As they strolled towards the hotel, Van Delden rattled on innocuously about the price of food and the weather. Guards were posted beneath the floral baskets on either side of the doors. They were wearing old-fashioned spiked helmets, and Innes momentarily recalled the excitement he'd felt at lifting one from a dead German. He'd discarded it a few weeks later. Dispatch riders in long leather coats and soft field caps were waiting at the curbside with their motorbikes, and their burly sergeant had stopped a lady of mature years to make a fuss of her little dog. Innes narrowly avoided becoming tangled in its lead, a piece of clumsiness that, he reflected, was proving rather too typical.

The kiosk was in the middle of a small *pavé* traffic island, close enough to observe the comings and goings at the hotel without exciting suspicion. The enterprising Weber had opened a public restaurant between the hotel and the city's Opera House, and it was through this their contact was hoping to smuggle Innes inside.

'Have you read the paper?' Van Delden slapped it against his chest. 'Here.'

'What? Now?'

'It says the British have launched another attack in France. It also says it was repulsed: of course it would say that, wouldn't it? Anyway, look as if you're reading it while I see if I can buy some cigarettes.' He turned towards the kiosk then checked: 'Here he comes.'

A small man in hotel tails was approaching the traffic island. He paused to let a horse and coal cart pass, then skipped the last few yards to stand a few feet from them, hidden from the hotel by one of the city's ornate street lamps. He felt in his pockets for a cigarette and felt them again for a light.

'Monsieur?' he said, gesturing to them with his cigarette. Van Delden sauntered over but only for the few seconds it took to oblige him.

'He'll smoke his cigarette, then go back,' he muttered to Innes. 'We wait five minutes, then follow.'

Restaurant Weber was decorated in the rococo style. Its fluted Corinthian pillars and monstrously high ceiling, gilt mirrors, and a polished floor reminded Innes of a picture he'd seen of the Hall of Mirrors at Versailles, the more so because many of the tables were occupied by officers of the Germany Army. They were too busy with lunch to consider the elderly looking local businessman and his son who drifted up to the front desk and gave the name Roels. They said they wanted a quiet table and didn't mind in the least that a reservation had been made for one close to the cloakroom. But the maître d'hôtel was French and proud, and ready to bully them into accepting a table of his choice. A German officer on a nearby table settled the matter by guffawing loudly, his voice bouncing round the restaurant. The older man exchanged a pointed look with the maître d'hôtel. 'Yes a quiet table by the cloakroom will suit us very well.'

They were shown to the far corner of the restaurant, behind one of its white columns and a large tropical fern. There were half a dozen tables close by and five of them were empty. An elderly lady was bending arthritically over her soup at the sixth. She looked as if she was dressed for a children's birthday party in an extravagant display of bows and frills. A tilted mirror to the left of Innes offered a view of the restaurant as a sinking ship, with the other tables, the waiters with trays of coffee and water, and the maître d'hôtel at the front desk sliding out of the bottom of the frame. Van Delden looked at his pocket-watch.

'We should order. At two minutes to midday you must go to the cloakroom. Our contact will be waiting for you.'

'He's sure Engelmann isn't there?'

'That's why he came to the kiosk. You have the money? He's the sort of patriot you need to pay.'

It was always possible to buy more than the ration in a good restaurant. Innes ordered a simple fish dish, a slice of bread, and if he was lucky, a little butter. The fish would probably be cold by the time he got back to the table, and he was too on edge to enjoy an appetite anyway.

'Eat mine too,' he said.

'I will. You're supposed to be sick,' Van Delden replied. 'But don't be more than fifteen minutes.' He sounded nervous. Waiting was always worse. Innes dumped his napkin on the table. 'It's time.'

He tried to concentrate on feeling ill as far as the gentlemen's lavatory. It wasn't that difficult with a cat's-cradle of knots in his stomach. Racing down a flight of stairs, eyes to the front, he walked with the single-minded purpose of a drunken officer who has only seconds to make the door of the *estaminet*: he'd always managed to.

A German in a suit was washing his hands and inspecting his face. It was the sort of mirror that showed every blemish, every line, and the fine grey hairs in his moustache. Innes knew he was German because he said *guten Tag* as if the cloakroom had been annexed by the Reich. *Guten Tag* to you too, Innes thought, now would you please leave. Fifteen minutes wasn't long and he was spending too many of them in a cubicle waiting for the clunk of the cloakroom door. First he heard it open, and the German offer another *guten Tag*, then he heard it close. The assistant manager was standing at a basin washing his hands with chamomile scented soap. Their eyes met in the mirror, and his were frightened, like a doe's.

'Let's go,' Innes said in French.

'I can't, it's too dangerous,' he said.

'Is Herr Engelmann there?'

'No, but if they find out—' He picked up a towel to dry his hands. They were nice towels. The place was doing its best to keep its standards high.

'You agreed with our friend to take me to his room, nothing's changed, so come on, let's go.'

'Well, I need more money,' he said.

'Money?' Innes grabbed the collar of his tailcoat and thrust his head over the basin. 'Do you know what will happen to you when the war's over?' The little snake was trying to wriggle free, but he was too small and not in good shape, and he cracked his head against one of Herr Weber's brass taps. Innes bent close to his ear. 'If you let me down my friends will find you, do you understand? Heard of the safety-pin men?'

He felt a surprising sense of exhilaration playing the bully, and a little shame too. However the assistant manager was a patriot again, and his view was now 'for god's sake get it done quickly'. He bounded up the back stair only pausing at the door to the guest corridor to catch his breath. On the other side, the German side, the side with thick blue carpet and engravings of Flemish seascapes, art deco light fittings, and polished half-panelling, the business of cleaning and tidying was still underway.

The assistant manager walked half a stride in front of Innes, as if he was leading a new guest to a room. The maids were

303

collecting dirty linen and making a mountain of it on a laundry cart, while a bell-boy was checking the rooms were adequately supplied with stationery. They saw one guest, a burly member of the German administration, who asked for his shirts to be washed and pressed by the following morning. Room 306 was at the end of the corridor. The manager produced a master key from the sleeve of his tailcoat, knocked lightly for form's sake, then unlocked the door. 'Please hurry, won't you . . .' he whispered.

It was a comfortable room, but by no means the best. There was nothing at first glance that offered a clue to the personality of its occupant. The furniture was heavy, highly polished and probably German, the ornately carved bed quite overpowering. There was a wardrobe – he would have to go through the jackets – a chest of drawers – those too – a bedside table, a desk – a suitcase beneath that – two armchairs, a water closet, and a small bathroom. Innes had spent rather too much time trying to find a way into Faust's room and not enough time thinking about what he was hoping to discover there. He glanced at his watch and wondered if the old policeman was doing the same in the restaurant.

On the bedside table there was a photograph of a plump middle-aged lady with two younger, plumper women who were plainly Engelmann's daughters. Inscribed on the back, *from your loving wife, Greta.* In the drawer, family letters, the most recent one from Greta, in which she described the shortages in Berlin and the anger and disillusionment she met in the bread queue. There was a Hebrew Bible in the desk and a copy of Goethe's *Faust.* Tucked inside the cover, Engelmann's *Soldbuch,* confirming he was a well-paid employee of the military and that he was working in Antwerp for an organization called the *Kriegsnachrichtenstelle* or War Intelligence Centre. There were some more personal papers of no real importance, cash, newspaper cuttings, and another one of Springer's business cards with the number and address of the Mephistopheles. Beside an ashtray on the desktop was an expensive-looking pipe.

The assistant manager was fidgeting, wearing a hole in the rug.

'I know,' Innes said, pulling the suitcase out from under the desk. 'Why don't you make yourself useful.' He glanced at the wardrobe to indicate where to begin: 'Go through his jackets, I'm looking for bits of paper, even old receipts.'

The suitcase was empty, and the chest of drawers was full of grey long johns and wool socks that badly needed darning. Did Greta know? Herr Engelmann wasn't a practical man, he wasn't a vain one, and Innes thought he was probably careful with money. His letters and books suggested he was well educated and thoughtful, a loving husband and father. He was a Berliner, he was probably Jewish, and he was a spy, but that much Innes knew already.

'Anything?'

'No,' came back the answer.

Innes walked over to the wardrobe. 'Let me.'

His boots in the bottom, his shirts and suits on the rail: 'You went through his jackets?'

'Yes, yes, I did, honestly. Very carefully. Now please . . .'

Innes glanced at his watch again. Did he have the time to check? No, but he was going to anyway. Pockets, linings, collars, hats, and the heels of his shoes: nothing.

'That's it, then?' The assistant manager sounded desperate: 'Because it's almost half past. People will be asking for me.'

Yes, they should go. What sort of spy would leave anything of value in his hotel room anyway? But there must be something . . . something. He hadn't checked the bathroom. He would check the bathroom.

'Monsieur, there won't be anything in there,' he heard the

assistant manager say. 'The room has been cleaned already.' He was probably right, but probably wasn't enough.

Scissors and razors and powders; all the usual gentleman's accoutrements, even a very small bottle of cologne. No secret vanities, no secrets he wouldn't be willing to share with a nosy maid or bellboy.

'All right,' Innes muttered, 'all right.' His eyes wandered round the bathroom again, because . . . think. He bent his head a little, trying to conjure an image of Engelmann in the room with his papers, and his gaze fell for a moment on a bathroom bin. He hadn't checked that, nor it seemed had the maid, because rooting around in it he found an old Berlin newspaper, an empty toothpaste pot, some clippings from Engelmann's moustache, and two pieces of paper scrunched into tight balls. Slowly, painstakingly, he began to smooth the folds from the first piece. Engelmann's handwriting, just snatches of a letter, fragments of sentences that didn't seem to make any sense: *you will appreciate the difficulty we will face if . . . I cannot agree that a transfer to Brussels will help us prepare for the coming offensive.*

Engelmann was a careful man: he plainly preferred to draft sentences on scraps of paper to be sure he was striking the right tone. With letters to authority Innes liked to do the same thing. Behind him the assistant manager was pacing and turning and sighing. Patience, patience, just the second ball to unwrap, then they would go. This piece was a torn half of hotel stationery, and the first thing to draw Innes's eye was a name: *Springer.* It read:

Springer – needs to offer something substantial
B needs urgently

That's where it ended but for three more short lines. Engelmann must have struggled with the name of a French village, he'd tried a number of different spellings. But it wasn't the village that jumped off the page, it was a man's name, a name that brought to mind a pinched and frightened face, eyes tightly shut, lips mumbling a prayer as he soared upwards into a night sky: Petit of the Suicide Club, sent against reason to work as a spy in the occupied territories. The lines read:

Agent Petit?
Saint-Amand-les-Eaux?
especially after Cambrai

The assistant manager was shaking Innes's shoulder. 'Now, monsieur. *Now!*'

'I've found something . . . my own scrap of paper.' The manager honestly didn't give a tinker's cuss. It was evidence. More than that, it was proof, something to show Ramble. 'In your Faust's own hand,' he could say to MacLeod and Charteris. He rolled it into a ball and picked up the bin. It had to go back, right at the bottom beneath the newspaper and the clippings from Faust's moustache. He stepped back into the bedroom, his gaze roaming over the furniture. 'Now we can go,' he said, but the contact was already opening the door.

The peculiar thing was that Innes did feel quite sick. The waiter was clearing away the plates and Van Delden was doing his best to sound solicitous. 'What a pity, but you're feeling better?' The waiter turned his back for a second and the old policeman shot Innes a look like thunder.

'I'm still a little unwell,' he said. 'Was the fish good?'

'Would you?' said Van Delden, catching the waiter's eye. 'We want to leave.'

The tables in their little corner were occupied now, and their nearest neighbour was a captain of artillery dining with a younger woman. She looked awkward; he looked hungry. Van Delden scooped the napkin from his lap and dabbed his lips. 'What in God's name were you thinking?' he muttered behind his hand.

Innes leant forward a little. 'Sorry' – his forefinger tracing small circles on the cloth – 'our friend the manager needed some encouragement.'

'I see.' He dumped his napkin on the table. 'We should leave.'

'You've asked for the bill, haven't you?'

'As soon as possible,' he said under his breath. His voice was strained, and looking up from the cloth Innes noted his high colour. 'The mirror . . . take your time. Do you see?'

Innes's gaze drifted to the reflection, and to the maître d'hôtel who was showing a couple of well-dressed middle-aged men to a table at the top of the frame. Further down its right edge a sommelier was offering wine to an officer with an arm in a sling, brandishing his corkscrew and fawning in the best tradition of wine waiters everywhere. Then a movement at the bottom of the mirror caught Innes's eye. A party of uniformed civil servants was pushing chairs from a table to leave, and as it did so it drew his gaze to a grey head at the very edge of the frame. With a little shudder he recognised Faust, chopped at the neck and delivered in profile on gilt, like a John the Baptist. He was sitting behind the nearest pillar, and with four long strides Innes would be able to join him.

'Careful,' he heard Van Delden mumble through his teeth.

'He can't see us,' he replied.

Van Delden sighed. 'No, but she can.'

Sitting full face clear across the table was the woman he'd seen on the pavement outside the General Government building. She was listening to Faust with the easy confidence and steady gaze of a superior. There was something in her manner – he'd recognised it in the field-glasses – a certain presence, a thoughtfulness, a spark in the eye – it was difficult to describe precisely. He had no proof, but he was sure she was the Fräulein Doktor. He could imagine brushing past her in a university corridor, perhaps somewhere in Mathematics or the Physical Sciences. She was blonde – he was right about that – but with dark eyebrows, and she was very pale – he was right about that too, but a little closer to thirty than she'd seemed through the binoculars.

Van Delden was leaning closer. 'Don't stare.'

'How long—'

'About twenty minutes ago. They came in together. He's done most of the talking.'

Innes glanced back at the mirror just as the waiter with their bill was passing the Fräulein Doktor's table. She was lifting a glass of water to her lips. It hovered there. Faust must have said something to make her smile. She replied, but just a sentence or two before she was interrupted by the sound of breaking glass. There was a startled hush in the restaurant as the eyes of almost everyone turned to search for the guilty man. But the Fräulein Doktor glanced at the mirror and she saw the only other person who wasn't interested in the culprit staring back at her. Innes looked away at once: that was probably a mistake. His face was tingling because the tables were turned and she was watching him in the mirror.

He must have walked past her on his way out but he resisted the urge to look down. He turned back to the body of the restaurant as a waiter was helping him into his coat, but he couldn't see her for bodies, not even a reflection.

They caught a tram to the south of the city. A gendarme and a German checked their papers at the Southern Station stop, but there were no difficulties. The new safe house was in a working district near the river. There was a ship basin at the bottom of the street, and most of their neighbours had worked in the docks before the allied blockade of the enemy had reduced river traffic to a trickle. The place was empty but there was some food, a little tea, and a small supply of coal.

'Go easy on the coal,' Van Delden said, 'stay inside, light a fire if you must, but only in the back room.'

Innes tried to thank him but all he wanted was to be away.

When Ramble found him five hours later he was dozing on the couch. The fire was almost out, and she set about coaxing it back to life.

'Here,' he said, 'let me.' She was plainly exhausted and it was shaming to see her on her hands and knees. He made her tea and brought her bread and some pickled herring from a jar.

'Well, tell me, did you enjoy your grand meal at the Restaurant Weber?'

He sat beside her, his arm about her shoulders. 'I didn't manage a mouthful,' he said. 'Your man Van Delden ate it all.'

That made her laugh.

'When the war's over I'll take you there,' he said.

She smiled a little sadly and touched his face lightly with her fingertips. 'You're very sweet.' They sat in silence for a while. 'Now you can speak to me about Faust,' she said.

He told her about the pieces of paper he'd found in Engelmann's bin, that Springer needed to offer something 'substantial', that B needed it urgently. He was in no doubt that 'B' was Captain Bennett, the Army's man in Rotterdam. And at the end of the line there was dear old Faust, the master spy, fishing for a suitably impressive-looking piece of nonsense with which to bamboozle the British.

She sighed. 'You mean Faust is a German spy?'

'Yes. Faust and Springer are enemy spies.'

As regular as clockwork, every fortnight a package of false intelligence was sent to GHQ. Only, there was something that didn't make sense. Put simply, why the good news? The enemy's bread ration cut – source *Faust*; food riots in one city and a mutiny in another – *Faust*; the great German Army cracking – *Faust*; and one more heave-ho to collapse the Reich – *FAUST*. Perhaps the enemy was just hoping to sow confusion and false hope. Perhaps he knew he was undermining Field Marshal Haig with false promises.

There was another explanation. It had come to Innes in the hours he'd spent watching the fire die. Graham said the source material was seen by such a small circle at GHQ it was impossible for those outside it to know for sure which pieces of intelligence from the occupied territories were from agent Faust. Perhaps some of the material GHQ was designating *Top Secret FX* wasn't Faust, perhaps Charteris and MacLeod were dressing up low-grade intelligence from other sources as something special by reclassifying it as *FX*. Were they capable of that sort of dishonesty when lives were at stake? They wanted to please Haig, to ease his burden and boost morale: yes, it was possible to imagine. Just. He didn't say so to Ramble.

She was pushing him, trying to make him listen. 'What do you want to do?' She grabbed a handful of his hair and gave it a tug. 'Listen to me, Alexander. Your Faust . . . what do you want me to do?'

'I don't know.' He took her hand and kissed her palm. 'There's something else. The second piece of paper mentioned an agent called Petit. He is—he was a British agent. It seems Faust wants to arrange for Petit to send a piece of intelligence to GHQ, probably by pigeon. I know this Petit. I saw him take off in a balloon. I'll never forget his face, he was frightened, he wasn't ready, but he was a patriot.'

'I'm sorry.'

'I prayed with him.' Innes sat, gazing at the fire. 'And what about the others? MacLeod has sent a dozen men – perhaps more since I left GHQ – are they spies too?'

She shuffled on to her knees and reached up to kiss his temple and smooth the frown from his brow with her thumb. He turned to look at her dark eyes and she smiled, and he pressed his head to her chest. They sat like that for a while, the fire hissing and spitting. 'You know, Alexander,' she said at last, 'this agent, Faust, he *may* be working for your British Army. All your pieces of paper prove is that he's working for the Germans too – or pretending to. He would have to do that, wouldn't he?'

'I know,' he said. 'Yes, I know. Springer, Faust, even Petit – one or both sides; or one side for some of the time and the other side for the rest. Who to trust? How is one to know?'

'That's why we're soldiers, not spies,' she said, emphatically.

'You think you can trust soldiers?'

She frowned. 'Don't you? I know, not all soldiers. Your Charteris . . .'

'His Faust works at a German War Intelligence Centre – the *Kriegsnachrichtenstelle*. Have you heard of it?'

'Here?'

'Here in Antwerp. And there's a woman I've seen him with twice now – she must work there too. I think she's the Fräulein Doktor. Faust listens to her. I know its strange, but I'm sure she gives him orders.'

Ramble was trying not to smile.

'The Fräulein Doktor may be in charge of this War Intelligence Centre.'

'She's clever, a clever woman.' She stroked his hair. 'I will ask our friends.' Then she reached up with both hands to remove the pins from her own, shaking it down over her shoulders.

'What about the network?' he said. 'Have you heard any more about Lux?'

She frowned and placed a finger across his lips. 'Later.' Then she cupped his face in her hands and leant forward to kiss him passionately.

24

A Coup de Main

I T WAS AN address in the old town only a mile away, but
Cumming could see he would have the devil of a job
persuading someone to drive him there. From night sea to the
bright lights of Boulogne, it was as if a curtain was parting on
a boisterous stage crowded with marching soldiers and nurses
and the wounded from the battle at Cambrai waiting to board
hospital ships. The wind was whisking ferry smoke south-west
and stirring the steam under the covered concourse at the Gare
Maritime into a luminescent fog. From the top of the destroyer's
gangway, soldiers waiting for the Front train seemed to slip in
and out of it like so many shadows of the past, as if the station
was haunted by those who went before – like his own son, Aly.

'Can I help you, sir?' the officer of the watch said.

'I can manage, I can manage,' Cumming replied. Hooking
his stick on his arm, he hauled himself up on to the gangway
and made his way down, a steady step at a time. An Army
officer in a trench-coat was pushing through the crowd on the
quay and as he came closer Cumming noticed he was wearing
the red and blue armband of the Staff. 'Hello, Graham.'

'Sorry, to drag you here, Captain,' he said.

'I thought you wanted to be discreet . . . meet in the town.'

'The chaos, as you see . . .' Graham opened his arms to the
quay. 'You wouldn't get there and we haven't time to waste.'

'We?'

'I'm parked at the station, can you walk there?'

'Of course I bloody can,' he said.

'Then it will be safer to talk on the way.'

But Graham was uneasy handling the large motor car in the narrow streets of the old town and had to concentrate on his driving. As he ground through the gears, Cumming shouted, 'Why couldn't you trust it to a coded letter?' And Graham shouted back, 'I think you'll find it's worth your while.'

They passed through a double gate in the ramparts and parked in a cul-de-sac at the west end of the town's basilica.

'I have a girlfriend who lives here,' Graham said without embarrassment, 'and her neighbours are used to seeing my motor in the street.'

Perhaps Graham's friend was hiding, because another Staff officer opened the door to them, a short man with a boyish face and an engaging smile. He said his name was Marshall and he knew Captain Innes.

There was a fire in the sitting room and Graham directed Cumming to an armchair beside it. 'We are of the soldiers' party,' he said, waving Marshall to another, 'but you know I am willing to do all I can to see the back of Charteris before he does more damage to the Army.'

He was standing at a side table with a bottle of whisky and a nest of crystal glasses. Everything else in the room, the furniture with its pastel patterned fabric, the rugs and china animals, must have been chosen by Madame. 'Haig all right?' Graham lifted the whisky bottle. 'Does your prejudice permit?'

'I am completely free of prejudice,' Cumming said, 'and free, incidentally, of what you call "party" allegiance.'

Graham smiled. 'Of course, and trusting in your judgement and our understanding, I asked you here to meet Major

Marshall. He has information to share with you about the source, which, in the right hands – yours perhaps – will finish Charteris.'

'By *the* source you mean Faust.'

'Precisely.' He handed Cumming and Marshall their glasses and took the armchair between them. 'So much has happened in the last few days. My mother wrote to tell me church bells were rung in England to celebrate our victory at Cambrai?'

'Yes, I heard the Westminster Abbey bells.'

'A victory after so many months of toiling to no great effect. Four miles in the first four hours with only four thousand casualties. Imagine . . . After Ypres. And now we are busy surrendering all the ground we've taken, and everyone is dismayed again.'

'"Gallantly resisting the enemy's counterattack while inflicting many casualties", *The Times* said this morning.'

Graham smiled. 'Is that what Repington wrote?' He leant forward confidentially, his whisky balanced on his knee. 'What the newspaper people really want to know is, why wasn't our Third Army ready for the counterattack – Mr Lloyd George too, I shouldn't wonder. What would they say, what would the public think if they knew? Because, Captain, this catastrophe could have been avoided – should have been avoided. Come on Marshall . . .' Graham turned. 'It's your story.'

Marshall had been sitting with his head back and his eyes closed, an intense frown on his brow. 'It's been a difficult few days,' he said. 'Where to begin? Well, with a confession, Captain. I'm not as convinced as my friend Graham here that sharing this with you will help the Army, or is even a very wise thing to do.'

Silence for a moment as Cumming leant forward to glare him. 'Well, perhaps you should have thought of that before you dragged me here. Graham, what do you have to say?'

Graham looked unperturbed. 'As your man, Innes, discovered in his time with us, Captain, loyalty is greatly prized at GHQ, and honesty rather less so – even when thousands of lives are at stake. Simply, senior officers do not like a sneak. A reputation for insubordination would follow us both like a bad smell.'

'I see.' Cumming picked up his glass and held it to his lips reflectively. 'I quite understand your situation. Of course, you have my word, I will keep your name out of this, Major.'

Marshall smiled a little sheepishly. 'I'm not as brave as Innes, I'm afraid.'

'Or as foolhardy,' Graham chipped in.

'That's as may be,' Marshall said, 'but he's the reason we're here; his network, your Ramble network, Captain. Perhaps he told you – I plot the enemy's order of battle for GHQ; not just the number and whereabouts of his divisions, but his reserves too. I think we do a pretty good job, but it would be almost impossible without intelligence from your network. This ridiculous rivalry between your service and ours . . . disgraceful, really.' He shook his head in frustration. 'But that's by the by . . . the thing is, I was involved in the intelligence briefings for Cambrai. As you know now, the plan was for a surprise assault on a weakly defended stretch of enemy line – a *coup de main*. Everything seemed to be going very well, and we were confident the enemy was unaware of the preparations. Then . . .' Marshall sighed heavily. 'Then I received some fresh returns from your spies – "watchers", you like to call them, don't you? They were reporting a very marked increase in enemy activity along an important section of railway track that runs along the Front at Cambrai. Three new divisions were being transferred into the sector as a reserve – thirty thousand additional troops.

'I needed to be sure, of course, so I visited Third Army and interrogated some of its prisoners and checked the air

317

surveillance. Then I took all the evidence to Charteris.' Marshall looked down at his glass, as if he were trying to capture an image of the scene in the crystal. 'I laid out my bits of paper and I said to him, "Our enemy is reinforcing his line at Cambrai with three reserve divisions." Quick as you like, he said, "No, no, Marshall, you're mistaken. It's a bluff. The Germans are trying to deceive us, those divisions are still on the Russian Front. Look, they're not even on the GHQ intelligence map."'

Graham snorted contemptuously: 'Fool.' He turned to Cumming. 'It's Marshall's map, Captain. His people are the ones who keep it up to date.'

Marshall's face had hardened. 'And I said so. "I brought the intelligence straight to you," I said, "but if you'd prefer to see it on our map first that could be arranged." He lost his temper. "Insubordination," he said, and "downright rude", and he spilt a cup of tea over his desk.'

Graham said: 'He doesn't understand that after months of putting up with his slapdash ways, Marshall is at the end of his tether.'

'That's as may be, but the source?' said Cumming, impatiently. 'He mentioned his source?'

'That his source was indicating no unusual activity in the sector.' Graham brushed his knee with the back of his hand as if he were sweeping away a fly. 'You knew he was talking about Faust, didn't you, Marshall?'

'He said he was receiving intelligence from a source in the sector. I *inferred* it was from Faust.'

Graham shook his head incredulously. 'The truth is, he isn't willing to inconvenience the Field Marshal with the facts. Damn it, he admitted as much.'

'His exact words were . . .' Marshall closed his eyes. '"If the Chief thinks the Germans are reinforcing Cambrai, it will shake his confidence in our success." And I'm afraid I lost it a bit . . .'

'Quite right,' Graham interjected.

'I said, the lives of thousands of our men were at stake, and I was confident the Chief would want to be appraised of *all* the facts. It would be shameful to keep him in the dark. Charteris would hear none of it – sent me packing.'

'Bloody fool. Enough to drive a man to strong drink.' Graham got up and walked over to the table. 'Another?' He pointed to the bottle. 'Marshall hasn't finished yet!'

Someone was moving about upstairs. 'Your friend?' Cumming lifted his gaze to the ceiling.

'Don't worry, she doesn't speak much English,' Graham said. 'Lovely woman but not very bright.' He walked back with the whisky and poured some for Marshall. 'You didn't let it rest there, did you? I advised Marshall to take his evidence to the Director of Operations, tell him Charteris was suppressing vital intelligence – lying isn't too strong a word – *lying* to his commander-in-chief.'

'Which I did.' Marshall stood up and placed his glass on the chimney-piece. 'I told him I was no longer willing to serve under Charteris, but he persuaded me to stay and say nothing to anyone, because that wasn't in the best interests of the Chief. He wanted me to watch Charteris and monitor our intelligence, and report to him in private.' He bent over with his hands to the fire for a moment. Cumming couldn't see his face but when he spoke his voice rose in anger. 'It hasn't made the blindest bit of difference. He's done nothing.'

'Because he's as useless as Charteris,' said Graham. 'The first time the Chief heard of the enemy's reserves was when they met our advance. And there we have it. The Boches have launched their counterattack and we are busy surrendering all the ground we took a few days ago. Back to square one.'

Marshall turned back to Cumming. 'A failure of intelligence, people will say, and they would be correct, but it could have been avoided if BGI had acted swiftly and with integrity.'

There was a long silence that not even Graham seemed inclined to break. Cumming could hear his girlfriend clumping around upstairs and wondered whether she was attempting to drive them from her home.

'Well, Captain, what do you think to that?' Graham said at last.

'I think I'll have that drink now, if you please.' Cumming was gazing into the fire, fingertips to his lips. 'You were right to bring this to me. Is it one man's weakness or is it a German plot? Is it both?'

Marshall said, 'How can one tell?'

Graham handed Cumming his glass. 'Faust is manipulating Charteris. What's more, I'm prepared to bet Charteris suspects Faust is unreliable, and that's why he isn't ready to let the rest of us examine the raw intelligence.'

Cumming frowned. 'That's quite an allegation.'

'I suppose it is, but that's my opinion, and I know the man. I've worked with him for two years. Faust is convenient, something to tell the Chief.'

'But too good to be true, it seems.'

'Yes. I believe so.'

Cumming held his glass to the firelight, turning it reflectively. 'But do you think Haig will believe so? Innes's experience with the Suicide Club is not encouraging. Perhaps you will acknowledge, your Chief is a man of decidedly fixed opinions.'

'If he has a fault it is the very natural one of excessive loyalty to old Staff comrades who are not up to the job.' Graham flopped back into the armchair beside Cumming. 'After Passchendaele and now this debacle . . . he has to be able to count upon his Staff for sound intelligence and to speak—how did you put it, Marshall?'

'*Sine timore aut favore* – without fear or favour.'

'Without fear or favour, yes,' Graham drawled. 'I'm sure Mr Lloyd George demands nothing less from his people – those people who take such an interest in our affairs at GHQ. When you tell them about this, I hope you draw them to the correct conclusions.'

'And those are, Major Graham?'

'That Charteris has to go at once and others should follow – MacLeod for one – and there needs to be an immediate investigation into the reliability of source Faust.' Graham leant forward earnestly. 'But Captain, you won't find a senior officer at GHQ who doesn't believe the Chief is still the man to win the war. I hope your friends in government—' He smiled wryly. 'I hope *Sir Maurice* will recognise where the fault lies, see the wood for the trees. I'm bound to say I know Sassoon is urging our friends in government to do the same.'

Marshall shook his head. 'I don't enjoy this sort of politics, Captain. Use what I've told you for the good of the Army and our country.'

'So say all of us,' said Graham, rising from his chair. 'We must return to headquarters or the BGI will send out a search party.'

Cumming and Marshall followed his example. Sensing that they were preparing to leave perhaps, Graham's lady friend was making her presence felt with more force. 'A woman with spirit,' he said, glancing to the ceiling with something like a smirk, 'and large feet.'

But in the dark hall he turned back to Cumming with quiet seriousness. 'It's Bureau business, I know, but Marshall and I were wondering about Innes?'

'Oh?'

He held up Cumming's coat. 'Innes is in Belgium?'

'You know, I never speak of such things.'

'Where else, if he's investigating Faust? But it seems to me we have confirmation of an unreliable source. If things are coming to a head—'

'You're concerned for his wellbeing? He would be touched.'

'Yes, I surprise myself.'

Cumming thought for a moment before slipping into his coat. '*Some* confirmation of an unreliable source, perhaps, but not German, and not enough to satisfy your Field Marshal Haig. Or do you disagree?'

'I'm sure the Chief will see – Charteris will go now.'

'Are you sure?' Cumming picked up his gloves and hat from the hall table and turned back to them. 'Let's see, gentlemen. I don't need to remind soldiers that plans full of promise have often come to nothing in this war – sometimes with very unfortunate consequences.'

25

The Father of Lies

THEY WERE WOKEN an hour before sunrise by an urgent knocking at the front door. Innes began stumbling round the dark bedroom in search of his trousers. Ramble stepped naked to the window and peered through the drapes into the street. 'Be calm, it's only Monsieur Van Delden.'

'Something's wrong.' Innes was shivering with apprehension.

Ramble snatched up her dressing-gown and was still putting it on as she padded down the stairs to the door. He heard it open and close and voices in the hall. There must be something *terribly* wrong if a man as careful as the former policeman was hammering blue murder on the door at that hour. The noise would have filled the empty street, drawing their neighbours to bedroom windows too.

They were waiting for him in the back room. There was no more light than a thin blue hint of the dawn through the curtains. The fire was out but they were standing either side of it anyway, Ramble holding her dressing-gown tight at the neck against the cold, the punctilious Van Delden so distracted he was wearing his cap in the house.

'Your prostitute, Mademoiselle Eve, she's dead. They found her body in the river,' he said flatly.

'She was murdered?'

Ramble reached out to touch Innes's arm.

'You think it was Springer?'

She hesitated: 'There's something else, Alexander . . .'

'A friend came to see me,' Van Delden explained, 'someone still inside the gendarmerie. He warned me the Germans were asking questions about me. Then he told me about the girl, Eve. He said they were looking for a Monsieur Thomas and that he met the description of a man seen in my company: tall – about one-ninety – about twenty-five, dark brown hair, blue eyes, moustache, sometimes walks with a limp. They are saying you killed the prostitute, monsieur.'

That poor, poor girl. He'd talked of duty, then used her. He shivered, but not so they could see. Van Delden was speaking and Ramble replied, but Innes wasn't listening.

'I killed her, Maria. You said I would, you warned me.'

'Don't be silly,' she said, sharply. She reached up and turned his shoulders so he was facing her. 'You didn't beat her, you didn't murder her. Feel angry, Alexander, but don't feel sorry for yourself.' She shook him gently. 'Are you listening to me?'

He nodded.

'I want some coffee and I expect you do too,' she said to Van Delden. 'We must talk this through, decide what to do. One of you, please, light a fire.'

Innes remembered the look he'd exchanged with the Fräulein Doktor in the restaurant mirror. Perhaps that was all the time it took for such as she. It was a clever plan to turn a British spy into the murderer of a prostitute. Poor ignorant Eve, used by careless men and a devious woman. He closed his eyes and groaned, but very quietly, so quietly Van Delden didn't hear him. He was sitting on the couch wringing his cap and jogging a chair impatiently with his foot. Innes was kneeling at the hearth trying to blow some life into the stuttering fire. The kindling was damp, just a few black twigs from a park or square. Poor Eve. Fire and brimstone was what he was threatening to bring down upon them all.

'She was badly beaten,' Van Delden said, 'murdered, then thrown in the river.'

'Do you think she was interrogated first?' Ramble had dressed in a black skirt and blue blouse and was sitting at the hearth cradling her cup of coffee. 'What I mean is, were they the sort of injuries you would inflict if you wanted to kill someone quickly?'

Van Delden pursed his lips thoughtfully. 'She was badly bruised – punched – her face was a mess. Rope marks on her wrists – perhaps they tied her to a chair. Yes, my friend thinks she was questioned first. Then she was killed by a single knife thrust' – he patted his chest – 'to the heart.'

'She will have told him about you, and Alexander, and me – and the Shoe Market,' Ramble said.

'Him?'

'Springer. It's the sort of a thing a man like that would do to a woman.' She turned to gaze at Innes. 'Don't you think so?'

He nodded.

'The Fräulein Doktor's men will question the boys in the shop downstairs,' she said. 'They won't get more than descriptions of us all, and they have those already. But you must leave, monsieur . . . you have a sister in Bruges?'

'If I must.' Van Delden slapped his cap on the arm of the couch in disgust.

'How did they know?' said Innes.

'Al-ex-ander,' she said, dragging the syllables of his name incredulously. 'That poor girl wasn't capable of keeping a secret.'

'He had to beat it from her, didn't he?' he said, angrily. 'Beat her face to a pulp.'

He looked away, and for a while no one spoke, but he knew she was watching him.

'I need to deal with him,' he said, meeting her gaze at last.

'You can leave it to our friends,' she replied.

'No, I need to know the truth about Faust . . . all of it.'

She gave him a hard level stare. 'At any price? What about our work – the network? Are you ready to put all that at risk? What if he's trying to lure you – trap you?' She lifted her hands in frustration and let them fall back. 'And who do you need to know the truth from, Faust? Springer? Will you know it if you hear it? You should go now, Alexander. It's time to leave. Take your story back to your Monsieur C and leave us to do our work. Isn't that what he would want?'

'I don't know what he wants. Feel angry, you said to me; I do. This is my affair, and I need to finish it.' He closed his eyes. 'It starts here, you see, with them, and it ends over there, in the mud at Ypres. You can't imagine . . . The Fräulein Doktor's destroying our network, and soon there will be Faust and no one else. But they won't believe us at GHQ because too much is at stake, they have too much to lose.'

'Oh, Alexander.' She clutched her head with both hands. 'What if Springer's trying to trap you for this woman. It's madness.'

'It's the last Monday of the month,' he said. 'He'll visit the Mephistopheles tonight.'

Springer was still at the club, and that was good because Innes wasn't sure he would have the guts to be. He was plainly not a man to let the small inconvenience of a dead prostitute get in the way of business. But there was a second doorman, and he was a bear of a man too. From time to time he stepped outside to pirouette in the street, trying to catch a suspicious movement in a doorway or a window. Wet snow was gusting along it and collecting in the cracks between the granite setts, swirling in doorways, pricking Innes's hands and his face, seeping into the fibres of his coat; smearing the red light above the name of the club on the buildings opposite.

It was a filthy evening and it was a quiet evening, even for a Monday, and it was one of the two evenings every month when Faust visited the Mephistopheles. On a night like this, there was a chance someone would drive Faust to the club in an official car, but Innes didn't think so, because he was a man who belonged in a cheap suit and in a crowd, shambling slightly, careful not to look the world too closely in the eye. Innes expected him to walk to the Central Station and catch a tram, and Ramble had arranged to have him followed by someone with a curfew pass. Innes had tried to make her promise to stay away. 'What would be the point?' she said. 'I'd only break my promise and commit another sin. Now isn't the time to do that.'

One way or another the long trail was going to wind up at the Mephistopheles. Innes touched his coat pocket and felt the heft of the service revolver.

'You know Springer will have something,' Ramble had said to him, 'and he'll kill you without a second thought – or one of his men will. Remember what he did to Eve? You know enough for your field marshal. Just do what you must.' He'd promised her that he would shoot first – for Eve. He'd shoot Engelmann too. He glanced at his watch, the one his kind civilised doctor-father in Edinburgh had given him: almost midnight. The last workman had trudged by with his hat low and his collar up five minutes ago, and it was twenty minutes since a curfew patrol had passed the girls' school at the bottom of the street. Ramble was waiting at the baker's as before.

'It's time,' he said when she came to the door. Her nose and the cuffs of her coat were dusted with flour. Reaching behind her head he pulled her close. 'What are you doing? Not now,' she whispered sharply, but she didn't resist. He kissed the flour from her nose, then he kissed her properly.

'Stay here, won't you?' he said. 'Promise me. Whatever happens.'

She smiled weakly. 'Remember, shoot straight. That's all you have to do . . .' Her eyes were glittering and she bit her lip, trying to choke a rush of feeling.

'Look, here,' and reaching up she began arranging his scarf over his mouth and nose, pulling the coat tight across his chest.

'I love you,' he muttered.

'Go on.' She pushed him gently. 'And shoot straight.'

Out of the baker's then, walking purposefully, as anyone would on such a night, the wind buffeting his back, the taste of the sea on his lips. Just fifty yards along the street was a short rough cobbled lane with stables and gates to the backyards of houses, shops, a timber yard, a club. For the convenience of clients leaving late there was a dim white light over the old servants' entrance at the rear. Lily had shown Innes out at about one o'clock on his last visit, and he remembered how little trouble she had taken to secure the door. But this time it was locked – Innes shook it gently – bolted top and bottom. There were night lights in two of the first-floor rooms at the back of the house and iron bars at all the ground-floor windows. The glass panel above the door was just out of reach. It would be better to wait a while. The Germans liked to creep away in the early hours, especially at the beginning of the working week – veterans and cavalry excepted, Eve had said. Innes pressed his back flat against the wall beside the door, right hand in his pocket round the butt of the revolver. He would wait about half an hour, no more than an hour, then he would fetch a ladder from the timber yard in the lane. The glass strip above the door would be tricky and noisy, he would try to force a first-floor window, like the one at the old priest's house. Was it madness? That depended on his luck. Lucky Lazarus. He expected it to be quiet inside. Faust was very discreet and he would try to avoid meeting his countrymen. 'Such a nice gentleman,' according to Eve. 'Like you,' she'd said. Poor Eve, she'd set her bar rather low. Poor, poor Eve, who had soothed him once from his nightmare of the grave. He closed his eyes and pinched the bridge of his nose, but only for a moment, because he could hear Lily the door-keeper's tinkling laugh, as false as water. Bang, the top bolt; bang, the bottom. Innes checked the safety catch of the revolver with his forefinger. The rattle of the chain and the door was opening. Goodnight, monsieur, *à tout à l'heure*, and thank you for the gratuity.

Monsieur the German captain was at the bleary stage of drunkenness when even placing and adjusting a hat can take an age. He didn't notice Innes step sideways to the door.

'Hello Lily,' he said, barging inside. She was too shocked to stop him, and the German too slow to prevent him slamming it shut.

'Don't shout, don't scream,' he said, his hand over her mouth. 'Did Eve talk to you about me?'

She looked terrified.

'Springer found out?'

She closed her eyes, tears springing through her lashes.

'You know it wasn't me who murdered her, don't you? I'm a British soldier, did Eve tell you? I'm working with the people trying to free your country. Please, I'm going to take my hand away, please don't scream.'

Outside, the German was banging on the door and shouting. Innes lifted his hand and her chin dropped at once, a curtain of her fair hair falling across her face.

'Are you all right?' She was shaking. 'I won't hurt you, believe me.'

'I know,' she said in a small voice. 'I know.' Her chest and shoulders rose in a sob. 'I know.' Innes wanted to comfort her, but all he could think of was the infernal racket the Boche soldier was making, and that sooner or later someone in the house was going to investigate. 'Lily, I must—' But before he could finish she lifted her head and shouted, 'Please, Captain, I'm all right.'

They heard an oath in German, and he must have stumbled away.

'Good girl. Here.' Innes offered her his handkerchief. 'Will you help me?' He held her shoulders and bent to look her in the eye. 'I won't let him hurt you. Look at me, Lily. I won't let him. Do you believe me?'

She sniffed and wiped her nose on her knuckles. Then she swept the hair from her face, and he was surprised by the determined look she gave him. 'What do you want?'

'Where is he?'

'In the drawing room with Jan.'

'Jan?'

'The doorman. He's expecting someone.'

'Faust?'

She nodded.

'And the other doorman?'

'Gone,' she said.

'And no one else?'

'A German with Isabelle on the second floor.'

'Can you lock her door – lock him inside?'

She sniffed, then nodded again.

'Please do it for me. Do it quietly. Then stay away from the bar, stay out of sight, do you hear?'

He dropped his coat quietly at the drawing room door. The revolver was in his right hand and he'd slipped the safety catch; his left was on the door handle. Someone inside was playing the piano without grace, without feeling. He tried to breathe deeply, tried to picture the room, because he would

330

be stepping out near the stage and there were two more doors at the far end, near the bar. The music stopped suddenly as if they were playing a party game. Turning the handle he stepped inside, the revolver raised in front of his face. Springer was at the piano and his man was lounging in an armchair a few feet away. He slipped his hand into his jacket and tried to rise.

'I'll shoot' was all there was time for Innes to say. 'No' died on his lips as the revolver kicked and the doorman was thrown back in his chair. His eyes were still open, his mouth too, perhaps he was trying to mutter something, but there was a dark red circle on his shirt and the burgundy wallpaper was glistening. The percussion of the revolver seemed to reverberate for the rest of his short life.

'Just one muscle, just one, and I'll kill you, too,' Innes said. Springer was staring at his doorman. 'Take off your jacket . . . slowly.' He gestured with the revolver. 'Now, turn around.' Then he slapped Springer's pockets. 'All right, sit down.' Springer did as he was told, watchful like a sleek cat, but not afraid, it seemed to Innes. That made him even angrier. 'I'm trying to make up my mind whether to shoot you now or wait for your friend Faust and shoot you together.'

Springer's thin face betrayed nothing. He pondered the question, then said in English, 'Please don't make another mistake, Captain.' His small brown eyes flitted up to Innes's face and away. 'If I may advise you—'

'You may not.'

'Leave now. Go back to Rotterdam. Tinsley, isn't it? Go back to him, that would be wise.'

Innes looked at his watch. 'When will Faust be here?'

Springer shrugged. 'I'm not sure he'll come. Perhaps he heard you shoot my man, Jan; someone will have. Perhaps he was expecting you to come here.'

331

'Get up.' Innes waved the revolver at him. 'Over there.' He wanted Springer in one of his deep leather armchairs. 'Comfortable?' He dragged the piano stool closer. 'We'll wait,' he said, settling with the gun in his lap.

'Wait for what? You know I work for Captain Bennett, don't you?'

'I know Bennett thinks you work for him.'

'I do work for him. I work for the Germans too. That *is* how it works, Captain. It wouldn't work any other way.'

'Is that your excuse?'

'But it's the truth. Not very convenient, is it?' He smiled, weakly.

'You give Bennett whatever Faust prepares for you.'

'Y-e-s.' He drawled the word like an undergraduate aesthete. Where had he acquired such educated English? 'Faust is your Army's most highly placed asset, the best spy you have here. I collect intelligence from the girls here too, but I can't speak for its quality, that isn't my area. I'm a businessman, you see – a trader, you say in English? – that's all.'

'Not a trader – a profiteer, and the worst sort. You disgust me.'

'Do I?' Springer smiled faintly. 'Your GHQ is very happy. You might like to bear that in mind.' His gaze drifted to the revolver. 'Captain Bennett would be very sorry to lose me. He's anxious to protect a valuable source. That's why he warned me you were here.'

Innes felt another surge of anger. It must have been in Breda or in the wood, or the barn door – he'd left it open. 'He didn't tell you to betray Father Albert or Monsieur Luyten.'

'To protect, Faust, yes. Bennett said I should do—'

'Or to murder Eve.'

Springer's hand strayed to his beard, then to his grey slicked hair. A nerve was jumping in his left eye.

'Did *you* beat her to death? I don't suppose you did it your-self. Was it him?' Innes glanced at the body of the doorman. 'That's all the reason I need to shoot you now.'

Springer moistened his lips. 'I was sorry. Faust knew you were visiting her, you see. That was my mistake. You're rocking the boat – isn't that what you say – rocking the boat, and Faust's frightened. He told Frau Schragmüller, you see. Sooner or later she would have questioned Eve, and I couldn't let that happen. Eve would have told her about the bits and pieces the girls collect for me from our German patrons.' He moistened his lips again. 'So, yes, I killed her.' He hesitated. 'And you killed her too.'

Clever Springer must have had a conscience once, because he knew precisely how to insert his blade in someone else's. 'Frau Schragmüller works for the *Kriegsnachrichtenstelle?*'

'Well, are you going to shoot me?' Springer wanted to bargain. 'I'm much more use to you alive.'

'That depends on whether I believe you. Pale, petite, about thirty – people call her the Fräulein Doktor?'

Springer considered this for a moment. 'Yes, that's Schragmüller. Would you like a drink?'

Innes lifted the revolver. 'Answer my questions. What is this War Information Centre?'

'If I tell you that, my life will be worth nothing.'

'It's worthless anyway. You say you're working for us, answer my questions, or I'll shorten it here and now.'

'And what will your GHQ say? I don't think you realise how much they value Faust . . . value me.'

Innes cocked the revolver.

'All right.' Springer raised his hand. 'A school for spies. Fräulein Doktor Schragmüller is in charge. Faust is Schragmüller's agent.'

'And Petit?'

'Petit? I don't know him.'

'A British spy – he flew across the lines in a balloon.'

'A member of your Suicide Club? Oh yes, they know all about that. Yes, that's Schragmüller. Your Petit is dead – shot; the others too – but Schragmüller keeps them alive on paper and sends pigeons back across the lines with intelligence she wants to feed the British.' He frowned. 'She doesn't miss anything.'

'You're frightened of her?'

He shrugged. 'Of course. I'm careful. You're making life very difficult . . . and for Faust.'

Innes stared at him coldly. 'Don't you care about your country? You can see what the Germans are doing here . . .'

He closed his eyes and shook his head impatiently. 'I do what I can to get by – I've told you – and your people need me. Who holds the enemy closer? This is for prostitutes and liars and men like me who do it for a profit, or do you think the Germans whisper their secrets to priests like your Abbé Buelens? Let me tell you my friend, spying is messy like your trenches. There are casualties. That's the nature of the thing, isn't it? You pushed your priests and your banker and your grocer's widow into the front line, and now they're in prison or dead.'

'Because of you.'

'I have to protect myself and your Army – protect Faust . . . Like your generals sending their men into those battles that drag on for ever – for the greater good, the final victory. It's the same isn't it?'

Innes didn't have a chance to reply. Someone was at the door behind the bar. He was rising to fire when Ramble burst into the room. 'You've been so long!' She was struggling to catch her breath.

'What are you doing? You shouldn't have come!'

'What did you expect? I waited but—the gunshot, what

are you thinking?' She brushed past Springer on the couch without noticing, then checked and turned to look at him. 'Who—'

Innes gestured to the doorman.

'Then shoot him – now!'

'I'm waiting for Faust.'

'Too late. Alexander, do it!'

'There's one thing I still need to know. Faust's intelligence – it's always what the British want to hear – do you understand? Why?'

Springer was hunched over his knees, his gaze fixed on Ramble. Perhaps Eve had spoken of her, perhaps it was the businesslike tone of her 'shoot him'. Fear was very apparent in his face for the first time.

Innes waved the gun at him again. 'Tell me!'

'I don't know about the intelligence . . . Fräulein Doktor Schragmüller . . . she . . .' He was struggling to collect his thoughts.

'Alexander, shoot him!' Ramble said again, and she stepped closer to stand at Innes's shoulder.

'Schragmüller says generals only believe what they want to believe . . .' Springer pressed his fingertips against his forehead. 'British, German – the same – give them what they want to hear and they believe you. And they want to hear they're winning. The British—'

'Shoot him. Alexander. Can't you see what he's doing?' She grabbed his arm. 'Shoot him before they come.'

'No.' Innes caught her wrist. 'Springer . . .'

'You can't shoot me . . .'

Innes, raising his voice: 'Go on.'

'Schragmüller – she says the British trust Faust because they hear what they want to hear and when it's time to tell them what she wants them to hear they believe that too.'

335

Springer's eyes were fixed on Innes. 'But Faust is working for Captain Bennett . . .'

'Passing on these lies?'

'In his position, he has to. That's how it is, how it has to be.' He sounded desperate, and he was perching so close to the edge of the chair his chin was only inches from his knees.

'Alexander, don't listen to him.' Ramble's voice shook. 'Do it, before it's too late. Please do it!' She was frightened too.

Innes raised the revolver and took aim.

'Captain Bennett – I'm the contact – your Army . . .' He was shaking, hands raised with the palms to Innes. 'Because I'm more use alive – my girls . . .' He switched into French to speak to Ramble. 'I can help you here – warn you. Your network – the German officers they tell me . . .'

'Give it to me, Alexander,' she said quietly.

Innes was suddenly unsure. 'He might be useful. You said so yourself.'

'That was before Eve, before Lux.'

'I don't know.' He didn't think he could kill the man. 'What purpose would it serve?' Wasn't it all a pointless waste anyway?

Ramble reached for his wrist. 'Give me the gun, Alexander. Give it to me,' and she dug her nails into the back of his hand, forcing him to loosen his grip. Springer was moving. He was out of his chair, he was turning to run. Innes watched in a daze. The crash of the revolver made him start. Ramble had taken it from him but she'd missed, and Springer was trying to slip between the chairs, stumbling towards the door behind the bar. Ramble followed, the gun in both hands. Her second shot hit him in the back and threw him forward across a chair. The third was closer, a *coup de grâce*.

But it wasn't over because Innes could hear footsteps and an order in German.

'Alexander!' She was dragging him back towards the stage door.

'Here.' He took the revolver from her. 'You must go – for the network.'

'No! You too,' she said, 'you must come with me.'

A German soldier was crouching by the bar. Splinters shivered from the door-frame and another bullet hit the wall. Someone upstairs was screaming. Innes took Ramble's hand and they ran for the stairs and down to the back of the house. 'Let me,' he said, opening the door to the lane. They could try to find a way through the timber yard or one of the houses opposite. He was so sorry he'd made a mess of things. He reached inside and drew her out. 'They're probably in the street.'

'Perhaps, but if we run—'

The lane was dark, the cobbles wet and uneven, and Ramble slipped and almost fell after only a few yards. He tried to support her, tried to keep her in the shadow by the wall. The Germans would be in the lane soon, perhaps they were at the end of it already. But he would protect her. He reached into his jacket – six more bullets, and two still in the chamber of the gun. He could hear her breathing heavily, he could hear the rustle of her coat and the click of her boots, and that was all he could hear: the silence was unnatural, and he wanted to tell her so.

They were near the end of the lane and the street ahead was still empty. He held her, pressed her back against the wall, bent to whisper in her ear: 'Something's wrong. Wait, I'll look.' After a pause: 'I love you.' She lifted her eyes to meet his with an achingly sad smile. 'No, it *will* be all right,' he wanted to say, but instead he turned away and began to edge along the wall towards the street. Just a few seconds, a few yards, and he heard her sharp intake of breath. Then he heard footsteps.

There was something in their urgency that sent a chill through him. A short man in a bowler hat was standing a few feet from her. He must have sprung from a doorway. Innes couldn't see his gun but his body was set ready to fire.

'Drop it,' he shouted in Flemish. He was using Ramble as a shield. 'Drop your gun now.'

The soldiers in the Mephistopheles must have known one of their vampires was in the lane.

'Hey, here. I'm here,' the man shouted, and he craned a little to the right so he could see beyond Ramble into the street. 'It's Schmidt. I'm here – they're here.'

In little more than a heartbeat Innes knew his world was going to turn upside down and he was powerless to prevent it happening. It was the same the second before the blast that had buried him in the dug-out. He saw Ramble rise on her toes. He saw her pitch forwards with her arms open as if she was intent on embracing the secret policeman like a lover. He saw the policeman force her away with a forearm. Then he heard the shot and saw her body jerk. He tried to catch her but she collapsed sideways and her head smacked against the cobbles. The policeman fired at Innes from point blank range but somehow managed to miss. Innes's shot hit him in the middle of the chest. Perhaps he was wounded, perhaps he was dead; Innes didn't wait to see him fall. Ramble was lying on her side, one arm above her head, the other beneath her body, knees bent as if she was pretending to ride a bicycle. He knew she was dead because he knew the awkward way of the dead and their stillness when the ghost has gone. Her dark eyes were open, her lips were open, there was blood at her temple and in the cracks between the stones; and when he swept her hair from her forehead there was blood on his hand.

He bent to kiss her cheek and say 'I love you' and 'I'm sorry'. Then he closed her eyes. He wanted to lay her body straight

338

but there wasn't time, because he could hear their boots and their rifle bolts and their shouting, always their shouting. Slowly he got to his feet and turned towards the street. They were advancing cautiously along the walls, dotting in and out of doorways. Then a high-pitched voice, a woman's voice, called for 'silence'. She gave the order – 'Light' – and a second later Innes was caught in the beam of a torch. Its circle seemed to lap at Ramble's body. The woman – Fräulein Doktor Schragmüller, he supposed – was calling upon him to surrender. Perhaps she'd planned for this to happen from the beginning. If so, she'd won. Shielding his eyes he lifted the revolver higher, high and wide enough to be sure he wouldn't hit anyone. Then he fired his last shot and they fired back. A bullet struck his thigh and as he crumpled another hit him in the side. Through a haze he could see Ramble's body lying only a few feet away. He was surprised he didn't have the strength to reach across and touch her, but he could feel her rough cross pressed between his chest and the cobbles. When he closed his eyes he saw a small church on a windswept hill above a shore; he saw an old priest kneeling at its door with a guttering candle; a white marble headstone. Then he saw no more.

December 1917

You will agree that it is very necessary the War Cabinet should have the fullest confidence in the opinions and judgement of officers of your Staff, and this they will not have so long as Charteris remains Director of Military Intelligence.

The Secretary of State for War, Lord Derby to Field Marshal Sir Douglas Haig, Telegram, 7 December 1917

26

Bury it!

WAR CABINET WAS over but its members were gathered in the ante-room of Number 10 raking through the ashes of their meeting. Cumming knew them by sight, of course; fortunately they were familiar with only the first letter of his name at the bottom of official papers. The old Boer rebel, General Smuts, with his distinctive white spade beard, was talking to Bonar Law, the chancellor of the exchequer; and former governor general of India, Curzon, was in conference with Derby, the bucolic secretary of state for war. At the door of the Cabinet Room, their mandarin, their man of secrets, Maurice Hankey, was listening intently to someone, probably the prime minister. He glanced into the ante-room and Cumming caught his eye before he resumed his conversation with his hidden interlocutor.

Perhaps it had been a difficult meeting, perhaps there were to be more meetings, because no one was in a hurry to leave, although Cabinet must have lasted an hour longer than it was expected to. Cumming could sense the gloom; anxious faces; quiet conversation, when men of standing generally find quiet very difficult. It was a troubling time, the worst he could remember. That morning the *Times* editorial had declared it was 'no longer satisfied' and was calling for the removal of 'blunderers', and that seemed to be a fair representation of the public mood. For the most part, the newspapers were directing their fire at the country's senior soldiers, but sooner or later they were going to ask why her politicians had let the slog at Passchendaele go on for so long; why the country was preparing for a fourth Christmas at war with victory apparently no closer. There was the memory of a dead man or the knowledge of a wounded one in every house. Cumming had thought a lot of his own son in the last few days. Poor old Aly had been the same age as Innes and an officer in a Highland regiment too. Did he blame anyone? No. Was there a different way? He didn't know. That was the job of the men gathered there in the ante-room, sipping their coffee, talking so quietly he was reminded of mourners at a funeral. Gazing round the walls at the portraits, he wondered if any of the great statesmen of the past would have been more capable of meeting the challenge than the politicians of the present day.

Sir Maurice was approaching. In the doorway behind him now, Mr Lloyd George was speaking to a young woman – one of his daughters, or his secretary perhaps.

'I advised the Prime Minister not to see you, I'm afraid,' Hankey said, following Cumming's gaze. 'I think he's more involved in this business than he should be. Shall we? I've borrowed Jones's room again.'

The dark picture of Lord Liverpool that had hung over the mantelpiece was gone and another prime minister had taken his place. A bit of a duffer called North, Hankey said. They had used the office three months before when Innes had sent his first report from GHQ, and it was still untidy but this time there was a lively fire. A gust of rain rattled the window; through it Cumming could see a Number 10 clerk scurrying between the garden suburb and the house.

'Your camp is bigger,' he observed, 'and it's muddier.'

'It is both those things. A hut is a thoroughly unpleasant

place to be in winter – but necessary. Please . . .' Hankey gestured to a seat. 'Tea?'

Cumming declined both, electing to stand with his stick wedged against the brass grate. 'Is this going to be difficult, Sir Maurice?'

'Difficult?' Hankey was in the process of transferring some papers from a chair to the desk. 'Do you think Jones's house is a pigsty too?' he said, crossing his legs, his hands clasped in a ball on his knee. 'Difficult? I don't think so. The Prime Minister is very sensible of your efforts, Cumming, and if this matter has proved anything to him, it is the importance of keeping the Secret Service Bureau free of Army interference.'

Cumming nodded. 'Naturally, I feel the same.'

Hankey lifted his balled hands to his lips as a man might in prayer. 'First let me say, there is to be a purge of the Staff at GHQ: Charteris is going. Sir Douglas was left with no choice. He's insisting on keeping him in some capacity – inspectorate of transport, I think – but the new man will be free to bring his own people into Army intelligence. Haig's chief of staff is going too – I expect there will be others.'

Cumming frowned. 'I'm surprised.'

'That Field Marshal Haig wants to keep him in some capacity, or that the Prime Minister is permitting him to stay?'

'Both. The man has done untold damage.'

'Untold? Yes. Well, I can only guess at Haig's motives . . . but they've been together through thick and thin, as they say, and the Field Marshal thinks well of him in spite of all the evidence to the contrary.'

Cumming snorted incredulously.

'The Prime Minister feels the same as you.' Hankey began to rise. 'Do you want to smoke? Jones will have an ashtray.'

'No thank you.'

'You're sure?' he said, settling back in the chair. 'Where

345

were we? Yes. Put simply, Cumming, it is Sir Douglas's personality that is at the heart of this whole story.' He paused again, considering his words carefully. 'In confidence . . . there is someone on the field marshal's staff, someone I very much respect.' His tone implied this placed his contact in rather a small circle. 'He says Sir Douglas will not tolerate anything that contradicts his idea of how a thing *should* be. Charteris knew that and was generally disposed to tell him what he wanted to hear. So, there you have the problem: if all one needed to do to win the war was to say "we're winning" many times, we would be in Berlin eating off the kaiser's china by now. Fixity of purpose is often a good thing; fixity of mind, never. That, my dear Cumming, is why some men are fitter to be leaders than others. Of course, even good ones go astray, and at those times they must be ready to listen to honest advice.' He smiled weakly. 'I digress, I know. It is just that my present situation allows me ample opportunity to observe such things – and that touches on your next question, I think.' He paused, inviting Cumming to speak, stroking his bald head rather forlornly. His hands were so small, everything about him seemed small, except his moustache and his brain, of course.

'The Prime Minister has read my report?'

'The War Cabinet read your report, although there will be no mention made of it in my minutes.' He pursed his lips and his moustache lifted into a Gothic arch that made him appear even more doleful. 'No mention should be made of it anywhere.' He paused again, and seemed momentarily at a loss for words, which was strange because Cumming was quite sure he knew what he was going to say.

'I understand the implications, Sir Maurice. Public confidence in the leadership of the Army would undoubtedly be dented if it was generally known that its most trusted source was a German double agent.'

'More than dented, Cumming, more than dented . . .' Hankey was almost out of his seat. 'After Passchendaele, public trust is wearing very thin. The Prime Minister is seething . . . frankly, he doesn't believe a word Haig says. A few months after promising us victory Sir Douglas is warning us of the possibility of defeat. He says he's short of men, and that he expects the Germans to attack in 1918. The Prime Minister is of the view that he should have looked after the ones he'd got more carefully. No, more than a dent, Cumming, a scandal at this time would threaten the country's resolve to keep on to the end.' He sat back and took a deep breath. 'The Prime Minister has asked me to go to France with General Smuts and find a replacement for Haig – if we can, of course.' He paused and picked a speck of something from his tunic sleeve. 'But that is the future, and my concern today – the Prime Minister's concern – is Faust and the Suicide Club and this woman you call the Fräulein Doktor. How many people know about this?'

Cumming said there were one or two people in the Bureau, Tinsley in Rotterdam – the Ramble network had brought the intelligence to him – Graham and Charteris and MacLeod and some others at GHQ, and the War Cabinet, of course. Could its members be trusted to keep their own counsel, he enquired facetiously.

'That's too many,' said Hankey.

'Some of them know only a little.'

'Bury it!' Hankey leant forward, hands in a fist again. 'Bury it, and the new BGI will be ordered to do the same. The fact that Charteris was drawing from a polluted well is something we can afford to forget. This is not for the history books.'

The telephone made them both jump. It stopped as Hankey

was rising to pick it up, and the sound of its bell was replaced by a stentorian voice in the corridor. The door opened suddenly and a small man with red hair and round glasses stepped inside the room – his room, Cumming supposed.

'Sir Maurice. Sorry,' he said, in the sing-song voice of the valleys.

'I think we've finished, haven't we?'

Cumming said, 'Not quite, Sir Maurice.'

'Then would you permit me another minute, Jones?'

'Of course, of course.' Jones was turning but checked: 'the Prime Minister was asking for you, Sir Maurice.'

'I'll be there directly.'

Jones closed his door and there was a sort of silence. The fire crackled, the wind shook the glass, and after a few seconds Cumming spoke. 'There's one thing we haven't addressed, Sir Maurice – my man, Innes. Or are you hoping we can bury him too?'

In fact the chances of Innes surviving were rather slim, although Cumming didn't say so, and even if he managed to pull through he was unlikely to be of service. Cumming was still considering the efficacy of bringing him back as he collected his hat and coat at the door of Number 10. It wasn't certain he would be able to anyway. 'Was this fellow a spy?' the permanent secretary at the Foreign Office had asked when he raised the possibility. 'Then there's nothing we can do.' So Cumming had included it in his report for Downing Street. 'The Prime Minister wants to know why?' Hankey had said. Why this one man among the thousands of autumn casualties? Still of use, Cumming had replied, and important to know the full story, but that was eyewash really.

The rain had stopped but it was blowing harder. Squinting at the flag in front of Whitehall Gardens with a sailor's eye, he decided it was backing south-easterly. The troop ships would be having an uncomfortable time in the Channel, and for most of the new men it would it be a first experience of the sea. Aly had never had good sea legs. He would sit in the stern of Cumming's yacht with his gaze fixed on the horizon to combat his nausea – but he made the effort for his old man. No surprise he elected for the Army. Innes was a different sort of chap, a bit of an intellectual really, decent, likeable. There wasn't room for sentiment in the spying game, Cumming had always said so, but walking back along Whitehall he reflected that no matter how he dressed it up, his determination to see Innes home owed more to his heart than to his head. Would he be going to this trouble for a scallywag like Tinsley? Not a bit of it. In truth, he felt guilty. Graham had warned him Innes was 'crocked' and unfit for duty, and that may have played some part in what had taken place in Antwerp. Tinsley had hinted at something of the sort. It was impossible to say for sure, because Innes was in a military hospital, Lux was in prison, Ramble was dead, and their network was shot to pieces. Their only source was an old policeman called Van Delden, who had slipped out of the occupied territories on a barge. Faust was a double agent, he'd said, Springer too – but he was dead – and Captain Innes had found proof in a hotel bathroom that an enemy espionage centre in the city was using the identities of captured Suicide Club members to send the British false intelligence. Cumming had taken his testimony to Hankey, who informed the prime minister and the secretary of state for war. A politician's plot, Field Marshal Haig said, and he refused to believe it at first, but it didn't matter because everyone else did.

Major Graham had been given the job of carrying out an investigation because he was acceptable to both sides. He was still turning over stones at GHQ. Under the first he'd found the Army agents in Rotterdam and the story of drugs, and payments and prostitutes. Under the second he'd discovered an order from Colonel MacLeod authorising them to warn Springer he was being watched by a British spy with the code-name Lazarus. 'To protect Faust,' MacLeod said in his own defence. Under the third Graham had expected to discover Charteris, but MacLeod was refusing to confirm that he had known and approved of the order.

Cumming nodded to Spencer the deskman in the hall of the Court and hobbled over to the lift. What was left of his leg was aching. He didn't like to use the Rolls for visits to Downing Street – it was a little showy for the head of a secret service. Spencer must have tipped off Groves, because she was waiting at the door of the Bureau.

'Colonel Browning was hoping to speak to you, I've put him in your diary for two o'clock,' she said, 'and the meeting you wanted me to arrange for you at the Foreign Office is at half past five.'

He asked her to find out if Thomson at Special Branch was able to see him. If there was any difficulty she should say 'at the request of the Prime Minister'. There would be difficulties with Thomson, there always were, but he'd anticipated those.

'Tinsley thinks they will accuse Innes of killing a prostitute,' he'd said to Hankey. For good measure he'd held an imaginary headline in both hands: *British spy sentenced to death for the murder of a tart.* A decorated officer betrayed by his own army and humiliated by his enemy. After Passchendaele, 'enough', Cumming had said, although he would have found it difficult to explain the link between the two. Hankey must have understood anyway, because he asked Mr Lloyd George to give authority for an exchange of spies. Thomson had two Germans in custody, but only a prime minister could force him to give them up.

Miss Groves was at his office door: 'Assistant Commissioner Thomson will see you at Scotland Yard at three o'clock.'

'Very good. And, Captain Innes's sister is a nurse here in London, find out where, would you.' He wanted to tell her he was doing all he could to bring him home.

In the days that followed the business of spying continued as always, with Cumming preoccupied by revolution in Russia and the capture of Jerusalem from the Turks, which lifted the spirits a little. He found a replacement for Innes, a young South African officer who spoke good Dutch, and tolerable French and German. He was joining Tinsley in Rotterdam with orders to patch the Ramble network, activate old contacts, and recruit new ones, and he would have to find some way of dealing with the Fräulein Doktor. A German offensive was expected in the spring and the staff at Army intelligence were clamouring to know where. On a wet Monday a few days before Christmas one of its officers came to visit Cumming in person. Major Stewart Graham said he was round the corner at the War Office for a couple of days and wanted to stay 'in touch'.

'A veritable warren,' was his judgement of the Court. 'Do you like being up here?'

'It isn't a warren, it's an eyrie,' Cumming said, 'with a fine view of government.'

'And you're the old bird at the top,' Graham replied.

They sat in Cumming's office and drank tea with a cake Groves had arranged to be delivered from the Savoy. It was the fag end of a dismal day, at the fag end of the year, a year they might wish to forget but would never be able to.

'The Army's short and morale's at rock bottom,' Graham said. 'No one in the line understands why it all went on for so long at Ypres. "Who was the idiot who thought we could fight through that mud?" an old Guards chum asked me the other day. I was too embarrassed to say, "Fight through it and win the war, Dick, you were supposed to finish 'em!"'

'But he's gone,' Cumming observed.

'Charteris? No he's still at GHQ and the Field Marshal still consults him – seeking reassurance, Sassoon says. It's a difficult time. Imagine. A commander-in-chief who is not trusted to choose his own staff?'

Graham looked down at his cup, lost in thought for a moment. Was he losing faith too? He seemed less cocksure than he had been in Paris-Plage. Cumming asked him if the new BGI was making a difference.

Feeling his way, he said, things would be better in time. But it was Faust he wanted to talk about, not the future. Yes, he'd been told to 'bury' Faust and the Suicide Club and the general mess at Army intelligence, but he wasn't quite ready to. 'You deal with liars all the time, Captain, don't you?' he said. 'You'll understand. You see, all those half-truths, little lies, false expectations amounted in the end to one very big lie – that we were ready to win and the enemy was ready to lose.' He lifted his thumb and forefinger to his lips as if pinching a thought. 'So now I try to count the men we lost at Ypres in small lies. Not just Charteris's lies – all of us who let it happen for so long, and a field marshal's hubris too.' Difficult to admit, he said, because he was of the soldiers' party. He smiled his old sideways smile. 'Innes didn't like me much, but I admired him for having the guts to tell Sir Douglas the truth. He wasn't much of a politician, was he? Or even much of a spy, it seems. Are you going to get him back?'

'The Boche are taking their time to decide. The Foreign Office isn't hopeful. He's still very poorly, too poorly to execute. A priest has been to see him – he's a Roman, you know, but of course you do.'

'You heard about that?' His gaze dropped to the edge of Cumming's desk for a moment. 'I feel a bit guilty – not about

352

Charteris and the Catholic thing – that I encouraged Innes to pursue Faust.'

Cumming leant over his desk with his arms crossed and peered through his monocle at Graham. 'You know, Major, Lazarus had . . . has a certain talent for making people feel guilty.'

Graham nodded. 'That business with the dug-out . . . has it occurred to you that he might not want to be rescued this time?'

The priest at the prison was reportedly of the same opinion, but Cumming didn't say so. A smart fellow, Graham, there might be a place for him in the Bureau after the war.

He was on his feet, ready to leave. Dinner with his stepfather and the secretary of state for war, he said. They shook hands before Graham pinched a final thought. 'Have you heard? MacLeod – the colonel in charge of the Suicide Club – he blew his brains out in a Paris hotel. Guilt, I suppose. I didn't think he was the sort to take his own life.'

Cumming was wrong about the Germans. The permanent secretary at the Foreign Office contacted him to say so on Christmas Eve. 'I don't know why, perhaps they think he's going to die anyway,' he said. After dragging their feet for a fortnight they wanted it to happen in days, at the border near Breda. Cumming drove into the East End to see Innes's sister. Groves had rung the Bethnal Green Military Hospital to warn her, but he was late and she'd returned to the wards. He found her there with the bad cases, the ones the ward sister described as the fifty-fifties; two neat rows of iron bedsteads, like a battalion of invalids trooping its colours. They were the men of Ypres. They'd rattled back to dear old Blighty without their arms and their legs and their faces, rescued from the mud like Lazarus, and even if they survived they wouldn't be whole again. As he watched and listened to their agony he wondered if any of them would care to read the field marshal's despatch – he had a copy, although it wouldn't be in the *London Gazette* until Christmas Day: 1 million German casualties and 131 enemy divisions defeated in 1917 by 'less than half that number of British'. 'What a lie!' Hankey had said when Cumming had telephoned him about Innes. 'Pray it's Charteris's last.'

Miss Innes was walking towards him with a straight back and long stride. Her eyes were the same blue as her brother's and she had the same fine features. Her dark brown hair was held in place by a starched hat and her uniform was starched white with a red cross. She looked exhausted, but she tried to smile.

'I wanted you to know, he's coming back,' Cumming said.

'Back?'

'The Boche have agreed to the swap.'

'Oh,' she said. Her chin was trembling and there were tears in her eyes, and her chest and shoulders lifted in a sob that came from and expressed a tight core of feeling held in check for many months, because it was not just her own pain but the pain and buried grief of many. Cumming could see tears welling through her fingers, and as she bent forwards they plopped on to the floor between them.

'There, there,' he said, although he knew it sounded foolish. 'Miss Innes, is there someone I can—' He took his handkerchief from his pocket. 'Would this be of any use?' She was struggling to breathe. 'Come, Miss Innes, this is good news, we should be happy.'

Author's Note

A great deal will be written about the First World War at this time of anniversaries. *The Suicide Club* is a story but it is drawn from real events and in casting a field marshal and a prime minister among my characters I feel bound to say something about their depiction, the history, and my sources.

It is hard to think of an event that divides people more than the First World War, or a time in which the gulf between popular perception and scholarly opinion is greater. Stop and ask people in a street for their views – as I have done for the BBC – and they will speak of trenches and mud and sacrifice, and many will say it was a war not worth fighting and blame the politicians and generals for 'the waste'. Most scholars disagree. They argue that popular opinions of many aspects of 'The Great War' have been shaped by the failure to offer soldiers returning home a land 'fit for heroes', by class struggle, another war, by bad 1960s history, and the poet's 'pity of war'. The terrible cost of the victory, they say, should not obscure the essential justice of the country's call to arms. Britain went to war in 1914 for the same reasons it went to war in 1939, namely to fight German military ambition and to honour her treaty obligations to a smaller country.

One figure represents this gulf between popular and scholarly understanding of the war more than any other – Field Marshal Sir Douglas Haig. For many, he is still the butcher and the blunderer. Most historians take a different of view. The scholarly consensus is of a man with a stoic sense of duty and of his own destiny, who was supportive of innovation and ready to learn from mistakes. Not a military genius, but, in the words of Winston Churchill, a man possessed of 'an exceptional greatness of character'. Lloyd George never tired of abusing Haig, heaping opprobrium upon him for the conduct of the Passchendaele offensive in particular. But his fury at Haig and his generals reflected his own sense of guilt and personal failure. Although he was strongly opposed to Haig's plans, he was unwilling to take responsibility for rejecting them or for bringing the fighting to an end sooner. It was always his 'most painful regret'. Prime minister and field marshal made mistakes, as all politicians and soldiers have done and will continue to do. Both men responded with calm resolve to the German offensive in the spring of 1918 and played a significant part in the final victory. In this they were more fortunate perhaps than Charteris, who was not presented with an opportunity to rescue his battered reputation.

For the character, thoughts, and words of Douglas Haig, I drew on his diary and correspondence in the National Library of Scotland, from the published diary of Brigadier John Charteris, and from a long list of secondary sources, in particular works by John Terraine, Gary Sheffield, Brian Bond, and Gary Mead. David Woodward's study *Lloyd George and the Generals* was useful for the struggle between the politicians and the soldiers in the autumn of 1917, and I would like to thank my old BBC colleague Detlef Siebert for his help in obtaining copies of the Cabinet's War Policy Committee papers from the National Archives in London. The published diaries and memoirs of the War Cabinet's secretary, Sir Maurice Hankey, were an especially important source. For the general military and political situation, I consulted histories written by Hew

Strachan, Max Hastings, and John Grigg. Robin Prior and Trevor Wilson's *Passchendaele: The Untold Story* and John Terraine's *The Road To Passchendaele* were my principal sources for the offensive itself.

'I had a long talk with [General] Macdonogh. He is quite of my opinion,' General Sir Henry Wilson wrote in his diary on the eve of the Passchendaele offensive: 'Charteris is a dangerous fool because of his ridiculous optimism and because he is also untruthful'. Senior members of Charteris's own intelligence staff were of the same view. One of his most perceptive critics was, Major, later General, James Marshall-Cornwall, who I have taken as the model for the character of Major Marshall in my story. It was Marshall-Cornwall's warning of German reinforcements at Cambrai that Charteris brushed aside. I am indebted to the Military Intelligence Museum at Chicksands for allowing me to consult Marshall-Cornwall's papers and for guiding me to the unpublished diaries and memoirs of a number of other intelligence officers. Tellingly, when Charteris fell ill, it was Marshall-Cornwall who took on the duty of reporting to Haig. 'I was appalled to find what a mistaken view he held about the German troops confronting us,' he observed: 'he seemed to think that they were on the verge of collapse. I tried tactfully to give him a different impression, but found that his ideas on the subject were obstinately fixed.' Another witness to Charteris's melancholy influence on Haig was Major Stewart Menzies, who rose through the ranks of the Secret Intelligence Service after the First World War to become its chief during the Second. Menzies is credited by some with engineering Charteris's downfall. I drew on his background and service for the character of Major Stewart Graham.

Charteris believed most of the optimistic intelligence assessments he placed before his commander-in-chief, but there were times when he chose to hide the true situation or was unable to communicate it properly. Haig was guilty of doing the same in some of his dealings with the prime minister. Charteris noted on more than one occasion that 'the Chief' went further in his optimistic claims than the facts could honestly support. Insights into this and aspects of the relationship between the two men can be found in Michael Occleshaw's *Armour Against Fate: British Military Intelligence in the First World War* and in General Sir Kenneth Strong's *Men of Intelligence.*

The same reckless optimism was responsible for the formation of the espionage unit staff at GHQ called 'the Suicide Club'. 'A long argument with the BGI who wants us to turn everyone into getting agents through the line,' a senior member of Charteris's intelligence staff noted in his diary: 'he has no clear idea . . . what they are going to do when they get through or how they are to communicate, but he pictures us pushing men in by the tens.' In the end, the few who did make it across in balloons were picked up by the Germans and shot.

In the interests of the story, I chose to omit any mention of the *other* director of military intelligence. British intelligence-gathering in the First World War was plagued by a tangled web of command and control. There was a particularly sharp rivalry between GHQ in France and the director of military intelligence at the War Office in London, General Sir George Macdonogh. A thoroughly professional intelligence officer, Macdonogh was much more cautious in his assessment of the strategic situation and the German Army's capabilities in 1917. Haig and Charteris tried to dismiss him as a pessimist of 'the deepest dye', as a man compromised by his religious loyalties. 'I cannot think why the War Office Intelligence Department gives such a wrong picture of the situation,' Haig noted in his diary on 15 October 1917, 'except that General Macdonogh is a Roman Catholic and is [perhaps unconsciously] influenced by information which doubtless reaches him from tainted [i.e. Catholic] sources.' Naturally, Charteris was of the same opinion. A few days after the end of the Passchendaele offensive, he wrote to his wife complaining that Roman Catholic officers were to blame for the criticism of GHQ's operations. They were 'half-hearted about the whole war and have never forgiven Douglas Haig, unjustly, for being Presbyterian'. He had a very low opinion of the 'professional pessimists' in Downing Street and the War Office, and of Macdonogh in particular, 'who takes a hand against both Douglas Haig and me'.

More than just an expression of the Scots Presbyterian prejudice of the day, these intemperate observations reflect something of the siege mentality at GHQ in the autumn of 1917. In the same letter Charteris dismisses Lloyd George as 'incompetent', Winston Churchill as a 'glory' seeker with 'no judgement', the former British commander-in-chief in France, Lord French, as an 'incompetent old fool', and one of Haig's rivals, General Sir Henry Wilson as a 'black leg' and an Irish 'intriguer'.

So much has been written from the perspective of the soldier in the trench over the years, most vividly by those who fought themselves. My story is of the Staff and spies and resistance, but for Innes's memories of the Front I drew on the diaries of Catholic officer Edwin Campion Vaughan (*Some Desperate Glory*) and Scottish officer Alexander Stewart (*A Very Unimportant Officer*). From John Lewis-Stempel's history *Six Weeks: The Short and Gallant Life of the British Officer* I took the idea of a survivor called 'Lazarus' and much fine detail. Glasgow University Library has a moving website commemorating the service of its lecturers and students in the Queen's Own Cameron Highlanders (http://special.lib.gla.ac.uk/exhibns/month/sep2005.html).

The British Army ran a number of intelligence networks in Belgium, including one that was code-named 'Faust'. By the autumn of 1917 the best of these had been seriously compromised by the Germans. Three of the Army's networks (Faust, Felix, and Negro) were run by double agents working for German intelligence. The Felix network was based in a brothel, where Belgian prostitutes passed on intelligence from their German clients and were paid for their service in drugs supplied by their British intelligence contact. For the history of British espionage efforts in Belgium I consulted Christopher Andrew's *Secret Service* and Keith Jeffrey's *MI6: The History of the Secret Intelligence Service*, and for colour, the papers of military intelligence officers Kirke, Woolrych, and Kirkpatrick at the Imperial War Museum in London. Marthe McKenna's account of her war work, *I was a Spy*, was an excellent source for life behind enemy lines. So too, Henry Landau's memoir of Secret Service Bureau operations in Belgium and the Netherlands, *All's Fair*.

The Roman Catholic Church was very active in organising intelligence-gathering in the occupied territories, and for a time a network organised by the Abbé Buelens was one of the most successful. There was a Belgian agent with the code-name 'Ramble', but she was much grander and younger than the Madame Maria Simon of my story. German espionage operations in Antwerp were run by the redoubtable Dr Elsbeth Schragmüller, 'an extraordinary and well-educated woman' her commanding officer, Colonel Nicolai, later recalled: 'expert at handling agents, even the very difficult and the sly ones.'

Finally, a very big thank-you to my editor at Hodder, Kate Parkin, for her guidance in shaping the story; to my agent, Julian Alexander; and to my friends and my family for their encouragement and boundless patience.

HISTORY LIVES

at Hodder

From Anya Seton and Mary Stewart to Thomas
Keneally and Robyn Young, Hodder & Stoughton
has an illustrious tradition of publishing bestselling
and prize-winning authors whose novels span the
centuries, from ancient Rome to the Tudor Court,
revolutionary Paris to the Second World War.

––––––––––

Want to learn how an author researches battle scenes?

Discover history from a female perspective?

Find out what it's like to walk Hadrian's Wall in full Roman dress?

Visit us today at **HISTORY LIVES** for exclusive author
features, first chapter previews, book trailers, author videos,
event listings and competitions.

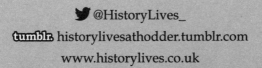

In the best books, the ending often comes as a shock.
Not just because of that one last twist in the tale,
but because you have been so absorbed in their world,
that coming back to the harsh light of reality is a jolt.

If that describes you now, then perhaps you should track down
some new leads, and find new suspense in other worlds.

Join us at www.hodder.co.uk, or follow us on
Twitter @hodderbooks, and you can tap in to a
community of fellow thrill-seekers.

Whether you want to find out more about this book,
or a particular author, watch trailers and interviews, have
the chance to win early limited editions, or simply browse
our expert readers' selection of the very best books,
we think you'll find what you're looking for.

And if you don't, that's the place to tell us what's missing.

We love what we do, and we'd love you to be part of it.

www.hodder.co.uk

 @hodderbooks

HodderBooks

HodderBooks